HELL

Lying there, I look around, tell you what I see
It's a sliding door and sixteen bars locking out on me
A six by seven room, a sink. a toilet on the floor
I've already read forty times the writing on the wall
Looking around this rancid place I realize I'm in jail
They described it in the Bible, but instead they call it Hell
Fed through the bars, food not fit for a pig
Oh, I wish I had a shovel for a tunnel I would dig
A bull walks up and down the hall, "asking how do you do?"
When deep inside his ugly heart he doesn't care about you
Ten minutes a day, you get to walk the corridor
You had better save your problems they heard them all before
The real joy comes every second day, because of the rule
You get to take a shower but don't forget to say thank you
Down the hall is a hole they use it as a threat
Just to show you that there is a worse hell yet
Laying here I look around, tell you what I see
A place I can't adjust to a place not for me.

Rest Stop
Chapter 1

Saturday, 5:45 a.m.

The Goddamn bell...seven years of Goddamn bells. That was Bobby's first thought on this new day.

"Hey, bro, you going to breakfast?" Bobby rubbed the traces of sleep from his eyes, turning to see Pauly standing there with his always-present childlike grin.

"How do you do it, you big fuck?" Bobby said as he sat up on his bed.

"Huh, do what?" Pauly replied in his baby Huey voice.

"For four years I've known you, two of them as my celly, and in all that time, every morning you wake up with that stupid fucking grin. Don't you ever hate waking up sometimes in this rancid fucking place?" Bobby said to Pauly with a look of bewilderment. Not waiting for a reply, Bobby climbed out of bed, pulling on his pants.

"They got grits and bacon this morning. Let's go, and we'll beat the lines," Pauly answered without even thinking about what Bobby just said.

Bobby pulled on his shirt and slipped into his thongs. He did not say so but he loved the grits at Prigg Cottage. Inside the walls, the grits were always mushy.

The reality hit him as they walked towards the chow hall. He was at the Cottage, one of the last two steps before hitting the street. It had been seven years since he had walked the streets. Seven years he had been paying for a split-second mistake. He thought of his temper and whether seven years had taught him how to control it. How many times on lonely nights he had thought, if he had not killed the asshole, if the ax had only glanced off his head, maybe only knocked him out. If a baseball bat would have been in reach, a pool-stick. Why did it have to be an ax? The newspaper headlines, *AX MURDER IN EUGENE*, surely did not help his case either. Bobby's thoughts broke as he felt a hand slip into his back pocket. It was Billy.

"I put some smoke in your back pocket bro, for dessert," Billy said as they came to the end of the chow line they were hoping to beat. Many cons liked the grits at Prigg.

"All right, you got your visits from that sweet thing," Bobby said, making a feel of his back pocket, making sure there wasn't a lump to bring about a shake down. The last thing he needed now was to be busted with some pot, two weeks before he had to see the Board.

"Yeah, sweet Charlene showed up bringing me just a taste for a trial run. She wanted to see how easy it was to get stuff in. She found out how easy it was, I think it excited her. She'll be back this afternoon with a full ounce," Billy snickered to himself thinking how he had manipulated Charlene over a three-month period. First, have the little lady fall in love with him; then, turn her into a mule. This was his third conquest in the eight years he had been down, making young girls into mules. He only had ten days before he was to see the parole board. This would be the third time. He had always been in and out of trouble with drugs, fighting, homosexual activity and a big mouth. He might have been out on the street three years earlier. It had been eleven months since his last fuck up. This time he had to hit the street. He could not handle it anymore, he thought.

"All right, it's party time," It was Jesse. If you were in need and were into it, Jesse gave the best head in the joint. "I told you my sister would come through, didn't I Billy? Didn't I, Billy?"

"Yeah, you did good, Jesse, but she wasn't any lay down. I had to lay a lot of my shit on her and it took three months of my talents," Billy replied, patting Jesse on the ass. Billy had been the biggest user of Jesse's talents over the years.

"Yeah, I know, she would never do it for me. She said she was too scared, but I knew you could do it," Jesse said, pushing Billy's hand off his ass. He hated Billy for doing that so everyone else could see. Jesse was not proud of the fact that he sucked dicks. He went on talking.

"I called my mom last night, and she told me that Charlene is coming to see you today. My mom sure is pissed that I ever gave you my sister's address and about you being in here for robbery and rape. She says Charlene's really in love with you. Well, my Mom thinks you're just using her to bring you drugs, for whatever you can get; that you'd just drop her when you get out. But I told Mom that you're not like that," Jesse said, looking right into Billy's eyes, believing what he just said.

"Sure, Jesse, I wouldn't use your sister. You, I would, but not your sister. Besides, you probably give better head than your sister," Billy remarked, which made Bobby and Pauly laugh.

"Why you always got to say shit like that?" Jesse asked with a hurt look in his eyes.

"Just kidding, Jess," Billy replied as he picked up his tray and made his way through the chow line.

The four of them sat down and scoffed down their breakfast, wanting to get out in the yard and get high. It had been over a week since the clique had any good smoke. The four of them had tripped a lot together over the years. They had been on the same softball team, worked out in the weight pile every day, and covered each other's backs when necessary. Now they were really close to getting out about the same time.

"Too bad Michael couldn't be here with us," Bobby said as he took a hit of the joint. "Umm," he said as he held his breath and said in a deep voice, "Good shit!"

"Yeah, he blew it. Trying to play psycho, thinking they would send him to the hospital, and that they would let him out sooner. That backfired on him, 'cause they do think he's crazy, so they may never let him out," Pauly said as he blew out his share of smoke.

"Trouble is I don't think Michael is faking it, he's one crazy son-of-a-bitch," Jesse said as he sucked on the last of the joint.

"You shouldn't talk, you fag cock-sucking asshole, about someone being crazy," Bobby quickly replied. He could never understand anyone turning to another guy to get off. However, as soon as he said it, he knew he was out of line. It was not his business what other people did. Besides, Jesse was all right for a fag, Bobby went on thinking. He had a heart, too. Jesse had stuck a nigger who tried to force him to have sex. He might be a fag but at least, he didn't do it with niggers.

Bobby hated blacks. It was a black that he killed.

"Cool it, Bobby, Jesse don't deserve that shit," Pauly was quick to defend. Pauly believed in the brotherhood, one for all and all for one.

"Yeah, I know. Sorry, Jesse, just feeling tight today," Bobby said with sincerity.

"No problem, Bobby," Jesse quickly replied. Bobby scared the shit out of him. Jesse had seen Bobby go off a time or two, and that was one person Jesse never wanted to have pissed at him.

"That's pretty good smoke your sister scored, Jess. You say she's coming back this afternoon?" Bobby cracked to break the tension he always seemed to cause.

"Yeah, she'll be here at one," Billy answered without giving Jesse a chance to answer. "She got the stuff from Animal, but it still wasn't cheap $200 for the ounce. Which reminds me dig in people. Let's have what cash you got. I've only got that hundred we took off that punk."

Bobby sat down on the grass and quickly looked up at the only watchtower that had any kind of view. The guard, Kamoza, was clean down the other end of the walkway talking to another guard. How easy it would be to get out of this place, Bobby thought. However, this is what they want. It was minimum security

5

and if a person were to fuck up, it was here before he hit the street that they wanted him to do it. Bobby thought about Animal, and how Animal used to say when he hit the street this time he was going straight. No more drugs, no more burglaries, all he wanted was to be free and never come back to prison again. As Bobby pulled off his shoe to get the money he stashed, he snickered to himself. How many people had Bobby known over the years that had said the same thing and were now inside the walls? Some had come and gone a couple of times in the time he had been there. Most of them swore they were not coming back either. Now Animal was supplying most of the joint with most of the smoke coming in. It was just a matter of time before someone would snitch him off, and Animal would be back again.

"I've already got half of the shit sold," Billy cracked as he put the forty dollars Bobby gave and the sixty dollars from Pauly inside the balloon with the hundred dollars he already had.

"I don't know why you keep doing that shit, brother," Bobby said as he watched Billy put his hand behind him and down his pants to slip the balloon up his ass. "You're the one packing the shit in, and the one selling it. Putting out the word before you have the stuff. Someone's going to snitch you off, you'll be back inside the walls and we'll be right behind you after we have to kill some asshole who snitched on you."

"You always get so paranoid, Bobby. I hear what you're saying, but I'm real careful about who I do business with," Billy quickly said to defend himself.

"Yeah, sure, whatever, let's go work out," Bobby came back. Knowing it was stupid to bring it up, Billy did things his way. They headed to the weight room. They had been working out together as a team for three years now. They all had unbelievable builds, Bobby best of all. He had not missed one day of going to the weight pile, except for the times he was in the hole, in the seven years he had been down. It was their way of escape. The hour or so they worked out everyday provided them with a form of power.

They all had their shirts off, proud to show off their builds and tattoos. Jesse was on the bench-pressing 200 pounds and Pauly was saying, "Two more, come on, one more," when a young kid came walking over.

"Billy, can I talk to you a minute?" the young kid said, as if he did not want to interrupt.

"Sure kid, talk, what's wrong?" Billy came back as if he was concerned.

"Well, you said when I gave you that hundred bucks, it was to make sure I didn't have any problems and if there were any, I was to come to you."

"Yeah, I sure did. Why, someone giving you some trouble?" Billy asked.

6

"Yeah, that nigger Duggan came over to my locker this morning and just reached in and took a carton of Camels. I asked him what he was doing. He says, 'Shut your white punky ass mouth, or I'll turn you over and fuck your li'l white ass.' I just shut up and he left. Then I came and found you."

Billy looked at Bobby who had his teeth locked. Everyone could see what he was thinking. They knew he hated niggers. What Bobby was really thinking was how weak this punk really was. The kid should have come flying off his bunk with anything he could grab and busted the nigger's head. Then he remembered who the kid was. He was busted for joy riding with some other kids. He was the only one over eighteen years old. Therefore, the judge thought he should teach the kid a lesson and gave the kid a year. The kid never even went inside the walls. They sent him straight to Prigg Cottage. Three or four months here, and they would spank his bottom and let him go saying, "Go and sin no more, son."

Then his thoughts went to the situation. If it had been some white dude, they would have just gone to the guy and told him to back off. Nothing was wrong with taking advantage of these young kids. They were natural prey for everyone who had done any time. But a nigger, Bobby's thoughts kept going. And I never liked that Duggan anyway, maybe I should...

His thoughts were interrupted by Pauly, "Don't start getting riled up Bobby, it ain't shit, bro."

Billy looked at the kid and said, "How much money you got, kid?"

"More money, what was that hundred for?"

"That was for membership, when we got to do something it costs more."

"I only have $20.00 left," the kid said.

"Well, it's going to cost you $50. But bring twenty to lunch, and I'll give you a week for the other thirty. Now get out of here, don't worry about it. We'll take care of it."

The kid just nodded, turned and walked away.

Bobby tapped Jesse on the shoulder and said, "Get up, Jess, It's my set." Bobby lay down on the bench and told Pauly to go to 240. At the beginning of 15 reps, Billy started speaking, "I'll go to Duggan and ask him to back off."

Pauly was counting.

"We going to ask for the kid's smokes back." Jesse asked.

"14, 15. One more, bro. "Bobby did it too easy."One more," Pauly said again. He reached to pull the bar onto the rack. However, Bobby kept going. "23, 24," Pauly was counting aloud while Billy and Jesse watched Bobby's muscles rip. "28, 29," Bobby took a deep breath, gave out an agonizing yell and said, "Thirty." He put the bar in the holder without Pauly's help.

"I'm going to see Duggan personally," Bobby said between breaths.

"We're getting too short for any kind of trouble, bro. Just let Billy take care of it, okay," Pauly said in a serious voice. More than anyone else, Pauly wanted out of this place for good. He had an old lady and a kid on the street. His old lady had hung in there for five years. His kid was only two years old when he was busted for manufacturing crank in Eugene.

Pauly had everything going for a person who was about to get out. His father-in-law owned a tree farm in Springfield. Therefore, he would fall right into a good-paying job and a wife who had hung in there. He had seen many guys lose their old ladies while they were down. In fact, almost everyone he knew, including Bobby.

He wanted to make it right by his kid. "Dustin, oh, Dustin," he said to himself a thousand times, "When I get out, I'm going to show you the best Dad in the whole world."

Pauly had known Bobby, at least something about him, before he even came to the joint. Bobby was one of his customers on the street. Boy, those days, money, more than you could spend. Cook up one batch a month and you could live like a king. That was probably what made my old lady stick it out with me. We always lived high on the hog when we were together, until I was busted that is. His mind just kept wandering.

Pauly knew about Bobby's old lady being raped by some black guy in Eugene. They never caught the person. However, all of a sudden there were many blacks being beaten up in the Eugene area. Then a black burned one of Bobby's fronts. Bobby caught up with the guy and killed him with an ax. At least, that was the story he heard. Bobby never talked about it much.

"All right, Pauly, go with Billy and Jesse, and tell that nigger to back off. I'm going to take a shower," Bobby said as he grabbed his shirt and headed for the shower. He was pissed.

He knew Pauly was right. He did not need any trouble. He was pissed because he really did not know what was pissing him off. That nigger did not do anything he had not done to other punk kids. In the joint, if you do not have a heart, you do not have zoo zoos and wam wams, munchies, you take shit off everybody, even turned out to do homosexual activities. Bobby remembered kicking that Mexican's ass, the second day he was at the joint. Hurting him bad, too. To get the message out, fuck with me and you know you fucked with someone. The message was worth a week in the hole. If Bobby had only known his reputation had beaten him to the joint, it might have saved him a week in the hole.

He did not even know himself, how strong he had become. He had become a breathing monster. He could snap a man's back before he knew what he was

8

doing. He was a good-looking person with long blond hair and a clean-shaven face. He only stood about 5 feet 10 inches, but he packed 190 pounds of solid muscle.

Duggan was on the handball court, standing there with five of his black friends when Billy, Pauly and Jesse walked up.

"Hey Duggan, you got a minute?" Billy said, stopping four or five feet short of the group. He knew it was not cool to invade a man's space.

"You got something to say to me, you can say it in front of my friends, Billy," Duggan answered. Duggan and Billy had done a few dope deals together inside the walls. Even though Duggan did not like whites and Billy was not fond of blacks, people would build that kind of respect for each other over the years.

"If that's how you want it. We need you to back off from that kid you took the box of Camels from this morning. He paid us his membership dues and we got to look out after him, if you know what I mean," Billy replied.

"Yeah, that's no problem, Billy. Just don't go making a habit of it," Duggan replied as if he did not give a shit.

It would have ended right there, but Jesse had to get in the act. Jesse hated blacks, too. Everyone had heard the story about Jesse stabbing the nigger who tried to take some of his ass. What most people didn't know was Jesse had stuck the black after he had already taken his ass.

"You need to give the kid back his carton of smokes," Jesse said in a king shit voice.

"Fuck you, you little fag. I respect Billy, but when the likes of you pops an order at me, I say fuck you, and fuck you, too, Billy. You can go and tell that to your nigger killing ax murderer, too. He don't scare me none, there ain't no ax for him here," Duggan said as he took a threatening step forward. One of his friends put a hand out, stopping him, only to make him say, "You guys don't own every punk that comes into this joint like you think you do."

"Yeah, we do," Billy, said as he grabbed Jesse's arm and started to walk away, "If they're white, we do."

When they got around the corner, Pauly smacked Jesse on the back of the head and said, "You dumb fuck, who gives a shit about a box of smokes? We ended it and you got to open your stupid mouth."

"Fuck that nigger. Bobby will take care of his ass," Jesse replied, rubbing the back of his head.

"That's what I'm afraid of, you asshole. So, now it's all right if Bobby goes down to take care of Duggan, a fight breaks out, and we get in the middle of it. So we all end up inside the walls, all because you can't keep your fucking mouth shut!" Pauly said in a pissed voice.

"Oh, fuck it! It ain't going to be like that," Jesse said.

"Pauly's right, Jesse. We took care of it and you blew it. You know Bobby's going to want to do something that might bring the shit down on all of us," Billy said. They all headed back to tell Bobby the news.

Bobby was lying on his bunk reading a science fiction book when the guys got back and told him the story. Bobby just stared into the ceiling for a minute, then said, "Jesse, go get your blade and bring it on back here."

"Now hold on, Bobby. It ain't come to that brother," Pauly was quick to say.

"I know bro. I'm just going to scare that nigger a little," Bobby replied. Pauly knew better. Bobby was not the type of person to just threaten someone. He just went and did it. Pauly also knew there was no arguing with Bobby, either. Jesse smiled and went to get the knife he had stashed.

"Well, I'm going back to reading my book. See you guys for lunch," Bobby said as he retrieved his book from his stomach and continued to read.

Pauly did not like it. He did not like the way Bobby was acting. He did not like the way Jesse smiled when Bobby told him to go get the knife.

Pauly, on the other hand, never took anything seriously. His philosophy was, "whatever will be, will be." When it came to playing the hand, he was always there for whatever was called for.

"See you at lunch. I'm going to go catch some z's before lunch. I got a feeling some shit's going to come down'" Billy said and went his bunk.

"Hold on, Billy. Would ya?" Pauly said, "I got the same feeling about some shit coming down. You know we don't need any shit right now, Billy."

"Then I suggest you don't go to lunch Pauly, because that's when I think it's going to come down."

"Come on, Billy; don't talk to me like that. I'm not saying I ain't going to be there. I'm just saying we don't need any shit."

"Hey, bro, I ain't talking to you bad. You don't have to prove yourself to me. You've done that more than once. What I'm saying is, you got a prime old lady on the street, a seven year old kid that needs a daddy, and nobody's going to say anything if you don't show up for lunch."

"Yeah, sure, see you at lunch," Pauly said as he walked away.

"I got the blade, bro. What do you want me to do with it?" Jesse asked.

Bobby did not put down his book, but replied, "Hang on to it until the lunch bell goes off, then bring it over to me." He went back to reading his book. Jesse walked away feeling good. Duggan would learn he should never have talked to him as he did.

Bobby was reading how Conan, with one swipe of his sword, removed the head from the shoulders of Hagan, the evil wizard. Bobby could picture himself as Conan.

When the lunch bell rang, Jesse was there within seconds. Without saying one word, he handed the knife to Bobby. It was a homemade knife done in the shop. Just a piece of steel with two edges as sharp as razor blades with two pieces of wood taped onto the end of it. Bobby put it in his pants and tucked his shirt around it.

A minute later, Billy showed up and said, "Let's do this trip without Pauly. He's got something going for him that we don't."

"Why, did he say he wasn't going to lunch with you?" Bobby asked.

"No, he'll be here. I just think we can do it without him," Billy remarked.

"Yeah, I agree with Billy," Bobby said.

"Let's just go," Jesse added.

As the conversation ended, Pauly walked up. "I'm hungry, let's go eat.," he said.

They all headed for the chow hall. Bobby went to the opposite side from where they normally ate. This was the side where the blacks entered. Bobby did not look to see where the guards were. He knew that there was always one at each entrance and two in front at the food section.

Kamoza was one of the guards stationed where Bobby normally entered. He saw the clique walk in on the other side. He knew that this was unusual and kept an eye on the group. It did not take long for Kamoza to see what was going on. Duggan was rapping with a few of his friends. He and his friends did not see the clique come up behind them.

Bobby did not remember grabbing the blade out of his pants. In fact, until that split-second, he was not sure what he was going to do. He put a death hold around Duggan's neck and said, "I don't need an ax, nigger." And Bobby's hand came up.

Duggan did not know how a bar of steel got around his neck. He heard someone say something. He felt a sharp pain in his back, but was not aware that a blade had just penetrated his liver.

Kamoza blew his whistle.

A friend of Duggan punched Bobby in the head. Bobby fell, leaving the blade in Duggan's back. Duggan's legs gave out and he fell to the floor. Pauly grabbed a tray and smashed it against the head of the person who struck Bobby. The second the guy hit the floor, Billy's foot landed on his face and broke the guy's jaw in two places. Another black said, "Hey, man, what's going on?" Jesse landed a kick to the person's balls and an upper cut that broke his nose.

Bobby was quick to his feet. The clique looked around to see if any more of Duggan's friends would come to his rescue. They all just stood there with their mouths opened. Kamoza was on the phone calling reinforcements. The clique turned and headed out of the chow hall. An army of guards met them.

"That's the guy who did the stabbing," Kamoza said, pointing to Bobby. Three guards quickly seized Bobby. The other guards surrounded Pauly, Jesse and Billy. They were marched toward the holding tank. That was where prisoners were kept before they were sent behind the walls. There was not a hole at Prigg Cottage.

They were put in the holding tank and the iron door slammed closed.

Jesse was the first to speak, "Fuck, they're having meatloaf for lunch. I wonder if they're going to feed us before they send us back. Did you see that nigger's nose caved in?"

"Goddamn, Bobby, I think you killed Duggan," Billy said in a low voice.

"Blood was shooting out his back like a fucking faucet," Jesse added.

Pauly sat there with his head in his hands, not saying anything. Bobby leaned back, staring at the ceiling. He said to nobody in particular, "We should have done it a lot smarter than we did. I blew it, guys, and it looks like I got you all involved in a jackpot. Sorry."

"What the fuck!" Billy cracked, "What's done is done--too late now to be sorry."

"Well, I ain't doing another seven years for some asshole nigger. They ain't going to get me back to the walls. Not alive anyway," Bobby said.

"What do you got in mind, bro?" Jesse asked.

"I don't know, but when the time comes, I will. Be ready all, except for Pauly. You ride this one out. You got something going for you out there. They ain't got you on nothing except for fighting."

"Oh, fuck you! You don't really believe that shit, do you? They're going to burn all of us for this shit. You make a move, count me in."

"All right, bro, I just wish I'd listened to Billy and Jess. They said to do this shit without you. I'm just sorry I got you involved."

"Like Billy says, what is is. So fuck it."

The door opened and the three guards came in with handcuffs and started to put them on the clique. Bobby tightened up his hand. His wrist swelled up a good half inch. The guard clamped the handcuffs on him. They walked out and slammed the iron door. After seven years, Bobby was used to slamming iron doors. However, he was tired of it and said to himself, "That's the last one I'll hear."

"Jesus," Jesse remarked, "I really thought I saw the walls for the last time. Looks like that's the end of that dream."

"Fuck, and Charlene is coming in twenty minutes," Billy said which seemed to be the only thing bothering him at that moment.

Charlene, twenty minutes, a car. That answered the question going through Bobby's head at that moment.

"What are you thinking, bro?" Pauly asked with his head still between his hands. He knew Bobby too well. He knew he was not thinking about going back to the wall. In addition, it scared him, because whatever Bobby was thinking, it included the rest of them. Bobby always did the thinking for the clique. Jesse and Billy needed someone to do that for them maybe he did too.

"We're going to take a swing on getting out of here. I fucked it up for all of us. The board isn't going to give any of us any advantage now. I'm really fucked. Kamoza saw me put the blade to Duggan. That was the second nigger I killed. They're going to life me for sure. I'd rather die."

Pauly's head came out of his hands. His face turned right to Bobby, but his thoughts were still his own. Bullshit, I never did need Bobby to do my thinking, I never did. I went along because it was the way to get by inside the walls. I have to think of Patty and Dustin. I'd rather die, that's what Bobby said, and he meant it too.

"Tell us what you got in mind, bro. We're in, you know that," Jesse said along with Billy, nodding his head.

Pauly's thoughts changed, looking at Jesse and Billy. He knew they would do anything Bobby suggested. Bobby gave him an out and instead of taking it, he had to say, "Count me in. Was it too late? He didn't even want to hear what Bobby was about to say. He knew it would be some off the wall idea. One that Bobby just thought of in the last few minutes. In fact, he probably didn't have an idea. Bobby's next words confirmed that.

"I don't know for sure. I do know in the next few minutes about three or four guards are going to come through that door, lead us out to a waiting van, put us inside and take us to the walls. We all know that once we're inside the walls, there ain't no getting out. So whatever's got to be done has to be done between this cell and the van. I think I can get my left cuff off, there's some room to play with. If we can get lucky and Charlene is there with her car that will answer what we do after we overpower the guards. Billy, pull off this cuff," Bobby spit all around his wrist and stuck his hand out to Billy. Billy didn't hesitate. He gripped on to Bobby's cuff. And with no thought of any pain that Bobby might feel, he began to pull.

Bobby had no thoughts of pain. His skin was being torn from his hand as he pulled away from the cuffs and Billy's grip.

Jesse got down between the two sets of hands and began to spit all around the cuff. The cuffs came off.

Bobby gave out with a soft, "ahhh," and with a final pull, the skin on both sides of his hand and the cuff came off.

"All right," Jesse said wiping off the blood off that had gotten on his lips.

All right, Pauly thought. All right, what? So what if he got the cuff off? Now what?

"When the guards show up, every one stand in front of me. I'll hang onto the cuff the best I can without them seeing. When we get outside, I'll make my move. You guys, do whatever you can. One of the guards is going to have a key to the cuffs. We got to be sure to get that. Billy, you still have the $200 you leistered?"

"Sure do!" Billy replied.

"Good, we're going to need money. I know a place we can score some guns."

Money, guns. Jesus, fucking Christ, man. What the fuck were they talking about? This is no plan, they are dreaming. Pauly's thoughts kept going. I do not want any part of this. He had to try to talk them out of it.

"How about the guards in the towers? They'll just blow us away when we take off running," Pauly said, hoping it would bring everyone back to reality.

"Yeah, I thought about that," Bobby answered, "We're not going to run. We lay the guards out, hop in the van and get out of Dodge."

Fuck, now he is reaching, Pauly was thinking. He just got that idea. A few minutes ago, they were going to take Charlene's car out of Dodge. Fuck, Bobby is watching some kind of movie in his head. For the first time since he had known Bobby, Pauly saw him as a lame brain.

"I know a place we can lay low, not two miles from here," Jesse remarked with excitement, "A good buddy of mine always got good drugs and can score us some pussy with just a phone call."

Nobody got to respond to Jesse's statement. They all turned to the door, as they heard a key go into the lock.

"This is it guys, let's do it," Bobby said in a low voice.

"Do what? Do fucking what, Bobby? What's the fucking plan?" Pauly's mind was going a mile a minute, "Jesse's already got us getting high and getting laid. Billy's acting like there's not a question in his mind."

Bobby stood up in the back of the cell. The other three stood in front to give him cover. Bobby's mind was racing, the cell door swung open, and two guards stood there. Two, was that possible? Would they only have two guards to transport them to the walls?

Bobby wiped off the blood on the side of his pants. His hand was really bleeding, "Look at my guys. They don't know what the fuck I'm going to do. I know Pauly don't like it. He is probably right; the guards in the tower will blow us away. But what the fuck man, I ain't got any choice. I ain't staying behind the walls the rest of my life. That fucking nigger, I should have done it smarter. God damn, my hand hurts."

"Let's go, guys. There's a van waiting for you outside," said a guard. Bobby knew this guard from the clothing room inside the walls. Good sign, he thought, they must be short-handed."

They walked past the guards standing on each side of the door. Bobby got by without the guards noticing the missing cuff on his bleeding hand. A couple drops of blood dropped on the tip of his shoe.

"Hold up, right there," the other guard said when they reached the last locked door before they exited onto the street.

The guard walked past the four inmates to a speaker box, pushed the button and said, "Officers Cox and Turnbell transporting four inmates back to OSP."

A buzzer went off. The guard pulled on the door, opened it, stood to the side and said, "Let's move, guys."

One guard walked ahead. The four inmates followed. The other guard closed the iron door and tailed behind. As they made their way down the stairs, Bobby looked to see if there was another guard waiting at the truck. He could not believe they would only use two guards. No guard, Bobby could not believe his luck.

The lead guard went to the back of the van and opened the two back doors. Jesse, Pauly and Billy waited for Bobby to make his move. The rear guard moved to the other side of the van. Jesse climbed up into the van.

Cox, the guard from the clothing room, felt something trickle on the tip of his shoe. He looked down and saw it was blood. He looked up to see where it came from. He never knew what hit him. Bobby's left hand came up, using the hard part of his palm to hit the bottom of Cox's nose. He followed through with a blow that pushed pieces of Cox's nasal bone into his brain. Cox was dead before he hit the ground.

Turnbell turned enough for Jesse to get both hands over his head and put a paralyzing chokehold on him. Billy, always good with his feet, was quick with his favorite kick right to the nut sack, hard enough to help Jesse pull Turnbell into the van.

Pauly was eyeing the watchtowers, expecting a fury of bullets. There was not a guard in sight. He looked around to see how many people were coming to the guards' rescue. There was no one around. Bobby spoke first, "Help me get Cox into the van."

As Bobby directed, Pauly seized Cox by the arms and looked right into his face. He could not believe what he saw, or that it could have happened. One look told him that Cox was dead. It was not the blood because there was little blood. It was Cox's eyes. They said, "I'm dead." There was just a blank stare. Pauly could not believe the look. His nose was not where it should have been. Pauly did not even see Bobby hit the guy. Did he do that with his hand?

"Get in, I'll drive. Find the fucking keys and get those cuffs off you. We're out of here!" Bobby continued.

Bobby made his way to the front of the van looking around; there was not a soul in sight. He said under his breath, "Thank you, Lord." Amen came out of his mouth when he saw the ignition keys dangling. He started the van and slowly drove away from Prigg Cottage.

Before they were 100 yards off the property, there was a knock on the window. It was Billy.

"That's Charlene coming down the road, bro," Billy yelled through the window. Bobby stopped the van in the middle of the road. He got out, went to the back, opened the door and said to Billy, "Stop her, get in the car with her and follow us. Pauly, come ride up front with me."

They both did as they were told, along with Charlene, who could not believe her eyes. Billy got in the driver's side, told Charlene to move over, made a U-turn and followed the van. Bobby could not believe his luck; things just kept falling into place.

"Well, we did it, bro," Bobby said as he put out his palm. Pauly just looked at Bobby and without thinking gave Bobby 5.

"How's Turnbell doing back there?"

"Jesse put him out with a choke hold. He's still breathing, which is a lot more than I can say about Cox. You really did a number on him!"

"Got in a lucky punch is all," was Bobby's cold reply.

"Here, give me your hand. Let me take that cuff off," Pauly said still looking at Bobby and thinking it is all over now. No Patty, no Dustin. A guard has been killed, Duggan has been killed, and it is all over. "Boy, you sure fucked up your hand," was all he could say.

"Yeah, hurts like a bitch too," Bobby, replied.

"Tell me, bro," Pauly came back, "And tell me straight, 'cause I ain't Billy or Jesse. You got some kind of plan? I mean, we're in some shit. The nigger doesn't matter but we've done in the guard. We're talking FBI, every cop in the state, and every Boy Scout looking for a do-gooder badge. I mean, unless we got a plan, they're going to pop us. You know what I'm saying?"

"Hey, bro, first off, I ain't ever done you anything without respect. Billy and Jesse are family, but you're different and you should know that," Bobby came back acting like he was hurt about the way Pauly asked his question.

"In the second place," Bobby continued, "I just got up a few hours ago with none of today being planned. It all just happened. I can't believe half of this shit myself. But it happened. I mean in a few hours, I killed a fucking nigger, killed some asshole guard, I'm driving down Interstate 5 with my brothers, and there's not a bar or a slamming door in sight. Yeah, I got a plan, one major plan. One big goal and this you can count on. I'll never see another set of bars. I'll never hear one more slamming fucking iron door. But other than that bro, I agree we better come up with a plan for getting out of this shit and this state real fast. First, we got to dump the van and the guard in the back. That's where Charlene and her car come in. I know a place I used to hunt out by Sweet Home where we can dump the van. Then we head to Eugene and pick up some guns, because whatever plan I come up with, it's going to take guns. I do have one plan in mind; let me know what you think of it."

"Lay it on me; I am all ears," Pauly answered. He was anxious to hear some sort of plan.

"You remember The Wizard, my old celly?" Bobby asked.

"Sure, he's one hell of a dude. But he's gone straight, hasn't he?" Pauly answered with a question.

"Yeah, he got married to a fine young thing, even got a kid. Anyway, when we were cellies we used to lie in bed at night and tell each other our scams. Those we had done and those we thought about doing. Well, The Wizard had this hot one and he never implemented it. But we both believed it would be a winner," Bobby stopped in a train of thought.

Losing his patience, Pauly said, "Well, go on I'm listening."

"Rest stop," Bobby answered as a smile crossed his face.

"Huh?" Pauly responded and then added, "And what the fuck you laughing at?"

"Oh, just thinking about The Wizard. Never knew anybody like him. Yeah, rest stop, rest area, you know, what you see along the highways," Bobby's thoughts went back to The Wizard. Maybe he should give him a call. The Wizard would come to his aid. No, he had done all right for himself. He does not need to be tied up in this shit. Yeah, he owed him at least that much.

"What the fuck are you talking about? I still don't get it. Talk English would ya?" Pauly asked, breaking Bobby's train of thoughts.

"OK, bro, picture this," Bobby went on, "people go to Las Vegas with a pocket full of money they're going to blow. I mean, like an average of 1,000 bucks."

"Yeah, so?" Pauly interrupted.

"Bear with me, would you?" Bobby continued, "Now 60 miles before they get to Vegas, there's this rest stop. It's their last chance to take a piss before they hit the big city and start blowing their money. With me so far?"

"Yeah, so far, go on," Pauly answered, becoming more interested.

"Anyway, that's it. We take over the rest stop and save the people a trip to Las Vegas." Pauly just looked at Bobby in bewilderment. Bobby continued, "Not only that, we're in and out of the place in less than half an hour with, are you ready for this?" Bobby went on, not waiting for an answer, "Twenty to forty thousand dollars."

Pauly never was what most would consider a diehard criminal. In his eyes, he was a bootlegger. He made speed. The best speed around. He took pride in his work. He only used the best ingredients. If a batch did not come out right, he would dump it rather than push it off on someone, and maybe make someone sick. His customers knew this and when they wanted the best crank around, it was Pauly's speed they bought. Now somehow he was mixed up in a double murder and a prison escape in a stolen van. And now he was listening to how he was about to get involved in a gangbang robbery with guns. He never used a gun for crime in his life.

That was as of this morning. It hit him all at once; his life would never be the same again. In addition, listening to Bobby confirmed that. It sounded good. Maybe with enough money he could get out of the country, somewhere where no one could find him. He would send for Patty and Dustin when he got things together.

"Well, Pauly, pretty hot, huh?" Bobby asked, breaking Pauly's thoughts.

"It's a plan I never would have thought of. You know, bro, I've always been a cooker, but this is kind of out my league. So, I ain't got much choice, I'm sticking with you all the way," Pauly ended as he turned around and looked through the back window to see how Jesse was doing.

Turnbell was handcuffed, and a rag was sticking out his mouth. Jesse was sitting there smoking a cigarette.

"How are they doing back there?" Bobby asked.

"Jesse's got him bound and gagged. What are we doing about Turnbell?"

"I've been thinking about that," Bobby replied, then went on, "We're not going to hang around in Oregon very long. But we've got to be here long enough to cop some guns. By now every cop in the state is looking for this van. In about five minutes, we will be off the road, out of this van and in Charlene's car. We will be back on the road again, and heading to Eugene, where I can get some guns. I don't know about Turnbell, do you think we should do him in?"

It was ironic that no one at the prison knew what had happened. No one had seen anything. As far as anyone knew, the van with four prisoners should be pulling into OSP by now.

"Do him in? Kill him? No, no way, Bobby," Pauly's heart was racing as fast as his thoughts. He was not religious, but he knew when something was just flat out wrong. To kill this guard in cold blood was wrong. The guy probably had a family. It was an unthinkable evil. Had he ever really known Bobby?

"No!" Pauly answered, "Why, I mean, what's there to gain by killing him? We just keep him handcuffed to the van and before they find him, we'll be long gone."

Bobby did not like the way Pauly had freaked out. The way he said no, like no matter what they all decided, it was going to be his way. What the hell, he already killed one guard. They could not hang him twice. Of course, Turnbell was never a bad bull. He did his job but never fucked with you when it was not called for. Pauly was probably right, they would be long gone by the time they found the van. It could be by the time they found the van Turnbell would have died of thirst.

"I didn't say I was going to kill him. I just asked you if you think we should," Bobby answered as if killing the guard was the last thing on his mind.

The van pulled off the main road and headed down an old logging road. Billy and Charlene were right behind them.

"It's hard to believe it's been eight years since I've been here. And it seems like yesterday," Bobby said, "If my memory is right and they ain't changed this place, there's a bend in the road just ahead, then a road that turns to the left that heads to an old cabin."

Ten seconds later, they came to a bend in the road. Down a road to the left about 200 yards, they came to an old cabin that was now burned down except for a few logs.

"Son-of-a-bitch, they burned it down!" Bobby said as he got out of the van. Billy was out of the car in seconds. He ran over to Bobby, picked him up in a bear hug and screamed, "We fuckin' did it, and we're fuckin' free!" He kissed Bobby on the cheek as he put him down.

Jesse pounded from inside van and yelled, "Let me out of here!"

As soon as Pauly opened the door, Jesse came flying out, threw his hands around Bobby and Billy, and said, "Just like in the movies, I mean fucking slick, man!"

"I skinned the first deer I ever poached in that cabin 20 years ago. Pisses me off that someone burned it down," Bobby said. "I'm going for a quick walk alone, and do some thinking. Make sure Turnbell ain't going anywhere and I'll be back in a few minutes."

"Take your time, bro. It's been eight years since I've had any pussy. I ain't waiting for another eight minutes," Billy said as he looked over at the car. Charlene was just getting out. "Get back in there, baby. I'm going to show you what I've been talking about during visits." Charlene just smiled.

"Not until I give my baby sister a kiss," Jesse said as he walked over to his sister. He gave her a big hug and a kiss, and then said, "Does this mean that you're not going to be a virgin anymore?" He smiled as he ran his fingers through her hair. What Jesse knew of love was what he felt for his little sister.

"With you as a big brother, I doubt if she was still a virgin after she learned how to walk," Billy said, giving Jesse a push, "Out of my way, man. I got some catchin' up to do."

"You take it easy on my little sister, Billy," Jesse said seriously.

"Billy's the one in trouble, big brother," Charlene said as she threw her arms around Billy. Her hands went to his ass and squeezed.

"Ohhh-weee!" was all Billy could say as he led Charlene to the back seat of the car.

Bobby walked out of sight, stopped by a fallen log, lit up a Camel and sat down on the log. He took in big breaths of fresh forest air. He always loved the forest. The only memories he had of his father were those times his dad had taken him hunting. His fondest memory was when he was about seven years old, camping out with his dad and waking up cold one night. He had slipped out of his sleeping bag and into his dad's. His dad did not yell or tell him to get out. All his dad did was put his arms around Bobby and hold him. Bobby had never felt more secure or safe in his life than he did that night. He took in his dad's scent, one of the only times Bobby could remember being next to his father without smelling booze. Bobby never had that secure feeling again. His mind at that time did not allow all the ugly visions he had of his father. The uncalled for beatings he and his brothers received. The broken nose his mother got when his dad had lost his temper because she stood up for the boys. No, the only thing going through Bobby's mind right then were nice thoughts.

Here he was in the woods, a million miles it seemed from the problems of that very morning. However, the nice thoughts could not last long. They stopped when he thought of his brother--how he had been murdered, stabbed ten times. No doubt over some stupid drug deal that went sour. Then reality hit him and he started to think about the present.

He wondered if they had police helicopters out looking for them. Could they tie him in with Charlene's car? He knew they had to get out of the state fast. He thought it would be better to split up. They would be on the lookout for four people together. Should he go to Maggot's place in Eugene, to get the guns? The cops would be looking for him in his old stomping grounds, but they had to have guns. Should they dump the broad? Sure would like to lie close to her. Bobby's mind kept wandering. Is that plan of The Wizard's really something to do? One thing Bobby knew for sure, they all had to get out the vicinity very fast. He dropped the butt of the Camel, squashed it out and headed back to the guys.

Pauly and Jesse were laughing, but in a way, they were envious of Charlene's car bouncing up and down.

"If she weren't my sister," Jesse thought.

"If Billy would share," Pauly thought, "No, I better not ask him. Boy, is she a moaner," Pauly went on thinking, "Sweet, young, firm little tits." Five years, four months, seventeen days, no, eighteen days now since he and Patty had been under the sheets together. Pauly kept track of his days without any loving on a calendar. He had a habit of announcing the fact to the clique every day.

Bobby walked halfway back, and then turned around to take one last view and draw in some deep breaths. He could see pieces of Green Peter Lake through the mass of trees. He remembered going water skiing there with his brother when they were just kids. He got an ugly rush, a chill of some sort. He did not know what it meant, but he did not like it.

"How did things come to this?" Bobby's thoughts went on. All he had to do was cool it, two or three more months. He could find a job. Pauly would be better off. He had his old lady, a kid, a good job. How stupid, big deal! So what if that fucking nigger moved in on that green nose kid, it was not his problem. Why did it even piss him off? He didn't get to finish the book he was reading.

"Hey, bro, we better get on the move," Pauly opined.

"I used to ski on that lake, with my family," Bobby came back.

"Oh, yeah, is that Foster Lake?" Pauly asked.

"No, that's Green Peter. Foster Lake's on the other side of those hills."

"Come up with any ideas, Bobby?" Pauly asked.

"Not really, other than what we've already talked about. I know we got to get a move on. It wouldn't surprise me if they had helicopters out looking for us. Do you think they've tied us in with Charlene's car?"

"I don't know bro. This is all new to me, other than watching cop shows. For some reason though, I think we're safe with Charlene's car, for a while anyway."

"Billy's all done getting his pussy?" Bobby asked.

"Yeah, they were just finishing up when I came to get you. She sure is a cutie, I sure would..."

"Forget it. We don't need any kind of strained relations between the brothers. But I hear what you're saying. Let's take care of what we got to do. Then we can think about getting some pussy. Anything on the radio about us yet?" Bobby asked getting back to reality.

"No, me and Jess been listening, and not a word about us. You think they even know yet. I mean, is it possible that no one saw us and they haven't missed the van yet?"

Pauly did not know how close he was to being right. It was just a few minutes ago that a guard who was going to have lunch and play some pool with the guard, Cox, had even inquired about the van which should have been at the prison by now.

"No way, we've been lucky but not that lucky," Bobby answered, and then went on, "I got to call Maggot and have him meet us along the freeway and bring us some guns. Right now, let's just get the hell out of here."

As they were walking back, Pauly said, "I've been thinking about the rest stop idea. You know, it could work. I mean who has ever done it before. It's just dumb enough to work."

"Well, it's the only idea we got right now. So that's the one we're going to shoot for," Bobby said as they came in sight of the van and the car.

Billy was tucking in his shirt. Jesse was sitting on a log smoking a big fat joint. Charlene was squatting next to a bush taking a whiz.

"Hey, all right, come here and take a hit off this shit Charlene copped for us," Jesse yelled out as if he did not have a care in the world. In fact, Jesse did not have a care in the world. His life had always been one of living the now. Even in prison, he had adjusted instantly, this was the now, this is what he has to do and enjoy it for what it was. His mind did not think of how serious their situation was. He was with his brothers, his real sister and had a fat joint in his hand. What the hell, life was going pretty good, right now.

"Jesus, what did you do? Roll a cigar?" Pauly said as he reached for the joint and drew in a deep long hit.

"Jesse, I take back what I said about you giving better head than your sister," Billy announced as he joined in for his turn on the joint.

"Fuck you, Billy, and if you ever tell my sister any of that shit, I'll kill you!" Jesse said in a firmer voice that he had ever been heard to use. In fact, they were all shocked. Billy could rip Jesse's head off, and Jesse knew it. However, Jesse was ready to go at the moment if Billy did not say the right thing.

"Hey bro, just joking. You know, I'd never say anything to your sister like that. It's all joint shit and that stays between us, okay," Billy said.

It calmed Jesse down. He replied, "Yeah, no problem, it's just that my sister is the only thing special in my life. And you know she's the only one in my life that has ever looked up to me. Well, just don't say that shit. Besides those days are over. I ain't doing that shit no more."

"Fine, brother, fine, I agree from now on all we eat are the finest looking beavers, suck on the firmest tits and fuck the best snatch there is around."

"Sounds good to me," Jesse said and joined in the laughter.

"Well guys we got some planning to do," Bobby said as he took his turn on the joint.

"What's the plan bro? So far you've done all right," Billy remarked slowly, blowing out smoke.

"Can a girl get in on some of that dope?" Charlene asked.

Bobby handed her the last of the joint. Everyone stopped what they were doing and stared at this sweet young thing. The way her lips sucked in, her little turned up nose, the scent she had that these guys had only imagined the last few years. They could smell the lovemaking she had just endured. She looked up, saw everyone looking at her, and remarked, "Did I interrupt something or what?"

"Well, we were just going over the plans we have, little darling. But, know it or not, you're part of them. So, I guess I'll just go on. First, do you want to be in on what we're going to do? I mean we're in some pretty heavy shit. And it's not too late for you to get out of it."

"Hey, Billy's my old man. I go where he goes, same thing with my brother. And don't worry about me being in the way. I mean, I ain't ever done any time or nothing, but I'll pull my own weight. I haven't been Mother Teresa in the past. Besides, I'm rushing, and I'm excited. I didn't expect any of this when I got up this morning."

"Don't feel like the Lone Ranger. None of us did when we got up today," Bobby replied.

He went on, "That's what I'm getting at, Charlene. This has been ad-lib, spontaneous. We had no plan and we got no plan, other than one thing: none of us plans to go back to the walls. And we're ready to do whatever we have got to, to make sure we don't. A nigger has been killed and, more important, I killed a guard. He's lying in the back of the van, right now, cold as ice. Now we have to decide what to do about the other guard. Anyone got any ideas?"

"Do him in and get the fuck out of here," Jesse replied, trying to act like it was no big deal.

"No way, bad karma, man," Pauly came back, "Cox was killed, well, because we had no choice. Besides, Bobby and me already talked about that. There's no way they'll even find him or the van before we're long gone."

"What do you think, Billy?" Bobby asked.

"Turnbell was always an all right guard. No sense in killing him if he ain't going to be no trouble. I'm with Pauly."

Turnbell lay inside the van feeling totally helpless. Cox, his good friend, was lying dead next to him. He could hear the cons talking, but could not make out what they were saying. It was enough to hear his name mentioned. That scared him. Just last night, he was bowling with Cox. In fact, just an hour or so before, he was trying to think of a way to tell Cox to shut up about bowling a 216 game. He was glad he did not say anything now. Were they going to kill him? Was that what they were talking about now? He heard a girl's voice and wondered where she had come from. He thought of his two daughters and Cox's three-month-old son. He began to shiver and to pray.

"So be it, Turnbell lives. Pauly, go check on him. Make sure he ain't going nowhere. Billy and Jesse, you guys climb in the trunk; the cops are going to be looking for four guys. Let's make it two guys and a girl going down the freeway." As usual, Bobby was taking control.

Pauly opened up the back door of the van. Turnbell suddenly turned to the door. He could not speak because of the gag, but if he could he would have said, "Please don't kill me, please let me live." Pauly walked over to him and checked on the handcuffs and the bar they were attached too. He was not going anywhere. Pauly spoke, "Turnbell, I don't know if it will make a difference. But you're going to live because I voted for you to live. You know I had nothing to do with Cox getting it either. I'm just hoping you will say so when you make your report. Also, I would appreciate it if you would tell my wife this was nothing I planned. Just something that happened and it is too late to turn back now. Tell her I love her and that I ask her to forgive me."

Turnbell looked at Paul. His eyes saying thanks. At that point, in time, he was going to do everything that he was asked to do. He watched as Pauly walked out and the van door closed.

"He ain't going anywhere," Pauly said to Bobby as he made his way towards the car.

Pauly rode shotgun with Charlene in the middle, as Bobby drove a car for the first time in eight years. Jesse and Billy were smoking another joint inside the trunk. They were all headed somewhere.

THE TRIAL

Way up in the mountains, so far from it all
A crystal clear lake, not yet polluted by man
Trees of life standing so proud and strong
Form my castle. For I will be king while I can.

"Come, animals, have no fear of me.
"What's that you say graceful deer?
"Yes, I'm here, because now I'm free,
"For living in peace is all I care."

"Could not find peace with your own?"
Said an owl so wise.
"I wish to forget my old home.
"Could you at least give me a try?"

"Your race is destructive, they are slowly
Tearing us down
"They burn our homes, and kill us for sport,
"How do we know you won't be the same
If you're around?"
I heard what the fox said, and gave it much
thought.

"I wish you no harm, as I defend myself.
"I just want to live in peace.
"My knowledge could be your wealth,
And I agree that man is the beast."
"Just what knowledge do you think you own,
Man?"
Asked the giant grizzly bear.
"Do you think you're strong enough to live
off the land?
"Without a mate you'll live in despair."

"Oh," I replied, "I'll be strong enough to survive.
"And, you're wrong, for I won't be alone.
"I have much will to stay alive,
"And my woman will be here when I finish our home."

"No," they shouted with anger and hate.
"You will start the circle over again,
"For you will have children as sure as fate
"And animal and man cannot remain friends."

Way up in the mountains so far away from it all
Are the bones of one lone man
He fought brave and very strong
And died saying, "I will be king while I can..."

-Rest Stop- Chapter 2

Saturday, 1:37 p.m.

"Missing? What the hell do you mean missing?" asked Warden Glass with no great concern at first about an inmate transportation van that could not be found.

"We can't seem to locate a transportation van with four inmates aboard."

"What four inmates? Get your ass up here!" he yelled into the phone. He then called the assistant warden.

"Lockney."

"Yes."

"I think we got troubles. Come on over to my office."

"Be there in a second," Lockney's first thought was about the stabbing over at Prigg Cottage that morning, trouble between the blacks and whites. He had not told the warden yet; he was waiting to get the report. He is going to be pissed that I did not tell him right away. His thoughts ended as he walked into the warden's office.

"What's cooking, Chief?" Lockney said as he sat down on the chair in front of the warden. It always made him think of the movie, *It's a Wonderful Life* with

James Stewart, the way he sat like a boy in trouble looking up to his daddy who was about to give him a big lecture.

"You know anything about a missing van with four inmates aboard?" asked the warden.

"What? No, there was a stabbing over at the Cottage this morning. I was waiting to get the report before I came and bothered you with it," Lockney did not get to finish.

The warden's face told him to shut up. He sank even lower into his chair as the warden began to yell, "Didn't want to bother me with it? There is a stabbing, there is a van missing with four inmates inside and God knows what else. And you don't want to bother me with it? Let me guess how many inmates were involved in that stabbing. I will take a wild shot. OK, let's say four!"

The warden stopped there, looking over his glasses and down at Lockney, suggesting that he had better start talking, and it had better be good.

"I don't have any of the facts myself yet, Chief. There was a stabbing in the chow hall and a small fight. I had them lock up the ones who were involved until we could transport them back here. I called transport and told them to go to the cottage and pick up the four inmates involved."

Lockney knew that would not satisfy the warden and was thankful for the knock at the door. Officer Cravens stuck his head in the door and the warden spoke, "Come in Cravens, have a seat. I hope you can shed more light on what is going on. Start from the beginning."

"I don't know a whole lot, warden. Mr. Lockney called me up this morning and told me he wanted four inmates transferred from Prigg back here. We were right in the middle of the shift change, so I grabbed the first two officers available and sent them to pick up the inmates."

The warden cut Cravens off, "Two officers? There was a stabbing, four inmates involved and you sent two officers? Oh, this is getting better. Who were the two officers?"

"I didn't know it had been a stabbing, Warden. Anyway, I sent Turnbell and Cox."

The warden cut in again, only this time he had lost all his composure, "Cox works in the fucking clothing room. What is going on here? We have a stabbing and we sent two inexperienced officers to pick up four cons. Shit, I can't believe it. Who got stabbed? Who did the stabbing? Somebody had better start giving me some answers. Go on Cravens, what else do you know?"

"As I said, Warden, I didn't know anything except that we were to have four inmates picked up at Prigg. About an hour and a half later, the van still was not back, so I called over to Prigg. They told me that the van had left over an hour ago with two officers and four inmates. That is all they knew. Therefore, I went the regular route to Prigg to see if maybe it had broken down along the way. When there was no sign of them, I came back in and that is when I called you. Warden, for all I knew the four inmates just needed transportation back to the walls to go to the dentist. I mean it happens all the time."

The warden cut in for the last time, "Sure Cravens make sure it's not your fault. Well, since you like to drive so much, get your ass in a car, get back over to Prigg, and get me a full report. I want to know names and numbers. This is top priority. I want everything dropped. Cravens, your ass isn't cleared. You should have notified someone before you took it on your own to go looking for a broken down van. You have cost us some valuable time. Now get over to Prigg."

The warden ended his conversation with a flick of his hand, and then picked up the phone, "Miss Simpson, call the state police. Ask them to come to the prison. I think there has been a prison escape and a kidnapping."

He hung up the phone and looked dead into the eyes of Lockney, "What's with you, Lockney, what were you thinking? You didn't think a stabbing was important enough to tell Cravens what he was having transported?"

Lockney had known the warden since the first day he was assigned to the position by Governor Strubb. Glass had been sent in to clean up after a big riot the previous warden could not control. Lockney had never heard Warden Glass swear, even when he let Gary Gilmore go to a motel and he escaped. Gilmore went on a crime spree that ended up in Salt Lake City with the killing, in cold blood, of a gas station attendant.

However, when the Oregon newspaper headlines read *NEW WARDEN LETS MURDERER GO TO MOTEL FOR SEX,* Lockney remembered, the warden said, "Fuck."

Was it the fact that the warden was now worried about his job? Strubb had just lost the election. Governor Attier's policies about prison reform were a lot different from that of Warden Glass. Right now, Lockney was not too worried about the warden's job. He had to start thinking about his own.

"Cravens is full of shit, Chief. When I called him this morning, I told him there had been a stabbing, and to take caution when bringing the four prisoners back to the prison." Lockney looked dead into the warden's eyes. He knew he was lying through his teeth and he could see the warden knew it, too. In reality, Lockney just was not thinking at the time. Stabbings happened all the time, so when he called Cravens, he had told him just what Cravens had told the warden. Cravens had no future to protect. He did not have a chance of being the next warden. Lockney also knew that if Glass was let go that they would want him to be the next warden.

"OK, stick to that story. But for now tell me everything you know so I won't feel like an idiot when the state police get here." The warden was pleased that Lockney was not stupid enough to be the fall guy.

"It was 11:30 a.m. when I got the call from Prigg that there had been a stabbing in the chow hall involving white and black inmates."

"Oh my God, this gets worse by the minute. All we need is a race riot. Okay, go on."

"They tell me they have the guy who did the stabbing and the three inmates that were with him."

"Who was the one that did the stabbing?" the warden interrupted.

"Hang on to your chair, Chief... Robert Smallwood."

"The ax man, that's good. That is a feather in my cap. I told the board not to release Smallwood from custody. It is on the record that I strongly contested his release. My exact words were that Robert Smallwood was a threat to the institution and would be a greater threat to the public if he were released."

"Good, we'll play that up."

"Who was it that got stabbed?"

"This part you're really going to like--Lavon Duggan!"

"That doesn't surprise me. What does surprise me is why it took so long. He caused me a lot of trouble over the years. When he was president of Uhuru and started all that prejudice stuff with the papers, he sure caused me heat. Well, is that it? Anything else you can tell me?"

"No, that's all, right now. I would like to add that I was wrong in not telling you right away. It won't happen again."

"Well, so much for that. For right now, you better head over to Prigg and keep a lid on the place. Let's get any hot blacks out of there and back inside and quick. I am a little worried about Cox and Turnbell. Oh, the other three that are with Smallwood, I imagine that is his clique--Atterberry, Brown and that little fag that was always running with him. What was his name?"

"Sweazy, I think. I'll get all their files pulled and back to you, Chief."

"Get me all four of their visiting lists, too. The police will want to see them."

"You got it, chief. I'll get someone on it and head over to Prigg," Lockney said as he headed out the door.

The warden picked up the phone, "Miss Simpson, call Larry Miller from Channel 5. Buzz me back when you get him. Thank you." The warden went into heavy thinking.

This could turn out to be a blessing in disguise. If they had listened to him, Smallwood would still be inside the walls. He was concerned about the safety of his two guards, of course, but they were secondary to his job security.

He knew all about Robert Smallwood and his clique. He knew about his hatred for blacks. He knew he had killed one with an ax and he knew that he was also behind the stabbing of the black a few years back. He just could not prove it. He knew that most of the white inmates respected him. He knew he would put Smallwood in the hole any chance he got. Smallwood was bad news. He laughed to himself. This time, Robert Smallwood is good news.

The phone broke his thoughts. Miss Simpson told him the police had arrived.

HOT SUMMER DAY

Hot summer day with all the heat
Angry souls and high walls meet
From the Board that speaks of your fate
That gives you the time you must wait
Of the badge with its power over blue
The pride he feels when he tells you, "Do"
All builds up with times corrosion
Until one day, hate meets explosion
Looking for changes to unlock the gate
Striking at themselves an inner hate
Most follow a leader or two
Each watching what the other will do
Yelling demands that are out of line
Breaking the monotony of unchangeable time
Ripping apart a badge without a face
Only to have another take his place
White on black until red is shown
Beating into the hate that's grown
Rape of the kid with the pretty face
Death of the rat that spoke a trace

Destruction is heard smoke is seen
Deprived manhood comes out mean
Hot summer day turns into night
Talks go on for what is right
A city of numbers, calm with cool
Looking to the leaders for what to do
When like a mist, the gas appears
Bringing forth the curtain fear
Dignity leaves when you fall to your knees
Yet pride keeps you from saying please
You fight with hate it is all you own
Hate needs food, and hunger has grown
The battle is over, but no one won
The fight for manhood is never done
Hot summer day with all the heat
Angry souls and high walls meet.

-Rest Stop- Chapter 3

Saturday, 2:38 p.m.
"Maggot?"
"Yeah, who's this?"
"It's me, Bobby Smallwood, is it cool to talk?"
"Yeah, sure, what's cooking? I heard they sent you to the cottage?"
"Sure did, I was there a couple of hours ago. Maggot, listen up. I stuck that fucking nigger, Duggan, at Prigg. They popped us for it and were taking us back to the walls. We overpowered the guards and got away. I need your help, bro. You going to come through?"
"Wow, heavy. You on the square, Bobby, I mean, no shit?"

"Serious as a heart attack, and there ain't no time to bullshit. We got to get out of this state and quick."

"Hey Bobby, no problem. Tell me what you need."

"We need guns. Don't worry about money. We just hit a 7-11. Also, any clothes you can round up for four of us."

"Four of you? Is Pauly with you?"

"Yep, Jesse and Billy, too."

"Where you at?"

"Remember where we grew those humongous pot plants right before I got busted?"

"Yeah, sure, outside of Springfield."

"Yeah, we'll meet you there. How many pieces are you holding?"

"I ain't got many. Business has been booming. I'm sitting on a sawed off shotgun, I know you like that, and two .38's. I can get my hands on a few more, but I have to go to Albany to get them."

"Ain't got the time. Bring what you got and any clothes you can and get here as fast as you can."

"OK, bro, this is heavy. Give me about forty five minutes, I'll be there."

"I won't forget this, Maggot."

"Hey, you don't owe me thanks, you got this coming," Maggot hung up the phone and then began thinking. What am I getting myself into? He turned on the TV to see if there was any news about a prison escape. There was nothing on but soap operas. He turned off the TV and went to the radio. Pink Floyd was playing *The Wall*. He left the radio on full blast and went to gather some clothes he no longer wanted.

Did they really knock off a 7-11? Were they really going to pay him for the guns? Did he want any part of this? What did he really owe Bobby? Sure, they were brothers in the joint, but that was two years ago.

They had a pot growing enterprise before Bobby was busted. Bobby had always scared him though. In the joint, it was great to have Bobby as a friend. No one would fuck with you. Of course, if it had not been for Bobby he might never have been busted in the first place. It was Bobby who convinced him to smuggle some smack into the joint. Someone got wind of it and snitched on them to Warden Glass. Maggot was busted cold. They even had cameras on him when he made the pass. He got ten years for that, of which he served three. He had just gotten off parole a month earlier. He had no plans to go back to prison again even though he took that chance every day being an ex-con in possession of firearms.

He knew it was a risk helping escaped cons. He was wondering whether to help them or not. While he was shoving clothes into a bag, he thought of Pauly.

He always liked Pauly. They used to cook crack together. He decided he had to do it, if only to help Pauly. If he had known there was a guard killed, there would have been no way.

As he removed the floorboards to get the guns he had stashed, he thought about Bobby's wife. Maggot had been screwing her for years, and he was not the only one. He could only guess, but he had always thought that she was never raped by anyone. Someone must have seen Bobby's wife with a black guy and before it could get back to Bobby, she had already come up with the rape story.

Maggot had been closer to Bobby's brother, Harry, than he ever was to Bobby. In fact, Maggot was the one who ripped off the drugs from those Mexican dudes who thought Harry did it. Harry paid the price. God help him if anyone was to ever find out. However, no way, Harry was the only one who knew. What a stand-up guy, stabbed all those times and Maggot never said a word about him.

Yeah, this was one way to pay Harry back by helping his brother. He put the guns, sawed off shotgun into the bag, and headed for his car.

Bobby felt just a little bad that he lied to Maggot about having the money to pay for the guns, but he knew Maggot enough to know he was a greedy son-of-a-bitch. For sure, he did not want to say anything about a guard being killed. One thing for sure about Maggot, he was lacking hard-core balls. Bobby was not positive that Maggot would show up. He knew Maggot always blamed him for his bust in the visiting room, even though Maggot did not have the balls to say so.

It blew Bobby's mind that there was still nothing on the radio about the escape. He wondered how long it would be before they would find the van and the dead guard. Then there would be shit coming down.

Billy, Jesse and Pauly were talking about Bobby's plan of taking over a rest stop. Charlene sat in the background, rolling joints and listening.

"It sounds easy. I mean think about it a second. When people pull into rest areas, it's only for a minute. They stretch their legs, take a quick piss, hop back in their cars and they're off," Billy said, really hyped up on the idea.

"When Bobby first told me the idea, I thought it was simple too, in fact, too simple. I started to see where the weakness was, and I found a real flaw in the plan."

"What? Jesse cut Pauly off.

"You ever been on Highway 15? It's all desert country. Sure, the plan is good as far as locking people in the bathroom after we take their money and jewelry. However, let us say that all goes well; we got a sack full of money, forty thousand bucks according to Bobby in a half hour's time. All right, so everything is hunky-dory. Now, what?"

"I ain't following you, brother," Billy, answered, "We got the money, and we're free. We head for Mexico."

"I know what he's saying," Charlene said as she passed the three guys each their own joint. "I've been to Las Vegas with my Mom. There's only one main road, in and out. The rest is desert. One road block on either end of the rest stop fifty miles down the road, and we're busted."

"Oh!" responded Jesse.

"Oh, yeah," said Billy under his breath.

"Right," answered Pauly.

"Hey, wait a minute, sis," Jesse broke in, "Either way, you're not going to be part of this. As soon as we score some other wheels, you're going back to Mom's. I was crazy to let you get this far involved."

"Hey, big brother, don't start that shit on me now. I've grown up without a Daddy, and it's too late for you to start acting like one now. Billy is my old man and the only guy I'm listening to these days. And no matter what, we both want to be together. Tell him so, Billy."

"Well, your big brother got a point, babe. Whatever we end up doing is going to be pretty heavy. I mean, our lives are pretty messed up right now. We got nothing to lose, but you do, baby. If everything works out good, I will send for you. On the other hand, you're a big girl and you can make your own choices. Sure, I want you with me, but the bottom line is not me, not your big brother, not anyone. If you want to take a chance of ending up in prison, that's your choice, baby. At least, that's how I see it."

"I'm with Jesse on this one. I'm not for bringing some sweet young kid down with us," Pauly added.

"Hey, fuck you guys! What makes you think I'm this sweet, innocent kid? Just because you dumb fucks were busted for the shit you did, doesn't mean I am a Virgin Mary either. I'm just smarter than you guys are. And shit, you all keep talking like you were already busted and heading back to the joint. I'm for positive thinking and for getting away with anything we do."

"All right baby, I hear you. You get my vote," Billy quickly said, thinking, I'm getting to like this woman more all the time.

"Fuck it, you're not going to listen to me anyway," Jesse responded.

"Well, the main one you're going to have to convince is Bobby anyway. He's the one calling the shots," Pauly interjected.

"Oh, I can convince Bobby. I've seen the way he looks at me."

"Hey, I don't know if I like how you said that."

"Don't worry Billy, I know how to shake it but not break it."

"Don't play games with Bobby, sis. He ain't about playing with."

"You know, one thing I don't understand is how scared you all are of Bobby. Like he is the only one with brains. I've known guys like Bobby before. I know how to handle them."

"You better listen to your big brother, lady," Pauly warned, "Bobby ain't like anyone you've ever met. Just back off from Bobby."

"They're right, baby," Billy agreed.

"Shit! OK, I'm not saying I'm going against Bobby. I'm just saying he doesn't scare me like he does to you guys."

"Talk about the devil, looks like that's Bobby coming back," Jesse announced.

Bobby pulled the car up. Everyone was smoking on a doobie. Ripped out of their minds, he thought. Oh, well, why not?

"Hope you saved one of those for me."

"I surely did, darling. A big one, just for you," Charlene cooed as she walked over to Bobby and handed him the joint. At the same time, her tongue ran around her lips in a suggestive way.

Bobby did not understand what that meant. He was not sure if he liked what she just did. On the other hand, he was not sure if he understood it. Was she just fooling around? She did it so no one else could see her do it. Bobby just shined it on but thought, "If she gives a sign, Billy or no Billy, it's been seven years since I had any pussy. She has the cutest ass."

Billy broke his thoughts, "Hey Bobby, you told us to do some thinking about the rest stop thing and we all like it. Only, we came up with one small problem.

Well, we don't see any until it's time to leave. But ten minutes later, someone we robbed is going to get to a phone or a CB and, being on a desert highway, we'll be popped before we get fifty miles."

"Great, glad to see you've all been thinking. And you're right it is a problem. In fact, I brought up the same thing when me and The Wizard were talking about the idea. How the hell do you get away once you get the money?"

"Yeah, and what did he say?" Jesse asked.

"He said you all don't get away. Some of you are going to be busted. This is how it will come down. After we make our score, everyone takes his share. We all take different cars. Two of us head south and two of us head north. Bottom line, we're all on our own once we hit the road. I don't want to know where you're going and I'm not telling you where I'm going. There is no doubt that one or two of us won't make it. That's it, unless one of you got a better idea. That's the one I'm stuck on."

"Boy, I didn't figure we were going to bust up," Jesse said, as the others were deep in thought. They were all shocked. Somehow, they all envisioned that they were sticking together. Billy did not like the idea. He never was good at doing anything on his own. Nevertheless, it did make sense. Pauly was somewhat relieved. He could not see himself with too long of a future running crazy with the clique.

Charlene was the first to talk, "I think it's a great idea."

"Oh, are you in this too?" Bobby said with skepticism.

"If you let me, Bobby, everyone said it's up to you," Charlene said.

"So far, you've been a fine lady. Only when it gets down to the shit, I don't know how you hold up. I mean, I don't know you good enough, lady. It's not because you're a girl, either. I've known many women who are more standup than a lot of guys. Let me do some thinking on it, lady. I'll let you know, later."

"Did you get hold of Maggot?" Pauly asked, knowing he cut Charlene off from saying any more. Bobby says he will think on something, best to let it go until he did.

"Yeah, I did. He should be here in about half an hour with guns and any clothes he could get. I had to bullshit him about having plenty of money. I told him we hit a 7-11. Knowing Maggot, he ain't going to do anything, unless there's something in it for him."

"We got that two hundred dollars. We can give it to him."

"Na, Maggot has to wait for any money we give him."

"He's going to be pissed," Billy, answered.

"Not half as pissed as when we take his car."

"Hey, I know Maggot, too," Pauly spoke, "He's not going to take that lying down. Hey Bobby, we can't go doing our brothers wrong."

"I don't like it either, Pauly. We ain't got much choice. By now, I'm sure the cops have figured out that Billy had a visit this morning from Charlene. One call to DMV and they will know what kind of car we're in. We'll do Maggot right when we pull our gig off. We'll send him all his dues."

"We'll shit his car. We can always steal a car anywhere. If we get busted in Maggot's car, it will bring heat down on him." Leave it to Pauly to always be looking out for the brotherhood.

"We can't risk it. All we want to do is get out of Oregon and taking a chance on a hot car is too big a chance to take. Maggot will understand. I'll make him an offer he can't refuse."

"Shit, now you're going to act like the Godfather. Okay, if you can get Maggot to go for it, no problem."

"If I can't, I'm going to take it anyway. But we all agree to give Maggot ten percent of what we get, OK?" Bobby looked at everyone. They all nodded their heads except for Pauly, who just said, "Whatever."

Bobby had a different motive that he did not let anyone know about, his brother Harry. Bobby always felt Maggot knew a lot more about Harry being killed than he ever let anyone know about. He could only guess. Either way Maggot had to be used right now. What if Maggot, like Pauly said wasn't going to take it lying down? Maggot would not have enough balls to stand up to him he knew. What if just taking the guns and his car burned him enough to snitch them all off? That was a pretty heavy thought. Snitches were the lowest form of life when it came to cons, lower than child molesters did. Child molesters, you beat up and turned into cocksuckers. Snitches, you killed.

Bobby took the last of his joint. He had to come up with some answers and he had to come up with them alone.

Pauly had walked off into the woods. Billy and Charlene climbed into the back of the car for another lovemaking session. Jesse turned to Bobby and spoke, "I'm not so keen on my kid sister going with us, Bobby. You think you can talk her out of it?"

"Your sister is a big girl now, and she wants to go, Jesse. As far as this trip is concerned, we could have uses for her. But like you, I'm a little worried, different from you though. What kind of shit's she been into in the past?"

"Nothing as big as she thinks it is. She's sold a lot of dope, done a few burglaries, stole a car or two, but mostly, she's been lucky. What we're getting into is way over her head."

"What we're getting into is way over everyone's head, Jess. I don't know I still ain't decided. I will by the time we hit the road. I think we'll wait until dark. We got any more numbers rolled?"

"Yeah, sure do," Jesse, replied

"Give me one, would ya?"

Pauly watched two chipmunks chasing each other. He envied them a life without care and worries. Free, no decisions. He wanted to think about anything but Patty and Dustin, but it didn't do any good. The thought that he would never see them again seemed much too real. He was afraid that Bobby was going to get them all killed. Even if this thing worked, life would never be the same. He'd have to leave the country. His mother would disown him. He remembered what his mother had said on her last visit.

"Paul, you messed up but you're being given another chance. You have a beautiful wife and child and you have your mother, but if you ever mess up again,

I'll never have nothing to do with you." The memory of his mother saying that was the last Pauly could take. He began to cry.

Bobby was trying to think of an excuse to go over to the car and get a shot of Charlene naked, when he heard a car coming. He got his excuse. He walked slowly and stopped a few feet short of the car. Charlene mounted Billy and had her back riding him. She had seen Bobby watching but didn't seem to mind. In fact, as she rode Billy, she looked right into Bobby's eyes.

"Get dressed, you guys. Maggot's here," Bobby said as he pounded on the hood of the car. He turned and walked away, hiding his erection from Jesse.

Maggot hated driving his car on this old road. He should have taken the old pickup. "Damn," he said to himself, as he hit another bump. He thought of the money he just had spent putting a new suspension system on his baby. Mostly, he brought the car to show it off to Pauly. He'd told Pauly all about it when the latter called him from Prigg Cottage, the night he got there. He thought about the old days when he and Bobby grew some of the best pot around. Sticky green buds, that shit went for $200 an ounce now.

He remembered coming out without Bobby and pulling three or four plants at a time, and stashing them. Bobby never did know. What the hell, Bobby never did much but supply the seeds and help him move the stuff when it was ready. He listened to the radio all the way out. Nothing was said about a prison break or a 7-11 store robbery.

He even wondered if it was some kind of a joke of Bobby's. Something he and Pauly had cooked up just to see if they could get him to do it. That thought went away as he rounded a curve. He saw Billy Atteberry getting out of the back seat of a car pulling up his pants, with some little chick right behind him.

He laughed out loud. Not only had they broken out of prison, but they already had some pussy. He pulled up alongside the other car and there, to his left, was the one and only Bobby Smallwood, smoking a fat joint with Jesse, the fag. Maggot got out of the car, laughing.

"You always knew how to do it up, Bobby. Just got out this morning, you're on the run; you already got some bud and some pussy," Maggot ended with a laugh, looking at the girl who was glaring at him.

Charlene didn't like this guy right off. Who does he think he is, saying that shit about me? She could see how he got his name. The fucking guy looked like a maggot. "What a gross individual," she thought.

"Got to do what you got to do," Bobby said joining in Maggot's laugh as he walked to him and gave him a hug.

"Where's Pauly?"

"Right behind you, you fat homosexual!" Pauly said as he stepped out of the woods and joined in on the hugs.

"God damn, prison life has been good to you. You're looking great," Maggot said as he stepped back and took a look at Pauly.

"Don't make a difference for you. Inside or out, you're as ugly as ever," Pauly replied.

"Well, I got my image to hold up, you know. So, tell me how the fuck did you guys pull this off?"

GUESS

You are a spectrum, nature's product
An output of the mind
The hue of beauty
Yet, a forgery of the blind

A panorama from the composite of the mist and sun
Kinsman to the wind
Your unchangeable contour
The myth of gold at your end.

-Rest Stop- Chapter 4

Saturday, 2:57 p.m.

"Mr. Miller for you on line three, Warden."

"Thank you, Miss Simpson. Hello, Larry, how are you?"

"Fine Warden, just fine. Sorry it's taken so long for me to get back to you. I wish I'd called into my office and got my messages. I was just down in Salem doing a news story on the new governor. I could have stopped in."

"You may just want to pack up and come back down here, Larry. We got a hot story and I just found out it's getting hotter."

"What's going on, Warden?" Miller asked, a little suspiciously. Warden Glass was always the last one who wanted anything on the news about the prison. No news was good news. Stay out of the limelight and you're doing a good job. At least, that was how Warden Glass felt, unless it was something that would make him look good. Warden Glass was a true politician.

"We had a prison escape, four inmates. You might remember the axe murderer from Eugene. He was one of the four. Also looks like two guards have been kidnapped and hurt in the process. The police just told me they found some blood in the place where the escape took place. Besides that, it all started with a stabbing inside the prison. White inmate stabbed black inmate. And again, our axe murderer was the one who did the stabbing."

"Robert Smallwood, isn't that his name? I covered that story, five or six years ago."

"It was seven years ago, but that's the boy."

"You're right, Warden, this is a story. I've got enough for a news report with a full story for the six o'clock news. Give me some more details and I'll get something on Channel 5, right now."

The warden provided Miller with all the information he had. He emphasized that he had opposed Smallwood getting a release at his parole hearing. He was primarily concerned about the safety of his two guards. He had most of what he told on a piece of paper with a heading saying, "Things to tell Miller."

After they hung up, the warden tore up the piece of paper and buzzed Miss Simpson, "Miss Simpson, get me Mr. Lockney over at Prigg. Then would you have a TV brought to my office?"

The warden was pleased with the way he handled Miller. This might be the break he hoped for to get on the right side of the new governor. The warden didn't like the next thoughts. He had to call the wives of the two guards. He couldn't wait for them to hear it on the news. He had met Mrs. Cox at a baby shower his wife had given, a few months back. He hated his wife for doing those things but she wanted to get involved and her thing was children. Baby showers, children events, Easter parties, Halloween, Christmas parties, etc. If only they could have had kids. The phone rang.

"Yes."

"Mr. Lockney, line two."

"Lockney what's going on over there?"

"It's real quiet, Chief. The police just left."

"They find anything else?"

"Two different types of blood. They interviewed the watch tower guards, but they didn't know anything."

"How could that be, Lockney? I mean, if there wasn't blood I would have thought the escape took place on the road back to here. But with the blood, and now two different types, well something must have happened there."

"I know Chief, it doesn't make sense to me either. I'm going to talk to the watch tower guards myself. The police got an APB out on the van."

"By now, I doubt very much if they're still with the van. What I'm worried about is when they find the van, what will be inside? Any trouble with the blacks over there?"

"Like I said, they're not taking it as a black and white thing. And, with the guys who did it being gone, well, there's no one for them to really be pissed at."

"How's Duggan doing?"

"He's at the hospital in intensive care, probably going to lose a liver, but word is he won't die."

"Well, I guess that's good. Any idea why Smallwood stabbed him?"

"As always, nobody knows anything."

"Well, keep on searching. I got to go, I just got a TV. I called Channel 5 and I want to see what they've got to say about this."

The warden hung up the phone and told Miss Simpson to switch the TV to Channel 5. *The People's Court* was on and Judge Wapner was saying he would be back with his decision and it went to a commercial. Two more ads ran, then a news commentator came on and said, "New governor plans a war on drugs. And a daring prison escape this afternoon, resulting in the kidnapping of two prison guards. Those stories and more, tonight on Channel 5 Eyewitness News at 6 p.m."

Judge Wapner was saying something when the warden turned off the TV. Son-of-bitches he thought, they're going to wait till 6 p.m. before they say anything about this. That's three hours away. The cons will be out of state by then. The phone rang.

"Warden, Mr. Lockney on the phone."

"Put him through. What you got, Lockney?"

"I just got the escapees visiting lists and here's something interesting. Inmate Atteberry had a visit scheduled this morning. And listen to this, his visitor is the 19 year old sister of Jesse Sweazy."

"Yes, that is interesting. Call the police and see if they can locate her. What else you got off the visiting lists?"

"The only other one who gets visits is Paul Brown. He's the only married one. His wife and his seven-year-old son visit, and twice a year, his mother comes and sees him. Smallwood has three people on his list, but it's been three years since he had a visit."

"Give the police the names on Smallwood's list anyway. Who knows what it might stir up."

"I watched the thing on Channel 5. They sure didn't say much, Chief."

"Yeah, I know. I think I'll call the radio stations. By the time the TV gets around to broadcasting, the cons will be long gone. In fact, I'm going to call them. You keep turning up stuff over there. Call me when you get anything."

The warden called the three radio stations he was familiar with and gave them the story about the prison escape and kidnapping. He knew the chances of the police finding the cons were slim. More escaped cons were caught because they made it to the news media and some citizen turned them in. The warden knew the police would be looking out for any stolen cars. Knowing Smallwood as he did, he respected his intelligence enough to know stealing a car would be a last resort. Smallwood's first move would be to turn to someone he or his partners knew. The phone rang.

"Warden, a Mrs. Cox would like to speak with you."

"Miss Simpson, tell her I'll be right with her, please."

Oh God, how did she find out? What am I going to tell her? I don't know that much. I've got to tell her something.

"Hello Mrs. Cox, how are you?"

"Fine, Warden Glass. Warden, I hate to bother you but I'm a little worried. John is usually home by 1:00 or 1:30, or at least he always calls when he's going to be late. I was just watching TV, and they said something about a prison escape and two prison guards being kidnapped. Please tell me John isn't one of them."

"I was just going to call you, Mrs. Cox. Yes, John is missing with the four escapees right now. But I wouldn't be worried at this point. Usually what happens in these cases is they let the guards go as soon as the convicts feel safe," the warden's voice was overtaken by Mrs. Cox crying.

"Please, Mrs. Cox, John's going to be all right. They won't do anything to him, they know better. Please Mrs. Cox, don't cry. It's going to be all right."

"I'm sorry, Warden. I'm just so scared. I've always worried about John working there. That something like this could happen."

"Mrs. Cox, please trust me. John's going to be all right."

"Oh, Warden, I pray so."

"He will be fine, just don't worry. How's the new little baby?"

"He's fine. Please, Warden, will you call me as soon as you hear anything? Please..."

"Yes, I will, Mrs. Cox. You'll be the first I'll call. I promise."

"Thank you, Warden," her voice faded into a cry as she hung up.

Victor and Kathy had been going together since the eighth grade. They were both going to graduate that year from Lebanon High. They loved their special parking spot and the wild keggers they had there with the rest of the gang. They were there the night the old cabin burned down. What a party that was. They turned left to their favorite spot where they could lay the blanket out so they could see Green Peter Lake while they made love. They were both shocked to see a white van parked there. Victor stopped the car short of the van. He got out taking a look around. He heard a noise from the inside of the van, like someone was kicking it. He went to the back of the van and opened the door.

SILENCE IS GOLDEN

The sand slowly disappears,
As four feet sink out of sight
Pushing sand to the side
Hands together with heart, head against
Shoulder
Looking at the sun starting to smolder
like a wax less candle.
The endless look of silver with
a golden beam.
The ocean and sun, together as one,
Except for them
The beach is theirs and God's
Eyes meet their rhythm together
Speaking in silence
The power of the universe, the strength
of time
Speak not in voice, just look, for it comes
The language of the heart
Bodies meet to fulfill the craving of touch
Ahhh, the heart skips a beat
The feeling overcoming with harmony
The combination of two becoming one
The magnitude of giving for surpassing
The wanting of taking
The swarming of vibrations
Stirring and the blending togetherness

She looks at him in oneness, and says
"I've got sand in my ass."

-Rest Stop- Chapter 5

Saturday, 3:15 p.m.

Maggot listened to the story about how they made their escape, mostly from Jesse and Billy. Bobby cut them off.

"Maggot, where do you have the guns?"

"In the trunk, in a big bag," Maggot threw Bobby the keys and added, "Also, I stopped along the way and picked up a case of beer. You'll find that in the back seat."

"Ahh, Maggot, I could kiss ya. As ugly as you are, I could kiss you," Billy said all excited about the beer.

"Well, I kind of figured it had been a while since you guys got to tip a nice cold one."

"Eight years for me, brother. Except for that potato shit we'd cook up, I haven't had a drink for eight years. You know I would lie in bed at night, and the first thought was always about pussy. The second was an ice cold beer."

Maggot looked right at Charlene, and then said, "Looks like you already accomplished the first part of your dream. The second part is in the car."

"Yeah, Billy, give me a hand," Bobby said as they sauntered to the car. Bobby opened the car door and stooped down like he was reaching for the beer. He said to Billy so Maggot couldn't hear him, "Billy, don't forget Maggot thinks we took off a 7-11. For now, I don't want him to know any different. Just wanted you to know before you got too far into the story."

"No problem, Bobby, I remembered. Quit playing me like I'm some fucking idiot, would ya?"

"I'm not, brother, just thought I'd remind you, that's all," Bobby came back defensively. The only trouble was Bobby did think of Billy as some kind of an idiot. And there was no doubt in Bobby's mind that if he didn't say something to Billy, he would have forgotten the story he had told Maggot to get the guns out there.

"You're going to have to tell him sooner or later."

"I know but I want it to be later, OK?"

"Yeah, OK."

"Well, what are you waiting for? Get to opening some of those beers you've been dreaming about. Leave me one, take the rest over to the troops."

Bobby opened the trunk and took the bag out. The first thing he felt was the sawed-off shotgun. A strange feeling came over him, a feeling of power, indestructible power. Pauly had joined him at the back of the car. He saw the change in Bobby. Like Bobby, it was like he had just reached a climax. It scared him.

"Good looking piece," Pauly remarked.

"Yeah, it is. It's beautiful. You know, this is the first time since we got out that I really feel safe. Hey, Maggot," Bobby yelled, "Where's the ammo?"

"In that brown bag by the spare tire," Maggot yelled back. He went back to listening to the story Jesse was telling about the fight in the chow hall that morning.

Bobby put two 12-gauge buckshot shells into the shotgun and with a flick of his wrist snapped it shut. "There should be two .38's in there, bro. Get them loaded and bring them over, would ya?"

"Sure," Pauly answered. It had gone too far. There wasn't any turning back now. His earlier thoughts of Bobby getting them all killed were even stronger now. But what could he do? He thought back to when they were talking about the escape and how he figured Bobby would never pull it off. He was wrong then, maybe he was wrong now.

Bobby joined the group, just as Maggot asked, "One thing you got to tell me, how the hell did you rob a 7-11 without having a gun?"

Before Bobby could say a word, Billy started to speak, "You should have seen it, Bobby was fantastic. We're almost out of Salem when Bobby says to pull into this 7-11 store. We didn't know why, but we did it. Bobby told us to wait, so we were watching. He walked in there like he owned the place. He jumped over the counter, knocked out the clerk with one blow, opened up the till, grabbed a fistful of money, came walking out like he just went in and got a Big Gulp or something. It was great. You had to see it to believe it."

Bobby was impressed. He didn't think Billy had a quick-thinking brain in him. It was a great story. He couldn't have done better. Billy looked at Bobby and was pleased with Bobby's look. "See?" Billy seemed to be saying with his eyes, "I told you, I wasn't an idiot."

"You never cease to amaze me, Bobby," Maggot said looking at Bobby with real admiration, "You like that piece, don't you? I knew you would," Maggot ended, referring to the shotgun Bobby was holding.

"Love it, just what the doctor ordered. To me it's like holding a woman," Bobby answered and his eyes went to Charlene who looked back at him, as if to say not like holding this woman. Bobby made up his mind right then that he was going to have some of that, the first chance he got.

"Jesus, hand me a beer before they're all gone, would ya?" Bobby said, looking at the empty cans already piled up.

"Billy already had four beers," Jesse remarked.

"That's right, and I'm going to have a fifth in a minute."

"That's what they're for. Snooze, ya lose," Bobby remarked, still thinking about getting close to Charlene and hoping Billy would drink himself to a passout.

"What have you been up to since you got out, Mag?" Bobby asked.

"Same ol, same ol...selling a few drugs. But the money is in guns. I got a few guys that go out and boost them. One of my guys likes to rob pawn shops, another guy specializes in burglaries. But it doesn't matter; I can off every gun I get my hands on. Even more, now that I'm off parole. Don't worry about some nosey PO coming around. Went and got me an old lady. You know her, Pauly. Remember Jerry Carr's old lady?"

"Yeah, sure. You know Jerry, Bobby, he's at the walls. You know the guy we get the yeast off, works in the kitchen."

"Yeah, so you moved in on his old lady?"

"More like she moved in on me. You know how those coke whores are."

"Jeez, and here I was thinking it was your good looks," Charlene said, cracking everyone up.

"Who is this chick?" Maggot asked.

"That's my woman," Billy answered in a voice already sounding drunk. Eight years without a beer, then drinking five in five minutes would do it to most.

"My little sister," Jesse spoke up with pride.

Maggot wanted to crack, "Does she suck as well as you do?" But he decided against it.

"Well, glad to meet you, little lady," Maggot said instead.

"Likewise," Charlene replied, but didn't mean it.

"What are your plans, Bobby? I imagine whatever they are, it's better if it's a long way from Oregon."

"That's our plan for now. And as soon as it gets dark, we'll be working on doing just that."

"What are you thinking, Mexico bound?" Maggot asked, but as soon as he did, he knew it was a stupid question. Bobby wouldn't tell him his plans.

"Na, I'm thinking about the other way, Canada most likely," Bobby answered. He wasn't planning on telling Maggot shit.

"Yeah, up there, you got places you can hide out. But really, I don't want to know where you're going. The less I know, the better," Maggot replied in hopes it would clean up his stupid questions.

Bobby knew this small talk was leading to getting his money for the guns. Bobby decided to make it easy for him, "What do we owe you for the guns?"

Maggot didn't flinch. He came out like a shoe salesman, "$150 a piece on the .38's, $250 on the shotgun and I'll throw in the ammo."

Bobby laughed to himself, "And I'll throw in the shoe horn." God damn Maggot, he only paid maybe $50 a piece for hot .38's and maybe $100 for the shotgun.

"Sounds fair enough, bro, and again from all of us, thanks for being there when we needed you."

"Hey, no problem, glad I could help," Maggot replied with pride while thinking he should have hit them up for more on the guns. He said, "Yeah, I could have got a lot more for those pieces. But shit man, what are brothers for?"

"I won't forget this either, Mag," Pauly said in a meaningful voice.

He didn't like the way Bobby was doing Maggot. Maggot deserved better. After all, Maggot wasn't a lame. He used to be one of the clique. What was Bobby doing? Did he forget that Maggot was a stand-up guy? Why did he tell Maggot they were going to Canada? If the cops did come on Maggot, he would say the opposite direction that he knew, which would make Bobby's plan backfire. The cops would go in the direction they were really going. Then Pauly remembered Bobby's plan to take Maggot's car. That 1969 GTO was his baby. That's all Maggot would talk about when Pauly would call him on the phone at night. It ain't right; we can't do Maggot like that.

Maggot's expectations for Bobby to reach into his pocket and pay him the $550 didn't happen. Oh well, he wasn't going to push Bobby for the money. He knew he would get it.

"Yes, indeed, feeling all right. We need some music," Billy broke into the silence, "Hey Maggot, you got good sounds in that car of yours?"

"You ain't heard better. Go ahead, turn it on. Got a lot of good tapes, too."

"Got any Led Zeppelin?" Jesse asked and started towards the car with Billy.

"Does the Pope shit in the woods?" Maggot replied, to be funny.

"Well, we got about two hours of light left. Hang out with us, Mag, shoot the shit. I'm going for a quick walk in our old planting grounds. When I get back, I'll pay you for the shit, okay," Bobby said out of the blue.

"Yeah, no problem, bro," Maggot said, going right into a conversation with Pauly. As Bobby walked off, Maggot caught Bobby's eyes going to the chick. Maggot picked up the look. It said, "You know where to find me." Fucking Bobby, he was something else.

Charlene picked up the look, too. She wanted to find Bobby some place alone. There was an animal type of attraction in Bobby that Billy didn't have. An appeal that had grown more intense as the day went on. When Bobby was watching her ride Billy, she loved it. She had power; she looked right into his eyes and imagined it was him she was riding. She was familiar with the way he looked at her. He was hooked. Yeah, this was her chance, but first she had to deal with Billy.

Bobby heard Led Zeppelin's *A Whole Lot of Love* playing as he walked out of view. He wondered if Charlene picked up his look. He thought of his trips on acid listening to the same song now playing. It was fading but he knew the song by heart. Charlene should give Billy some head. As drunk as he was, he would pass out right after. I ain't ever going back to prison again. Look how beautiful this is, I could live here the rest of my life. Never have to see another person and it wouldn't bother me. I'm going to eat her until she melts in my mouth.

"Hey, baby, what do you think of these duds?" Billy yelled as he stepped out from behind Maggot's car wearing some of the clothes Maggot brought.

Charlene looked and couldn't help but laugh out loud. There was Billy dressed in some of Maggot's huge clothing. Maggot weighed 260 pounds and was only 5' 9". She also had to laugh at the style of the clothes. Billy had on a red floral shirt and green striped pants. She laughed even harder when she thought about the fact that Maggot really wore that stuff and no doubt thought he was really cool in it.

"Well, shit, you guys didn't give me much time to go and get anything custom made," Maggot replied, pissed. He didn't know that shirt was in there, he wanted to keep it.

Charlene walked over to Billy and threw her arms around him and said, "Oh, sweet cheeks, maybe these clothes ain't so bad. I can get at that cute little ass of yours a lot easier."

"See how easy you can get around to the front," Billy said wanting to show off the beer hard-on he had.

"Oh...yeah, forget the sweet cheeks. I just found something sweeter," Charlene said in a soft, seductive voice. She placed her lips to Billy's ear and sucked the lobe ever so lightly.

Bobby's thoughts just minutes earlier of Charlene putting Billy to sleep were in progress. Again, Bobby's thoughts had been right. When Charlene was done pleasing Billy, he fell off to a gentle sleep. Charlene got up wiping her face and pulled the huge green pants over Billy's thighs to cover his nakedness. She slowly got out of the car on the other side so no one would see her. Right now, it wasn't them she wished to see. She made her way to the woods in the direction she saw Bobby go. After five minutes of walking, she heard voices. She crept forward until she could make out what they were saying and who was talking.

"I just don't feel right doing Maggot this way," Pauly said in a stern voice and body language, hands to hips, looking right into Bobby's eyes.

"How else can we play it, Pauly? Tell me what else can we do? We ain't got the money for the guns. By now, the cops have tied us into Charlene's car. Sure, I know Maggot's going to be pissed. But brother, I'd rather have Maggot pissed than us looking at the walls again. This ain't a game anymore. When Maggot finds out why we did him like we did, he'll still be pissed, but believe me, he'll be cool. We got no other play, Pauly. Do you understand?" Bobby said as he watched Pauly's body language.

Bobby topped it off by saying, "Besides, as soon as we're clear of Oregon, you can personally call Maggot and tell him where his car is," Bobby stopped talking, placed his hands on Pauly's shoulders, looked him in the eyes and said, "We're doing what we got to do, bro. Dig?"

"Yeah, I know. I just don't like it. But you're right. I think we should tell him, though. Maybe he'll understand a little sooner," Pauly said giving Bobby a soft punch in the chest.

"I don't like it either, bro. And sure, I plan on telling him. Of course, I'm going to do it with this little baby in my hands. As you said, Maggot's not going to take it lying down. And I'd hate to see that little fat man come at me."

"Nah, I don't think you got to worry about that. Nobody is that dumb to go up against you. You won't need that shotgun. You forgot that Maggot was there the day Charlie Tatum took a punch at you. I think when Maggot got paroled, Charlie still had his mouth in wires," Pauly said, and they both began to laugh.

"What were Billy and Jesse doing when you came out here?"

"It was funny, you should have seen it. Billy put on some of the clothes that Maggot brought which were all Maggot's by the way. Anyway, Charlene started reaching down Billy's pants, and the next thing you know Billy had her in the back seat. Jesse was rapping to Maggot. You know, I think if I get half a chance and Charlene wants to play ..."

"I know what you're saying and who knows what the future holds. Only the phantom knows," Bobby said, giving Pauly a punch in the chest. He said, "I'm going to hang out here and get some ideas. Go make sure everything is going smooth. I'll be up in a few."

"OK," Pauly replied and made his way back to the camp thinking, "I guess we don't have much choice. I hate it but Bobby was right. We've got to do what we've got to do."

Charlene held her breath as Pauly walked by her. She was lying on the ground behind a clump of bushes. Dumb fuck, didn't even see me, she thought. Her desire for Bobby increased seeing the way he controlled Pauly, the way he controlled everyone. In just a few minutes, she would show Bobby what it was like to be controlled.

Pauly was dumbfounded. Why was Charlene trying to hide? She reminded him of a little kid. Hide your eyes behind your hands and if you can't see anyone then no one can see you. So Bobby was going to get some of that pussy. That cocksucker," he went on thinking, "Only the phantom knows. When all along he was waiting to move in on her Well no problem, it had to be his turn next." He laughed again about her trying to hide, three feet away in broad daylight. He joined Maggot and Jesse in finishing the rest of the beer.

Bobby wondered if Charlene understood the look he gave her. He thought she had. He turned around to see if there was any sign of her, and there she was just standing there. She looked so cute, so young, and so frail.

"So only the phantom knows. Knows what?" Charlene said as she slowly walked towards Bobby.

"I'll be damned. Where were you hiding?" Bobby said as his mouth dropped open. She excited him in ways he had forgotten. The way her hair blew softly in the wind. He could make out her firm little nipples.

"Right over there behind those bushes. I heard what Pauly said he would do to me if I gave him half a chance and what you said about the phantom. So tell me what the phantom knows."

Charlene stopped two feet short of Bobby and put one hand to her hip. She thought she had a strong urge to get closer to Bobby, but the urge she had now was by far stronger. She wanted to keep walking right into his arms, but she wanted him to make the first move.

"I didn't see you. Did Pauly see you?" Bobby said, wishing she would keep on walking right into his arms. For a second, he thought she was going to do just that.

"Nope, he almost walked on me, but he didn't see me." Her heart was pounding. She couldn't remember ever feeling like this. She had to have him, must have him now. She saw her chance and reached for his hurt hand and said, "Oh, I bet that hurts like a bitch."

She took Bobby's hand and put it to her lips. She looked right into his eyes as her mouth went around his middle finger and slowly sucked it in an up and down motion. That was all that Bobby could take. For the first time in over seven years, he was feeling things he thought had died, emotions he had forgotten. He pulled her to him. Their lips met in a frantic kiss. Bobby's hurt hand was forgotten as it went to the cups of her ass. His other hand was at her neck pulling her in a deeper kiss. Her hand went inside his shirt and rubbed the chest that minutes ago she was wondering about. Her other hand followed suit with Bobby and went to his ass. She pulled up his shirt and reached down his pants and began to squeeze his naked ass.

They fell to the ground. She worked at pulling his pants off. His thoughts of eating her until she melted in his mouth had vanished. All he wanted now was to be inside of her, feel himself enter her. She lifted her ass so Bobby could pull her pants from her while she kicked off one shoe. He pulled her pants off with one quick pull. He positioned himself to enter. She spread her legs then reached for his manhood to place it inside of her. He lost it. He was coming all over her. She said, "No, no, not yet!"

He fell on top of her and whispered in her ear, "I'm sorry, seven years along with the looks of you. I just lost it, sorry."

She wished he didn't say anything. She could have gotten him back up again. She still had his cock in her hand and could feel it going soft. She rubbed it against her anyway, her legs still wrapped around him. Her desire hadn't left, but her thinking was back in order. She knew now that she was in. No doubt that she would be going on the trip. She knew she could work him up again, she knew the power of her mouth. She had forgotten how many guys had bragged to her about her remarkable abilities, how she was the best they ever had.

But, she thought it best to end this trip with Bobby right now. As much as she wanted it to go on, she knew she still had something Bobby wanted. It would work on him now more than ever. Yes, she went on thinking, "Bobby may control everyone, but I control Bobby."

"It's all right, Bobby, I understand. Billy did the same thing," Charlene lied to Bobby. Billy had fucked the shit out of her, but she could see Bobby was pleased to hear it.

Bobby rolled off her. He wondered how long it had been since he told someone he was sorry. At least he meant it. He wasn't sure who he was sorry for. He sure wanted to show her a thing or two. Oh, well, it was a good start.

Charlene wondered as she looked at Bobby's bare chest if tattoos did something for her, somehow turned her on. She did admire the one on his arm, a rainbow of stars and the words, "Born to Die" under them. It was the only tattoo that life wouldn't change.

"Where was Billy when you left?" Bobby asked as he pulled up his pants.

"He fell asleep. Too much beer, I guess."

"Well listen, lady, for right now you're Billy's old lady, and I don't need extra problems."

"Hey, you don't have to say no more, Bobby. What happened was just between you and me, mainly because I want it to happen again. So darling," Charlene said as she stepped into her pants, "Don't worry about me screwing anything up."

Bobby was getting to like this little lady. What was that word The Wizard would say if someone had a lot of balls? Oh, yeah, moxie she had a lot of moxie.

"We better go back at different times. Go now, I'll show up in about 10 minutes."

Bobby's eyes stayed on Charlene as she walked away. His thoughts were still sexual. She had the nicest ass he could remember. He was getting aroused already, and he knew it wouldn't be long before they would be together again.

Charlene returned from the woods cautiously so Pauly, Jesse and Maggot wouldn't see her climb in the back seat of the car where Billy was still asleep. She snuggled up to Billy and began to massage his stomach.

"Hi, baby," Billy said in a yawn. He put his arms around her and pulled her into a kiss.

"Have a nice sleep, babe?"

"Yeah, felt good. Any beer left?"

"Don't know, babe, I've been in here with you."

"Let's go see," Billy said as he crawled out of the car, Charlene right behind him.

"Oh, the love birds arise!" Jesse yelled out, "You guys fucked your way through all the beer, none left."

"You assholes," Billy answered.

Pauly was bewildered. He didn't see Charlene get back in the car. He was watching, too. Maybe he was wrong about her and Bobby getting it on, there hadn't been very much time since he had seen Charlene trying to hide from him.

No one replaced the Led Zeppelin tape when it played through. Maggot's top-notch cassette player automatically went to the radio when the tape was done. No one seemed to mind, it was on a good station playing old rock-and-roll. No one seemed to hear the news come on until the radio said something about a prison break. All their heads turned towards Maggot's car. There wasn't a sound but the voice on the radio.

"A prison escape from a minimum security release center in Salem today has turned into a full-scale manhunt with the discovery of a murdered prison guard in the small town of Sweet Home. This story and all of today's news on K-ROCK radio. First, some plans our new governor has for the war on drugs."

Everyone looked at each other. Maggot was surprised that the van had been found so fast. Maggot thought, "Oh shit, Oh shit."

The news commentator was saying something about the governor's idea of mandatory sentences for distributors of any drugs. Then something about when children are involved, that a 15 year minimum should apply.

The newsman finished up his story about the new governor, continuing, "The escape of four inmates from Salem's Prigg Cottage today has resulted in at least one death. The notorious axe murderer of Eugene, Robert Smallwood, was one of the four inmates who got away in a prison van, taking with them two prison guards as hostages. Reports have just come in that the van was found by two young people out on a walk in the small town of Sweet Home, 35 miles southeast of Salem. In the van, one prison guard was found handcuffed and alive, but quite shaken and unable to be of very much of help at this time. The other guard wasn't so lucky. He lay dead next to his friend since the escape. When asked how the guard might have died, one sheriff's deputy was quoted as saying, "He was beaten brutally to death."

"It started about noon today inside Prigg Cottage, a part of the prison system used for inmates close to parole. I talked to Warden Glass and this is what he told me: 'A stabbing took place at 12:02 p.m. today in the chow hall. The four inmates responsible were handcuffed and led to a holding tank to be transported back to the main prison'."

Maggot jumped up, shaking his head, then said, "This is bullshit, this is too heavy man. I don't want any part of this shit."

"Sit down, Maggot, and listen to the news. I'll explain it all in a minute," said Bobby, standing there with the shotgun in his hands. Maggot did as he was told and the news went on.

"'During transport back to the prison, the four inmates overpowered the guards and escaped in the prison van. We believe, at this time, they had outside help and a getaway car.' That was all the warden was aware of as of news time. State police have set up road blocks on Highway 20 and Interstate 5. An all-out manhunt is now in progress. Here are descriptions of the four inmates. Anyone with information should call the state police."

"Robert Smallwood, 37 years old, 5 feet 10 inches, blond hair, blue eyes, well-built, weighs 175 pounds, in prison seven years for the axe murder of a Eugene man in 1977."

"George William Atteberry, 33 years old, 5 feet 9 1/2 inches, dirty blond hair, green eyes, well-built, weighs 168 pounds, in prison eight years for robbery and rape."

"Jesse Arnold Sweazy, 27 years old, 5 feet 8 inches, dark hair, one brown eye, one gray eye, well-built, weighs 155 pounds, in prison almost five years for a rash of burglaries he was convicted of in 1979."

"And Paul James Brown, 36 years old, 6 feet 2½ inches, light brown hair, blue eyes, weighs 235 pounds, in prison since 1980 for manufacturing illegal drugs. He was due for parole in thirty days."

"All four escaped convicts have a variety of tattoos. All should be considered armed and dangerous. Do not try to apprehend any of them. If you have any information on the escapees, please call the state police. The identity of the slain officer is being withheld until notification of the next of kin."

The three-month-old baby boy in Sweet Home didn't understand why his mother screamed. It hurt his ears, he began to cry.

"Turn the radio off, Jesse," Bobby commanded.

"Damn, Bobby, I had the right to know about the guard getting killed," Maggot tried to say with a firm voice, but he was high-pitched by the time he finished.

"Would you have come?" Bobby asked.

"I don't know, I just ..."

"You just would have done nothing, Mag, you wouldn't have come and I can't blame you. I might as well tell you the rest of our plans. First of all, we never knocked off a 7-11. So we ain't got any money to pay you for the guns. But you know I was kind of figuring that you owed me from years ago when we were in the pot growing business together. When you would come out and steal five or six plants a week."

"Huh, what are you talking about Bobby?" Maggot was quick to his own defense, but wondered how Bobby ever found out. "Oh God, please don't let him know about Harry," he thought.

"Ahh, never mind, it don't matter now. Anyway, we ain't got any money. But that's not how it's going to stay. We're all off for a big sting and, if it works out, you're cut in. Ain't that right everybody?" Bobby asked, looking around.

Everyone said yes.

"Fucking fools, you ain't going anywhere. You killed a guard; you'll all be busted or dead before the day is over." He just wanted out of here. Fuck the guns, they could have them.

"Now the next thing I tell you, well, don't get upset 'cause it won't do no good. We're going to have to take your car, too, Mag," Bobby said in a voice meaning you ain't got any choice.

"No Bobby, not my car. Don't do me that way," Maggot came back sniveling.

"Maggot, you just heard the news report and they know we're running in Charlene's car. We got to take your car. But hold on you'll get it back. Tell him, Pauly."

"Hey, bro, we didn't want to do this thing to you, but hey, the car is not going to get hurt, I'll give you my word. You'll get it back. As soon as we cross the state line, your car will be parked, and I'll give you a call. I give you my word, I'll do that," Pauly said, believing every word he just said.

"It will be right up in Vancouver, not Canada either, the one in Washington. Within a week after that Mag, you'll be receiving your share of the job we pull," Bobby was doing all this pleading for a show.

Fuck, Maggot, he ain't got shit coming. If the rest of them weren't there, Bobby would beat the shit out of Maggot until he told all he knew about Harry getting killed.

"How about if I get you my pickup truck? Will that work?"

"Maggot, don't treat me dumb. Jesse, get a pair of those handcuffs and cuff Maggot to Charlene's car." Jesse as always, didn't even wait to question one of Bobby's orders. He just got up and headed for the car.

"No, no way, Bobby, you ain't handcuffing me," Maggot said and he started to get up.

"Sit back down, Maggot. I ain't playing no fucking game. Handcuffing you is for your own good, too. It will show the police we took your car by force. Don't make me get ugly, Maggot. I don't want to, but you know I will."

"Just do as he says, Maggot. You know we're in a world of shit, or we would never do you like this. We don't have any choice, do you understand?" Pauly cautioned.

Maggot didn't understand anything but that sawed-off shotgun looking into his face. He knew there was no stopping them, especially Bobby. He had better change his attitude.

"Yeah, you cocksuckers, but you know you owe me. I mean you better believe there's going to be some shit come down on me. The cops are going to want to know what I was doing out here in the first place. They will know I'm old buddies with all of you. But, not that you deserve it, I'll be standing by you, won't tell them shit. I'll probably be the one getting busted for some shit they made up. If you guys get busted they'll tie me in with the pieces you got. But fuck it, just go. Handcuff me to the fucking car. What are brothers for?"

"All right," Pauly burst out, "I knew you'd br cool when you understood. We won't do you any wrong that we haven't already done, and I'll see to it personally that you get your end of the money."

"Don't tell me nothing, but just for a laugh let me know what my end could end up being in this big score you all got lined up," Maggot said as Jesse was putting the handcuff on. Bobby spoke up.

"Your 10 percent cut alone is going to be between $5,000 and $8,000 buddy."

Maggot didn't believe it, but he did believe that they would have to pull something off to get enough money to live on, wherever they were going. What he didn't believe was that they were even going to get out of state. But first, his car would be shot with all sorts of holes, or Bobby would try to crash through a road block before he would stop. But then what if they did get lucky? Even the low end of $5,000 would be sweet. He trusted Pauly enough that if they did get away, he would be sent his share.

As Jesse was handcuffing Maggot to the door handle of Charlene's car, he said, "I want my car back, Pauly. You call me as soon as you get another. And I guess all I can do is trust you guys that you'll send me my dues when you pull the job. And don't expect no goodbye kisses either. Cocksuckers! Handcuffing me out in the middle of the woods. As dumb as these Oregon cops are, I'll probably be eaten by wolves before anyone finds me."

Pauly rubbed Maggot on top of his head and said as he made his way with the rest of the gang towards his car, "You'll get your car back and your cut. I promise you that."

"Good luck assholes!" Maggot managed to get out.

"Take care Mag, we'll be seeing you," Bobby said as he closed the trunk on Jesse and Pauly and climbed in the front seat with Billy and Charlene.

"You drive my car easy, Bobby. You hear me, treat her like a baby." These were the last words anyone would ever hear Maggot say to this group.

Bobby drove right through the middle of Eugene heading west. His plans were to get to the coast highway and go south. His plans were not to stop until they were in California. His plans so far had worked to a tee. His plans as far as he was concerned were going to keep on working.

HUMAN TEARS

My heart cries, as tears form in his eyes
Jumping through the air to hug me goodbye
I love you, we both repeat
Then through iron doors, I retreat
Seeing his face before me.

Crooked teeth but smile of life
He reminds me so much of my wife
It isn't fair, stays in my head
His father in prison, his mother dead
Seeing her face before me

Oh, buddy, I'm the blame
For that inside unreachable pain
Forgive me.
Then his words came back to me
He's only nine, so hard to believe
Dad, what's a little time
When we'll be together forever,
Seeing his face before me.

-Rest Stop- Chapter 6

Saturday, 6:28 p.m.

He was telling the lady on the phone that Monday at 6 p.m. would be fine, that he would have one appointment to cancel. But business has to always come first. If Monday at 6 p.m. was convenient for her and her husband, he would make sure that he would be there. "All right, see you then. Thanks for calling."

He hung up the phone and looked around. Two salesmen were pitching quarters. One was reading the newspaper. Two had been gone an hour and a half on a supposedly 45 minutes lunch. He loved it. He was taking a piss when the paging system said "Salesman line two."

"Bummer," he thought. He loved those phone pops. Half the reason he was always a top salesman was the fact that he loved working the phone. Half of his sales started with an incoming phone call. When he walked out of the bathroom, he saw line two still flashing. He couldn't believe it. The salesmen would always ask him how he got this sale or that sale. He would always tell them just being at the right place at the right time. But here was money calling out to them on the phone and not one of them took the call. He loved it.

He took the name and number from the caller and opened his phone log book. He wrote in Monday at 6 p.m., their names and what kind of car they were buying. He knew he didn't have an appointment at that time but telling customers you'll break an appointment for them obligates them to show up for their appointment. He was having a good day. He had already rolled one car and had a pretty good appointment tonight at 7 p.m. on a used pickup truck. He thought about having 15 units already out this month. Four more and he'd beat his own record. He had already won every spiff the dealership had put out so far this month. And no doubt with the sale this morning, he would take the weekend spiff money. He loved it. He knew he was the best salesman around, but what he loved even more was that everyone else knew it, too.

He was heading outside to see if any customers were hiding around the side of the building. Sometimes customers would hang back there not wanting to talk to a salesman just yet. He loved walking up to them ask if he could help them. Most people would say, "Oh, we're just looking." It was like a bell going off his head, "Yeah, just looking for a salesman. Well, here I am." He never made it out the door. The paging system called his name.

"Ken Rocmel, line three. Ken Rocmel, line three."

He hoped it wasn't his seven o'clock appointment canceling as he picked up the phone.

"Hello, this is Ken Rocmel, may I help you?"

"Honey."

"Hi, babe, I already got one out today, $240 deal."

"Honey, Bobby was just on TV. He escaped from the prison with three others."

"How did you find this out?"

"It was just on Channel 5, and that isn't all. A guard they kidnapped has been found dead in Sweet Home."

"Oh, damn, really Malerie?"

"I wouldn't fool around about something like this. You haven't heard from him then?"

"No. And I really don't want to hear from him. This is too heavy even for The Wizard to fix."

"Wizard? What are you talking about?"

"Oh, nothing, babe, just something Bobby used to call me when we were cellies."

"Ken, what are you going to do?"

"Do? It blows my mind. Bobby is so stupid. He had three months left. He was going to see the board from Prigg. You don't see the board from Prigg unless they are going to parole you. He blew it. So, I ain't doing anything. When did this all happen?"

"Today, about noon. Oh honey, I'm glad you're not going to get involved. Sometimes, I don't know if you're really happy being a family man."

"Oh, babe, I've never been as happy in my life as I am with you and Dane. Don't you ever go worrying about me backsliding. It took prison to show me what freedom was all about."

"I know, Ken, it's just that you and Bobby were so close."

"That was a long time ago. I know it's been six hours since this has all come down. He's long gone by now."

"What time are you going to be home for dinner?"

"I got a seven o'clock appointment that looks like a sale. So sometime about 9 p.m."

"OK, I love you."

"I love you too, babe. Don't worry," Ken said as he hung up the phone.

Malerie was worried. She was never quite sure what Ken was capable of doing. She'd known him since he got out of prison. Many people wondered what it was that attracted a girl as sweet and innocent as Malerie to Ken. She was a beautiful girl, 19 years old, and a year out of Lebanon High.

He was 14 years older than Malerie, had been married four times, a con man from the days he traveled with the carnival. He had spent four years in prison for bank robbery and kidnapping and had a son only seven years younger than she was. She had to raise the boy because his first wife, the boy's mother, had died. Ken sure wasn't the tall, dark and handsome kind. Ken stood 5 feet, 5 inches tall with a good build. What could she have possibly seen in Ken?

The answer had come to Malerie a day after she met him. She loved his personality: the way he would keep her laughing, his ability to see all things in life as funny. With his big talk, his big plans, he had a way of explaining them to whoever would listen and make it sound so believable.

Malerie was glad that Ken didn't follow the pack. Every time she went to the prison with Ken to visit Bobby, the convicts she saw had tattoos all over them, even on their faces and necks. Ken didn't have any tattoos. He didn't believe in them. He said it was like having a road map to your identity if you were ever on the run. Besides, feelings change with life. Why have a tattoo of something you might have been?

It didn't matter now, anyway they had Dane. She loved Ken and planned to spend the rest of her life with him. One thing about being married to Ken, her life would never be boring. She continued to worry.

"Salesman line one," squawked the pager.

Ken ignored the page and walked outside not looking for customers. He was really bummed out. He couldn't believe that Bobby would do something so stupid. He had beat the time, he licked it, he was going to hit the street in a few months, tops. Oh well, too late now. He really blew it.

He laughed to himself when he thought of how he used to always call Bobby "kid." Bobby was two years older than Ken. They would stay up all night talking. Ken was one of the few people, in fact the only person, Bobby spoke his true inner soul to. And Ken knew Bobby could kill someone without thinking about it first. Most of the convicts knew that about him. He was a scary man. No one messed with him. He scared everybody, but not Ken.

Ken knew how to control Bobby, and Bobby let him. The whole time that Ken and Bobby were cellmates, Bobby never went to the hole. Not that Ken wouldn't use Bobby's image to collect debts on the gambling and various other ventures he controlled. Ken was a regular entrepreneur in prison scams. That was why Bobby called him "The Wizard."

Ken thought of the time that some dirtbag was going to stick him for some overdue football bet. Bobby got wind of it and the guy ended up in the hospital with cracked ribs. The guy never made it back to population again. He spent the rest of his sentence in protective custody. No, he never did have any trouble along those lines with Bobby as his backup.

Ken wondered if Pauly was one of the guys who escaped with Bobby. No, one thing about Pauly, he had moxie, one of the few guys he'd met in prison who was a realist. Ken's thoughts switched from the past to now when he saw the state police pull onto the lot. He wondered what took them so long.

Ken waited outside and watched as the police went through their antics, flashing their badges and asking where they could find Ken Rocmel. He saw the secretary point to him. He lit up a camel and watched them walk towards him.

"Howdy gentlemen, I imagine you're here to talk to me about Bobby Smallwood."

"This is Detective Bowen and I'm Lt. Camode. What can you tell us about Robert Smallwood?"

Ken laughed to himself. The lieutenant's name sounded like a toilet. Boy, what a different feeling it was to have cops in front of you without worrying why. He was clean--no longer a lawbreaker-- unless you can count smoking a little weed.

"Can't tell you anything except my wife called me about ten minutes ago and told me that Bobby escaped. That was the first I knew."

"Did she tell you he killed a guard?" Lt. Camode asked, as he tried to analyze Rocmel. He was in charge of this case, and he personally wanted to be in on the interview with this guy. He was positive that Smallwood had outside help on the escape. Rocmel was a perfect candidate, an ex-celly of Smallwood's who still had regular visits with him. The guy would even bring his wife and baby. An ex-bank robber, huh. There ain't no such thing; once a thief, always a thief. This guy knows something and I'm going to get it out of him.

"When was the last time you talked to Smallwood?" the detective asked him, already knowing the answer. He had Smallwood's visiting file in the car. It was right after Smallwood got sent to Prigg Cottage. He was surprised by Rocmel's answer.

"About three nights, no four nights ago. He called me from Prigg Cottage." Ken saw the cops eyes flicker. He wondered if he said something he shouldn't have.

"Did he tell you about his escape then?" Lt. Camode asked hoping Rocmel was stupid enough to say yes.

"No, we just talked about the same old shit we'd always talked about."

"What might that have been?" asked the detective.

"Nothing that's going to help you. He asked how the wife and kids were. I said fine. I asked about Prigg Cottage, he said something about the food being a lot better. I reminded him that I knew because I was there. I asked how some of the guys were doing up there--who'd got out, who'd come back. Just shit man, he didn't say anything about any escape. In fact, it blew my mind. He was telling me the opposite of an escape. How he was looking forward to getting out and getting a job, an old lady and become a citizen. He was tired of prison."

"You know what I think?"

"What's that, lieutenant?" Ken came back sharply.

"I think you know a lot more than you're telling us. I think Smallwood had this escape planned for a long time. You know what else I think? I think you helped him to escape, which means you're in on a murder beef. I think you ought to take a ride with us downtown."

The lieutenant watched Rocmel's reactions as he sounded off. He wanted to see if he could get this guy to warm up and fall to pieces, saying all he knew as long as they would give him a break on the murder.

Ken couldn't believe this guy. First, they came popping off questions from all sides, like he was going to get confused or something. "Now he's really reaching, trying to scare me. He's a joke, he's not even good at it," he thought.

"Hey, lieutenant, you're just wasting my time and yours. I can't tell you anymore downtown than what I've told you here. The ride downtown doesn't scare me, lieutenant. I'm off parole and there ain't a whole lot you can do to me. But I'll tell you this, you probably won't understand it, but I'll tell you anyway. Me and Bobby were real close. There's a kind of love you get for someone when you live in an eight by ten cell together for two years. And for that reason, Bobby wouldn't contact me."

"You're right, Rocmel. Explain it to me."

"You see lieutenant, if Bobby had got away clean, didn't hurt anyone, there wouldn't have been much heat on him, and he just might have tried to get hold of me. But he killed a guard. He's not going to bring that kind of heat down on me. Would you like to know what I think?" Ken asked without waiting for an answer, "I think you're barking up the wrong tree looking for a long range plan. I think it's something that just happened, nobody planned it. It just happened, and it escalated from there."

"Do you know Charlene Sweazy?" the lieutenant asked like he didn't hear a word Rocmel was saying.

"No, can't say I do," Ken answered but immediately thought of Jesse Sleazy. So Jesse's with Bobby.

Ken didn't mind prison at all. Out of 1800 inmates in the prison system, Ken didn't think any of them had it better than he did. He was activities director, he promoted events, and once he got Barbara Mandrell to give a concert inside the prison. That made him a hero with everyone, including Warden Glass. He would announce all the shows, whether entertainment or the boxing matches. He had his baseball team which Bobby and Jesse were both on. Boy, could Bobby play a mean third base. He slept most of the day if he wanted to, played handball, wrote poems, and got three square meals a day. Many times Ken had told people that if there would have been women in prison he would have stayed. Ken Rocmel always made the best of the worst.

"You aren't going to say you don't know Jesse Sleazy, either."

"No, I ain't going to tell you that. He was a good buddy of mine when I was inside the walls."

Jesse was quite a character. Billy would always tell Ken that he should give Jesse a try. But Ken would always shine it on. He'd wait to have the real thing when he got on the street. He thought of the night he married his fourth wife in prison. No such thing as a honeymoon. Billy told Jesse to go to Ken's cell and give him one. Ken thought seriously about letting Jesse show him if he'd like it or not. But as soon as Jesse touched him, he told Jesse to leave. He was like Bobby, just could never get off by another man.

"Good buddy, huh, good enough for you to help him escape?" asked the detective.

"Come off it, would you? I tell you, I don't know anything that is going to help you. I've told you everything I know."

"Well, you're not being helpful. How about George Atteberry or Paul Brown?"

"Ahh, shit," Ken said, thinking out loud, "Yeah, I know them both. I sure hate to hear that Pauly's on the run with them. He ain't that hard core." It didn't surprise him one bit hearing that Billy was with Bobby, especially with Jesse being there. Those two were in love, they just didn't know it.

"And you haven't heard from any of these people, is that what you're saying?" asked the lieutenant, now thinking that what Rocmel was saying made a little sense. That didn't mean he believed him. He was glad he got the OK to put the wire tap on Rocmel's phone and the man hours to have one of his men follow him.

"That's what I'm saying lieutenant, and that's all there is to it. I mean, I hate that this happened. I hate to see Bobby in trouble again."

"Trouble isn't the word. This time we're going to burn him," answered the lieutenant. He wanted Smallwood and his buddies worse than he ever wanted to catch anybody. As far as he was concerned, Smallwood killed a cop, a brother, one of his own. Whatever it took, he was going to see to it that the escaped cons were all going back to prison or hopefully, in Smallwood's case, the morgue.

"I understand where you're coming from, lieutenant, but I really don't know any more than I've already told you. So if there's nothing else, I really need to get back to work."

"Just know, Rocmel, you're on a fine line, and if you're holding anything back, I'll find out and see to it personally you pay the price."

"One more time, Lieutenant, I broke the law six years ago. I'm married now, raising two kids, got a good job and no plans of having any trouble with the law. I don't know anything I haven't told you. I'm going back to work, see you later." Ken turned his back on the police and walked back into the showroom.

"You want to bring him in, Lieutenant? I believe the same thing as you do that he knows more than he's letting on."

"No, let him go. Even if he does know something, we won't get it out of him. Besides if he does have something going, he'll do us more good being on the street. If he knows where Smallwood is, he'll lead us right to him. For now let's get back to Salem. I want to talk to the warden again."

All the salesmen were waiting to hear what the police wanted with Ken. Some were hoping that he was getting arrested so they would get a shot at spiff money again. Everyone knew Ken had been to prison for bank robbery. Some even admired him for having the guts to do something like that. You could never tell it by looking or talking to Ken, he seemed such a mild manner guy.

Ken told everyone why the police were there. Then he went about his business, or so they thought. Mostly he was thinking about Bobby. He hoped what he told the cops was right, that Bobby had made a beeline out of state. That even if he didn't, he would have enough sense not to try to contact him. Ken wondered who this Charlene Sweazy was. Did Jesse get married? No, he wished he knew more about what had happened. Then he thought of the salesman who was reading the newspaper and went over to him.

"Anything in the paper about a prison escape?" Ken asked the salesman, whose eyes were glued to the paper. He was probably the only person in the dealership unaware that the police had been there.

"Prison escape, no, why? Has there been one?" He answered peeking over the top of the newspaper.

"No, just wondering if there had been one today," Ken answered.

The salesman gave him a weird look and went back to reading the sports page, thinking how much he hated that guy, "Thinks he's such a hot shot. I've been selling cars for twenty years. I forgot more than he knows. Next month, I'll beat him."

Ken would have to wait till he got home to watch the 10 o'clock news to find out most of the details. He'd learned in prison during a riot that newspapers usually printed one side of a story; the same thing was true of the TV newscasts. He went outside to get the car ready for his seven o'clock appointment.

Lt. Camode was on the radio, "Any word on Charlene Sweazy yet?"

A voice came back, "Still haven't located her yet. Have contacted her mother, who's quite worried, but doesn't put it past her being talked into helping them by her brother and Atteberry. Over."

"Well, that's the best lead we have for now. Has the APB gone state wide?"

"Yes, and we have also contacted all surrounding states. Over."

"Breaker, Lt. Camode, come in," one of the officers in the field interrupted.

"This is Camode, come back."

"Lieutenant, this is Sergeant Saunders. We've located Patty Brown. Over."

"Good, where?"

She just pulled into her driveway and went in the house. Over."

"OK, just observe. Don't let her go anywhere, but don't go up to the house either. I'm on my way there, 15 minutes tops." The lieutenant hung up his radio. The warden would have to wait. He had that gut feeling that Brown's wife wasn't involved, even though she couldn't be located for the last six hours. And she was the most active visitor any of the escaped convicts had.

Patty Brown had spent the night at her boyfriend's house. She went over there right after getting off the phone with Paul. Paul was sounding good, really positive. He told her within thirty days they would all be together. The waiting was over, five years of waiting. He told her how much he loved her and Dustin, and that he would spend the rest of his life making it up to them. How he was going to work for her father, and work hard. That he was going to make her proud of him. She believed him.

She was going over to Danny's to tell him they had to end their two year affair. She had gone three years without ever being with anyone while Paul was in jail. Then she met Danny one night just after she moved to Salem from Eugene. She wanted to be closer to the prison for her visits with her husband. She got a job at a small bakery.

Patty had met another girl that was visiting her husband up at the prison and they became friends. Her name was Story and her husband was in for murder. He had killed a guy in the course of a robbery. He got life without the possibility of parole. Story had been visiting for six years and had no plans of stopping. But, it didn't slow her down on her social life. She had three or four boyfriends she saw regularly and kept her eyes out for more. Story talked Patty into going out dancing one night, and that's when she met Danny.

Patty explained to Danny that she couldn't get involved with anyone because she loved her husband. Danny didn't push her. He said that he would just like to be her friend. He had a good job and was a perfect gentleman. He was also somewhat of a hunk. Story couldn't believe it when Patty told her she had been out with Danny three times and still hadn't gone to bed with him. Story explained the facts of life to Patty.

"You know, Patty, you don't have to love a guy to hop in the sack with him. I can't believe you've gone three years without being with a man, then meet a guy like Danny and keep him hanging. I don't care what Danny tells you or how nice he is. If he doesn't get some pussy pretty soon, he'll cut you loose. Believe me, I know."

Patty thought about what Story had told her. In fact, it worked for her. She didn't want to lose Danny as a friend. She really enjoyed being with him. She would lay in bed at night after a date with Danny and, for the first time in three years, see a different face than Paul's when she masturbated.

On their fourth date, she spent the night with Danny.

Patty and Danny created their own little world. Story was the only one who knew they existed. Patty told everyone that she had a night job Monday, Wednesday and Friday at Weyerhauser in Beaverton. She told them her hours were7 p.m. to 3 a.m. Since it was too late after work to wake Dustin up, Grandma and Grandpa would get him off to school.

She also claimed to work sometimes on her day off. She used that lie for the times that she and Danny would go fishing. Patty loved being with Danny, but she loved Paul more. She never let Danny forget she was going to end their relationship as soon as Paul was out of prison.

Paul always told Patty he would understand if she went out one night, met a nice guy and something happened. He said it would be all right with him. Then he'd always add, but don't make it with the same guy all the time. Only Patty knew differently. She knew, from his letters, it drove him crazy at night wondering if she was with a guy while he lay in the bunk above Bobby's, snoring. So she lied to Paul, too. It was for his own good. He couldn't handle the truth.

Last night, she was going to tell Danny, to end it right away. She needed to start adjusting to Paul coming home, and she had to get used to not being with Danny. But when she got there, Danny had a beautiful dinner, with candlelight, and a big bottle of champagne, so she decided to hold off another day. They made beautiful love and she fell off to a peaceful sleep.

When she woke in the morning, Danny was gone, off to play golf with some of his friends. She got out of bed, showered, dressed and headed to her mom and dad's house to pick up Dustin. She promised to take him to the Portland Zoo that day. She did just that.

She and Dustin had a wonderful time. Dustin made out like a bandit, his grandfather said, when he walked in the house with two balloons and a stuffed kangaroo. Dustin gave his mother a big kiss when she had to leave to go to work. He thanked her for taking him to the zoo.

Patty had decided that tonight, no matter what, she was going to tell Danny that their affair was over. She kissed her mom and dad, with her mother saying good-bye as she always did, "You drive carefully, darling."

Patty had to stop by the Circle K to get some cigarettes. As she started in the door, she saw headlines in the paper: *Massive Manhunt for Escaped Convicts.* She walked over to take a closer look. Prison stories interested her since Paul was in one. Paul usually knew the guys the story was about. Below the headlines were the words, "One prison guard found dead, second one freed from stolen van found in Sweet Home." Patty just breezed over the start of the story until it told of the escape at Prigg Cottage. She almost lost her breath when she saw the name Robert Smallwood, her legs got weak and she dropped the paper when she saw Paul's name. "Oh God, no! Oh God, no, no, no," she screamed. Patty raced back to her car. She had to get home. Paul had probably been trying to get hold of her all day.

"Oh Paul, why, why? I know Bobby had to be the one to get you messed up in this, but after five years with only thirty days left, how could you let it happen," she asked aloud as she drove. And a guard was killed. Oh God, everything was over. She pulled into the driveway and raced into the house, not paying any attention to the car parked across the street.

Danny finished 18 holes of golf and was sitting in the snack bar with his two buddies drinking iced tea. They were watching the news to see who had won the Bob Hope Golf Classic in Palm Springs when the report about the prison escape came on. Danny's heart raced but for a different reason than Patty's. He was saying, yes, yes, yes and thank you, God. He loved Patty and the fear of their

70

relationship coming to an end terrified him. Whenever he tried to get Patty to talk about a future after Paul got out, she would always cut him short. He knew that she liked him a lot but that she would never let herself fall in love while she was waiting for Paul. This was the break he needed. He had been trying to call her every ten minutes for the last hour.

Patty was in the door two minutes when the phone rang. She ran to the phone praying it was Paul.

"Hello."

"Hi, Patty, this is Danny, you all right?"

"Oh Danny, you heard. I don't know what I'm going to do!"

"Yes, I saw it on the news. Do you want me to come over?"

"No, I just got to think this out. I'm hoping Paul will try to call me."

"What will you do if he does call? You're not going to get involved, are you Patty?"

"I don't know what I'm going to do. I just don't know. Oh, why did he have to do this? Listen Danny, I better get off the phone. I'll call you later, OK?"

"Yeah, but please, Patty, don't do anything stupid." He wasn't sure she heard the last part before he heard the dial tone.

A minute later, the phone rang again. It was a friend from work telling Patty that the police had been there a few hours earlier looking for her. A man in a van parked down the street from Patty's house with headphones listened to the conversation. He made notes of the conversation under the last entry which said,

6:47 p.m.: a man named Danny called. Conversation indicates that Mrs. Brown has not made any contact with Paul Brown. She did remark that she hoped her husband would call and that she had no idea what she was going to do if he did call.

6:50 p.m.: a girl described as Susan called telling Mrs. Brown that the police had come to the bakery looking for her around 4:30 p.m. When asked by the caller if Mrs. Brown had anything to do with the escape, Mrs. Brown replied, "Oh God, no, I just found out about it myself." She again ended the conversation with, "I better go just in case Paul is trying to reach me."

Patty hung up the phone with new thoughts. No doubt the police would be looking to question her. Maybe, like Susan, they thought that she had helped in the escape. She went to the window and looked. There was a car with a man sitting in it across the street. Then a car pulled in her driveway right behind her car, two men got out and made their way towards the house. Patty went to the door and opened it.

"Mrs. Paul Brown?"

"Yes."

"I'm Lt. Camode and this is Detective Bowen, may we come in?" Without waiting for an answer, the two men made their way into the house. Patty closed the door, walked into the living room and sat down on the couch.

"Any of you have a cigarette?"

"Have you heard from your husband, Mrs. Brown?" Lt. Camode asked as he handed her a cigarette.

"No, I just found out about it before I got home. I took my son to the zoo and on the way home I saw a newspaper with the story about the escape." The lieutenant and Patty made eye contact as he lit the cigarette. He read that she was telling the truth.

"You say you've been at the zoo with your son? What time did you get there?"

"We were there all day. I picked him up about 11 a.m. and just dropped him off before I came home."

"Doesn't your son live with you?" the lieutenant continued.

"Yes, but when I work he stays with my mom and dad in Eugene."

"You said you picked him up this morning. Did you work last night?" asked Detective Bowen, already knowing the answer. He and the lieutenant were at the bakery that afternoon.

"No, I don't work nights at the bakery. And why ask me a question when you already know the answer. My friend from work just called before you guys got here and told me you were out there asking questions."

"Where were you then, Mrs. Brown?"

"That's none of your business."

"I'm afraid it is our business, Mrs. Brown. You don't seem to understand that there has been a murder. That somebody helped your husband to escape, and whoever that someone is, is in big trouble."

"Well, it wasn't me. I told you I didn't know it even happened until just a little while ago."

"You have any way to prove you were at the zoo this afternoon?"

"Yes, out there in the car there's a coupon book. Oh yeah, also a parking stub from the zoo," Patty said almost boldly, thinking that should remove any doubts from their minds. The lieutenant motioned the detective with a flick of his head to go look.

"Lieutenant, can I ask you a question?" Patty asked before the detective returned.

"Sure, what is it?"

"Tell me, what really happened? I mean just two days ago when I talked to Paul, everything was fine. He knew he just had 30 more days to do. He was saying how he wanted to go to work, take care of me and Dustin. I totally believed him. Now it's all over. I just can't believe that Paul would have anything to do with murder. Paul's just not like that. Can you please tell me what really happened?"

"I wish I could Mrs. Brown, but at this point we really don't have that information. I can tell you this, Paul wasn't the one who killed Officer Cox. In fact, he might have been instrumental in keeping Officer Turnbell, the other officer alive. I interviewed him and he verified that it was Bob Smallwood who killed Officer Cox. Also, Turnbell said that Smallwood and the others wanted to kill him but your husband talked them out of it. I'm not going to lie to you, Mrs. Brown, Paul's in a lot of trouble. But it's something he might be able to get himself out of if he will help us to catch the others."

"What do you mean?" Patty asked as the detective came back in the house waving the zoo program and ticket stub.

"I feel your husband is going to try to get hold of you, either by phone or through one of your friends. Either way, it doesn't matter, you got to get him to tell you where they are. Things are not going to get better. Things are only going to escalate and get worse. This so-called friend of your husband is a coldblooded murderer. He won't hesitate to kill anyone who gets in his way. And so far your husband isn't guilty of murder, but he had a witness this time. Paul wasn't involved in the knifing in the prison. So far, your husband is guilty of escape from a minimum security prison and that's about all. If you can talk him into telling you where we can find the other three, I'll do everything in my power to see to it that things go easy for your husband."

The lieutenant was lying through his teeth. He didn't give a shit what Officer Turnbell said. He wanted to burn all of them, but he wanted Smallwood more than anybody else. Maybe Brown would be dumb enough to tell his wife where they were hiding.

"Are you telling me the truth, Lieutenant? You mean if Paul was to turn himself in, he would only be charged with escape?"

"No, I didn't say that. I said if he were to help to catch the others, then and only then, would I see to it that escape was all he was charged with. Your husband hasn't got a long criminal record like the others. And as far as I can tell by reading his file, your husband doesn't appear to be dumb. How he got involved in this harebrained escape, I don't know. It's not too late for him, but he's got to help us. Do you think you'll be able to make him see that this is his only way out?"

Patty ate it up hook, line and sinker. The lieutenant could see what she was thinking.

"Is there something you can tell us now that might help out, Mrs. Brown?"

"No, I was just hoping he would call because I know what he's feeling right now. He's wondering how he got himself into this mess. How bad he must be feeling for me and Dustin. How he must be thinking his life is over and that there's nothing he can do to change it. If he does call, and if I know Paul, he will, I'll tell him what you just told me. I do think he would do whatever it takes to get out of this mess. I know for a fact Bobby Smallwood got him into it. But Lieutenant, I need a guarantee, something in writing, something he'll believe. Then believe me, I'll talk him into helping. He'll do it for me and Dustin."

"No problem, I'll go and see the D.A. and have him type something up. But in the meantime, if he calls you just have to take my word that I'll do what I said I would. It's getting late and I might not be able to get to the D.A. until morning. But I promise if your husband helps in the capture of the other three, no charges other than escape will be made against him. Okay?"

Patty thought hard and deep. She had no other choice. She was about to agree when the phone rang. All eyes turned to the phone then back to Patty. She got up to answer the phone. The lieutenant grabbed her by the arm and said, "Do we have a deal, Mrs. Brown?"

"Yes, but you better remember your promise."

"I will," the lieutenant said as he let go of her arm and she made the phone by the third ring.

"Hello."

"Honey, are you all right?"

"Oh hi, Mom."

"Oh honey, we just heard about Paul. Why would he do something like that when he was about to get out?"

"Oh Ma, I don't know, just stupidity, I guess. I'll call you later Mom; right now the police are here."

"You're not in on any of this, are you Patty?"

"No, Ma, I just found out right after I left your place. Ma, I got to go, I'll call you after the police leave, bye." And she hung up the phone.

"One other question before we leave, Mrs. Brown. Do you know Charlene Sweazy?" the detective asked.

Patty shook her head while she ran the name through her head and answered, "No, should I?"

"No, just one of our leads we're trying to track down."

"Here's one of my cards, Mrs. Brown. If you hear anything at all, you call that number, day or night, I don't care what time it is."

"Yeah, okay, but you get that letter to me as soon as possible."

"I will, but just remember this: this is the only chance your husband's got. If he doesn't do it he'll go down with the rest of them."

"Don't worry, Lieutenant, I know how to get through to my husband. You just go get through to that D.A."

"Don't worry about that, I always keep my word," answered the lieutenant as they made their way out the door.

They were in the car, pulling out the driveway, when Detective Bowen asked, "Can you make a promise like that without talking to the D.A. first?"

"I can make any promise I want, but it ain't worth spit without prior approval. The way I see it, if Brown is going to call, it will probably be tonight. I got her put off until morning about the letter from the prosecutor, so chances are there may never have to be a letter. For right now get on the horn and call the van. Find out if that was really her mother who just called."

Detective Bowen got on the radio understanding why the lieutenant made a promise.

Two hours later, the lieutenant was sitting in front of his TV set watching a cop show. He had just finished a wonderful meal his wife had fixed. The phone rang.

"Yes."

"Lieutenant, this is Bowen. They just found Charlene Sweazy's car in Eugene. Also, handcuffed to the car was an ex-con named Dick Ellis. He says they tricked him into meeting them and that they took his car."

"All right, let's get an APB out on these guys right away."

"Already done, lieutenant."

"Good, you say Ellis is an ex-con, did he know the guys who escaped from the joint?"

"Affirmative. That's how he says they tricked him. He was told by Smallwood that he got out on parole and just wanted to meet him to celebrate."

"What did he say about who was with Smallwood?"

"They're still together including the girl. Eugene police wanted to know what to do with Ellis. Word is that he deals in guns."

"Oh shit, that's all we need is Smallwood running out there with guns. I want to talk to this guy. Call Eugene, see if they'll bring him up to Salem and I'll meet you at the office in an hour."

INNER BATTLE

There is a place locked within the inner depth of my mind

The total contentment of peace, I've longed to find
Not an outer place of material that can be touched
But the truth of life without the common crutch
Of flowing through living without the remorse
A plan of existing that God would endorse
The taking of bad without all the excuses
Remembering the paranoia is the one who seduces

And what of this place you have longed to consume
Is it not a figment and just one to assume
Do you fantasize what you wish to predict
Forgetting that reality will always restrict
If this place is real it will remain disguised
Or if it did appear would it be recognized?
So put away your dreams and ease the strain
For you will never find this untouched domain

No! There is a place and it will be found
And in that direction I will stay bound
I'll search till all possibilities are explored
You will find my efforts won't go ignored
And why listen to you and be misguided"
You forget we are but act divided
So to your permission I will not concede
You will find my optimism will succeed.

-Rest Stop- Chapter 7

Sunday, 3:10 a.m.

California Highway Patrolman Keith Ribbons hated these fights with his wife. They seemed to happen whenever there was a shooting or an auto accident involving another highway patrolman. She would want to know when he would be returning to college to finish his engineering degree. She would remind him of his promise to be a cop for two years, at the longest three, while he went to night school. That had only lasted four months. He used the excuse of getting through his one year probation period, before returning to college at night.

What Keith had never confessed to his wife was the fact that he loved being a cop and had no plans of ever returning to school. He would tell her one day, but he thought it better to wait until she had the baby. He laughed inside when he thought of that, because that's what he told himself when she was going to have the first baby.

He had to end the conversation when he looked at his watch and saw he was running ten minutes late. He kissed his wife good- bye, reminding her that if ever he were an engineer he could have been in an auto accident like the highway patrolman that got in the accident yesterday. He neglected to say anything about the fact that the patrolman was chasing a robbery suspect.

Keith loved walking out his door to the highway patrol car sitting in his driveway. He was allowed to take his car home at night because he patrolled the Oregon-California border which was too far away from base. Besides, he was able to handle 24 hour on-call duty, another thing his wife hated. Most of his calls dealt with traffic in one form or another. There was very little crime in his neck of the woods.

He got in his car and started it up. He loved the sound of its engine, the power he knew it possessed. He picked up the radio and called in that he was on duty as of 3:11 a.m. Immediately, orders came back to him. He was to proceed to the Oregon-California border on Interstate 5. He was to be on the lookout for a 1969 blue GTO. They were looking for four male suspects who escaped from the Oregon State Prison. Also, they could be in the company a 19 year-old girl. They were to be considered armed and dangerous. Officer Ribbons was also informed not to try to apprehend them, if found.

It took the patrolman nine minutes to get to the destination. If he hadn't had that fight with his wife or if he could have made the trip in seven minutes instead of nine, this story might have ended differently. Just two minutes earlier, a 1969 Pontiac GTO had passed by heading south on Interstate 5.

"Turn the radio down, Bobby. They're trying to tell us something back there," Billy said as his hand continued to rub Charlene's ass in the back seat.

Bobby turned the radio off. He couldn't get a good station anyway. As soon as he did, a voice screamed from the trunk.

"I got to fucking piss, pull this fucker over," Jesse,who, besides having to piss, was really pissed. He had spent more time in the trunk than anyone else. Bobby never had to get back there once. Jesse didn't think that was fair. So what if he was the shortest, big fucking deal. This was it once they stopped; he wasn't getting in the trunk again.

Pauly wasn't too happy being back there either. It had been almost four hours since they stopped for gas. All four guys had got out and sent Charlene to fill up the tank. As big as Pauly was, he was getting cramps in muscles he never knew he had. Pauly didn't argue with Bobby because Bobby was right. He wasn't taking any chances. Pauly was pissed too, not so much for having to be in the trunk, but for how everything turned out. He still couldn't believe it. He prayed to God that it was all just a dream that he would wake up not in this trunk, but on his bunk back at Prigg Cottage. Less than 24 hours ago that's where he was. He still couldn't believe it.

Bobby saw what he was hoping to see: *REST AREA 8 MILES*.

He knew it was time to change cars. He figured by now the police had found Maggot handcuffed to Charlene's car. Even if Maggot didn't say anything, they would still be looking for Maggot's car. He felt more comfortable since they crossed over the Oregon border, but in Maggot's car he still felt uneasy. Maggot's car was the last thing tying them to Oregon. The rest area would change all that.

"Hold on, brother, we have a rest area coming up in about five minutes, OK?"

"Fuck," was all Bobby heard come back. Then Billy spoke.

"Think that's smart, all of us pulling into a rest area and letting people out of the trunk?"

"Yeah, I don't think there will be many people there this time of night. If there are, they pull in, take a piss, hop back in their cars and go. That is until the right car pulls in."

"What do you mean, the right car?" Billy said as he sat up in the back seat.

Bobby had the rear view mirror adjusted so in addition to the road behind him, he could get a view of the back seat. He had found himself with a hard on more than once watching the antics going on there. Charlene also got up pulling her blouse closed, but not before Bobby got a look at her tit sticking out. Charlene knew he could see.

"It's time we got rid of Maggot's car, and the rest area is the perfect place to drop one off and pick up a new one at the same time," Bobby answered, looking into Billy's eyes to see what he thought of the idea.

He didn't have to read Billy's eyes. Billy came right out and said, "Bro, you never cease to amaze me. You're always thinking, and thinking right."

"You get my vote too, Bobby," Charlene was quick to answer "What do we do with the people whose car we take? Not that I give a shit."

"We'll cross that bridge when we get to it, lady," Bobby answered as he began to coast towards the rest area exit.

Bobby reached under the seat, and pulled the shotgun out and placed it beside him. He didn't want some cop having a coffee break see a car on their hot list pull up alongside them. If there was a cop there, Bobby wouldn't take a chance. He'd blow him away without a second's thought. Bobby eased his grip on the shotgun as soon as he could see the rest stop was empty. He pulled right up to the restrooms and parked the car.

"Let me out of this fucking coffin," Jesse screamed.

Bobby got out and opened the trunk, thinking how stupid Jesse really was. He didn't know where they were or who they were next to but he was screaming. Bobby decided not to say anything. Jesse wouldn't understand anyway. It just made him remember not to count on Jesse when it comes to brains.

"It's about fucking time. I got to piss so bad I can taste it," Jesse said as he climbed out, his legs a little wobbly.

"Piss my ass, you better just wipe your ass 'cause I think you shit your pants right in my face," Pauly said as he unfolded out of the car, adding, "God damn, I didn't think anything alive could smell like your farts, asshole!"

Jesse ran towards the restroom saying, "You loved it. I had to take four hours of smelling your feet next to my nose." Billy and Charlene followed.

"How you doing, kid?" Bobby asked as he placed his hands on Pauly's shoulders."

"Damn brother! Don't make me go through that shit again. I mean that was a long time between stops. Are we out of Oregon?"

"Sorry about that Pauly, I just didn't feel comfortable stopping anywhere. I feel a little safer now that we're in California."

Pauly took small steps trying to get the blood flow back in his legs.

"California, huh, well that's something. What are our plans from here?"

"They haven't changed, we're going to do Wizard's plan. But I think we're going to dump Maggot's car 'cause I got a bad feeling it's on the hot sheets by now."

"But first, you're thinking of picking up a car here, right?" As much as Jesse could remind Bobby how stupid he was, Pauly could do the same with his smarts. Pauly was a thinker.

"Yeah, that's what I figured."

"Right on, brother. First we pick a car up here, take along Maggot's car, which would be found if we leave it here at the rest stop. Right, following me?"

"Yeah, I got you. Keep going."

He hadn't even thought about taking Maggot's car with them, he was just going to leave it at the rest stop. Pauly was right, it would be found too quickly. Right away, the cops would have an idea of which way they went. Why leave them a calling card.

Pauly kept going, "Then we dump Maggot's car off some place it won't be found for a while and head towards the rest stop near Vegas."

"You must've heard me telling Billy. That's the plan to a tee," Bobby was amazed. Except for a few points that would be better if Pauly didn't know, such as when they dropped off the guy whose car they stole, they were really going to drop him. No sense leaving another calling card to say what kind of car they were in. They'd also score a better change of clothes than what Maggot brought, plus any cash the guy happened to be packing. Yeah, Pauly was pretty smart.

"No, I couldn't hear shit. Four hours locked in a trunk smelling Jesse's farts gives a guy time to do some thinking," Pauly continued, "I'm still in the fog though, bro, on how things are going to be after we split up after the rest stop thing."

"I've already told you my plans. We just got to hope we make it. I don't think they're going to catch us all, might not catch any of us. We just got to hope for the best, brother."

The conversation was cut short by the flash of head lights pulling into the rest stop. Bobby looked around. He saw Jesse walking back. There was no sign of Billy or Charlene. He looked back at the lights coming, and saw yellow lights. He blew a sigh of relief. It was a truck.

Barry Newsome was wide awake when he pulled into the rest stop. He just had to piss, badly. Crisscross Meth tabs made him piss a lot, but they also allowed him to drive a thousand miles without any sleep. Tacoma to here in eleven hours, he was happy with his time.

Barry got a quick glimpse of what looked like some dude fucking a chick doggy style on the lawn. He shook his head and thought he had better get himself some poontang in San Francisco. He was starting to see things.

There was a lone car parked by the bathroom. Two guys were talking, a third had just got into the driver's side of the car. "Damn, that's an old GTO. My dad used to have one," Barry thought. He parked the truck, leaving the engine running but locking the doors. He kept the keys to the door on his key chain at his side.

He walked toward the restroom unable able to resist looking at the old GTO. He passed the driver. "Sure is a pretty set of wheels you got there, buddy," he said.

"Yeah, I like it," Bobby said trying to conceal the shotgun lying beside him.

"My dad had one just like this. I think his was a '68. Is this a '68?"

"No, '69, but '67 through '69 all look the same."

"Either way, you made it look good."

"Thanks," Bobby said as the man walked by Pauly and Jesse with a nod on his way to the bathroom.

Pauly walked over to Bobby and said, "You're not taking off a truck, are you Bobby?"

"No, what the fuck would we do with a truck? We'll just play it cool with this guy and let him go his merry way. But can you guys see how easy taking off a rest stop can be?"

"Easy as shit!" Jesse said. "In fact, why don't we take this one and the one in Las Vegas?" Jesse was serious.

"I mean how do we know what's inside that truck, it could be a load of fur coats."

"Slow down, Jesse, I hear you thinking, but getting away with just one rest stop's going to be hard enough. And we might as well do the one that's going to get us the most money," Bobby answered, thinking that, for a fag, Jesse sure had a lot of balls. No brains, but a lot of balls.

Pauly was beginning to believe this rest stop thing could work. He was sold on the fact that they could rob a rest stop, but the problem was getting away. He saw a chance of getting away with big dollars, if he could just solve the problem of the getaway.

Pauly's thoughts were broken by Jesse saying, "Another car pulling in." Bobby and Pauly quickly turned to check it out. Bobby's hand tightened on the shotgun. It sure wasn't a cop car. The lights were too close.

"Everything cool, Bobby?" Billy asked, walking up with Charlene wrapped in his arms, acting like he didn't have a care in the world.

"Yeah, everything's cool. There's another car pulling in. We need to check it out. And quit disappearing would you? Some shit may come down and I don't want to go searching for you guys, OK?" Bobby wasn't sure if he said that because

82

it was what could have been or that it bothered him to think of Billy fucking Charlene.

"Yeah, sure, bro, no problem," Billy responded.

A small Honda Civic pulled up two stalls away. In it was an old couple. They both got out of the car. The old man checked twice to see that his door was locked. The couple walked towards the restroom paying no attention to the riff-raff they had seen when pulling in.

"Nice old couple, they remind me of my grand folks, about as friendly too," Jesse cracked.

About the same time the old couple was pulling into the rest stop, 15 miles north a new Chevy van with a newly married couple was heading their way. Only they weren't going to be as lucky as the old couple.

"Honey, wake up. Honey, we're almost in California," Rich said in a soft voice just in case Kelly was in a sound sleep.

"Huh," Kelly responded.

"Two miles and we'll be in California, babe."

"Oh jeez, how long have I been asleep?"

"Well, let me say this. It has been eighty miles since you kissed me," Rich said as he ran his fingers through Kelly's hair.

"Well, we better not let it get to eighty-one," Kelly said as she leaned across the van and kissed Rich.

Rich couldn't understand how she could still send chills through him with just a kiss. There couldn't be a happier man alive than he was. They were married the day before and on their way to Red Bluff so Rich's dad could meet his new daughter-in-law. After a day there, they planned to honeymoon in Southern California, taking in all the sights: Disneyland, Knott's Berry Farm, Universal Studios and whatever else they could fit in during Rich's nine days off. He had to be in Seattle on the tenth day to get back to his job at Boeing.

Kelly, on the other hand, wasn't sure she wanted to go back to work. Rich had said he would rather have his wife work. Rich made pretty good money, and she loved to be spoiled. She was brought up spoiled--dance lessons, beauty school, leader of the Auburn High cheer squad. The only girl with four brothers, she once counted 73 pairs of shoes in her closet. She'd rather be a housewife, fixing dinners, watching soap operas and going shopping. She loved to shop.

"There it is, babe, welcome to California. Oh shit!" Rich instantly changed the subject, hitting his brakes while looking at his speedometer to see how fast he was going. "Eighty. Oh no."

"What's wrong? What's wrong?" Kelly said.

"I just passed a cop doing eighty miles an hour," Rich responded as he slowed to 65, looking in his rear mirror. The cop wasn't coming. "He's not coming, I can't believe it. Boy, this is our lucky day!"

Highway Patrolman Keith Ribbons clocked the van doing 77 miles an hour. He thought about going after it, but his orders didn't say anything about issuing tickets. He hated the boredom of these stakeouts, and for a second, thought about going after the van anyway, but dropped the idea and said out loud, "This is your lucky day, buddy."

Barry Newsome was sitting in his truck drinking coffee when he watched the old couple get in their Honda and drive off. He poured some more coffee and put the lid back on. Time to get back on the road, still had 500 miles to go. He noticed a couple join the three guys in the GTO. He wondered if maybe he wasn't seeing things when he first pulled into the rest stop. She sure was a cute little thing. It would be nice to hear her bark a few times, thinking of the "doggy" he saw when he pulled in. Oh well, he knew he could get laid in Frisco. That would ease the tension he was having.

Barry was ready to pull out as a Chevy van pulled in. A young guy got out and went around to the rider's side to open the door for a sweet young thing. They kissed and hugged, put their arms around each other and headed towards the restroom.

Lucky guy, Barry thought as he made his way back out to the highway.

Bobby saw the van pull in and knew right then that was the perfect rig. He watched the truck start to pull out as a young couple made their way to the restroom. The timing was perfect. The others had no idea what his thoughts were, he could tell by the looks on their faces.

"Jesse, go see if the doors are still open in that van," Bobby said, which got everybody's attention. Jesse did as he was told without hesitation, thinking maybe there was a purse or something to grab.

"Listen up," Bobby said in a voice that brought everyone closer.

"Yeah, the doors are open; you want me to check what's in there?" Jesse said in a loud whisper.

"Get in the back, Billy. We'll be leaving in that van. Lay back there and try not to be seen, you hear me, til it's time to show yourself." Billy did as he was told; climbing into the back of the van and getting under a blanket like it was waiting for him.

"What's your plan, brother?" Pauly asked, mostly wanting to know what he had planned for the young kids that were driving the van.

"You already know the plan Pauly, we grab a new rig and dump Maggot's car."

"Yeah, but the plan called for us taking a rig from some dude by himself, not a couple of kids."

"The van's perfect, bro. We won't hurt the people. As soon as we can feel safe, we'll dump them off," Bobby said as he strode to the car to grab the shotgun, checking first if he could see any headlights coming. He saw nothing.

Rich walked around to the women's restroom waiting for Kelly to finish. He noticed just one car and a few people standing in front of the car. They all looked like a bunch of creeps. He would be glad when he and Kelly pulled the hell out of here.

Kelly had a habit of sneaking up on Rich grabbing him and saying "boo." This was the first time she ever did it when it had actually scared him.

"Damn, do you always have to do that shit?" Rich said, regretting it as soon as he said it. He knew she didn't mean anything by it.

"I'm sorry," Kelly said, realizing Rich had a look on his face she had never seen before, "What's wrong, Rich?"

"Nothing, let's just get going. Sorry, I yelled at you," Rich said as he put his arm around Kelly, giving her a quick kiss on the cheek. He probably got worried for no reason, no sense telling Kelly. They started to walk back, Rich saw another guy get out of the car. He was trying to remember if he had locked the van up when they got out and remembered he didn't. They stepped up their pace.

"That's a cute little babe, huh, Pauly?" Jesse said in a whisper. His eyes along with everybody else were watching the young couple make their way back towards their van. That made Rich more paranoid.

She was a cute little thing, Pauly thought to himself. He didn't like this idea at all. He was scared, not for himself, but for what he thought might happen to this girl. For one quick second, the thought of rape even excited him. Pauly knew in Jesse's head it would be more than a thought, not to mention Bobby and Billy. Then Pauly saw Bobby walk by him with the shotgun behind his back.

Rich and Kelly were about ten feet from the van when they saw one of the guys coming towards them. Rich had an urge to make a mad dash for the van. The guy had something behind his back. Rich's heart started to pound.

"Where you folks heading?" Bobby asked as he kept going towards them.

"Get in the van and lock the doors," Rich said, giving Kelly a little push. He stood his ground, ready to confront this guy. He had placed fourth in wrestling in the state of Washington in his weight class. He could take care of himself if he had to.

Kelly all of a sudden got scared, more so because she could sense Rich's fright, but she did as she was told.

"We're on our honeymoon, going to introduce my wife to my dad in Red Bluff," Rich said as he saw Kelly had made it to the van. He no longer wanted to stand his ground with this guy coming at him; the guy had a look that terrified him. Rich made a dash for the van. Kelly had already locked the door. Kelly reached over and unlocked the door. Rich was opening it when he heard the words.

"You better hold it right there, buddy."

Rich turned to see the guy pull a sawed off shot-gun from behind his back.

"Don't hurt us. We don't want any trouble, please."

"Just shut up and nobody's going to get hurt. Billy come on out." Bobby's voice brought Billy out flashing the gun. Kelly screamed.

"What do you want? Please tell us what you want," Rich was able to get out.

"We're escaped convicts, and we are going to take your van. If you don't cause any trouble, you'll come out of this all right. Do anything stupid and you're dead. Do you understand?"

"Yes, we won't do anything stupid. You can have the van, just take it. We won't say anything to anybody. I promise. Just take the van and go."

"Just shut up for now, buddy. Pauly, put this guy in the trunk of the GTO. You and Charlene drive Maggot's car and follow us. We'll find a place down the highway and dump the car. Jesse, get in the van and get that girl in the back and all of you stay down back there."

Jesse did as he was told. Rich kept looking back at Kelly as Pauly grabbed his arm and led him to the back of the GTO. Pauly opened the trunk and helped Rich to get in, then closed the trunk's lid. Bobby jumped in only to find no keys in the ignition.

"Where's the key, girl?" Bobby said, turning back to Kelly.

"My husband has them," Kelly said as her whole body shook.

"Pauly, the guy's got the keys." Pauly went and opened the trunk, got the keys and gave them to Bobby. They all pulled out.

"Hey, pretty nice set up, huh, bro? Take a gander at that sound system," Jesse said as he checked out the inside of the van. Rich had really decked her out, putting all his spare time and money into making the van one of the nicest custom vans around. Then Jesse's eyes went to Kelly, lying on the bed portion Rich had just finished before they left for their honeymoon.

Billy wasn't so much interested in the van as he was with the girl. This sweet young thing lying next to him shook all over with fright. He sensed her fear, it excited him.

"This guy doesn't only have good taste in vans, he's also got it for picking a nice old lady," Billy answered as his hand went on to Kelly's leg. She quivered when he touched her. Billy liked that.

Bobby checked the rear view mirror. The GTO was right behind them. He wanted to get five or six miles down the road, then start looking for a place where they could dump the car. Then an idea came to him that could solve a problem he had been having all night.

He couldn't get Charlene off his mind. He wanted her, not just to fuck, but all of her. He couldn't stand to see her with Billy. All night long he had watched them getting it on in one way or another. How Charlene would look right in the mirror while she was giving Billy head, knowing Bobby was watching. He thought about how good it felt to touch a soft naked body. He wondered if Charlene was still laughing on the inside about him shooting his load like a high school kid yesterday. But his main thoughts were how he could get her away from Billy.

He justified having such thoughts because Billy had told Bobby several times how he was just using Charlene. Well, Bobby wanted her as his old lady. He felt they would make a good team. But how was he going to pull it off? Bobby knew he could handle Billy, only how was he going to get Charlene to dump Billy for him? Going down the highway knowing Billy as he did, he thought, once a rapo always a rapo. Well, the girl in the back could give Charlene her reason for dumping Billy.

Bobby knew Billy and Jesse thought alike. He turned to see Jesse smile at Billy as Billy began to rub Kelly's leg. Bobby knew the only thing holding them back was they weren't sure how to go for it. He decided right then to go a few more miles before looking for a place to dump the car. Also, he needed a roundabout way to give Billy and Jesse some encouragement.

"Hey, we travelin' in style or what? I be lovin' this van!" Bobby said in his black impersonation voice. Then he continued, "Yesterday at this time we were waking up to some shitty grits and another bullshit day. Now, we're going down the highway in a choice van with the sweetest little lady I've had the pleasure to feast my eyes on in over seven years. The first one done back there come up here and drive a spell, I ain't waiting another day. I got some business to take care of with that little lady," Bobby guessed that was as roundabout as it was going to get. It was all the encouragement Jesse and Billy needed.

Kelly wet herself. She could never even imagine this type of fear. She knew she was about to get raped, but staying alive was what she valued most. They were nothing but animals. "We're going to be killed, they're going to kill us," she thought. She felt a hand go between her legs, "Please don't, please," was all she could manage to get out.

"Oh man, the bitch pissed her pants," Billy said pulling back his hand and wiping it on Kelly's pants.

"Well, we better help the poor thing out of her pants, can't have her going around in wet pants," Jesse said as his hands went to Kelly's belt.

Kelly was able to say, "Please don't, please don't do this."

"Little lady, if you want to spend the rest of your life with that new husband of yours, the best thing you can do is just shut up. You see all of us have been in prison a lot of years, more years between us than you are born. And you see in prison, one thing you miss is sweet pussy like you. You can relax and enjoy this, because we don't plan on hurting you. If anything, you're about to be treated like a queen. Jesse help me lift her on the floor, this bed is too wet. What's your name, little lady?" Billy asked her and Jesse eased her to the floor.

"Please don't," Kelly pleaded in a whimpering voice as she felt someone unsnapping her pants.

"Shhhh," Billy said in a whisper in her ear. "Relax; now tell me your name."

"Kelly," she answered this time more like a cry. She felt her pants being pulled from her. "They are going to rape me. Oh God, they are going to rape me," she thought.

"Kelly, now that's a real pretty name. Don't you worry none, Kelly, think if you let yourself, you can really enjoy this," Billy ended before he started to kiss Kelly. Kelly just closed her eyes. She tried to tell herself to think of something nice, just let them do what were going to do, get it over with. Oh God, she hated this guy kissing her, his breath smelled like a toilet. She felt her panties not being pulled off, but being ripped off. She thought how she had bought them especially for Rich. How much he loved to see them on her. She heard the sound of a zipper and pants coming off. She felt something on her lips and knew what it was without opening her eyes. She had done it twice with Rich and hated each time. Rich had promised he wouldn't make her do it again. She heard someone say something like, "Take it!" She opened her mouth and thought about her and Rich at the Space Needle just two nights ago.

Rich was saying prayers he could remember from his church days. He promised God that if he and Kelly got out of this all right, he would start attending church regularly. He thought about Kelly being alone with those guys and made a solemn oath that if they harmed a hair on her head, he would kill them. Tear them apart with his bare hands.

"What do you think, Charlene, are we all out of our minds or what?" Pauly asked, knowing no matter what, it was too late to change anything now. There was no turning back.

"Who knows, if tomorrow we're all heading to Mexico with a sack full of money, then I guess we're pretty smart. If we get killed or busted, then I guess we're out of our minds. One thing I know for sure, it's too late now and the plan we have sounds like the best way to go. No sense worrying about it right now, we just got to do what we got to do. Personally, I'm going to feel a lot better once we ditch Maggot's car. That dirt road we just passed would have been perfect. I wonder what Bobby's thinking?"

Pauly wondered also what Bobby was thinking. Why did he have Charlene ride with him? He knew what Billy and Jesse were thinking. Probably by now, they were doing more than just thinking about it. That poor girl was being fucked by now. Yeah, that's why Charlene was riding with him, why Bobby had him drive the GTO. Bobby knew he wouldn't go for them raping the girl. That cocksucker was playing them all.

Bobby saw the old dirt road, and knew that was just what he'd been looking for. But he turned to see what was going on in the back, and it wasn't quite time yet. Billy was skull fucking her, and Jesse was pounding the shit out of her. The girl was lying there with her eyes closed. Bobby wanted to wait until Billy had his turn pounding her. He would have to figure out a way later to let Charlene know.

"Switch me places, Jess," Billy said between pants.

"Just a second, I'm going to come."

"Cocksucker, don't come in her. I want to eat her."

"Ahhhh... Oh Lordy!"

"You asshole, don't come in her."

"Too late, bro, sorry."

"You fucker, get off her."

Jesse fell off. Billy didn't want to eat her. Shit, he wasn't eating anybody's come. He just climbed on and mounted her.

The timing was perfect. Bobby saw another dirt road coming up. He didn't care how long Billy got to fuck her just as long as he did. Bobby really didn't want to get in on the action. In his own way, he felt sorry for the girl. He pumped his brake so Pauly would know to slow down, and then put on his blinker. What was he going to do about the girl and her old man? He bit his lip which was a habit when he was in deep thought. Take them both along. No, he didn't like that idea. Put them both in the trunk and just split? No, they would get out, and the cops would know what we're driving in less than an hour. Kill them. That thought lasted longer than the last. "What the fuck," he thought, "They can't hang you more than once. Karma...bad karma. I had no choice with the cop, but I do with these kids, or do I?"

"Hey, brother, you want me to drive?" Jesse broke Bobby's thoughts, "That little lady is hot to trot."

"We're just getting ready to pull off the highway. There's a dirt road coming up. I'll have to deal with the little lady later. It's going to be getting light soon and we need to get rid of Maggot's car before it does. Business before pleasure."

"That's cool," Jesse responded, "She's nice. I mean she feels real nice, you'll see. And as soon as you're done, I want some more. I mean, I forgot how nice it is to feel like a man. Whooo!" Jesse yelled like a wolf. It made Bobby laugh. The reason he felt like a man was because he'd been acting like a woman in the last five years.

"Don't stop yet, I ain't done yet," Billy yelled as he pumped like a madman.

"We've got to!" Bobby yelled back, "It's getting light and we got to dump the car. You better look out, the roads going to get pretty rough and you might snap your dick off," Bobby and Jesse laughed as the van pulled on to the dirt road. Bobby purposefully looked for bumps to hit. It made Bobby and Jesse laugh harder.

"Assholes!" Billy said as he climbed off Kelly and pulled on his pants.

Billy looked down at Kelly. She lay there naked, her legs still spread. Her eyes were still closed, but it didn't stop the tears from coming out. Kelly no longer cared if they killed her. She already wished she was dead. She felt dirty, contaminated, as if her life had just been taken away. Rich would never forgive her.

"Get dressed, little lady, we can't have your old man freaking out on us if he sees you that way, " Billy said as he knelt down to her face to face. He reached under her shoulders and shook her so she would open her eyes. She did.

"Now listen here, girl, my old lady is riding in the car behind us and if you don't want anything to happen to you or your old man, then you better make sure she doesn't find out what just happened, understand?"

Kelly wasn't sure what this guy was saying. She still could smell his rancid breath. She heard words but they didn't make sense. Kelly didn't know it, but she was in a state of shock. She felt him shake her again, heard him say understand, but she didn't.

"Hey, girl, do you hear me? Get dressed!" Billy said as he pushed her down and stood up. Kelly lay there looking up to the ceiling.

"Hey girl, what's wrong with you? Get dressed!" She still just lay there. "Jesse, give me a hand dressing this chick. She won't get dressed, she's just lying there."

"You better hurry, doesn't look like this road goes very far," Bobby said as he looked up the road about 200 feet where some old junk cars were. It looked like the road ended there. "Couldn't have planned it better," Bobby thought.

"Damn, come on Jesse give me a hand, would you?" Billy asked worriedly. They went to back looking for Kelly's clothes.

"There's no way we'll get these panties back on," Jesse said as he held them up, all torn to shreds.

"Come on, quit fucking around. Help me with these pants. Lift her ass up, and I'll pull them on."

"Wow, this chick really freaked out, huh?" Jesse said as he looked out the back of the van and saw Pauly and Charlene following them in the dust.

"Yeah, fuck, if your sister finds out what happened she'll cut both our balls off."

"She ain't going to find out," Jesse said as he began to button Kelly's blouse, then without thinking his lips went to her nipple and he began to suck.

"God damn it, Jesse, cut that shit out! I'm serious," Billy yelled as he felt the van coming to a stop, "Oh shit, come on. Help me sit her up."

Kelly wasn't sure what was happening. She felt herself being lifted up someone was buttoning her blouse. She saw some faces in front of her, but they were a blur. She felt the van stop.

"Make her look right. All right, Jess. I'm going to stall your sister as long as I can," Billy said as he climbed up to the front and got out the passenger door.

Charlene was already out of the car and making her way towards the van.

"Hey, baby, wait till you see this van, it's boss," Billy said as Charlene went into his arms. They kissed.

"Let's check it out," Charlene answered when they broke their kiss.

"First off," Billy replied quickly, "Who's got the weed?"

"It's in the car," Charlene answered.

"Go, roll us a big fat one, would you, babe? We got to celebrate; we're traveling in style from now on. And guess what, it's even got a bed." Charlene smiled and went, and did as she was told. Billy loved that about Charlene, she never asked questions, just did as she was told. He didn't want to blow it with her. Then he thought about the bed. He went to the van and yelled back to Jesse. "Hey bro, pull that sheet off the bed and turn the mattress over, would you? How's the girl doing?"

"She's fine, pretty as a picture. I think she's tripping because she's never had it so good."

Bobby was out of the van stretching. He couldn't see the highway but knew it was only 400 or 500 feet away.

"Hey, so far so good, huh?" Pauly asked as he walked toward Bobby.

"Yeah, check out this van, bro. We're traveling in style from now on," Bobby went around to the rear door, but found it locked, "Open this up, Jesse."

What was Bobby doing, Jesse thought as he finished turning over the mattress. He looked at Kelly, who was staring straight ahead, expressionless. Oh well, he thought as he reached over and unlocked the door, hoping the chick's old man wasn't out there to see her. He wanted her again really bad and this time all by himself.

Bobby opened the door and said, "Is this style or what?" All Pauly really wanted to see was the girl, and at first glance he saw her. She was leaning up against the back of the van, slumped over. Her hands were to her side, and her mouth just hung open. Her expression was blank.

"What's wrong with the chick, Bobby?"

"Nothing, probably just scared," Bobby answered as Billy joined them at the back of the van.

"Bullshit," Pauly thought. Her blouse wasn't even buttoned right.

She's just freaking out," Billy said, "She's just worried about her old man, that's all."

"The girl looks in shock to me. I've seen that shit before," Pauly replied not wanting to say what he really felt, but then he said it anyway, "You guys fucked her, didn't you?"

Bobby was quick to reply. He just put his hands up and said, "Don't look at me, brother. I was driving. But what the fuck, come on I'll show you the rest of the van." Bobby made his way to the front of the van. This was working out perfectly.

Pauly looked at Billy and Jesse. They didn't have to say anything. He could see the truth by the looks on their faces.

"You fucking rapos," Pauly said in disgust.

"Fuck, brother, don't get so pissed. There's plenty left for you," Jesse replied, not knowing why Pauly seemed so pissed.

"Fuck you!" Pauly said as he turned away.

"Hold on, Pauly," Billy said as he reached and grabbed Pauly's arm. Pauly turned and stared hatefully into Billy's eyes. He never liked being grabbed and now was the wrong time. Billy was worried Pauly might say something to Charlene. But Billy didn't want Pauly pissed at him either. Pauly was a big boy and not someone Billy wished to mess with. Pauly pushed Billy's hands off of him and kept staring.

"What's your trip, Paul? You all of a sudden get religion or something? What the fuck, we've been down a long time. The pussy was there, so we took some of it. I suppose you didn't think about it, huh? You've been pulling your pud so long, you telling me you ain't ready for some real thing?"

"It ain't that, Billy, and I know you don't understand. But we are in a world of shit. We got a lot more things to be thinking about than getting pussy. We killed a guard. I mean has that even sunk into your head yet? This ain't no fucking game anymore, Billy; we're running for our lives. I've lost everything that's ever been important to me. I'll never see my wife and kid again and it's tearing me up inside. This caper we're going on just isn't going to work. We've been lucky so far. I mean really fucking lucky that we got this far. And sure, it's been a long time without pussy for me and to tell you the truth, brother, yeah I've thought about pussy. I thought about fucking your old lady. How would you like it if I raped her?"

All of a sudden, it was Billy who was getting pissed. What gave Pauly the right to come off saying shit like that about his old lady? But before he could say anything, he saw Charlene get out of the car and walk towards them.

Billy said in a soft voice, "Fuck that shit for now. I don't want Charlene to know what happened, OK."

"Don't worry about me. Charlene's no dummy, she'll find out for herself, not to mention Bobby."

"What do you mean by that?" Billy asked, totally puzzled by what Pauly meant by "not to mention Bobby."

"Nothing, just forget it," Pauly said as he turned to walk away again.

"Hang on, Pauly, I just rolled a big fat one," Charlene said, not the least bit aware of what was going on.

"I'll pass for now," Pauly said.

"What's wrong with him?" she asked Billy.

"Oh, he's just worried about his old lady and kid. Hey, Bobby, Jesse, Charlene rolled us a fat one. Come and get it."

Jesse came out of the back of the van, closing the door behind him. He had heard most of what went on between Billy and Pauly, but didn't want to say anything in front of Charlene. Bobby joined them, asking where Pauly was going.

"He's on some kind of a bummer, saying shit like the plan we have ain't going to work. Worried about the cop we killed and shit like that. To tell you the truth, I'm getting a little worried about him, if you know what I mean," Billy said as he passed the joint to Bobby.

"Oh, he'll come through when the time calls for it. To tell you the truth, Pauly gave up more than any of us did. He had something going for him when he got out. It's all gone now. So I guess I can understand his bummer," Bobby ended by taking a big draw on the joint., "Think I'll go rap to him though."

Bobby took another pull on the joint and handed it to Charlene. They made eye contact and she smiled at him. He walked toward Pauly who was standing by the old junk cars. Pauly was smoking a Camel, wishing he hadn't said what he did to Billy. He somehow figured out what Bobby was doing.

Bobby wanted Charlene, and Bobby was playing Billy, Jesse and the young girl just to get his way. His feelings about Bobby were a complete turnaround from what he felt 24 hours ago. Bobby was playing him and Charlene, too. Pauly realized that Bobby was a master at manipulation. And the worst thing was there was nothing he could do about it. He was stuck in a web, and there were spiders all around him. There was nowhere to go. He was going to be eaten alive.

"Hey, bro, what's bothering you?" Pauly turned to see Bobby talking to him.

"Fuck, Bobby, why did you let them rapos take off that little chick?" Pauly asked seriously.

"First off, that ain't a little chick! She's like out of a magazine we use to jack off with. And what the fuck, Pauly, they didn't hurt her none. And what was I going to tell them? Their dicks got hard. They weren't going to listen to me."

"Oh, bullshit, Bobby, they'll do what you tell them and you know it."

"Maybe so, but I saw it as no biggie. I don't know why it's bugging you so much. You telling me you wouldn't poke that sweet thing if she gave you half a chance?"

"Yeah, sure, if she gave it to me, but I ain't raping nobody even if I was down 20 years."

"Well, that's you, brother, and I admire that in you. But Billy, on the other hand, would rather take it than have it given to him. That's the way it is. I mean I didn't think that I had rapo blood in me. But when those guys were back there laying it on that sweet piece and she's not fighting it, to tell you the truth, brother, my dick got hard. I don't know what to tell you, Pauly, other than don't let it bother you. Nobody got hurt."

"What are we going to do about them?" Pauly asked to change the subject. Bobby did have thoughts about what he wanted to do, but first he wanted to see what Pauly was thinking.

"I don't know. I think you did right picking the van it's perfect for keeping everybody out of sight and I don't feel like doing any more trunk time. And if we keep the couple here they'll be found and the whole world will know what we're traveling in. So I guess we got no choice but to take them with us. Is that what you're thinking?" Pauly hoped for just once, Bobby would agree with him. Yet in the back of his mind he was scared for the young couple. In Bobby's head it would be better if they were just dead. No way would Pauly go for that.

"Yeah, that's close to what I was thinking, except that guy kind of scares me. I'm afraid he might try to be some kind of a hero or something. When he finds out what Billy and Jesse did to his old lady, he could go off."

"Well, what do we do then? I hope you ain't thinking about wasting him." Pauly decided to come right out and say it.

"To tell you the truth I thought about it, but I guess Karma scares me. The cop, well, we didn't have much choice. With the kid, we do, so this is what I'm thinking. First of all, we can use another set of clothes, so we take his along with all his I.D. which I think you come the closest to fitting. We sink into his head that if he ever wants to see his new bride again that he better not give up any information when he's found. He should act like he got amnesia or something. Within 24 hours or so we'll let his lady go and they'll live happy ever after. What do you think?"

"First, I'm glad to see you talking about Karma. I was getting a little worried about you, bro. But I don't think that plan will work. First, we know the car will be found as soon as it gets light, and the guy's a square. The cops will get information out of him no matter how much you scare him. I say we got no choice, we got to take them both with us."

"Yeah, you're probably right. But let me tell you this, you better let the guy know this ain't no game. Karma or not, if he goes off, I'll kill him right where he sits. Make sure he believes it, Pauly. Let him know if he is going to play hero, he can cause his sweet young wife to get hurt also."

"That's no problem, Bobby. I don't think this guy is the hero type. I think he's just plain scared shitless."

"Good, keep him that way, because I ain't bullshittin', Pauly, I'll kill him fast." That wasn't quite what Bobby had in mind. He wanted to leave him dead. He knew Pauly would never go for it though. He was going to say that was the plan, knowing as Pauly had just said, that no matter how much they scared this guy the cops would get all the information they wanted from him. The others never would have thought of that, but leave it to Pauly to answer a question before you even asked him.

Then Bobby wasn't sure how he could kill the guy without the others knowing. Karma, fuck karma. When the time was right the guy was dead.

"Bobby, whoo, Bobby Jesse shouted running at them with a handful of money, "That chick had $345 bucks in her purse. Score, brother, you sure know how to pick the right rig."

"Good, we can use it. Pauly, go with Jesse and get that guy out of the truck. Strip him down to his shorts. See if you fit in his clothes. Then find something to tie him up, the chick too. We better get on the road, we ain't far from light. Make sure the guy gets my message, Pauly."

"Yeah," was all Pauly answered and made his way with Jesse waving the cash in front of Pauly's face. Bobby headed toward the van. Billy and Charlene were walking towards him.

"Who's keeping an eye on the chick?" Bobby asked as they approached. He felt for the van keys, they were in his pocket.

"She's scared shitless, just sitting there. She's not going anywhere," Billy replied, glad that Charlene hadn't noticed anything other than seeing Kelly sitting there scared shitless.

"Yeah, we'll go get all the shit we need out of the GTO. Don't forget the bag of ammo in the trunk. We got to get going before it gets light."

"OK," Billy answered without a second thought and loped over to the car.

"Charlene, do me a favor and keep an eye on the girl, okay?" Bobby asked in a way she couldn't refuse. Charlene loved the way Bobby seemed to show her more respect than he showed anyone else. She went back to the van, but not before she sent a look that said I like the way you're handling everything.

Bobby was hoping Charlene would find out what happened to the girl without him being the one that let the secret out. Maybe if she was alone with the girl, Charlene would be able to sense what happened. Or the girl would break down to another girl.

Rich had been doing a lot of thinking. One thought kept coming back in his head. They were going to kill him and Kelly. He had to do something. He felt the car pull off the highway and on to what felt like a dirt road. He felt around in the darkness of the trunk, and he came up with a tire iron. He felt the car come to a stop. He put his feet to the top of the trunk and waited for someone to pop it open. He heard voices. He waited. Break their heads open was all he could think. Come out swinging, hope that it was just one guy. Hope that guy had a gun. Grab the gun and blast away. Shoot to kill, get that son-of-a-bitch with that shotgun. Maybe he would be the one who opens the trunk. Yeah, it would surely be nice to bust his head open. Yeah, you assholes, this is one guy that's not going to lie down and just let you kill him. He waited.

"Gee, if the chick had this much money, I bet the dude is packing more," Jesse said as he got to the back of the car and waited for Pauly to open the trunk.

"Just cool it for a few minutes would you, Jess? No sense in getting riled up. We just turned this guy's whole world around," Pauly said as he slipped the key into the trunk.

"Fuck him!" were the last words Jesse would remember saying for the next nine hours.

The trunk flew open and, in what seemed like one movement, Rich leapt out of the trunk, bringing down a tire iron with all his might towards Pauly's head. Pauly got his arm in front of the blow. If he hadn't, Rich would have gotten his wish about breaking a head open. As it was, the blow was hard enough to break Pauly's wrist and send him flying backwards.

With another quick movement Rich brought the tire iron down on Jesse's head. Jesse's mouth was still open as his legs caved in. He fell to the ground, blood oozing out the top of his head. Rich stepped toward Pauly to finish him off. He raised the tire iron up but heard a noise right by him. Turning toward the noise, he saw a silver plated .38 pointed at his face. He didn't even see the flash. Rich fell over backwards dead, almost landing on top of Jesse, the tire iron still held tight in his hand.

Billy stood there with the gun smoking in his hand. Bobby was there in seconds with the shotgun cocked for action. Charlene jumped out of the back of the van and headed toward where the shot came from with the other .38 in her hand, leaving the back of the van wide open.

Kelly heard the shot and knew that Rich had just been killed. She was still in a daze, but her senses told her she had to get out of there or she was next. She jumped out of the van and ran down the dirt road toward the highway.

"What the fuck happened?" Bobby yelled.

"Fuck if I know. All of a sudden this guy came flying out of the trunk kicking ass with a tire iron on Jesse and Pauly, so I blew him away. I mean, I blew his fucking face right off," Billy answered, not sure if he was scared or proud.

Bobby went to Pauly and helped him up. Bobby could see Pauly was in pain. "What happened, bro?" Bobby asked Pauly.

"Fuck, I don't know. The guy just surprised the shit out of us. Don't be pissed at Billy, the guy was about to cave my head in when Billy blew him away. You better take a look at Jesse, the guy got him good."

Billy was already with Jesse holding his head up. "Mother fucker, he killed Jesse!" Billy screamed in almost a cry. Bobby went over to Jesse at the same time Charlene showed up and knelt down to Jesse. Bobby could see right off that Jesse wasn't dead. Blood didn't spurt out of dead people.

"No, he ain't dead. Hey, who's watching the girl?"

"Piss on that girl, this is my brother, Bobby," Charlene said as tears started run down her face. Bobby pulled off the flower shirt Maggot had brought and handed it to Charlene.

"Hold this on the top of that gash as hard as you can. Billy, go check the girl and pull the van over here. We got to get the fuck out of here," Bobby said as he handed Billy the keys.

"How you doing, Pauly?" Bobby asked.

"I think my wrist is broken, hurts like a bitch. Cocksucker, I just didn't expect it Bobby. I just didn't expect it."

"I tried to tell you the guy had hero in him. Damn it, we don't need this shit. Fuck!" Bobby screamed, not over Rich getting killed. In fact, that part couldn't have worked out better. But Jesse was hurt and Pauly's hand was all fucked up. He sure wasn't ready for the next thing he heard. It was Billy screaming.

"Bobby, the girl is gone! The girl ain't there."

"Fuck, what the hell is going on? Pauly, see if you can get any of the guy's clothes off him. Make sure you get his ID and money. Grab the ammo bag in the trunk. I got to find the girl."

Bobby ran over to the van.

"Where the fuck did she go, Billy?"

"I don't know. She wasn't there when I got here. What should I do?"

"Get the van over to those guys. Help Pauly get everything the guy has. Get Jesse loaded up, then pull the van down as far as the highway and let's do it quick."

"Got you," Billy said as he hopped in the van and pulled it over to the GTO.

Bobby couldn't believe this was all happening. He hadn't planned on killing the girl but now he wasn't sure. First, he had to find her. She could be anywhere. It was still dark, even though the first rays of light were starting to show. All she had to do was run into the woods and they would never find her. That meant they would have to ditch the van and get something else fast. He hated that thought he was looking forward to making the rest of the trip with the van. Bobby tried to scan the woods, but he saw that it was hopeless. It was pitch dark in there. He ran toward the highway, about 50 feet, and then stopped to try to hear anything. He heard nothing.

Kelly just knew she had to run. She looked to the woods but it was so dark, it scared her. She just kept going until she got to the highway. If she had turned north, she would never have seen those people again.

Barry Newsome was cursing to himself. He made it standard to always check his tires whenever he made a stop as he did at the rest stop a few miles back. Sure enough, the first time he didn't he got a flat tire. It was an inside tire to boot, a real bitch to change and no doubt it was already flat when he was at the rest stop. Sure would have been a lot easier to change it back there. "Oh well, got to do what you got to do," he said under his breath. He went to get a flare to place behind his truck. He lit the flare and went to get the tools to get started. He heard what he thought was a shot just down the road. He looked but couldn't see anything. What a weird time to be hunting, he thought, as he reached for his tools.

Kelly saw a flare. Her first thought was that it was the police. She ran toward what she thought was safety, screaming, "Oh God, help me, help me!"

Barry Newsome jumped with fright at the sound of a woman screaming. He turned to look and could barely make out the shadow of a woman running toward him. It must have something to do with the shot he heard. The girl ran right into his arms. There was a look in her eyes of total terror.

"Oh please, help me. Help me. We got to get out of here. Please, we got to go now."

"Slow down girl, what's happening? What's wrong?" Barry asked, recognizing her as the girl he saw at the rest stop.

"They're going to kill us. Please, we got to go. They already killed Rich. They're going to kill us. Oh God, they're going to kill us."

"I don't know what you're talking about, girl, but you quit worrying. Nobody's going to hurt you. I'll get on the C.B. and get the police here, OK? Now don't you fret? I won't let anything happen to you."

"Please, let's just get out of here. They're coming, look, they're coming."

Bobby heard the girl scream and took off running toward her. He had to get to her before any passing motorists saw her. When he got to the highway, he saw the flare, the truck and the girl in some dude's arms, thanks to the flood light Barry Newsome had set up. Bobby crept slowly on the side of the road hoping not to be seen. He wasn't. He got within 20 feet of them when the girl screamed. Bobby turned to see the van turn onto the highway.

Barry Newsome wasn't sure what was happening, but this girl had him scared shitless. No time for the CB. He had to get to the gun he kept under the seat. For twenty years he had been a truck driver and had always carried a gun. He had never needed it before.

"Girl, you get up in the truck. I'll find out what this is all about. Now, don't you worry any, I won't let anything happen to you." He grabbed the girl's arm to give her a hand up and at the same time saw someone walk out from behind the truck. Barry pushed the girl to the ground and went for his gun. Bobby emptied both barrels into his back. He fell in a heap right in front of Kelly. Kelly began to scream at the same time the van pulled alongside them. Billy came jumping out of the van with his .38 in his hand.

Bobby looked up and down the highway. There were no cars coming from either direction.

"Everything all right, Bobby?" Billy asked as he bent over to roll the truck driver over, "They don't get any deader than this guy," he said.

"Hey, this is that guy from the rest stop."

"Yeah, it is, isn't it? He sure picked a bad time to get a flat," Bobby said as Charlene joined them, "Hey lady, make that girl quit her screaming and get her inside the van. Billy, give me a hand. We got to dump this guy in the woods. First, take his wallet."

Billy did, and put it inside his belt. They covered him with what leaves they could find, and went back to the van. They headed south on Interstate 5.

FLOWING

Look around; think profound, all the sounds going around.
Listen, from deep within are the secrets,
The longed for answer lives within.
Sadness with the head never meet, happy is the cry I squeak
Looking, searching, for unknown
Yet, the party is a blast.
The hurt is comfort, sorrow is masked
Dying expressions never came, overlapping fears just the same.
Memories can't drive tomorrow's ship
Sailing into the sunset rainbows
Unforgotten breeze, blowing waste
Pictures of yesterday taste
Crying, yet tears never show
From yesterday sadness flows
A feeble attempt, to swoon degree
Of forever trying to end a spree
Heights never reached in human mind
A hunger to speak our inner sights
Long lasted visions into wastefulness
Claiming all that is not yet forgotten
Speak unto lost, mighty man
Shed no greedy cost, if you can
Tell the truth, heavenly beast
Words full of wisdom uphold
Waiting and yearning, at last paid
Like a bright light, it shone
Coming home to true reward. Let it be.

-Rest Stop- Chapter 8

Sunday, 6:45 a.m.

Highway Patrolman Keith Ribbons was glad when the call came in to end the stake out. He already figured that the escaped convicts probably went north heading for Canada. He was hungry and headed for a small restaurant down the highway 20 miles. He saw a truck pulled over to the side of the road and slowed down to thirty miles an hour to check it out. He saw nobody and figured the driver went to seek help. Not much he could do, so he was going to move on when he noticed a floodlight still shining. "Ah shit, better check it out," he thought. He pulled over in front of the truck. Walking around the side of the truck, he noticed tools on the ground and a flat inner tire. That seemed unusual. A driver was not likely to take off leaving his tools on the ground. The driver must be around. He looked inside the truck, nobody. He tried to open the door. It was locked. He looked behind him in the woods, thinking maybe the guy was taking a pee. He didn't see anything. He walked around the truck and tried the driver's door. It was open. Now he knew the driver had to be around. No truck driver left his truck door unlocked, even if he was only going to take a walk in the woods.

The officer knew there were no houses around. He would take one more look in the woods. He saw blood on the ground. He wondered why he didn't see it sooner. It was a lot of blood. He quickly went to the back of the truck. The door was locked from the outside. He went back to the blood, looking harder this time. He saw a foot print in the middle of the pool of blood. He looked a few feet away and saw the same foot print with a trace of blood next to it. He noticed a second set of prints, then another drop of blood in front of the truck--another drop of blood, then some more, all leading into the woods. He had seen enough. It was time to call for help.

Within 20 minutes, two other California Highway Patrolmen had joined Keith Ribbons, along with a county sheriff. They followed an easy trail of trampled grass and drops of blood. It was Keith who first saw the feet sticking out from under a clump of leaves.

The highway patrolmen knew not to disturb anything, but they did remove the leaves off the guy's face. One look told you the guy was dead, still Keith put his hand to the guys neck to feel for a pulse. There was none.

Within an hour, there were five detectives, an ambulance, and a helicopter at the scene. A call came in from the helicopter about an abandoned car about a half mile from the scene on a dirt road. Keith said he knew the road, and went with two of the detectives to show them.

"Oh, shit," Keith said out loud when they approached the car and saw it was a 1969 GTO. Keith explained to the detectives about his stake out last night as they approached the car. One of the detectives drew his gun. It took only a second to see the blood at the back of the car, and trail of blood leading to the trunk. To the officer's amazement, there were keys in the trunk. One of the detectives took a handkerchief, put it to the key and turned and opened the trunk. There was a man lying there with his eyes open, and a hole in his face where his nose should have been. Highway patrolman Keith Ribbons was no longer hungry.

"Ten egg McMuffins, 10 hash browns, and 10 milk," the girl driving the custom van said into the voice box.

"Would you like any apple or cheese danish with that order?" she was asked.

"No, thank you. Hold on just a second," Charlene turned and asked Billy what he said.

"Get me a cheese danish," Billy said in a whisper.

"Me, too," Bobby also responded in a whisper, "Fuck, just order five of them. I'm sure we'll eat them later."

Charlene turned back to the voice box and said, "Yes, we would like five cheese danish, please."

"Thank you for your order. That will be $26.47 at window one."

"It's been a long time since I've had an egg McMuffin," Billy said as he held Jesse's head on his lap.

"The bleeding stop?" Pauly asked.

"Yeah, it looks like it. I can't wake him up for nothing. I mean he's out cold. He might be worse than we know, huh?" Billy said as he looked at Pauly's hand which was badly swollen. "How's your hand doing brother?"

"Hurts like a mother fucker," Pauly answered. You could see the pain on his face.

"Charlene?" Bobby said in a low voice while they were waiting for their order, "Get a giant cup of ice, okay?" He turned to the guys and said, "Ice will help your hand a little, not much, but it's the best we can do for now. We need to get off I-5 and I'll feel a little safer. Then maybe we can get someone to take a look at your hand."

"Not much to look at, my fucking wrist is broke. Don't need to be no fucking doctor to tell you that," Pauly said in a loud voice without realizing it. He went to a whisper.

"Sorry, Bobby, I'm not pissed at you. I just can't believe I let the joker bust my hand. I know you tried to tell me," Pauly stopped short of saying, "It cost the hero his life." Then he remembered Kelly. She was lying in the corner. Her back was turned to the group. She never moved, or said a word, no matter what anyone said to her. But still they knew she was there.

They had gotten as far as Red Bluff when Bobby decided it was time to get something to eat. McDonald's was perfect; they didn't need to get out of the van. Everyone but Charlene could be hidden. Bobby was a little worried about Jesse. The gash in his head was about an inch deep. He might have had his brains smashed, any brains that he might have had, that is.

There had been very little talk since they left the dead truck driver. Kelly was put into the back with no problem. Charlene had slapped her and said, "Quit your screaming, bitch or you're dead, understand?"

Kelly stopped her screaming. She wasn't going to be killed. She wanted to live, she was going to live. These son-of-a-bitches weren't going to make her give them an excuse to kill her.

With one deep breath, Kelly quit screaming. She looked Charlene right in the eyes with an expression that said, yeah, I understand. You bet, I understand. If there was such a thing as a look of daggers, that was what Kelly gave Charlene. Charlene saw and felt it. She led Kelly to the van. Kelly got in and turned her back to everyone. She stayed in that position until they arrived at McDonald's.

During those three hours she never moved once. But she was thinking. Boy, was she thinking. She somehow accepted the fact that Rich was dead. She had seen a truck driver, who tried to help her, get shot in cold blood. These animals had raped her. But all those things didn't overcome her desire to stay alive. At least long enough to see all these people killed or go to the gas chamber. She had to stay alive in order to see these scum-buckets die. She would play whatever games were needed. She was going to get out of this.

"Hey lady, pull in that church parking lot. That's where we'll eat. The last place the police will look for us. And with all those cars in there and everybody inside the church praising Jesus makes it a perfect place."

"Gotcha," Charlene answered. She was amazed that Bobby never stopped thinking.

Bobby was right about the police looking for them. They didn't know what the convicts were driving, but every cop in Northern California had a full description of them and the girl traveling with them. There wasn't one cop who wouldn't like to make the collar on this group. It was the kind of bust that came with a promotion, an extra stripe, a step up the ladder, plus a sense of pride for catching cold-blooded killers.

Since Red Bluff was the first major city south of the killings this morning, there was twice the number of police out as compared to a normal Sunday morning. And again, Bobby was right. Seconds after the van pulled into the church, an unmarked police car went by with two police officers inside. Neither one of them glanced toward the church parking lot.

"How's the gas, Charlene?" Bobby asked between bites of cheese danish.

"Getting pretty low," she answered, licking salt from her fingers.

"I got to piss real bad," Pauly said while he held a bag of ice to his broken hand.

"I guess we all got to go to the can, but everyone heard the radio, they got us all down to a tee. Piss in a cup, if you got to. Shit, hold it. We got to get back out on the highway," Bobby continued as soon as he put the last bite of the Danish in his mouth, "My first thoughts were to get the hell off of 1-5, but I don't think that's the right move now. See, the cops will be thinking that we need to get off I-5, too. And besides, I-5 is too big for them to put up any kind of road block. I say, the cops are going to gamble on every other road except I-5. You follow me?" Bobby was looking right into Pauly's eyes.

"Yeah, I follow you, and its good thinking. Stay on I-5 all the way to L.A., then go east until we hit the I-15. Only thing I think is we ought to get out of this town and back on the freeway, like right now," Pauly said, thinking how good an idea that really was.

"As soon as we get gas we're out of this town. Lady, let's move it. There's a gas station just before we get back on the freeway. Pull into that one, and fill it up." Bobby said. Charlene didn't think twice. She just laid down the last few bites of her egg McMuffin, jumped in the driver's seat, started up the van and drove away.

"Let me see that," Bobby said as he hit Billy's hand. Billy moved the rag to show the gash in Jesse's head. It was as bad as he thought. Billy put the rag back to Jesse's head.

"She said anything yet?" Bobby asked, referring to Kelly.

"Said anything, shit, she ain't moved. If I couldn't see her breathing, I'd swear she was dead," Billy answered, as he kept applying pressure to Jesse's head.

If the convicts had only known how lucky they had been from the very beginning, but they didn't. They believed it was Bobby getting them through everything. Was it luck that no one at the prison had seen the actual escape at the beginning? Was it fate that made the police too late in finding Maggot? It was unknown what car they were driving. Was it destiny that a cop would have a fight with his wife, causing him to be just two minutes too late to save the lives of two people, and a girl from being raped? Luck or whatever you call it, things were still going their way.

Red Bluff Policeman John Unger began his day pissed. Today was his day off. He was looking forward to just sitting home, sipping a few beers and watching the 49ers kick Seattle's ass. Then he got the call to report for duty, something about a double murder. Just like he had done a hundred times before in the ten years he had been on the force, he did what he was told. He was still pissed, though. He went to the station house and was briefed about the escaped cons and the murders. He was to go out and stop any suspicious vehicles, especially ones with out of state license plates. He was not to apprehend them, as they were all to be considered armed and dangerous. If involved in a confrontation, he was to shoot to kill.

Wow, John Unger thought, they want these people bad. He'd still rather be home watching football. He picked up the keys to a patrol car and hit the street, but not before he made a bet with one of the new rookies for ten dollars.

Unger had been on the street two hours. He had pulled over three vehicles with out of state plates. None was even close to what he was looking for. He finished writing a ticket to one of the local kids for doing 50 miles an hour through town. He pulled out and happened to look into his buddy's gas station across the street, thinking if Joey boy was there, maybe he could get him to take Seattle and nine points for 10 bucks, when he spotted the van with out of state plates. He could see a girl driving, but no one else.

He drove too far before he decided to check the van and the girl out. He made a U-turn at the same time a call came over his radio, "Attention all units, robbery in process at the AM/PM on Front Street."

Unger was only four blocks away. He forgot the van, put on his siren and took off for the AM/PM.

Bobby had seen the cop's car, saw it make a U-turn. Bobby put his hand to the door handle when he heard the siren. He'd blow that cop away before he knew what hit him. But then the cop just kept going. Within two minutes, the van was going south at 65 miles an hour down Interstate 5.

Bobby climbed up in the front while Charlene drove. He pulled the back curtain shut. It had been over an hour since they had left Red Bluff. Charlene smiled at him and Bobby asked, "How you doing, lady?"

"I think I'm about to piss in my pants. You guys may be able to piss in a cup, but it's not so easy for us girls."

"Yeah, we could all use a break. The next one of those camp signs you see let's pull in, just make sure it can't be seen from the road," Bobby responded at the same time looking at Charlene. He really admired her. She was dealing with the situation better than any of them. He knew she was worried about her brother, but other than that she hadn't said shit about anything that has gone on. She did all the driving, took all the orders, and never said a word. Bobby knew she was no dummy.

She saw him looking at her, smiled and asked, "Something wrong?"

"No, nothing, I was just thinking how you're holding up better than the rest of us. I'm impressed."

"What's there to be impressed with? I'm doing what I got to do."

"Yeah, you are, you sure are," Bobby responded with a smile. Then he saw the sign, *Camp Area - 1 mile*. Let's check that camp area coming up."

Sid and Mary Clifton were waving goodbye to the last campers. And Sid was really relieved. They were a family with four of the most rotten kids he had ever seen. He would like to have choked that 12-year old who kept stealing his worms. And the fat dad who tried to make out like he knew everything there was to know about fishing. Mary was glad to see them go also. The wife would do nothing but complain about what a terrible life she had. And the way she let the baby run around for hours with a shitty diaper on!

Both Sid and Mary enjoyed their camping much better when they were alone. Sid would go off and do his fishing while Mary would pick a shaded spot and do her knitting. So they were always glad when Sunday came and the weekend campers would head back to the city.

They had sold their home two years earlier, bought the motor home and put the rest in the bank to buy a mobile home when they were ready to settle down. Sid had thought they would travel around the country for about a year, first. They had kids in Oregon, California, Alaska and Mississippi that they wanted to see. That was two years ago. They had made it to visit each of their children twice. Somehow the time just flew by. It didn't bother Sid. He worked all his life, went without many things so his kids wouldn't. He felt entitled to the way they had been living the last two years. And Mary was the kind of wife only a few men were lucky enough to have. Whatever made her husband happy, made her happy. She had no objections to the way they were living. She enjoyed a carefree life. Besides, looking at Sid was like looking at the boy she married 45 years ago, in his short pants and skinny legs, carrying a fishing pole and a bucket of worms. Sid loved this spot. They had stopped here four times before. They were planning to stay until Tuesday, then head up to Oregon and see their son and his family for the third time in two years.

Sid was almost to the path leading to the creek when he saw the custom van pulling in. Shoot, he said under his breath, hope they're just seers and not campers.

Bobby knew right off that this was just what he was looking for. After they pulled off the highway they saw a sign that said, "Camp area, one quarter mile." They came to a dirt road and saw two signs: a sign with an arrow pointing to camping, and a sign specifying no hunting allowed. Just as they were ready to pull onto the dirt road, a station wagon was pulling out. There were a bunch of kids in the wagon and camping equipment on the top of the wagon. Bobby didn't give them a second thought. He wondered how many other campers would be at this spot, and what he does about them. He would cross that bridge when he came to it, he guessed. He popped open his shotgun and double-checked to see if it was loaded. It was.

Pauly's hand was still very painful. It was hard to think about anything else. But, his thoughts went from his hand to Bobby when he saw him pop open the shotgun. Pauly was afraid that killing was becoming easier for Bobby. Three people were dead so far. He had a terrible feeling there were more to come. He wasn't too upset over Rich getting killed. The guy would have killed him with that tire iron, if Billy hadn't shown up when he did. His thoughts stopped. He felt the van coming to a stop, and went back to the pain.

Bobby couldn't have planned it any better, it was perfect. There was only one rig there, a big motor home. He saw an old lady sitting under its canopy in lawn chair knitting. He took a second look at the old lady. For a second she reminded him of his grandmother. That was all he could remember about his granny, that she was always knitting. He never forgot how much she loved the sweater she made for him. He wore it till he outgrew it. Then his little brother Randy wore it for years.

Bobby took a quick look around. They were surrounded by woods. He saw an old man coming out of the woods with a fishing pole and a bucket. He smiled to himself. Fishing, how he'd love to go fishing. Maybe he would. There was no rush. "Stay here till dark, it would be safer to travel then," he thought.

"Everyone, hold on a few more minutes, OK? Let me check it out. So far it's looking great. I'll be right back," Bobby said as he got out of the van, "What the fuck? There's only an old couple here, guess there ain't much to check out. Let's just stay cool; I'm not looking to hurt any old people. Billy, keep an eye on the girl until Charlene gets back, and we'll have her take her for a walk in the woods. I'm going to go say hi to these folks. I'll see if they got something to make that hand of yours feel better, Pauly."

Pauly was glad to hear Bobby say that about not wanting to hurt old people, but he also knew what Bobby said and what he did were two different things. For now he was glad they had found this spot. He got out of the van, heading for the woods holding his hand.

Billy got up, placing Jesse's head on a pillow. Jesse's head had quit bleeding all together. Billy got out and stood at the back of the van stretching. He looked at Kelly and said, "Hey girl, you got to take a piss or anything? Now's the time."

Kelly just lay there. She heard him; she had heard everything said since the slap in her face by Charlene. And she wasn't sure how much longer her kidneys would last. She hadn't gone to the bathroom since she peed her pants. She had thought that with just staying still and not responding to them that they would leave her alone. The thought of them raping her again terrified her.

"Well, go ahead and piss your pants again, I don't give a shit," Billy said, wondering if the girl had turned into a mental case.

"Hello there folks, how you doing today?" were the words Bobby found coming out of his mouth.

"Real fine, young man. How about yourself?" Sid responded not feeling real comfortable with this new group of people. One look told you they weren't campers.

"Oh, we're all just doing fine. On our way to L.A., thought we'd stop and stretch our legs. Looks like a real nice place."

"You got that right, young fellow. We've traveled up and down the coast for two years, no, in fact from one end of the country to another. And we haven't found a nicer spot than this. Also, some of the best trout fishing I've ever found."

"Oh yeah? No kidding? What kind of trout?" Bobby asked excitedly. He knew his fishing, he thought. He had been fishing a total of three times in his life. His dad had taken him each time. As the years went by, the three times turned into a hundred times in his head. In prison, he would always read all the Field & Stream he could get his hands on. So even though he had only fished three times, he still knew a lot about fishing.

"German Browns, maybe not the biggest. But, the best eating fish I'd ever had, and stronger fighters than some bigger ones that I've caught in lakes. Come on over, I'll show you a few we're going to fry up for dinner," Sid said with a change of attitude. Sid loved to talk fish and this young man seemed to know a little about fishing.

Oh, my goodness was Mary's first thought, feeling sorry for the young fellow. Sid would talk his ear off about fish. He had so many fish stories, and she meant stories. What was that they said about how to tell when a fisherman was lying, when their lips were moving? She laughed to herself. Oh well, she was glad Sid had someone to talk about fish.

"Where's the fish, Mary?"

"In the ice box, Sid, in the tin foil," Mary answered at the same time Bobby stuck his hand out.

"Hello, my name is Bob Taylor."

"Hi, I'm Sid Clifton and this is my wife, Mary. Glad to meet you. Come on in, I'll show you the fish," Sid said at the same time he let go of Bobby's hand. He walked into the motor home with Bobby following right behind.

"Now, are those some nice fish or what?" Sid said as he removed the tin foil.

"Boy, I'd say. Sure wish I had my pole. I'd sure like a chance at catching some of them," Bobby said as excited as a ten-year-old boy.

"That's no problem, son. If you folks aren't in a hurry, I got a few extra poles, plenty of worms. You're welcome to use them. If you like, you folks are welcome to join us for dinner. That is provided you're good enough to catch it."

A big smile came to Bobby's face as he said, "Really? You mean it? Boy that would be real friendly of you. There's nothing I think I'd like better."

"Well, sure I mean it. In fact, we could go right now if you'd like. I'd welcome the company."

"Sure, give me just a few minutes. All right if I bring someone along?" Bobby asked as he made his way out the door.

"No problem. I only have two extra poles though. Mary, these folks will be coming over for dinner if they can catch themselves some fish, that is. How many people with you, Bob?"

"There are five of us," Bobby answered thinking he better not count Jesse in just yet.

"That will be fine. And I'm sure two great big fishermen won't have any trouble catching enough fish for supper," Mary said, laughing to herself. Sid's way, know some folks just two minutes and already they're coming over for dinner.

"Give me just a few minutes, Sid, and I'll be right back."

"You're not going to believe it. The old man invited us to go fishing and to have supper with them."

"No shit?" Billy said as he looked over at the old couple and smiled at them. The old couple smiled back.

"Serious as a heart attack," Bobby said smiling.

Bobby looked over and saw Pauly coming out of the woods doing up his fly.

"Oh shit, I forgot your hand, brother. These old folks are real nice people. I'll go and see if they have something to make your hand feel better," Bobby said as he made his way back to the old couple.

"Mrs. Clifton?" Bobby asked in a most courteous way. "My buddy Paul over there hurt his hand real bad when we got a flat tire and the jack slipped. I was wondering if you might have some ice or something to stop the swelling."

"You better have him come over here and let me take a look at his hand. He might need more than ice," Mary answered really concerned.

"Mary was a nurse for thirty five years, Bob, and a damn good one. She knows what she's doing. You better have your friend come here so she can have a look at it," Sid answered, also in a concerned way.

"That would be great of you, Mrs. Clifton. I'll go get him," Bobby answered as he made his way back to Pauly.

"Talk about luck, the old lady's been a nurse forever. She wants to take a look at your hand, brother. I told them it got hurt fixing a flat tire when the jack slipped."

"He didn't get hurt as much as the truck driver did when he got his flat," Billy responded with a snicker.

Both Bobby and Pauly turned and looked at Billy with a look that didn't need any words.

"Excuse me, just trying to ease some of the tension," Billy answered knowing then that nobody needed to hear that shit.

"Think the people will be wise to how my hand really got hurt?" Pauly asked hoping the old lady could ease some of this pain he was feeling.

"I don't see how, it looks like a jack did it to me," Bobby answered with a slight snicker.

"Oh sure, give me shit when I crack something, then you can come back saying the same shit," Billy responded.

"Come on Pauly, let's get your hand fixed," Bobby said, ignoring Billy. Pauly cradled his hurt hand while they walked back to the old couple.

"Mr. and Mrs. Clifton, this is my friend, Paul and he's got a bad hurt hand."

"Hi Paul, I'm Mary and this old fart is Sid. And Bob, you stop that Mr. and Mrs. stuff if you want to have dinner with us."

"Sorry, Mary won't let it happen again. Did I tell you these were real nice people, Paul?"

"Let's take a look at that hand of yours, looks like it's hurting you quite a bit. Have a seat here," Mary said, as Pauly sat in the seat across from her.

"Hurts awful ma'am, I sure do appreciate you taking a look at it."

Mary took one look at Pauly's hand and knew right away by the off color that his hand was broken.

"You did more than hurt your hand son, I believe you have a broken wrist," she said as she gently felt it, "You should be getting yourself to a doctor as soon as you can, but for right now let's see what we can do to ease some of that pain. Bob, run on down to the creek with that plastic container over there and fill it up with mud. Sid, get inside and grab me that ace bandage, third drawer down in the bedroom. And the bottle of pain pills, second shelf, green bottle in the medicine cabinet."

Sid went and did as he was told thinking how much he loved his wife, how well she knew him. How many times over the years he had gone to her after looking for something for ten minutes or more, and she would go right to it. How well she took control of the situation.

Pain pills, super was Pauly's thought, along with the fact he liked this old couple right off, especially this old lady.

"You should only take one of these at a time, two if the pain's real bad, but here are three. They will probably make you real tired, but I think in your case, we'll make an exception. Grab Paul a glass of water, Sid."

"Would you prefer a beer, Paul?" Sid asked as he made his way inside.

"Yes, sir, I sure would."

"No, no, sorry, no alcohol with those pills," Mary was quick to reply.

"Yes, Ma'am, you're the doctor. Water will do just fine, Sid, thanks anyway." Sid laughed under his breath. By the time he was back with the water, Bobby was back with the mud.

Pauly laughed under his breath. If Mary would have known how many times he had popped a few downers and washed them down with a half case of beer, she would have freaked. He kept it to himself, but made a point to tell Bobby about it later. It would be good for a laugh.

The mud felt really good on Pauly's hand. He watched the old lady as she slowly wrapped the ace bandage around his wrist and arm. She was the first goodness he had felt or seen since he went to prison. It made him feel warm that there were still people like her in the world.

Bobby's eyes were also focused on the old lady. But his thoughts were a little different. How was he going to explain Jesse? After watching her work on Pauly, he knew she knew what she was doing. He wanted her to take a look at Jesse. His thoughts were broken by Charlene joining them.

"Sid, Mary, this is, ah Kathy."

"Hello there, young lady," Sid replied. Mary looked up at her and smiled. "Would you care for a cold drink?" Sid asked.

"That would be very nice, thank you very much."

At that point, Bobby just realized how these old folks automatically made the nice come out of all of them. He hadn't heard so much conversation without the word "fuck" in years.

"How about you, Bob, care for a beer before we head down to the fishing hole? Kathy, did you want a beer or soda?" Sid asked as he saw Bobby nod his head for the beer.

"A beer will be fine, Sid," Charlene answered while wondering why Bobby had given Sid his name, but yet she got stuck with Kathy. She was also careful not to say Pauly's name until she knew what name Bobby had given him.

"How about your other friends, are they going to join us?" Sid asked as he handed Bobby and Charlene their beer.

"I'll go check, but first I'd like to say something. Well, I ain't much on speeches, but I just want to say thanks. I mean, you folks been just real nice and we sure do appreciate it," Bobby wanted to say more but was cut short by Sid.

"Oh bull, we haven't done anything. In fact, my old girl there is just tickled to be able to do some nursing. So just save your thanks and run over and get your friends."

"Well, thanks anyway, what was that Mary called you, oh yeah, you old fart," Bobby said as they all gave out a laugh. Bobby headed for the van, Charlene right behind him.

On the walk over Bobby asked, "You get that chick to go piss yet?"

"She won't move. Talking to her is like talking to the wall."

"Well, we can't have her pissing in her pants. Go in there and talk to her woman to woman. Get her to go for a walk in the woods with you. Be careful though, lady, I think the chick flipped her cookies. She could do something crazy. When you're done, don't bring her over to the old folks. We don't want her going off or something in front of them. I really like them old folks and would hate to have to do something I don't want to. I'll tell them you guys are cleaning or something."

"Oh sure, both of you packing a beer. Where's mine?" Billy said, almost like he was hurt.

"That's why we're here to get you. The old folks want you to come over for one. Has the girl moved?"

"No, I think she's in the twilight zone."

"Well, come on, Charlene will get her to come around. Let's go do some fishing," Bobby said as his eyes caught a glimpse of Charlene's ass climbing into the van. He had to find a way to be alone with her. He was hoping if she could get the chick to start talking woman to woman to her, Charlene might find out about the rape. And that would be the first step toward getting Billy out of the picture.

"How's the old bitch doing on Paul's hand?" Billy asked.

"She's doing real good, and she's not an old bitch. She's the nicest old lady I've ever met. She reminds me of my grandma. I want you to be real cool around these folks, Billy. Talk like you're around your mom and dad, OK?"

"Jesus, fucking Christ, I didn't mean nothing by it. You guys sure been jumping on my shit. I know how to be cool. I already figured on it. I was just talking to you, not to them," Billy responded, pissed off.

"Yeah, no problem, I'll be cool," Billy said under his breath as they got to the folks.

"Sid, Mary, this here is Bill," Bobby said as Billy walked over to Sid and shook his hand.

"It's a real pleasure meeting you, sir." Billy said in a way that Bobby never thought he had in him, "Pleasure meeting you too, Mary." They both returned smiles.

"Well, that's the best I can do for what I've got. How's it feel, Paul?" Mary asked, hoping she had brought him some comfort.

"A hundred times better, Mary. I can't tell you how much I appreciate it," Pauly said, speaking as he really felt.

"Them pain pills will start taking effect real soon, too. That will bring the pain down some. You're still going to need to get in and see a doctor as soon as you can. Have some x-rays taken. It really didn't look very good," Mary said, wondering why they hadn't stopped at a doctor before coming here.

"Thought you wanted to do some fishing, Bob?" Sid said.

"I'm ready. Let's do it."

"Where's Kathy?" Mary asked. At the same time Billy looked at Bobby with a look like "Who the hell is Kathy?" Bobby still wasn't sure why he made up her name.

"Oh, you know how girls are, Mary. They wanted to go down to the creek and clean up some before they do any socializing."

"Does either of them knit?" Mary asked hopefully.

"I really don't know. Does your wife knit, Bill?"

"Huh?" Billy said on an impulse as he tried to analyze what was happening. "No, her mom did, but I don't think my wife ever learned from her," Billy replied in the only way he could, not knowing which one of the girls Bobby had said was his wife.

Bobby was impressed. He wasn't sure if he did it just to see if Billy was as smooth as he thought he was. Bobby put him on the spot. Billy had come through with flying colors.

"I'm going fishing. Whoever is going with me grab that bucket of worms, and there's a couple of poles right there," Sid said as he grabbed his pole and headed for the creek.

Bobby looked at Pauly, as he replied, "Don't look at me. All I want to do is lie down. The pain's gone away thanks to Mary. Think I'll try to get some sleep."

"I need to talk to my wife. You guys go on ahead, and I'll join you in a little bit," Billy replied, thinking of Charlene alone with Kelly. He wasn't sure he scared her enough about not saying anything about getting raped. He didn't want Charlene alone with Kelly until he was sure she had the message.

"OK, see you all later with our supper," Bobby said thinking only about fishing.

Billy was worried for no reason. Kelly had gotten his message loud and clear. Yet she hated him so much she thought about telling his girlfriend, or whatever she was, about what happened. The girl, the one they called Charlene had been inside the van trying to comfort her for the last five minutes.

"Look, Kelly, everybody's got to pee. Don't make it harder on yourself. You know I had to slap you, you were out of control. If I didn't, something bad might have happened to you. Hey, come on, let's go for a walk. Get some fresh air, OK? Come on."

What Charlene was saying made sense. She had to pee really bad. The slap did help to bring her back to reality. All of a sudden, Kelly turned to Charlene and said, "What happened to Rich?"

Charlene wasn't sure whether the girl had lost her mind or not. No, the girl hadn't lost her mind; all she had to think about was whether or not her husband was dead. Charlene felt sorry for Kelly and at first was at a loss for words. Charlene tried to think back and couldn't remember anyone saying anything about killing the guy. She couldn't remember anything being said in front of her.

"He got shot, but only in the arm. He tried to be a hero and they had to shoot him to slow him down. He's all right though. We called the police when we stopped at McDonald's and told them where to find him. Now come on, I know you got to pee." Charlene made her way out of the van hoping Kelly would follow.

Kelly lay there a few seconds thinking. At first, she felt like new life had crept into her. Rich was still alive. Oh, please, God, let this girl be telling the truth. Kelly made her way out the back of the van. She stood face to face with Charlene and reached out and grabbed her by the arms, looked her right in the eyes and said, "Please tell me the truth, and please don't lie. Is Rich really alive?"

"Yes, I'm telling the truth. Why would I lie? You see that guy laying there with his head split open? Well, that's my brother, and your husband did it to him. He was going crazy. They had to shoot him in the arm to stop him. I think he was real lucky they didn't kill him, but they think he's alive. Now come on, let's go piss," Charlene said as she pushed Kelly's hands from her arms. She couldn't look at the girl any longer. Kelly's eyes were burning right into her. They both headed for the woods. Kelly wanted to believe so badly, that she did. Her head cleared. She took deep breaths. She was feeling alive. Rich was alive. She had to start thinking of a way to get out of this and back to Rich.

Paul and Billy watched Bobby and the old man walk toward the creek as they ambled back to the van.

"I'll be a son-of-a-bitch, Charlene got the girl out. You know, at first, I sure didn't want your old lady going with us. I thought she would be a pain in the ass, but you know, she's been a real asset," Pauly said really meaning it.

"Yeah, I've been kind of proud of her myself. I'm a little worried though about her being alone with the girl, that she might say something about getting raped," Billy replied looking around to see if he could see the girls anywhere. He couldn't.

"It would serve you right if she did snitch on you," Pauly answered but wished he hadn't by the look on Billy's face. What happened had happened. Pauly had a new feeling for Billy, and he thought now was the time to tell him.

"Listen, brother, I really haven't had a chance to tell you about saving my ass last night. I mean, I guess I'm trying to say thanks."

"No biggie," Billy answered as he climbed in the van to take a look at Jesse.

"How's he doing?" Pauly asked.

"The bleeding stopped. He just looks like he's sleeping. You think maybe we should have that old lady take a look at him?"

"She did a hell of a job on my hand, and those pain pills she gave me surely have done the trick. In fact, I'm going to climb up there with Jesse and get some z's. But I don't know if we should let the old lady see him. Not much more that can be done anyway. Just let him sleep. He does look a lot better than he did a while ago," Pauly said as he grabbed a pillow and lay down next to Jesse.

"Well, I'm going to go find the girls. Catch you later."

Bobby couldn't believe it. He baited his hook, cast it out and within seconds, and had a fish on the line. Sid smiled watching Bobby. He was happy for him.

"I got one, I got one!" Bobby yelled like a six-year-old.

"Looks like a good-sized one, too," Sid responded as he watched Bobby work the reel. His first thoughts of Bobby being a knowledgeable fisherman diminished. Bob was jerking the pole too hard, and was reeling the fish in too fast. A good fisherman would savor the fight for as long as he could. He was surprised that Bob didn't lose the fish. Bob got the fish to shore and pounced on it. It was a good catch, about a fourteen inch German Brown.

"Wow, it's a beauty, isn't it?" Bobby asked with excitement.

"It sure is. I can't believe you caught it so fast. I've never been able to catch one that fast. You are a hell of a fisherman, aren't you?" Sid lied. He had caught many fish here within seconds of putting his hook in the water. He just wanted the kid to feel good.

"Oh, I just got lucky," Bobby answered beaming with pride. All that reading about fish had paid off.

Within half an hour, they had caught seven fish, really eight, but Sid had thrown one back thinking it was too small to keep. Bobby wondered if he should have kept the last one he caught after seeing Sid throw back a fish about the same size.

Ten minutes went by without either one catching a fish, which brought about a conversation.

"So what kind of work do you do, Bob?"

"Oh, nothing special, I'm a painter, houses mostly."

"Sure it's special. My dad was a painter all his life, raised eight kids, put three of us through college. Took real pride in his work. In fact, people would call from as far away as 50 miles to get my dad to do some painting for them. He was special all right. I think it all had to do with pride. No matter what you do, if you're proud of how you do it, then it's special," Sid answered thinking how long it had been since he had thought about his dad. Been dead thirty years, but he still missed him. Sid didn't say it was painting that had killed his dad. Twenty years of paint fumes had destroyed his lungs.

Bobby was thinking, what were the chances of him picking a job that Sid's dad did. Maybe he should have said he was a bricklayer.

"I've never thought about it that way, maybe it is special. I think I'd rather be doing something else though."

"What, for instance?" Sid asked.

"Oh, I don't know, maybe a fisherman," Bobby answered which made them both laugh. Bobby was loving this banter, talking to the old man. How he wished he could have had this kind of relationship with his dad. Sid talked for quite a while about his life and the things he felt strong about. The way the world was changing, how this new age of drugs and crime was bringing the downfall of the country he loved so much. About enjoying life the best that one can, not letting the problems of the world get in the way of the joy of life. Sid went on to say that he and Mary hadn't read newspapers or watched the news for years. If there wasn't anything good to hear, then it wasn't worth listening to. He'd answered a question Bobby was worried about. What if Sid and Mary happened to hear about them on the news? What might he have to do? He was glad. He didn't think he could harm them even if they did know.

They fished for another hour, catching a total of fourteen fish. Bobby caught eight to Sid's six, which brought the pride Sid had talked about earlier. Sid on the other hand, wasn't even keeping count.

"Well, I think we got enough for dinner," Sid said as Bobby pulled in the last fish, which was probably the biggest of the lot.

"Look at the size of this one, Sid," Bobby said as he held it up.

"That's a beauty all right, must be 18 inches. He's a meal in himself. Good job!"

"Maybe we ought to stay a little longer, while they're biting," Bobby said, not really wanting to leave. Fishing had let him lose track of reality. This seemed real; this was a world he never thought he would ever experience.

"Not good to take more than you need, son," Sid replied.

"Yeah, that's true," Bobby said, disappointed.

"The fish aren't going anywhere. If we need more, they'll be here," Sid answered seeing the disappointment.

Billy forgot all about fishing. What he wanted was to be between Charlene and Kelly before anything could be said about the rape. He hoped it wasn't too late. He saw the girls making their way out of the woods.

"Hey, there, good-looking," Charlene yelled, which eased the tension in Billy right away. She wouldn't be calling him that if she knew anything about the rape.

"Hey, baby, how's it going?" Billy said as he made eye contact with the girl. She took one look at him and a shake ran through her. She looked to the ground. Good sign, Billy thought. She was being humble.

Charlene walked over to Billy, put her arms around him and gave him a kiss. Kelly kept walking back toward the van. Her eyes explored the area. She saw the motor home, then the old woman sitting in her chair knitting. She wanted to make a break toward her telling her what these people were, but what could an old lady do? She had to stay cool, wait for the right opportunity.

"Let's you and me go for a walk in the woods," Charlene said as her hand roamed over Billy's ass, "I saw a nice log, I'd let you bend me over."

"Oh sweet lady, you're something else. I'm getting really attached to you. Pauly was bragging on you, saying, he thought you were going to be a pain in the ass, but instead you turned out to be a real trooper. How did you get the girl out of the van?"

"You'll be proud of me for this, then. She's been worried about the fact that we killed her husband. Hell, I told her we didn't kill him, only shot him in the arm. She ate it up. She believed it. We got to make sure no one blows it, and let them know what I told her. You know, you really can't blame her for the way she's been acting, with all the shit she's been through along with the fact that her old man had been killed. I kind of feel sorry for her."

"Good job, baby, I'm proud of you. Good thinking. As far as us taking a trip to Mr. Log, we got to wait on that for a bit. Pauly got some pain pills and crashed. Jesse's still out cold and Bobby's still fishing with the old man. We got to hang around to keep an eye on the girl. I think if we give her half a chance, she'll take off on us."

"My goodness, did you leave any fish in the creek?" Mary asked as Sid and Bobby laid the fish they had caught on the table.

"If Bob here had his way, there might not have been any fish left. He was catching them left and right. Look at this one he got," Sid said as he held up the last fish Bob had caught, "All the times I've fished here I never got one this size."

Bobby felt proud of his catch but remarked, "It was Sid's good fishing poles that did it. I'm going to run over and get some help, and get these fish cleaned up for dinner. Sid, I really want to say thanks. I enjoyed going fishing a whole bunch."

"No problem, Bob, I enjoyed the conversation. We'll do it again if you all stick around."

Bobby smiled and headed over to the van. He saw Kelly sitting on a rock outside the van, and was glad someone had urged her to come out of the van. No doubt it was Charlene. He was mad that he hadn't gotten Billy to go fishing with him. He didn't think there was enough time for Charlene to be alone with Kelly to find out what happened to her. The next thing he saw proved he was right. Charlene and Billy were by the woods with their arms around each other. He walked to the back of the van and saw Jesse and Pauly asleep. He looked at Kelly who was looking down at the ground. "Hey, Kelly," Bobby said but received no response.

"That's right, isn't it? Kelly's your name, right?"

Kelly looked up at Bobby and remembered two visions of him. The first one was of him back at the rest stop when they all first met. The second one was of him holding a smoking shotgun that killed the truck driver. She looked up at him with her red eyes and nodded. Yes, my name is Kelly and for as long as I live, I'll never forget you. But she didn't say anything. She just went back looking at the ground.

Bobby didn't like the look he got from her. He guessed he really couldn't blame her. He headed towards Billy and Charlene.

"Hey, brother, you catch us our supper?" Billy remarked as Bobby approached.

"Sure did, we're all going to eat like kings tonight. You should have come, Billy. I've never seen fishing like this."

"Wanted to, but those pain pills the old lady gave Pauly knocked his ass out, and that broad still scares me. I think she's just buying her time till she gets a chance to skip out on us. Anyway, I thought it would be better if I stuck around to keep an eye on her. Besides, I ain't much of a fisherman anyway."

"Yeah, good point, we better keep an eye on her. She said anything?"

Charlene told Bobby about the shot in the arm story. As she talked, Bobby's eyes roamed all over her. She had changed her clothes. She was wearing a tight pair of shorts and a sexy halter top. Billy caught his look and didn't like it. Charlene also saw him looking and ate it up. She had Bobby right where she wanted him.

"Good thinking, lady, like I said before, you never cease to amaze me," Bobby said as he was thinking how he was going to get Charlene alone. It wasn't going to be easy. He wondered if Charlene loved Billy. Had she only been playing games with him? He'd find out how much she loved him or even if she did when she found out her old man had raped Kelly. But still the question arose. How was she going to find out? He couldn't be the one. The only thing he could think of was Kelly telling Charlene. He would see to it that the girls got the chance to be alone long enough for Kelly to do some talking.

"Where did you get the clothes?" Bobby asked.

"Like them? My friend, Kelly, let me use them."

"Well, call that friendly of her, they look fine. Billy you know how to clean fish?" Bobby asked, dropping the subject, but wanting to say how nice she did look.

"Sure, I do. I'm an old country boy." They left to clean the fish.

He could swear his eyes were open, yet he couldn't see anything. There was a pounding in his head he had never felt before, a painful pounding. Was this a dream? Where was he? He couldn't remember anything. Jesse Sweazy, my name is Jesse Sweazy. He tried to talk but the pounding in his head made it come out as a moan. Slowly light started to show, but everything was blurry and nothing could be made out. He let out another moan when he tried to turn his head. He closed his eyes. This wasn't a dream. Something had happened to him. What, he couldn't remember.

"Hey big brother, how you doing?"

"That voice, I know that voice." He opened his eyes and could only see a shadow in front of him. Again he tried to talk, and again only a moan came out. This pain, this terrible pain, never had he felt such a pain. Like a hammer kept on hitting him in his head. A hammer? He saw a vision of a man standing over him coming down with a hammer, no, it was a lug wrench.

"Jesse, you all right, talk to me Jesse," Charlene almost yelled as she shook him.

"Ahhhh, don't," Jesse managed to get out when the pain increased with the shake.

"I'll get Bobby. You hang on, big brother."

Bobby, Bobby Smallwood, prison, the escape, the guy in the trunk, the lug wrench, big brother, Charlene, Billy, Pauly, the face of Kelly. It all came back in an instant. He tried to focus his eyes, but still everything was a blur. The pain seemed to be getting worse.

"Hey, Jess, how you doing, bro?"

"Bob, Bobby, I don't feel so fucking good. My head, I can't see, Bobby. Oh fuck, my head hurts, hurts bad, Bobby."

"Easy kid, easy, you took a bad hit on the head. The guy tried to kill you, but you're too tough of a motherfucker to let him. You'll be OK, just lay still. We'll get you some pain pills," Bobby answered to comfort Jesse. But he was worried about him not being able to see.

"I smell fish. Am I going crazy, or do I smell fish?" Jesse said for some reason through his pain.

"No, you ain't going crazy Jess, we've been fishing. Me and Billy were cleaning the fish. Going to have a big dinner, you hungry? Want to have some fish?" Bobby answered in a half laugh.

"No, I ain't hungry. I'm scared, Bobby. I can't see you, and my head is hurting real bad. Did you get that son-of-a-bitch that caved in my head?"

"Blew him away. Billy put a bullet through the middle of his face," Bobby answered without thinking. All hell broke loose.

Kelly had heard Jesse when he moaned the first time. It gave her some pleasure. She had been looking at him while he was asleep and wishing he would die. Hearing him moan made her feel good that he was in pain at least. When he moaned the second time Charlene had heard, and went to him. Kelly listened about him not being able to see. She hoped he was blind, yeah, chalk one up for Rich. He blinded the son-of-a-bitch. Kelly watched as Charlene ran to get Bobby. Hearing every word they said, she went running right toward Charlene screaming, "You bitch, lying fucking bitch!" Her fist hit Charlene in the back of her head, making her fall to the ground. Kelly started kicking her as Bobby jumped out of the van and grabbed her. Billy heard Kelly scream and ran over.

"You lied to me, you fucking bitch. Your boyfriend and your brother raped me. How does that make you feel? They raped me, your boyfriend raped me!" Then all her energy left her and she went limp in Bobby's arms and began crying.

Billy ran over to help Charlene up. She pushed him away.

"Is that true, Billy? Did you guys rape her?" Charlene asked looking right into Billy's eyes, which said it was true.

"Oh bullshit, she's lying. She just wants to get back at you for lying to her," Billy said as he turned his head, unable to look her in the eyes.

As sound as Pauly was sleeping, he couldn't sleep through all that. He woke up in time to see Bobby grab Kelly.

"What the fuck?" was all he said as he heard what was going on.

Sid and Mary knew something was wrong from the time Charlene came running to get Bob. They couldn't see Kelly attack Charlene, but could hear all the screaming, something about a rape. They just looked at each other, each not liking the profanity they were hearing.

"Kelly, now you listen to me. Your husband was trying to kill us. We had to stop him. And we lied to you for your own good. But you got to pull it together, or we're going to have to hurt you. Do you understand?" Bobby said as he tried to get her to look him in the eyes. It was out. Charlene knew what Billy had done. "Pauly, come, keep an eye on Kelly. I got to cover Sid and Mary and find out what they're thinking."

"You're lying, Billy, you and Jesse raped her when me and Paul were driving Maggot's car, didn't you? Don't lie to me!"

"Believe what you want, lady. I'm saying it's all bullshit," Billy remarked knowing it was useless. She wasn't going to believe him. He tried to get Kelly to look at him. The bitch thought she got raped the first time, wait until the next time he got her alone, if she lived that long. "I warned you. Damn it, I warned you," he thought as he turned away and headed for a walk toward the creek.

"Everybody cool it, none of that shit matters now," Bobby spoke up, knowing everything was accomplished.

"Bobby is it true? Did my brother and Billy rape the girl?"

"Charlene, I was driving the van. I don't know what happened," Bobby answered in a way that had to mean it was true, but didn't say so, "I'm going over to talk to the old folks. Everybody, let's try to maintain. We're all going to have a nice fish dinner. I'm going to see if I can get Mary to take a look at Jesse. I don't like the fact that he's not seeing."

Bobby headed toward the motor home, looking at Pauly who was shaking his head and looking right back at Bobby.

"Hey, Jesse, buddy, how you doing?" Pauly asked as he saw Bobby headed toward the old couple. He was a little worried that Bobby might have to do something to them if they found out what was going on.

"Pauly, that you brother?"

"Yeah, how's your head?

"Hurts fucking bad, but I'm not going to worry about that. I can't see shit. Am I blind? Am I going to be blind?"

Pauly looked at Charlene, who just shook her head as she climbed up next to Jesse, moving the hair out of his eyes. Kelly was sitting back on the rock with her head between her knees sobbing.

"You ain't going to be blind, big brother. You took a bad hit on the head. Your sight will come back in a bit, you'll see. Can you see anything?" Charlene asked, not knowing how much truth was in what she said.

"Yeah like, I can kinda make out your face. It's blurry and spinning. Where are we? How long have I been out?"

"We're safe and still in California. You've been out a long time, eight or nine hours," Pauly answered.

"Billy did that guy in, huh? The one that come flying out of the trunk?"

"Shhh, keep it down Jess. The chick's right at the back of the van," Pauly said in a whisper. Both he and Charlene looked over at Kelly who still had her head between her knees.

"What the hell happened? I can't remember shit," Jesse asked with a lowered voice.

"The guy went berserk, came flying out of the trunk with a lug wrench. He busted your head, then came at me, broke my fucking wrist. Was about to cave my head in when Billy showed up and wasted him," Pauly said in a whisper.

"Where's Billy? What was all that shit a second ago?" Jesse asked. It gave Charlene the chance to find out for sure if the rape did happen. She was pretty sure, but she wanted to be positive.

"Kelly told us what you guys did to her. I got pissed and Billy got pissed that I was pissed, and went for a walk in the woods. I'm pissed at you, Jesse. That wasn't cool."

"Jeez sis, it wasn't nothing. We've been down a long time. She's a pretty chick, and she was kind of asking for it. Don't be pissed at Billy. Really it was nothing," Jesse answered hoping Charlene would not be pissed at Billy. It didn't matter if she was pissed at him. Charlene and Pauly looked at each other. Pauly dropped his eyes. He didn't want to get in the middle of this.

"Hi, Bob, Mary's about to start cooking up the fish. How many in your group going to eat?" Sid asked, not caring to know what went on over by the van a few minutes ago.

"Sid, Mary, I feel I need to do some explaining, ahhh."

"Bob, we would rather not hear about it. It's none of our concern," Sid said interrupting Bobby.

"Well, I appreciate that Sid, but we need Mary's doctoring again. I think we owe you at least an explanation."

"Is Paul's hand still bothering him?" This time Mary interrupted.

"No ma'am, it's our friend Jesse. He got hit on the head real hard. He's got a deep gash in his head, and says he can't see."

"Oh my goodness, let me get the first aid kit and we'll go take a look at him," Mary answered without the slightest hint that she was interested in how he got the gash on his head, only that someone needed help and she was going to respond.

"Sid, the fish are all ready for the grill, go ahead and start them. Bob, you give Sid some help or he'll end up burning them. I'll go see your friend Jesse," Mary ordered. She got her first aid kit and headed for the van.

"Sid, I'm sorry about all of this," Bobby answered watching Mary walk over to the van. How he admired her and Sid. It was the first time in years that he had good feelings about people. That there was still goodness left. Sid heard, but pretended he didn't.

"You any good at cooking?" Sid asked.

"Yeah, I'll do the cooking if you want," Bobby answered.

"Wish you would. I hate cooking."

"Sid, don't you want to know about any of this?" Bobby asked.

"Not really, Bob, I learned a long time ago not to get involved in anything that doesn't concern me. So if you don't mind, I'd rather you didn't tell us anything. Let's just have a nice fish dinner and when you folks leave, we'll all say goodbye. That will probably be the last time we ever see each other. I got a feeling the less we know, the better. So get to cooking and quit trying to tell me your life story, okay?" Sid answered really meaning he didn't want to know anything. He already figured out that these people weren't just ordinary folks.

When he was fishing with Bob, Bob had taken off his shirt. The tattoo told Sid all he wished to know about these people. He said nothing to Mary, but was going to be real glad when these folks left. He wondered all along about Paul's hand, it didn't look like a wound a made by a slipping jack. Then the screaming about a rape. He owed these folks a dinner but once that was over, he'd be real glad to see them hit the road. And now some guy he hadn't ever heard about before had a broken head. Sure hope they leave soon.

"If that's how you want it, Sid, that's fine with me. But God bless you, 'cause there aren't many people like you and Mary."

"Quit yapping and get to cooking," Sid answered looking over at the van. He couldn't see Mary, just a girl sitting on a rock with her head buried between her knees.

"That boy needs a doctor, Bob. I put four stitches in his head and gave him some pain pills, but that was all. I can't do anything about him not seeing, or if infection sets in. I also think Paul should be seeing a doctor. I don't know what you've all been up to, and I don't care, but if you care for those friends of yours, get them a doctor. I've never seen a boy so brave. He just laid there without saying a word while I put a needle in his head."

"We plan to, Mary, when we get the chance. I do care about my friends, but there are reasons that Sid asked me not to tell you about. We can't right now. I thank you for all you did," Bobby said as he turned the fish over again, "I think these fish are about ready."

"You go get your friends while I put on some corn and potatoes," Mary answered also wishing not to know more.

Today's Game

I reach deep inside my head
For what I can't tell
Maybe a voice singing out to me
Everything is well
There seems to be a lacking
For knowledge of the truth
For questions that have no answers
Of long forgotten youth
For learning that I have known
And stored inside my head
It seems rather than remember
I enjoy being burned instead
For all the joy, I am yet to see
For happiness yet to come
There is always now to look to

And today has been fun
So stick tomorrow in another place
Today the smiles came
And life may be a lesson,
But I see it as a game.

-Rest Stop- Chapter 9

Sunday, 5:52 p.m.

FBI Agent Mitchell Zaga arrived in Sacramento this morning. He was mulling over the reports of all that had occurred since the GTO had been found with two bodies. He was awaiting a fingerprint report from Washington, D.C., in an effort to establish the identity of the victim who was found in the trunk of GTO. The trucking company disclosed that the driver of the truck was Barry S. Newsome. He had driven for the Almond Trucking network for eight years. He was forty-six-years old, and married with three children. He lived in Fife, Washington, a small town north of Tacoma.

Agent Zaga was having some difficulty putting this case together. How did the truck driver get involved? There had been no robbery. His freight of bottle caps ruled out any thought of hijacking. The gun was still under his seat. Only the truck driver's wallet was missing. Robbery was discounted as the motive. The extent to which the truck driver was involved was baffling. How did he get involved? Did the convicts simply drive down the highway and suddenly decide to shoot someone? He hoped not, and yet he knew if that were the case, the convicts would leave a trail of bodies leading to them.

It is a federal crime to cross a state line to avoid prosecution. The FBI had been notified of the prison escape. The escapees had crossed the state line and now the FBI was officially involved in the investigation. Unofficially, Zaga had been working on the case a day earlier. He had interviewed Dick Ellis, Warden Glass, and Assistant Warden Lockney. He had even talked to Turnbell, the injured guard. Agent Zaga always had a tape recorder whenever he conducted an interview. He took a recorder and an envelope from his briefcase. The envelope was marked, "INTERVIEW TURNBELL." Inserting the tape into the recorder, he thought, maybe he had missed something during the original interview. He turned on the recorder:

"Mr. Turnbell, my name is Mitchell Zaga. I am with the FBI. How are you feeling?"

"Fine. No, not fine, I feel like shit, true shit."

"Why did they hurt you Turnbell? What did they do to you?"

"To me? They did nothing to me. My friend, Johnny Cox, the person I bowled with a couple of days ago, a guy I worked with for two years, lay next to me dead. I can't...God, shit. There was nothing I could do. There was nothing I could do," Turnbell repeated himself.

"Easy there, Turnbell. Slow down. None of this is your fault. Just tell me what you do remember, everything that you can."

"Lordy, I already told everything to Lt. Camode. Can't you just look at his report? I really don't want to be bothered right now. I really don't."

"Sorry Turnbell, I've read his report, but I want to hear it from you. There are a few things missing there, a few things that do not make sense. First, not that I'm unhappy about it, but why do think they let you live?"

"I don't know, I thought I was a dead man. Johnny lay there with his eyes fixed on me, murmuring, 'They killed me, they killed me.' I was sure they were going to kill me too. I will say this, not that I give a shit what happens to him but I think Paul Brown had a lot to do with me being alive. I think he had a fight with that fucking Bobby Smallwood for not killing me. That scumbag, Smallwood, Johnny never saw what was coming. He was standing there and the next thing I knew, he was dead. Someone grabbed me around the neck, then everything went blurry...so blurry. I couldn't do anything. I could not do anything "

"Easy, Turnbell! You need to calm down. No one blames you for what happened. There was nothing you could do. It happened too suddenly for anybody to prevent it. Now, we want to catch these assholes, and we need your help."

"I didn't hear anything. I don't know which way they were going. I do know there was a girl with them, I am sure of that. I also know that they are dangerous and must be caught. I want to kill them. Oh God, Johnny's got a three month old baby, a little baby."

Continuing the interview, Agent Zaga asked, "Is there anything Turnbell, anything you can remember? Anything that will help us to catch them? Please try to think. Anything."

There was a long pause as Turnbell tried to remember. He shook his head, there was nothing more that he could remember.

"Did you see any guns? Do you know whether they had guns?" Showing the strain of the interview, "No, no I didn't see any guns," Turnbell responded.

"Did they say anything about guns, any suggestions about obtaining guns?" Wearily, Turnbell said, "No, I didn't hear anything about guns."

"All right Turnbell, don't you worry. We are going to catch these people. We'll lock them up for good."

"Kill them!" exclaimed Turnbell, "Yes, kill the assholes. Kill them all." The interview ended with Zaga saying sympathetically, "You take it easy buddy."

Rewinding the tape, Zaga listened to it again. As he listened, he thought, "Turnbell was right. There was no help here." He grabbed the next tape marked, "Tape # 2," which covered the interview of Dick Ellis/aka Maggot.

"Mr. Ellis, I'm Inspector Mitchell Zaga with the FBI. If you don't mind, I'll be taping this interview."

"That's fine with me," said the cooperative Ellis. "I have already told everything that I can to everybody else, but I'll start over with you. I suppose that's what you want to hear."

"Certainly, Mr. Ellis, I wish you would start right from the beginning."

Ellis began, "Sitting at home minding my own business, watching the ballgame, the phone rang. It was Bobby Smallwood, a guy I know from the joint. 'Guess what, I'm free, I'm out.' That's great, I say. Bobby and me were real close in prison together. We had some good times; we looked out for each other's backs. When he calls and says he is out, I'm real happy for him. When he says, 'Let's party,' well, I'm all for it. So I go out there and meet with him to party. The next thing I know is he smashed me alongside my head; he handcuffs me to this chick's car, got in my car and left. That's about the whole story. I don't know where they went, but I'm real pissed that they took my car."

"Ellis, don't take me to be a schmuck. You are not talking to one of your convict friends or some small town cop. You are talking to an FBI agent. What you have told me is not even, close to what I want to hear. I want to know who helped them to escape, every little detail, what guns you gave them and where you got the guns."

"Where they got the guns? Shit, I know they got no guns from me. I didn't see any guns. I already told the other cops that. I don't think they even had any guns. I didn't see any guns. I don't have no guns. They didn't get guns from me. I don't know what the cops are talking about. I don't know what the FBI is talking about. I don't know anything about no guns."

"Mr. Ellis, I don't care what you do for a living. All I care about is catching these escaped convicts. They have already killed a prison guard, and you know they are capable of killing others. If you are involved in this and they have your guns, you are in deep, deep trouble. This interview is over, mister."

Zaga remembered Maggot jumped out of his chair and stared him in the eye as he said, "I don't know anything about no guns, you want to talk about guns, then you go and talk to someone else. I don't care how you threaten me, I don't care how many people they kill, as long as it's with guns that I don't know about. Do you understand that Mister?"

Staring back at Maggot, Zaga realized that Maggot was a hardcore con. Zaga knew he would not get anything from Ellis that he did not want them to know. No doubt, Ellis was needed to get the guns. Smallwood would not call him up to party, knowing he was hotter than a firecracker. Nor would Ellis drive out there just to say hello. Yeah, he brought them guns. Zaga knew he had to play up to Maggot, to get the information he wanted. He decided he could best do that by dropping the gun subject.

"Mr. Ellis, I apologize. I had to take a shot to find out. I don't even know whether they got guns or not. However, hey, man, you can't blame us; we need to know if the people we are chasing can shoot back at us. Another reason I believe you is that if Smallwood had guns there would have been a shooting by this time. I had to take a shot; we needed to know if they had guns. You cannot blame me for trying, can you?"

With a sense of relief, Maggot replied, "Yeah, no problem, I understand. You were conning me." Zaga recognized a relief on Maggot's face that seemed to say all right I got this guy convinced.

"Do you believe me I don't know nothing about no guns?"

"Mr. Ellis, I believe you. Please, I had to take a shot. I had to find out for sure. Tell me this much Dick? Who was the girl? Have you seen her before?"

"No, I never saw her before today, cute little thing, though. She was with Billy Atterberry. I didn't like her much, she was a kind of smart ass little bitch, but I got nothing against her."

"So you don't think she was forced to go along?"

"Na, I don't think so. When I pulled up, she was getting out of the back seat with Billy, straightening out her clothes. I think Billy just poked her, it didn't look like she was fighting too much."

"Yes, you're right; she's with them for sure. We think she is the one who helped them escape. Anyway, Dick, you get this call from Bobby Smallwood and he asks you to come out 10 miles from your home to party? Why didn't he just come to your house to party?"

"Well, to tell you the truth, years ago, Bobby grew some pot plants there. I knew about it. I don't know what I was thinking. Maybe he just wanted to be away from the city. I really didn't care; I was looking forward to seeing him. I was glad he was out. He did not say anything about who was with him. I didn't think about it, I was so excited to see him."

"So you hopped into your car and drove over to Springfield?"

"Yep, I went to Springfield."

Zaga continued his subtle line of questioning, "When he called you, did he ask you to bring anything? Did he ask you to bring him food or drugs or clothes-- anything?" Shaking his head, Maggot answered negatively.

"How about beer?"

"Oh, yeah, he asked me to get some beer, which I did. I picked up the beer at the 7-11 store just down the street from my house, and drove out to the spot." Maggot was convinced that Zaga knew about the beer. There were beer bottles everywhere. He knew there was no sense in lying about that.

"So just the beer and nothing else, really? Zaga asked while he kept strong eye contact on Ellis.

"Yep, they didn't ask me for nothing else. Just pick up the beer and meet them at the spot."

Zaga stopped the tape there. Maggot said they did not ask for anything else. Then in the next breath, he said to meet them at the spot. That told Zaga that Maggot knew more than just Bobby Smallwood would be at the spot. Zaga just shook his head. He had learned nothing new. He knew that Maggot was lying through his teeth. He turned the tape back on.

"So you drove out there. Did you see anybody else along the way?"

"Nope, I didn't see anybody!"

"So when you got there, what happened?"

"Well, first, I was pissed. I hadn't been out there in years and that road was bad. I work hard making my car look nice, so I was pissed that I drove my GTO. I have a pickup, too. I could have driven that, but I wanted to show off my car. And it sure was looking good. Damn, I want my car. You guys got any word on my car yet?"

"No, not yet Dick, but I'm sure it will show up. We have three states on the lookout for it. When we get it, I'll make sure it gets back to you, okay."

"Yeah, OK, thanks."

"So, you pull your nice G.T.O. down the dirty old road and eventually, what did you see?"

"Well, the first thing I see is what I told you, I saw this chick getting out of the car with Billy Atteberry. And that was the first I knew Billy was with Bobby. I didn't know who the chick was. Next person I see is Jesse...I can't remember his last name."

"Sweazy." Zaga said aloud.

"Sweazy, yeah Sweazy. Him and Billy were, you know, kind of lovers in the joint. So that didn't surprise me to see Jesse with Billy."

"Go on."

"And then a good buddy of mine, Paul Brown shows himself. I'm real happy to see him. Then Bobby Smallwood appears; I am happy to see them all. I can hardly talk, we were hugging and saying hi, everything was hunky dory. The next thing I remember is we're all getting the beer out of the car and..."

"Hold on a second, you got out of the car and hugged everybody. You are saying that you saw Bobby Smallwood, Billy Atteberry, Jesse Sweazy, Paul Brown and the girl, but you did not know who she was. Did you know she was Jesse's sister, Charlene?"

"Uhmmm...yeah, that's right, they told me that. But I didn't know that at first."

"And nobody else was there?"

"Nope, nobody else, just those five."

"You saw no guns?"

"I never saw any guns. They never said one word about guns. At this point, I don't know what is going on, I know something ain't right, all of them getting out at the same time. But I figure they'll tell me in due time."

"So go on, what happened next?"

"Well, we got the beer out and we all started drinking. There was some weed being passed around, we're all smoking, drinking, having a good time. The next thing I know, I got whacked alongside my head, and I'm getting handcuffed to the chick's car."

"How did you know it was the chick's car?"

"Oh, I don't know, I guess it came up in the conversation earlier. Somebody said it was the chick's car, all I know is they handcuffed me to it."

"Did they tell you why they were doing this, I mean you guys being tight, well, that's not the way of the brotherhood, is it? And I cannot understand why they had to hit you. I mean, Bobby Smallwood had a pretty bad reputation, you wouldn't tango with Bobby if he told you he was just going to take your car, would you?"

"Shit, I would have tangoed with the devil himself if he tried to take my car. That's my baby. No way would I let him take her. I guess Bobby knew that, that's why he had to whack me first."

"Did they ever tell you why they were doing this?"

"No, they never did, before I knew what was happening, I was handcuffed to the car and they were driving away. I'm calling them all kinds of assholes as they drove off and that was the last I've ever seen of them. And that was it. They never said one word about them escaping. I was just waiting for hours; I thought the wolves would eat me before anyone found me. Then the police showed up, and that was the first I found out about any escape."

"And did they tell you where they were going?"

"They never said a word about where they were going. Not a word, I didn't even know they were going. I came to a party, and that's what I thought the meeting was going to be."

"They didn't take your wallet?"

"Nope, and I had a hundred bucks in it, but shit, they could have had my wallet, but my car, they took my baby. They took my life, can you understand that? Damn it, I'm the victim here, and you people are treating me as if I did something wrong. I want my car back, I don't care what you do to them, and I don't care. If I could help you, I would. I hate those guys, they were my friends, but I hate them now. They had no right to treat me like that; I didn't deserve to be treated like that."

Zaga remembered studying Maggot, trying to look him right through the eyes. Maggot stared right back, not blinking. This guy was possessed and wild; there is no way that he could break him down. He knew Maggot knew a lot more than he was telling. He also knew that Maggot had provided them with guns.

"Mr. Ellis, I just want you to understand, as of right now the statement that you just made will be the official one that goes on the report. If we find out it varies in any way, that you helped them at all, you are going to be in serious trouble. Those men are wanted for murder. There is no telling what they are going to do. If you want to save yourself, if you want to get your car back, then help us. Tell us everything you know."

"Mr. FBI whatever your name is, that report I just gave you is what happened. I don't care what you find out, or what anybody else tells you. What I told you is what happened. That's all I know. Can you help me to get out of here? They're holding me for no reason."

"I have no say on that Mr. Ellis. End of statement by Dick Ellis." Zaga said into the machine and then turned it off. Zaga sat there, recollecting the interview, he remembered saying to Maggot after he turned off the tape recorder.

"Now, off the record Maggot, you're lying through your teeth. You do not know who you are fucking with here. I am going to bust your ass. You brought those people guns, and I will prove it. You better pray they don't kill anyone with them, 'cause I'll get you for murder, I swear I will." Zaga grabbed his tape recorder and was making his way out of the room as Maggot carried on.

"Yeah, sure G-man, sure, you've been watching too many movies. I don't know nothing about any guns do you hear me? Do you hear me G-man? Hey, you asshole!" Maggot yelled as Zaga walked away.

Zaga snickered to himself, asshole huh? I will show you an asshole, if we ever do find his car; I will make sure he doesn't get it back in one piece. Zaga sat back thinking, this case was really bothering him. Too many questions needed answers. How did they escape so easy? How did they go undetected for so long? Did they have inside help? How did they make it all the way through Oregon without being spotted? Did they drive that fast? Had that much time elapsed from the time Ellis was found handcuffed to the car and when the APB goes out? Alternatively, were they just lucky? The truck driver kept bothering him. Why was he killed? He did not fit into the picture he was along the highway. Were these people just random killers? He wanted these people very much.

All the money his folks had spent on him to become a lawyer, a successful lawyer. He did not have the desire to stand in a courtroom all day. He wanted action. He wanted excitement. He had gone right from college into the FBI, he was not sure his parents would ever forgive him for going into the force after college. His heroes had always been the police.

Who was the person that was killed in the GTO? No doubt, it had to be the cross switch, where they got the car they were driving now. Find out this person was and you know what car they are driving now. How did the person die? Was it in cold blood?

Zaga's concentration was broken. A tall man standing in front of him was reaching out his hand. "Inspector Zaga, I'm Captain Don Gants with the highway patrol, can I be of any assistance?"

"Hello Captain, glad to meet you, Mitch Zaga," Mitch said as he stuck out his hand meeting the Captain's in a handshake. He was a tall man with bushy hair. He did not look old enough to be a Captain.

"How are we doing on road blocks, Captain?"

"Come on over to the map and I'll show you," the Captain answered as he went to the map and showed him all the roads, "To start off, Inspector, there are just too many ways that they could be traveling. For all we know, they could have headed back north."

"I kind of doubt that!" Zaga responded quickly.

"Me too, but it is a possibility. The way we figured, they headed south, probably southeast. Where, we don't know. We put out an APB statewide, all county and local agencies have been notified. We have surveillance all over the south, all along every highway except 5, where the murders took place."

"Huh, explain that, Captain."

"Well, the way we figure, the first thing on their minds would be to get off Interstate 5. We really couldn't concentrate on I- 5 anyway; it's just too big, too immense. We'd use all of our manpower on it. By dropping 5 we could cover every other highway, at least, somewhat."

"Yes, I see, that's good thinking, Captain. I don't think they would stay on the five either. I see what you mean by so many roads," Zaga said as he looked at the map, "I was going over your reports--looks like the convicts have at least two weapons. The truck driver was killed with a 12-gauge shotgun, the unidentified body with a .38. This report on the tire tracks has to narrow things down a bit. A big tire, your man says either a big sports car, or more likely a van or a pick-up truck. I rule out a pick-up because there are too many people. That brings it to a van, I'll bet you a dollar to a donut, these guys are driving a van."

"Well, it could still be a pick-up if they have two rigs. For all we know, there could be another dead body somewhere we haven't found yet. And, with two rigs, one of them could still be a pick-up."

Zaga listened to what the captain just said. He could see how he made captain so young. The guy was sharp.

"You're right, and good thinking, that hadn't even crossed my mind. However, for now, we don't have another body, or car missing, so let's have your people concentrate on a van. At least, as a priority."

"That sure would narrow it down," the Captain answered.

"Any luck on stirring up any witnesses, Captain?"

"No, nothing out there that time of the morning on a Sunday. There are no close residences...nothing close by. They were in the middle of the forest."

"What about this Officer Ribbon's report? He was on stakeout, looking for the convicts and the G.T.O.?"

"That's correct. It shows that he called in at 3:11 A.M. and it shows the stakeout at 3:20. Autopsy shows that the victim died between 4:30 and 6:00 a.m. That means our friends here, drove over the state line before 3:20. Now about 18 miles from the State line, is a rest stop where we found the bodies and the car."

"Rest stop, yeah, that makes sense. You pick up the car at the rest stop, you drive the car and the driver down to an old road, leaving your car and taking his." Zaga answered.

"That's only my guess. I've had some fingerprint guys out there at the rest stop, but nothing yet."

"No, I'm not worried if they find any or not. I think you called it right. There's one part of this I can't put together," Zaga was saying when the Captain interrupted him.

"The truck driver, huh?"

"Yeah, I mean, I understand their thinking, killing the driver of the rig they took. However, where does the truck driver fit in? That part's just got me puzzled. Is there anything else? Some proof of what went on?" Zaga asked with real hope.

"Well, to tell you the truth, that's all we have for now. Other than the reports, there isn't much more I can tell you..."

The Captain was interrupted by a knock at the door.

"Come in."

A young policewoman came in and said, "These are for the inspector, Captain, a finger print check from Washington, D.C." She walked over and handed the report to Zaga.

"Thank you," Zaga said and immediately began to read it, as the policewoman left the room. It was a piece of paper faxed from Washington. Captain Gants knew it was not good news by the expression on Zaga's face. Zaga said, "Shit," and handed the paper to the Captain. The Captain read it, "A check on records dating back to 1950 on all Military and Felons came up negative. Checking other sources now. Will inform. END."

"Well, our young murdered friend was never in the service nor has he had a felony. Which means a couple of more hours at least before they can check other sources. And in a couple of hours, our convicts are going to be out of state, if they're not already," The Captain said, looking at Zaga, who seemed to be in heavy thought.

"We can't wait for Washington; we've got to come up with something now. I.D. on his clothes, a tattoo? How about missing persons? Have you received any reports that could fit in?" Zaga asked hopefully.

"Good thinking, but I don't think we've had enough time. We don't even make a report until 24 hours after we receive the first call about a missing person. Then the people who reported the disappearance call again and we make out the report."

"We haven't got 24 hours. What are the chances of sending a notice to all offices to inform you of any missing person report that would involve someone traveling south on interstate 5?"

"Sure, we could do that, that's more good thinking," The Captain answered, seeing why the feds only hired college people, they're thinkers. Zaga went back to studying the reports, as the Captain left the room to get the memo sent to all stations.

"You know what, Bobby, I'm starting to get paranoid over this van," Pauly said as he saw a sign for Bakersfield--16 miles.

"Why, what's your thinking, brother?" Bobby asked.

"Well... ahhh," Pauly looked behind in the back of the van, everyone was crashed. Pauly was sitting up front with Bobby driving. Pauly took a toke off the joint and handed it to Bobby. Pauly spoke in a low voice, "You know we wasted that guy back there, so by now I figure the cops have found him. And with cops being cops don't you think they are going to run a fingerprint check on him? When they find out who he is, it won't take long to know what he's driving. I don't know, it's just a hunch, but for all we know the cops may already know what we're driving."

"That's good thinking brother, that's real good thinking," Bobby, answered, agreeing with Pauly.

"You know, you're something else, Pauly. I mean, man, your whole world has just come to shit. I hate to see you here with us. You don't know how sorry I am that because of me, well shit man, your life will never be, oh man, I'm trying to say I fucked it up for you. However, at this very moment, I'm sure glad you're with me. I mean, fuck man, you're the only thinker I got. I really hate to dump this van, I've come kind of attached to it, you think it would work if we did some plate switching?"

"I don't know, Bobby, when I get paranoid, I get paranoid. And I'm a big believer in going with your feelings."

"Good enough for me, I respect your feelings Brother. I don't know how easy it's going to be to get another ride like this, or even close, but let's try."

"The next exit is a small town just before we get to Bakersfield," Pauly looked out the window and saw a sign saying Oildale and an arrow pointing to get off.

"Might as well try here," Bobby said as he took the exit.

"How we going to cop another ride in broad daylight?" Pauly asked.

"It's not going to be easy," Bobby, answered as he came to a stop sign. "Wake Charlene up, we better let her drive into town."

Pauly went to the back of the van. Jesse was asleep on the cot. Charlene was lying on her back with only a pair of panties on, Billy wrapped around her. Pauly got an eye full of firm tits and, for a second, got an urge to give them a squeeze. Pauly looked over at Kelly, who was looking right back at him. He wondered if she had heard what he said to Bobby just now.

"Hi Kelly, how ya doing?" She just kept her stare, acting as if she was not asked anything. Pauly pushed Charlene's leg, "Hey lady, wake up, Bobby needs you to drive." Charlene woke up stretching, revealing her nudity; in fact, it excited her the way these guys drooled over her.

"Where we at?" She asked as she pulled on her blouse.

At the same time, Billy made a grunting sound, rolled over sending an arm across Kelly's legs. Kelly said, "No," pushing Billy's arm away. She moved to the corner of the van curling herself up into a ball.

Charlene looked a Kelly and felt sorry for her. Charlene was pissed at herself for letting Billy make love to her last night. Billy just kept pushing himself on her, when all of a sudden the thought of him raping Kelly turned from disgust to turn on.

"Come on, we can't stay at this stop sign all day," Bobby said as he climbed in the back of the van, just in time to see Charlene bend over to get her pants. The way her panties crept up the crack of her ass was instant excitement for both Bobby and Pauly. Bobby could not figure out how Charlene let Billy do it with her last night. He thought Charlene finding out about the rape would break them up, so he could move in on her. Last night looking in the back, hearing her moan with her legs wrapped around Billy, made him furious. However, it did not stop his want for her; it increased it.

"Which way?" Charlene asked as she climbed into the driver's seat.

"Turn right, there's an Arby's down the street, pull into the parking lot, while we all pull ourselves together," Bobby said as he pulled the curtains closed.

"Fuck man, I can see, it's blurry, but I can see," Jesse said unexpectedly.

"All right," they said in unison, including Charlene up front who added,

"Way to go, brother, I knew you'd pull through."

"How you doing, Jess?" Bobby asked bending over Jesse.

"Good, I feel fucking good. I'm hungry as a motherfuck, but I feel good, even the headache's gone away," Jesse answered as Bobby looked at Jesse's head.

"That old lady did a hell of a job on your head, looks as good as new," Bobby said aloud.

"Yeah, I remember an old lady. I thought it was a dream, where did she come from?" Jesse asked.

"Sent by the gods, brother, sent by the gods," Bobby answered.

"Want for me to pull up into the drive, Bobby?" Charlene asked as she pulled into Arby's.

"Yeah, might as well, Billy, get your ass up," Bobby said as Pauly gave Billy a soft kick.

"I'm up, I'm up, where are we, what's happening?" Billy said, rubbing his eyes.

"Stopping to get something to eat, thinking about snatching us another set of wheels. We think these are pretty hot by now," Pauly answered as Billy slipped into his pants. Billy looked over as Jesse and saw him looking right at him with a big smile.

"Jesse, you motherfucker, how you doing? Can you see?"

"I see your ugly ass, maybe I was better off not seeing."

"All right, fucking A, all right," Billy replied as he made his way over to Jesse, giving him a kiss on the forehead.

"What should I order, and I ain't got any money?" Charlene asked as she pulled up behind one car.

"Get 10 roast beefs, 10 fries, six large cokes. Pauly throw me that truck driver's wallet, would ya?" Pauly did what he was told, seeing how Bobby took care of everything, even what they were going to eat. Not that he minded he loved roast beef, but the way Bobby did not even ask.

"No mayonnaise on mine, sis," Jesse said as Bobby went into the trucker's wallet. The first thing he saw was a picture of the truck driver, his wife and three kids. Too bad, he thought, as he grabbed two twenties out and handed them to Charlene.

"What's wrong with the chick?" Billy asked, looking over at Kelly curled up in the corner.

"You touched her and she freaked out, can't blame her can you?" Pauly answered in a rough voice.

"Man, Fuck, let's not start that shit again. I think it's about time we dumped the chick, that's what I think," Billy replied in a serious voice.

"Can I take your order please?" A voice said from the box. Bobby held up a hand to quiet everyone down.

"Ten Arby's, two without mayonnaise, 10 fries, six large cokes, that's all, thank you," Charlene said, glad that the guys shut up.

"That will be $36.20 at window one," the voice came back.

"Let's just cool it guys, okay," Bobby said in a soft voice. Jesse had forgotten about the girl. He raised his head and looked at her. He did not want to dump her he wanted her for himself.

"When you get the food, pull over to the corner, over there," Bobby said, then continued, "Now listen, everyone, me and Pauly been talking, we think this van could be hot by now or at least warm. Either way, we think it's time we made a switch. I hate to give up this ride, it suits us just perfect, but it would be the smart move."

"How we going to get another one?" Jesse said, as he felt the stitches on the top of his head.

"I guess the same way we got this one. We don't want to just steal a ride, 'cause someone may miss it soon, and we don't need to be on no hot sheet," Bobby expressed as Charlene climbed in the back, bringing the food with her.

"Grab the cokes up front, would ya, Bobby?" She asked as she began to hand out the sandwiches. She went over to Kelly, laid a sandwich next to her, and said in a soft voice, "Listen honey, if you don't eat something, you're going to get real sick, and you don't want to do that do you?" Charlene felt sorry for Kelly. She was not the least bit mad at her for punching her in the head. After all, the poor girl just lost her new husband, and she did lie to her. Charlene would have done the same thing, only more so. Kelly grabbed the sandwich, opened it up and took a bite. She wished she wasn't hungry, but she was.

"We going to go to a rest stop to get another ride?" Billy asked as everyone watched Kelly eat her sandwich, without looking up.

"Na, too risky in the daylight. I think after we're done eating, we just drive around this little town until we come across a rig we like parked in someone's driveway. We go right up to the door, and kidnap them and their keys. We dump the van a few miles down the road, and we keep going with the rig we just snatched," Bobby said, impressed with his own idea. He just thought of it as he was talking. Charlene was smiling at Bobby, shaking her head with acceptance.

Jesse said, "That's a great idea, brother."

Billy, replied, "I like it, yeah, it sounds easy."

Pauly was impressed, "You did it again, Bobby, you truly amaze me. That's good thinking, let's do it."

"Glad you guys like it, I been thinking on it all day. Well, let's eat our last meal in this van," Bobby answered, enjoying his praise from everyone.

"Might as well have some tunes with our lunch," He remarked as he reached over and turned on the radio.

"All right, Pink Floyd. All in all, it's just another brick in the wall," Bobby sang as he took a bite of his sandwich. Everyone except Kelly was moving with the music as they ate. The sound system in the van was fantastic.

At that moment, they were all in a joyful mood. There wasn't a care in the world. They were going to come through everything with flying colors. Then, the song ended, and reality came back with a voice saying:

"And now, the 11:00 o'clock news. Top story of the hour is a massive manhunt throughout California for four escaped convicts from Oregon." Everyone in the back of the van froze in mid-bites, their jaws falling open. They just looked at each other. Kelly for the first time looked up and was pleased with what she saw. They all had a scared look on their faces.

"The escape began Saturday morning at a prison facility in Salem, Oregon. Four inmates, involved in a stabbing, were being transferred back to the main prison. They managed an escape en route to the prison. Word last received, they had outside help from a girlfriend of one of the prisoners whose brother was another of the escapees. The prison van was found several hours later. Two prison guards were found in the van. One was alive but in extreme shock; the other, a father of a young baby, was the victim of a vicious beating and did not survive. Nearby, police found a man handcuffed to a car belonging to the woman who is suspected of helping in the escape. The convicts had taken his car. The Oregon Police say the only reason this man, Dick Ellis of Eugene, Oregon, was alive was because he had known these convicts in prison.

Roadblocks were set up on the California-Oregon border, on the lookout for a 1969 blue GTO. However, it got through the roadblock. Police speculate they drove 18 miles more to a rest stop. At 7:00 yesterday morning the GTO was found with the dead body of an unidentified man, shot in the face at point blank range, in the trunk."

"You dirty, rotten bastards," Kelly screamed, and went into hysteria.

"Shut her up," Billy screamed, "I want to hear this." Nobody said anything to Kelly. They all knew it was not a nice way to hear about her husband. They all just leaned into the speaker closest to them, and listened.

"The truck driver, a husband and father of three, was shot in the back with a 12 gauge shotgun. The police have no clues in the truck driver's death. Their greatest fear is that the convicts are on a killing spree. To give you more inside details and a full description of the escaped convicts is FBI inspector Mitchell Zaga.

"The FBI and all police agencies are pleading for the public's help in apprehending these escapees. In all my years with law enforcement, I have never known a more dangerous group of killers. They will kill anybody who gets in their way. They will kill without provocation. Please listen to the following descriptions, after which I will give further details.

"The man whom we believe to be the leader of this deadly group is Robert Blair Smallwood, age 37, 5 feet 10 inches tall with the body of a bodybuilder. He has blond hair, blue eyes and weighs about 175. Smallwood is a convicted axe-murderer and is the most vicious one of the group."

"Bullshit," Bobby said as he reached to turn off the radio, "Fucking assholes, the most treacherous of the group, an axe-murderer, I don't need that shit. You hear the way they're trying to make us out to be the assholes of the earth...shot in the back, a father of three, the dead father of a three month old baby, who had been beat to death. Damn, I only hit the guy once."

"Shit, Bobby, turn it back on, I want to hear what they say about me," Jesse blurted out."

"Yeah, Bobby," Pauly said, "we might find out stuff we need to know."

"Besides, we need to know how much they know about me since I'm doing the driving," Charlene reminded the group.

"OK, OK," Bobby said as he reached to turn the radio on again. Bobby agreed that they did need all the information they could get.

"All the men have tattoos on their bodies; they are armed and considered to be extremely dangerous. If they are found, please do not attempt to apprehend them but call the FBI or your local law enforcement agency."

Jesse was disappointed, "Shit, they all ready told about me," he said.

"We are also looking for Charlene Ann Sweazy. Sweazy is 19, light gray eyes, blonde hair midway down her back, weight about 100 pounds. Charlene is the sister of Jesse Sweazy and the girlfriend of William Atteberry. We have evidence that she aided in the escape and believe she is still with the group."

As the broadcast continued, Charlene said to herself, "I didn't know shit about any escape."

The broadcast went on, "We ask for the public's help in the following ways:

If you see any of the individuals, please do not try to confront them. If your car has been stolen during the past, 12 hours call 1-(800) 947-7536. You may also call this number to report a missing friend or relative. These people must be found, and the sooner the better. As long as they are free, no one they meet is safe. If you have any information regarding any of these people, please call 1-(800) 947-7536. Thank you. "

"We will keep you updated on this story," said another voice, "Now for more news."

Bobby turned off the radio. They all looked at him with anticipation. He did not disappoint them. They had not swallowed the first bite of food they had taken when the newscast first began. Billy was the first to speak. "Well, they know we're in California," he said.

"You know I'm glad you got me to turn the radio again. Do you know what I picked up?" Bobby asked as he looked into their blank faces. He knew they had not picked up that information.

"Yeah, they have the whole state of California looking for us. I bet you if we go pick up a paper they got our picture on the front pages," Billy continued.

"We all ready know that, that's not news that they're looking for us in California, but you know what they told us that's going to help us make a necessary decision?" Bobby asked.

Pauly answered, "No, you lost me Bobby."

"They told us we don't have to get rid of the van."

"Why's that?" asked Jesse, "What do you mean?" They were all anxious to know.

"Did you hear what that news guy said about finding an unidentified body in the GTO?"

"Yeah," they blurted out simultaneously.

"The FBI dude asked people to call if they had a missing relative or friend. Well, that tells me that they don't know who he is, and if they don't know who he is, they can't know what car he was driving. Following me so far? So I say, let's fill this van up with gas and get the fuck out of California. Hand me the map, Billy."

Pauly watched Bobby unfold the map and begin to read it. Charlene and Billy looked over Bobby's shoulder and nodded in agreement. They gave no thought to the news about the three people being dead. Pauly didn't know that Cox had a new baby or the truck driver had three kids. He had not given a second thought. They all stood there looking at the map as though what they had done was of no consequence. Pauly thought that maybe their way was right. It was too late to think about what had been done. Maybe he should stop fighting Bobby and join him in his quest for survival.

"Yeah, look at this. We get back on 5, just past Bakersfield there's Highway 58 going east. We take that to Barstow, and take highway 15 to a rest stop before we hit Vegas. We can be out of California in a few hours," Bobby said as he looked at Kelly. Kelly had stopped crying. "What do you think," he said as he stared at Pauly.

"Seems good to me," someone said, another responded, "Sounds good to me."

Taking a deep breath, Pauly said, "Let's just do it. I'll feel much safer once we're out of California."

Looking at the gas gauge, Charlene said, "I don't think we need gas Bobby, we have more than half a tank, and we'd rather get gas in Nevada, wouldn't we?"

"Alright then, like Willie Nelson, we're on the road again," Bobby realized that he was getting tired. He had not had a bit of sleep since he was awakened by the bells at the cottage. He needed sleep more than anything else.

"Lady, you got it, drive us to freedom. Just head east on 58, I'm going to get some sleep. Wake me up when we get to Barstow," Bobby lay down about a foot from Kelly, placing the shotgun between them, asking, "Anybody got a joint rolled?"

"Yeah, take this one," Billy said as he lit it and handed it to Bobby. Bobby took a long hit. His thoughts went to the old couple, Sid and Mary Clifton. He thought how he had enjoyed the fishing, the deep breaths of fresh air, eating every bit of the 18- inch trout he caught. He thought about how much he liked the old woman' potatoes. He was glad that no harm had come to them. He didn't think they had cared what was going on--it wasn't their concern. He remembered how Sid just kept fishing and Mary continued with her knitting. He liked the old couple.

"Hey, I smell one burning back there, pass it on up here," Charlene yelled out. Bobby took a long toke, before he handed it to Charlene. His thoughts wandered as he held in the smoke. He thought he had designed a perfect plan. How could she make love to Billy after she found out about the rape? He didn't seem to want her as bad now as had thought he did. Maybe he was simply too tired to think straight. He blew out the smoke as his eyes grew heavy and instantly he began to snore.

Kelly eyed the shotgun, wondering how it worked. Did she just pull the trigger? Could she get them all? They killed Rich in cold blood. The guy seemed to have a tight grip on it, but he was asleep. It would not have bothered her a bit. She could do it for Rich, for being raped. They are animals and deserve to be dead. When she looked around, she saw the big guy looking right at her. This frightened her. Did he know what she was thinking?

Pauly looked at Kelly and felt sorry for her. He wondered what she was feeling, what she was thinking. Poor kid, he would see to it that nothing happened again. The van pulled onto Highway 58 and headed east.

IF ONLY A DAY

Once just a seed, not knowing, had a crave
Digging into the soil, the only way he could behave
Just far enough so, the rain could find its way to penetrate
With the strength of the sun and all the ingredients to germinate
The seed felt a change, a certain kind of power.
Forgetting what it once was, for now it was a flower

Growing as straight as nature had inbred
The pride to see it grow and fragrance spread
Upon the sands of days that ran too, slow
Of flowers, why mourn for them, or feel the woe
To follow its flowered desire is without grace
A flower plucked and left to dry in a casket vase

-Rest Stop- Chapter 10

Monday, 1:16 p.m.

FBI Agent Mitch Zaga was on the phone with the Portland office of the FBI. He was informed that Patty Brown had been interviewed by the FBI, but had received no further information. The wiretap was still in place. No phone calls had come from her husband. She had not left the house since she got home Sunday morning. The wiretap at the home of Ken Rocmel, Robert Smallwood's friend was still in place. No helpful information came from either wiretap. There was one reference to the case by Rocmel's brother Steve. Ken was quoted as saying to Steve on the phone, "It wouldn't surprise me if Bobby was at the rest stop right now." When asked by his brother what he meant, Rocmel replied, "Oh nothing, just something I and Bobby used to talk about when we were cellies."

Zaga wondered how much this friend of Smallwood knew. He couldn't know anything about the car switch at the rest stop in California. The remark was about something they used to talk about as cellies. Was the idea that if you ever needed a switch of cars a rest stop was the ideal place? Or was there more to it than that? Zaga wished he had the time and opportunity to interview Rocmel but he did not have either. He made a mental note that if they did not catch the convicts before they left California, he would have that interview with Rocmel.

Zaga made a call to Washington, D.C. A check on 87 million civil servants had not given any clues as to the unidentified body. He wondered if it were possible for a man to go through life without his fingerprints being on record. The truth was that it is possible--one percent of Americans have never been fingerprinted. The truth was that Rich was one of that one percent. Bobby Smallwood had just hit a hundred to one shot.

Mitch Zaga was unaware that Joe Quinton of Red Bluff, California, had called the highway patrol three times voicing his concerns that his son and new wife were overdue from a trip. He had identified their vehicle as a 1983 Custom Chevy Van.

Again, Joe Quinton asked if there were any reports on any accidents, and was informed that there were none reported. It was suggested that the newlywed couple might have taken the coast route, but Quinton knew better. He knew his son would have gotten in touch with the family if he were going to be late or change his plans. Rich had always been that responsible. Joe was mad that he could not get the time off from work to go to his son's wedding. He separated with Rich's mother when Rich was 11 years old, but every summer for the last ten years, Rich had come down to Red Bluff and gone fishing with his dad. Joe was real close to his son. He was getting quite worried. He got on the phone and called the Highway Patrol for the fourth time. Joe Quinton had heard the news reports about a truck driver being killed and some other unidentified body that had been murdered along Interstate 5. Not that he thought that it involved Rich in any way, but it made him more concerned, more worried.

"Highway Patrol, may I help you?"

"Yes, this is Joe Quinton. Ahhh, this is the fourth time I have called. I know you keep telling me there is nothing to worry about. However, my son was due here yesterday. He is newly married with his wife. I had thought he probably went the coast route or was just taking his time, whatever, but I am concerned. Ah, is there any way you can check or find out. I mean, I know there haven't been any accidents. I have been informed of that. He's driving a 1983 Chevy van, I'm just worried, I mean, is there some way you can help me?"

"Can you hold just one second?" a voice on the other end asked. Joe was put on hold. He was becoming irate. His worry was eating at him. He had called his ex-wife twice. She had not heard from Rich, either. She told him not to worry, trying to comfort him. As a rule, Joe was not the worrying type. Now, he just had a bad feeling, a big chill. He did not know how to explain it; he just didn't feel safe. He didn't feel safe for Rich. Something was wrong.

Dispatcher Eddy Seibel was away for lunch when a memo came through to notify the FBI of all new missing persons and stole car reports. His replacement read the memo and laid it on top of the desk. Just before Eddy Seibel returned from lunch, his replacement took a report on a family dispute and laid that on top of the memo. The replacement, having a date for lunch with his wife of two months, was glad to see Eddy Seibel return from lunch. He grabbed his hat and said as he passed Eddy Seibel, "Got a date with the wife for lunch, see you later."

"Still on your honeymoon, huh, kid?" Eddy Seibel said as he took his seat. He was about to pick up a report when the phone rang. He had taken a call from some person whose kid was missing, when he got another call. He put the person on hold and took a call from his wife, who wanted to know if he wanted pork chops or meat loaf for dinner. He chose the pork chops and told his wife he had to go.

"Sorry about that," Seibel said as he took the call he had on hold.

"Your name again, sir?" he asked, as he grabbed the report form.

"Joe Quinton, I live in Red Bluff," Joe Quinton said, and then he proceeded to talk very slowly.

"My son and his new wife are missing; this is the fourth time I've called. Please...uh, there have not been any accidents, I realize that, but I'm worried. They were coming along Interstate 5. They weren't going the coastal route. They were supposed to be here yesterday, about this time. My son always calls if there's any change in plans or if they are going to be late. He's very responsible. Please tell me what can be done?"

"What do you want us to do Mr. Quinton? I mean. I am sure if anything had gone wrong, we would have received a report. They were driving a van I believe you said. Can you give me a description? I have been away at lunch for the last hour. I'll check to see if something might have come up while I was out."

"I've given a description three other times, but here it is again," Joe said, trying to stay calm.

"They are driving a 1983 custom Chevy van, it's two-tone, it's very nice, and would have had Washington plates on it."

"I'm going to put you on hold again, Mr. Quinton, I want to check the latest reports, OK?"

"Sure, OK, thanks."

Seibel had been a dispatcher for the last year and a half. He was a patrol officer and been injured in an automobile accident in pursuit of a robbery suspect.

He returned to work as a dispatcher. He had no desire to return to patrol duty. He was happy to remain as a dispatcher until his retirement, four years away. Normally, he would get incensed when a missing person report came in. Within an hour or two, they always seemed to turn up. However, this guy, Quinton, was different. This was his fourth call; his kid was missing not hours, but a day. In addition, there was something about his voice that made him want to help. However, other than check the latest reports; there was not much he could do. He went to the computer and punched a key. All accidents in the whole state, during the past 36 hours were displayed. The only accidents on Interstate 5 were in the L.A. area, and none involving a van. He went back to the phone.

"Mr. Quinton, I checked all accidents within the state. There was none involving a van. Just a thought Mr. Quinton, but was your boy coming down from Washington?"

"Yes, he was, and I already called the Washington and Oregon police and they had no reports either," Joe answered. He was disappointed, knowing he would find no information about his son.

"Describe your son for me, would you Mr. Quinton?"

"Richard is 21 years old, brown hair and eyes, 185 pounds, fair complexion, no tattoos, a scar on the back of his left, no, right elbow, from a bike accident. He's with his new wife of four days. I've never met her, but Rich did send me a picture. Her name is Kelly, I think she's 19, cute little thing with blond hair and blue eyes."

"OK, Mr. Quinton, I'll make a report and get it circulated, and see if we can find out anything for you. Let me get your phone number. I'll call you with any information I get," Eddy Seibel stood up with the report he just took and was heading for circulation. He saw another report on his desk and picked it up. He would have something to read along the way. The memo he missed was now right on top of his desk.

FBI Inspector Mitch Zaga was looking at the autopsy report on his unknown victim. He was 20 to 24 years old, brown hair and brown eyes, 187 pounds and a fair complexion. There were no tattoos. One small scar on his back and another on his knee and a big scar on his right elbow. A blood test showed no drugs or alcohol. He died from a single gunshot wound to his head. Death was instant.

There were long blond hairs found on his person with a blood type of A. Zaga's first thought was that the hair belonged to Charlene Sweazy. He wondered how she had been so close to him for such a long period as to leave so many hairs. There was blood other than his own found on his right hand. Blood type B. This blood matched the blood of the tire wrench found at the scene of the crime.

This gave Zaga the first real clue that the man might have died attacking the convicts. You got one of them, though, didn't you buddy? You went down swinging, but you took one of them with you. Who are you, buddy? Who are you? If we could find out who you are, then we will catch your murderers.

Kelly had watched for an hour before she saw him loosen his grip on the shotgun. She continued to watch; a half hour later, he let go of the shotgun and rolled over. The big guy was up front riding with that girl. Jesse and Billy were both asleep. For the last 35 minutes, she had been building up courage. She wondered why she only remembered two names, Jesse and Billy--because they were the ones who raped me. They made me do such terrible things. I would kill them first. No, I have to kill the person lying down first. He is their boss, he is the closest, and he would take the gun back. Jesse and Billy have to die. Yes, that person killed the truck driver. Rich, oh Rich, I do not want to live without you. Kill them, kill them. They shot you in cold blood, Rich. They did not give you a chance. They raped me, honey, they made me suck them. Kill them, kill them.

Kelly jumped for the shotgun, and stood up as far as she could, pointing it at Bobby. Bobby, startled by the sudden movement, turned to see the shotgun in his face. He jumped to the far side. The barrels of the shotgun followed his face. He looked to the other end of the shotgun and saw Kelly's face. Kelly said, "Scum," and pulled the trigger. She pulled it again, then both triggers at once, then both again. She got scared, nothing was happening. Then she heard him say, "You got to cock it, you dumb cunt." She looked down at the same instant he snatched the shotgun away.

Pauly, thinking he heard somebody say something, looked into the back to see Bobby pointing the shotgun at Kelly. Kelly was standing up with a horrified look on her face.

"Bobby, don't!" Pauly yelled. Billy and Jesse jumped up to see what Pauly had seen.

"Don't what? I ain't going to shoot her. I just woke up with this chick pointing the shotgun in my fucking face, calling me scum and pulling the trigger. She was trying to blow me fucking away. Fuck man, what is going on? I can't go to sleep or what?" Kelly was still standing.

"Sit down girl, before I smack you on the head," Bobby sneered as Kelly slid down the wall and sat. "If this little pea brain broad knew she had to cock a shotgun before she could fire it, my brains would be all over this van."

"Shit, Bobby, who would ever figure she would try something like that?" Pauly said, still not sure he believed it.

"That's what you said about her old man being a hero, ain't it?" Bobby said violently, looking right at Pauly. He saw Pauly's eyes get big. It made Bobby laugh.

"Fuck, bro, she was going to waste me. Wouldn't that have been something? Bobby Smallwood wasted by the hands of Goldilocks," he laughed again, everyone joining in.

"What's so funny?" Charlene yelled out over the blaring radio.

"Kelly just tried to blow Bobby away," Pauly said under his breath.

"Huh?" Charlene said. She thought she heard Pauly say Kelly just tried to blow Bobby away. She turned the radio off.

"She got hold of Bobby's shotgun and tried to shoot him with it!" Pauly screamed, not realizing the radio was off until he was finished with his sentence. Everyone laughed again.

"And that's what's so funny? You guys are fucking crazy," Charlene said.

"Where the hell are we?" Bobby asked, as he looked at Kelly. He was not mad at her he admired her. She did what she had to do, or at least, she tried to. She had her head buried between her knees. He felt an urge to comfort her.

"We thought we'd let you sleep. I know you said to wake you up when we got to Barstow, but you were snoring away, brother. So, we let you sleep. Another 70 miles, and we'll be out of California. We're 15 miles from Baker," Pauly answered.

"No shit? Boy, I been asleep for a while huh? Feels like I just dozed off. How we doing on gas?"

"Not so hot," Charlene answered, "I was hoping we could make it out of California before we gassed up, but we're between a quarter tank and empty."

"You say Baker's coming up?" Bobby asked, while he was thinking about Kelly. Just what was he going to do with her? He knew she was not as lame as she was acting. He took a deep breath, thinking he was glad about her being lame about shotguns.

"Yeah, 15 miles," Pauly answered.

"Well, we better pull off there and get some gas. We'll hold off eating till we cross the border," Bobby said. He wondered if he had a chance at winning her over.

"Inspector Mitch Zaga, FBI, can I help you?"

"Yes, hello, this is Eddy Seibel with the California Highway Patrol calling you from Red Bluff. Anyway, I have a memo here saying you wanted to know about any missing persons or cars, especially vans along Interstate 5?"

"Sure do. Do you have something?" Zaga asked, trying to hide his excitement.

"I got every part of it, but in a way, I hope I'm wrong. This concerned father called about his overdue son, coming to Red Bluff from up around Seattle."

"I'm listening," Zaga answered, hoping this guy would get to the point.

"Anyway, his kid got married a few days ago. He and his new wife were on their way to Red Bluff, driving a custom van, along Interstate 5. They were due over 24 hours ago."

"You get a description of the kid driving this van?" Zaga asked this time excited revealing his excitement.

"Yes, sure did. His name is Richard Quinton, he's 21 years old, 185 pounds, brown hair, brown eyes, and a scar on his right elbow."

"That's our boy, what's your name again?"

"It's Seibel, Eddy Seibel, Red Bluff Highway Patrol."

"Good job, Seibel, anything about the van he was driving?"

"That's really too bad, I was kind of hoping this wasn't the kid, his father sounded like a real nice guy."

"I'm sure, Eddy, that whoever would have been killed, would have had a real nice father. What about the van?"

"Well, it's a 1983, two-tone, custom van, not sure about the colors--fixed up nice with Washington plates on it."

"All right, you solved this case, Eddy."

"What's this all about, Inspector? I know there were some dead bodies found up North. But that's it."

"Eddy, I have no time, what you just gave me should break this case wide open. Read the newspaper, it will tell you everything. And, thanks again, Seibel. I won't forget your name, thanks," Zaga said and hung up. A break, a big break. He picked up the phone to let the news media know.

Arty Thurman hated these slow days and was glad to see the motor home pull in. These rigs take 50 gallons of gas. Sure was a good looking motor home, he thought, as he turned the radio up so he could hear Mick Jagger sing while he was pumping gas.

"Afternoon folks, can I help you?" Arty Thurman said with a big smile.

"Afternoon yourself, fill her up with premium, would you? Do you have a rest room we can use?" a man asked as a woman came around the other side of the motor home.

"Sure do ,the cleanest in California. On the right side of the building, the doors should be open. You want me to check the oil?"

"No, oil's fine, just gas, thanks," the guy said as he put his arm around the lady, and they walked around the side of the building.

"We should be in Las Vegas by 5:00, hon," the guy said as he gave his wife a quick peck on the cheek. She made a kissing sound back as she opened up the door to the Ladies rest room.

Perry and Elaine Bartlett, from Billings, Montana had four days left of their two-week vacation. They spent three days with Elaine's mother in Wallace, Idaho, and another four days seeing the sights of San Francisco. They were on their way to Las Vegas after three days at Disneyland and Sea World. They planned to stay three days in Las Vegas before heading home. This was their first vacation in 19 years without any kids. They were really enjoying it. They just married off their daughter a month ago. Elaine looked in the mirror and wondered if she was going to be a grandmother before she was forty. She did not feel like a grandmother. In reality, she did not look like one either. She was a good-looking woman of 38, who looked 10 years younger. Perry looked in the mirror as he washed his hands. He swore he lost some of the grey in his hair; he was going to ask Elaine. She would have fun making a joke about it. He would tell her he lost some of the grey because she has been treating him like a king in bed during the whole vacation. He had been looking forward to getting to Las Vegas since the vacation began. He had a new system he wanted to try out on the Black Jack table. Moreover, since all the money they had left was vacation money, he could blow it without feeling guilty. He looked into his wallet. He knew he had three $100 bills in there that Elaine did not know about, they were still there. There was also $800 left in traveler's checks. Elaine had to have a couple of hundred in cash. She would play the quarter slot machines with that while he was trying out his new system on the Black Jack tables. Yeah, what a way to end a beautiful vacation. If only he could get lucky, it would be even better. He looked in the bathroom mirror as he headed out the door and said aloud, "Go get 'em, lucky!"

"I can't get no satisfaction," Charlene was singing as she pulled into the gas station.

"That Mick Jagger can really sing. I'm listening to the same song," Arty Thurman said, as he pointed to the speaker he had setting out front. However, he was really thinking about how pretty this little girl was that was driving. She looked all alone, unless someone was in the back of the van.

"You got that right, nobody can sing like Mick," Charlene answered as her head shook to the music, "fill her up with unleaded, would ya, darling?"

"Sure will. How's your oil?" Arty Thurman answered with a smile. This cute thing called him darling...made him feel good.

"You might check it if you don't mind," She smiled back.

"Part of my job," Arty answered, trying to see past the curtains into the back. He could not see anything. He walked to the gas pump remembering the time that woman from L.A. stopped to get gas and Arty had talked her into staying for dinner. The woman ended up staying the night with him. He put the gas in and set the pump on automatic. He noticed the Washington plates, which would be great to start the conversation. He did not want to move too fast. He would check the oil first, and then start the conversation when he went to her with his report. He walked by her and gave her a quick smile. She smiled back.

"Need you to pull the hood latch for me, ma'am," Arty said, sticking his head around the corner.

"Oh, sorry about that," Charlene said, as she looked down for a hood release. She liked the way he called her ma'am. She found the latch and pulled it.

"Got her filled up yet?" Arty heard someone say as he lifted the hood. It was the person from the motor home.

"One tank, the second one's still going," Arty answered as he pulled out the oil dipstick.

"Have a pop machine?" the motor home guy asked, interrupting Arty's thoughts of how he was going to start his conversation with the girl in the van.

"Sure do, right inside that door. You need change?" Arty asked, hoping he did not.

"No, I have some, thanks. Want a drink, hon?" Perry asked his wife as she came around the corner.

"I'll share yours," Elaine answered back, walking with Perry inside the office.

"Your oil and water were fine, ma'am. Where you from in Washington? My aunt lives in Puyallup. You know where that is?" Arty asked, thinking how different, compared to the woman he talked into spending the night with him, this sweet young thing was. All the difference in the world. That L.A. woman had to be twice the age this girl was. In addition, the L.A. woman was not even that good looking.

"From Tacoma," Charlene replied with the first town that came to her head. "Puyallup, nah, can't say that I ever heard of it."

"Get the gas and let's go, lady," a voice said from the back. A man's voice.

"Damn it," Arty thought, he knew she was too good to be true. In addition, how could she not have ever heard of Puyallup? It was right next to Tacoma! He heard the automatic pump shut off.

"Sounds like you're filled up, I'll go top it off," Arty answered. He was disappointed. At the same time, Mick Jagger quit singing and the announcer was beginning to speak, "And now an update on the escaped convicts from Oregon..."

"Listen to this; these guys are on a real rampage," Arty said as he made his way to the gas tank.

"We reported earlier about four Oregon escaped convicts responsible for at least three deaths since their daring escape from an Oregon prison on Saturday. Two of these deaths occurred in California. We just received information that they could be driving a two-tone 1983 Chevy Custom Van. We are asking anyone who might have seen such a vehicle to call 1-800-9476. It was last seen with Washington plates on it...."

"Shut it off!"

"What?" Charlene asked. Bobby reached up through the curtains and shut the radio off. It did no good, the radio at the gas station was saying, "there are four convicts, one that might be hurt and a 19-year-old blonde. They are considered to be armed and extremely dangerous..."

Arty had been following the story since it was first broadcast yesterday. All their photos were on the front page of the newspaper. The same time the radio said something about Washington plates on a van, was the same time he remembered the pictures in the paper. The girl driving the van was the same girl. His heart started pounding. He had a strong urge to run. He should have.

Bobby knew they were all in trouble now. He moved a curtain from one of the side windows. There was a motor home parked next to them. They had to make the switch, and they had to make it now. The gas station guy knew too much. He saw the gas station guy putting the pump back. He looked down the street. There was nobody around. He went to the other side and looked out. There was a man and a woman inside the office.

"Listen up, everyone. They made this van. Also, I think that gas station guy made us. There's a motor home next to us, we are going to take that. Billy, you got your piece?"

"Right here," Billy answered, pulling the .38 out of his belt.

"OK. We have to move fast. I'm going up front to come out the door. As soon as I do, you come out the back. Don't go flashing the gun, we don't want Mr. Citizen passing by to see anything crazy going on," Bobby said as he opened up the shotgun and looked to see the shells he already knew were there.

"What do you want me to do?" Jesse asked sliding his legs off the cot he had been sleeping on.

"You stay here and keep an eye on this crazy broad. Charlene, as soon as we take control, get all our shit together and get it in that motor home. You think you can drive that thing?" Bobby closed his shotgun. Charlene looked over at the motor home and said, "Just a big car is all it is, sure I can."

Pauly just sat there, waiting for his directions. He finally crossed over to Bobby's side. His directions came, "Pauly, you got your piece, right?" He answered by lifting his shirt to show his .38.

"There's a man and a woman in the office. They probably own the motor home. We're going to have to take them with us. You get out with me and get to them."

"Yeah," Pauly said in a way, like then what.

"And get their asses in the motor home without any hassle. Can you handle that?"

"Yeah, sure I can. We taking Kelly with us too?"

"Guess we've got to. She'll know what we'll be in."

"What about the gas station attendant?" Pauly asked, somewhat knowing the answer.

"I'll take care of him. We might as well hit the cash register while we are at it. You take care of that, Billy."

"My pleasure," Billy answered, "It'll feel like old times."

"Charlene, as soon as me, Pauly and Billy are out, pull the van around to the back of the station. Jesse, you can walk; can you make your own way? We need you to get the girl to the motor home. You think you can deal with that?" Bobby asked at the same time Jesse was trying to stand.

"Whoa, fuck. My legs are a little shaky. But, I'll deal with it, don't you worry."

"Good man. OK. We ready?" Bobby said as he put his hand to the door handle. He got a "yep" from Billy, and a nod from Pauly.

Arty Thurman did not know what to do. He memorized the license plate. He looked around, but he couldn't see anyone. The closest place to him was a fruit stand a 1/2 block down the street. He would just play it off as if he did not know anything, go and collect the money, then call the police as soon as they left. He heard movement inside the van. This was really something to tell his grand kids about.

He started up to the window when he heard the doors of the van opening. He looked behind him and saw a guy come from around the back. Two other people were coming around the front of the van. His heart started to beat faster, these people were murderers. One of the guys coming around the front of the van had a sawed-off shotgun at his side.

"Get inside the office, buddy," the person with the shotgun said.

"Wait on, guys, I don't know nothing," Arty was saying as he felt someone stick something in his back.

"You heard the man, get in the office." Arty turned to see a man holding a gun to his back.

Elaine and Perry were looking at a map on the wall and did not notice anything until a man said, "We'll be taking your motor home now, folks."

They turned to see a man with a gun pointing at them. "What the hell is this? A joke?" Perry reacted.

"No joke, mister. We're taking your motor home, and you folks are going with us."

"What's going on, Perry?" Elaine asked, scared to death.

"Look, friend, I don't know what this is all about," Perry said as he reached in his pocket and got his keys, "but, you have the gun. Here's the keys and take the motor home, I don't give a shit, but we aren't going with you. No way!"

Right then, Perry saw the gas station attendant get pushed through the door. Another person stuck a shotgun in his face and said, "Hey fella, you see this fucking thing? Well, it will blow your face into so many pieces they'll never put you back together. This ain't no fucking game. Whatever we tell you from this point on, you do--right then, right now. Understand?"

"Yes," was all Perry could manage to get out. He put his arm around Elaine. He couldn't remember being this scared, even after two tours of Vietnam. Maybe, it was because Elaine wasn't with him in Vietnam. He was scared for Elaine.

"Hey, how do you open this fucking thing?" Billy asked, getting pissed at the cash register.

"It takes a key, here," Arty Thurman said as he handed the key to Billy.

"Pauly, get these people out to the motor home. You got a back room here, fella?" Bobby asked Arty.

"We have an oil room," Arty replied, wondering why he asked.

"Show me."

"Come on, folks, just act regular. If you do as I tell you, then you won't get hurt, " Pauly said as he, Elaine, and Perry made their way to the motor home.

"Come on, you got to have more money than this, fella. Where do you stash it?" Billy said as he counted $87.00 dollars.

"That's all we have. It's been very slow today. I swear that's all there is," Arty said, telling the truth.

"You're lying. You got to have more than this. You hide it somewhere?"

"Fuck it, Billy, he's probably telling the truth. Come on, fella, show me to the oil room," Bobby said, pointing the shotgun at Arty's chest.

"Hey, I'm not lying, I swear that's all there is. Hey, you people aren't going to hurt me, are you? I mean, I ain't going to say shit to no one."

"Yeah sure, come on show me the room," Bobby said laughing to himself. They would be a block down the road before this guy was on the phone, calling the police.

"I'll go help Charlene get everything out of the van," Billy said, putting the money in his pocket. He thought about taking the change, but decided against it. He wanted out of there. He knew what Bobby was going to do to this dude. Arty felt it too. He had to do something--this person was going to kill him!

Bobby was not sure what he was going to do. He had nothing against the guy, but he couldn't let him live. Maybe he could just knock him out and tie him up. Hey, why not take him with us too? That thought never even crossed his mind. The more, the merrier, right? Yeah, the guy can be killed if he becomes a problem what the hell, we have to watch three people now, what's one more?

"No!" Arty screamed as he turned around, catching Bobby completely off guard, grabbing the shotgun with one hand and throwing a punch with the other. The punch caught Bobby in the forehead, making him lose his grip on the shotgun. Arty had the barrel with one hand and grabbed it with the other. He swung it full force like a club at Bobby's head. Bobby reached and got Arty's arm in motion, stopping the butt of the shotgun inches from his head.

Arty could not believe this guy's strength. The grip on his arm was like a vise. The look in Bobby's eyes was the most frightening thing he had ever seen in his life, which lasted three more seconds. Bobby's other hand went into Arty's neck. Arty was robbed of his last breath. Bobby grabbed the shotgun from Arty and brought the butt down on his head. There was a sound like hitting an empty box with a big stick. Blood hit Bobby in the face, which made him mad. He lifted the butt of the shotgun and hit Arty again. The first blow had already killed Arty Thurman. The second one caved in one side of his head.

"I was going to let you live, you dumb fuck!" Bobby noticed he was covered with blood. "Shit," he said, looking at the blood on his hands, "I was going to let you live." He grabbed a rag and wiped the blood from the shotgun and his face. All it did was smear it. He walked to the motor home wiping his hands on his pants. He saw Charlene in the driver's seat, the engine running. He climbed in and saw the expression on Charlene's face.

"Everybody in?" He asked.

"Yes," Charlene said as she swallowed.

"Let's get the fuck out of here."

Charlene pulled the motor home forward. There was a noise, then the sound of something hitting the ground.

"What the fuck was that?" Pauly said coming up front and seeing Bobby covered in blood.

"Ahh shit, Bobby, no!" Pauly's shoulders seemed to drop and he shook his head.

Charlene looked in the side mirror and saw the gas pump lying on the ground, "Shit, nobody took the gas pump out, we just ripped it out. What should I do?"

"Nothing, just get out of here. Ah shit, nothing, I decided to take the guy with us," Bobby said to Pauly, "Then, he attacks me, hits me in the head. He tries to bust my head with my own shotgun. I took it from him and hit him with it instead. Man, I got to get this blood off of me, is there a bathroom in this thing?"

"Yeah, that first door on the right," Pauly answered, not believing that the person attacked Bobby. Pauly feared that Bobby was enjoying killing. Bobby went to find the bathroom.

"Jesus Christ, Bobby, what happened?" Jesse asked, seeing Bobby.

"Shit, we had another hero, he attacked me, and I had to bust his head. Blood went everywhere," Bobby answered. From a corner, Kelly and the two new people looked at Bobby in horror. Bobby noticed that the man was about his size.

"Hey, buddy, you got any clothes in this thing?"

"Yes, in that closet over there," Perry answered pointing to it. Perry became scared seeing this guy covered in blood. He hoped the guy would not find the .44 magnum he had in there. It was his ace in the hole.

"This thing has a TV, a stove, a fridge, all the comforts of home. Even has apples," Billy said, taking a bite of one of the apples. The sight of blood on Bobby did not bother him at all. In fact, he thought it was somewhat manly.

"We're moving up in the world, huh?"

"Yeah, I guess we are, brother," Bobby answered as he picked up a shirt and a pair of pants. He went into the bathroom and closed the door. He noticed there was even a shower. He stripped and hopped in the shower.

The motor home, gas dripping out of a hole where a gas cap used to be, headed down Highway 15, eight people aboard. Forty minutes from Vegas.

ACCOUNTS RECEIVABLE

Borrowing from the bank of life
We have all made the loan
It comes when we are in need
Giving is the only payback known

Some continue to borrow, without thought
Making loans interest due
Payment is never forgot
Every day comes a certain clue.

The conscience receives the bill
There is no bankruptcy in giving
Leaving it all to your will
And the way you choose your living.

Well this lad borrowed, to full extent
Kept putting payment off till tomorrow
Giving felt cheated of rent
Tipping the scales to sorrow.

What comes around goes around
The bank of life keeps the books
For what I owe, I now pay
Why not, it is my debt.

-Rest Stop- Chapter 11

Monday, 2:37 p.m.

Jim Rushton dreamed he was playing poker. Texas Hold 'Em. He seemingly always dreamed about poker whenever he had been up all night playing. The bells he heard ringing fit into his dream. His mind flashed to someone hitting a jackpot on a slot machine. The bells kept ringing. It's a jackpot! He opened his eyes and saw that he was in bed. It was a dream. He had only heard the phone ringing. Answering the phone in the middle of a stretch, "Hello," Jim said.

"Jim, you still asleep, its 2:30 in the afternoon!" Mike, Jim's poker buddy asked.

"2:30, no shit. I didn't get home till about 8 o'clock this morning," Jim said as he reached for his glasses, "How did you do?"

"Lost my ass, mostly in that one pot against old George, when I flopped 3 Kings," Mike replied in a crying voice.

"Yeah, that was a bad beat. That fucking old George, he'll outdraw you more than any man I ever met," Jim answered putting on his glasses and watching the clock." It was 2:30.

"Bad beat, shit, it was worse than that--I mean I flop 3 kings. Old George calls my $125 bet, which I love, right? He's holding a pair of eights, the flop's king, king, ten. Then on turn one his eight comes. So now old George is hooked on." Jim cut Mike short.

"Well hold it, he's got a full house on the turn, you only have three kings. You had king what in the hole? Jim asked disinterestedly. This was just another bad beat story.

"I had king, queen of spades. Yeah, maybe I was the one that was hooked on after the eight flops. However, what could I do? I come out betting $100. George raises everything I got left in front of me. Shit, now I'm worried that he may have ace, king. I don't put him on pocket eights, Anyway, I call. River comes to add salt to the wound: in this case the eight. It could have been a queen, a ten, another king. Man that is just how my luck is going. I mean I'm worried after he puts me all in, but what am I going to do? Throw away my hand?"

"No you're stuck. Anyway, after you leave I get old George back for you. I catch him bluffing and call a $200 bet with two small pair. Cards run over me after you left. I could not do anything wrong. I ended up the only winner last night."

"No shit, you're lying," Mike said. Although he knew, it was the truth. When Jim is running hot, nobody can touch him. "How much you get?"

"Thirty three hundred fucking dollars."

"No, fuck you, really, thirty three hundred, no shit?"

"No shit. Boy was Howard pissed. I pull a beat on him and caught a river flush in a $1000 pot I had no business being in. Howard was talking about kicking my ass and shit. You know how Howard gets when you bad beat him. It was funny." Jim thought it was a bit funny about fat Howard trying to kick anybody's ass.

"Yeah, that's funny; I love it when Howard gets beat. I don't think Howard could kick old George's ass let alone yours. Hey, you see the paper today?" Mike asked, thinking he could put a touch on Jim for a few hundred.

"I ain't seen shit yet. You woke me up you asshole. But I'm glad you did, I'm thinking about going to Vegas, you want to go?"

"I'd love to, but I'm cash poor after last night. Besides I got a job I have to do in Victorville, tomorrow morning. I have to get up at four in the morning to be on time. It's a three day job. I could use a couple of hundred though, what's the chance of hitting you up before you blow it all in Vegas?"

"Fuck, I ain't blowing anything. I am feeling lucky. I am going to try my luck against the big boys. And besides, you still owe me three hundred." Jim knew he would give him the $200.

"Oh, maybe you forgot when you owed me $700," Mike answered nonchalantly.

"I was just pulling your chain. However, you have to get here before I leave. What's this about the paper?"

"Oh yeah, I didn't know you were an escaped convict."

"Huh, what are you talking about?"

"There is the picture of a guy on the front page of the paper who looks just like you. He killed three people so far. There's a $10,000 reward offered by some trucking company for the person who turns him in. So I thought I'd turn you in and we'll split the money."

"What the fuck you talking about?"

"Get your ass out of bed and get the paper. You'll see the guy looks just like you. I'll be over in twenty minutes."

"Yeah, see you in a bit." Jim took a wad of money from his pocket and began to count it. Forty four hundred and some odd dollars. That was correct. He had eleven hundred dollars and won thirty three hundred. He gave a self-aggrandizing smile thinking how lucky he had been. He was still feeling lucky. He thought of the time he went to Vegas with $300 and left with $1200. He hoped he could be as lucky on this trip. Like most gamblers, he did not remember the many times that he went home broke.

Jim went and got a newspaper. He saw the photos of four men and a woman flashed across the front page. He saw no resemblance of any of the men to himself. Maybe this person, Robert Smallwood, did look a little like himself, but hell he was a lot more handsome than that guy was. He read the article as he prepared his toast and coffee. The girl in the paper, he thought, was a good-looking chick.

Jim drank his coffee as he put some toilet articles in his overnight bag. He had decided to stay a few days before heading home. He would take it slow and easy while getting in a ten twenty hold 'em game and work his way up to the no limit game with the big boys. He had the feeling that this was his time. He could leave Barstow tomorrow about four and be in Vegas around 6 to 6:30. I will not be in any rush, he thought to himself. Get a room, something to eat and maybe some pussy before he started playing. He looked in his wallet to see if he still had the phone number of a waitress whom he had met--he did. Debby, that's right, skinny with big tits. He would call her when he arrived and invite her to dinner. This would be a fun trip.

FBI Inspector Zaga was boarding a small-chartered plane for a flight to Baker, California. About half an hour earlier, he had received a call from the Baker police informing him that the body of a gas station attendant had been found. It was an hour later before police realized that the van parked in the back of the station was the one listed in the APB. His convicts had killed again. Mitch was steaming mad that an hour had passed before the van had been tied to the crime. Small town cops, they were something else. They had no clues or witnesses, no idea what vehicle the convicts were driving by this time. Roadblocks had been set up about half an hour earlier while the killing had taken place two hours earlier. The Nevada border was less than an hour away from the murder scene. This meant that the roadblocks were practically worthless. However, overall it meant he was closing in on these ruthless killers. He alerted the Nevada Highway Patrol as well as the Vegas Police. He assumed that the killers were some place between Baker, California and Las Vegas on interstate 15. He would not be surprised if they were all in a casino having the time of their life. Again, the question arose as to what kind of vehicle they were driving. Would there be more bodies found?

Zaga initially thought to fly directly to Las Vegas. His suspects, he thought, would be at least that far by the time of his arrival. However, he would have no leads to help him to find them. Maybe he could get some information at Baker that the local authorities did not have. He would go north on I-15, the same direction the convicts went. He had no doubts that he would get them but would they commit other murders before they were apprehended. Whatever happened to Richard Quinton's wife? Would her body also be found somewhere along the highway? Or was she still held captive? The inspector's plane took off.

Monday, 3:59 p.m.

"That's our baby," Bobby said excitedly as he saw the sign, REST *AREA 2 miles.* Pauly, Jesse and Billy took a look, "Get back there, Billy and keep an eye on those people. I don't trust that dude, he's another hero type."

"OK. I just wanted to see," Billy wondered why Pauly wasn't told to keep an eye on the people but he followed orders. With gun in hand, he walked to the back of the motor home.

"Well, we made it brother, somehow we made it," Pauly said, amazed. He never believed they would get this far. Four people had been murdered in the process but he had made it. He still questioned whether Bobby's way was the better way. By this time, he even believed Bobby's story about being attacked by the gas station attendant. The red mark on Bobby's face did look like a blow to his head. "What's the plan Bobby? We going to take over the rest stop as soon as we pull in?"

Bobby coolly replied, "Oh no, we're going about it slow and easy. There is no rush; we have all the time in the world. There ain't a soul in the world that can tie us to this motor home. I'm thinking about waiting till dark. I don't know for sure. We'll pick our shots. What's your thinking?"

Happy with Bobby's answer, Pauly said, "Sounds smart to me."

"We better get in the back, we're pulling in now. When we get in there, lady, park as far away from anybody as you can. There will be a parking site for cars and another for trucks and motor homes, pull in on the truck side, okay," Bobby said as he ran his fingers through Charlene's hair.

"Got you, darling," Charlene said, showing her thrill by the touch of Bobby's fingers in her hair. She wanted to be with Bobby again, but this was not the time. She was getting tired of Billy and could kick herself for making love with him after he had raped Kelly. Bobby was more her type of man. There were very few cars and only two trucks as she pulled into the rest stop.

"Listen folks," Bobby said to the three sitting on the floor. "We're pulling into a rest stop and we'll be here for a while. I can tell you what our plans are, you would find out anyway. We've come all the way here to rob this place. For you two new folks I want you to know we mean you no harm. If we did, you would've been dead already. We're escapees from an Oregon State Prison. Now this ain't no game. We've already killed four people to get this far. I'm telling you this so you won't try anything stupid. I won't fool with you. In fact, if you behave yourselves properly we will part company in a short time, and you folks will be none the worse off. You will have your motor home back and everything will be fine. Where were you heading before you ran into us?"

"Vegas," Perry Bartlett answered.

"Well, what do you think of that, we won't even take you out of your way," Bobby said, suggesting they were doing them a favor.

"How about their money and these clothes I'm wearing, Bobby," Billy asked, wondering why he didn't think of it sooner.

"Yeah, we will be taking your money and these clothes I'm wearing. The shirt is a little tight though, guess you can't have everything. Where do you keep your money?" Bobby asked as he looked at the woman. She was attractive and looked much younger than her husband looked. Perry reached in his back pocket and threw his wallet on the bed. "That's all we have in cash," Perry said as Jesse searched the wallet.

"$67 is all you got?" Jesse asked. He had missed three $100 bills, which had been stashed behind some photos.

"We have traveler's checks. You can have them if you want, but I don't think they will do you much good," Perry answered, delighted that he had hidden his other cash.

"Where they at?" Billy asked as Perry looked at Elaine. He was not sure where she had put them.

"They're in my purse, in the closet," Elaine managed to say.

Perry thought about the gun. Please do not find the gun. Billy found the purse on the top shelf. He grabbed it but missed seeing the brown leather case hidden under a robe. He laid the purse on the bed and opening it, he found additional cash.

"What's this, pickled herring?" Jesse laughed, "Maybe his old lady was holding out on him."

"A hundred and forty bucks. Hey, now this is getting to be fun. Where are those checks you were talking about?" Billy asked Elaine, as Perry took a deep breath. Billy had missed the gun.

"Should be in there in a brown envelope," Elaine said in a near whisper.

"Oh yeah, the $100 bill things. What can we do with them?" Billy asked as he counted them. "Damn, there's a bunch of them."

Holding out his hand Pauly said, "Let me see them."

"Fuck, there are eleven of them, that's $1100 bucks," Billy announced as he handed them to Pauly. For the first time Billy took a long, look at Elaine. She showed intense fear. He liked it when women showed fear. He began thinking how he could get her alone.

"The guy is right. These ain't going to do us no good. You got to have a picture I.D. to cash them," Pauly said.

"Give them back to them then," Bobby said as he felt a hand rub across his ass. He turned to see Charlene had joined them.

"Give what back?" she asked as she smilingly looked into Bobby's eyes.

"Oh, some travelers checks that ain't no good," Billy said as he tenderly put his arm around her. She pushed him away. Not understanding her motive he asked, "What's with you?"

"I've been doing some thinking and I'm still pissed at you. I'll talk to you about it later," Charlene said as Bobby saw his plan finally coming to life.

"Talk to me about what? What's your trip now?" Billy asked defensively. He really did not care because his thoughts were now concentrated on Elaine.

Charlene was deeply disturbed. She said, "I'll talk to you as soon as we get a chance to be alone."

Billy just shook his head and walked to the front of the motor home where Pauly joined him.

Bobby pulled the curtain back and looked out of the window. From where Charlene had parked, there was a good view of the entire rest area. He could see the entrance to both the women and men's rest rooms. There were four cars parked and one was entering the area. There were two trucks. The driver of one of the trucks was sitting inside the cab eating. He could not see the other driver. One man walked out of the restroom while another was entering with two small children. The guy leaving the restroom went to the truck where the driver was eating. He got into the truck on the driver's side and pulled away as Bobby closed the curtain.

"It's perfect. It is just what The Wizard and me used to talk about. Good choice on the parking, lady," Bobby said," It gives us a great view of the whole place."

With obvious pride, Charlene said, "Glad you like it." She was now anxious to please Bobby in any way she could.

"You want me to fix us all something to eat? They got food in the fridge."

"Yeah, we're going to be here for a while," Bobby directed Pauly and Billy to remain in the back, saying, "We don't need some citizen who has seen our pictures on TV or in the papers to spot any of us. If you have to use the can, use the one in here. I don't want anybody going outside. I think we'll wait until dark. We'll see. But once we get started, we will have half an hour to get what we can and hit the road. I guess now is a good time to start making the plans. Everybody be cool but take a look outside, then let's put our heads together and decide just how we're going to do it."

They all went to the window and looked out. Jesse spoke first, "The bathrooms are right there. I say we just hang out inside of them and take people off as soon as they walk in, take their shit and push them in one of the shitters, and just keep doing that for half an hour."

"How about the people who are riding with them that don't have to take a piss or anything, how long they going to wait before they come looking?" Pauly asked. He said this to show that Jesse was in accord as Bobby.

"Yeah, the same question crossed my mind. I mean I agree with what Jesse just said. The bathrooms are where I planned to keep the people after we take them off, but we need to keep some kind of control of what's happening out on the parking lot."

Billy interrupted, "Why can't we hit them as they pull into the rest stop?"

"That won't work. We don't have any control on how fast people will be pulling in, and then how do we get them from their cars to the bathrooms to keep an eye on them after we rob them. I mean, if we had twenty guys on an assembly line it would work."

Charlene quipped, "There's only five of us." None of the group ever thought of her contributing any ideas. Her observation took the group by surprise.

"That's true, I didn't think of that," Billy said in agreement. He had hoped to ingratiate himself with Charlene.

Pauly listened in amazement at their stupidity. He was even appalled at Bobby's moronic approach. They'd all forgotten about the getaway that they said wasn't going to be difficult. Bobby had been so sure that his plan for the robbery as well as his getaway plan would be successful. Pauly wanted to listen to the expressions of the others first. He was confident however, that his was the superior plan.

"So why worry about people coming into the bathroom to look for anyone? When they come into the bathroom to look, we'll take them too," Billy spoke as though he had solved the problem all alone.

"Nah, we got to come up with something better," Bobby said. Looking out the window at the three telephones he thought aloud, "We have to knock out those phones, too. Otherwise, there will be too many people wandering around and we could lose control. We have to do this with five people. We're going to make our getaway in the cars that are parked outside, so we need to know what cars belong to what people. I don't know. We have a lot more thinking to do. But as I said, we're in no rush so let's keep talking. You're awfully quiet, what are you thinking, Pauly?"

Pauly was thinking how crazy the whole thing was, that Bobby had come all this way, had all this time and had never developed a plan, "Well I'm thinking about a number of things. I think I have a plan that will solve a lot of our problems."

"Well, what are you waiting for, let's hear it," Bobby was not surprised that Pauly would come up with an excellent idea.

"First off, I've never liked the idea about our getaway plan. I never liked the idea that some of us would make it and some of us would be caught. It seems to me that such a plan is inadequate. It's subject to the way the cards fall," Pauly replied.

Bobby interrupted, "Hey I never said that was the plan. It was the only one we had at the time, though. You got a better one lay it on us, I'm sure we're all interested." They were all interested; they were all tuned into Pauly.

Perry Bartlett, who had heard the entire conversation, decided they were all absurd. Yet for some reason he was no longer scared. The idea these people had, as imprudent as it was, was understandable. It was so crazy that it might even work. He hoped, however, that causing harm to himself or his wife, Elaine, would not be a part of the plan. He didn't want any trouble and the sooner this plan pulled together the sooner he and his wife would be free.

"Okay, this motor home is our plan," Pauly continued, "Those people in the corner are a part of our plan," Pauly paused expecting an interruption which came immediately from Bobby.

"You lost me, brother."

"OK, listen," Pauly continued, "Our problem is getting away after we hit the rest stop, right? The danger is that as soon as we are gone a hundred people will be on the phone or CB calling the police. There is only one highway to get away on, and we would soon be cornered."

Bobby said, "I'm still lost, Pauly."

"Let me finish. To pull it off we have to take this place off without anyone knowing," Pauly paused, wishing to be stopped. He rather enjoyed the fact that no one else had put this plan together. This time no one broke his chain of thought. With open mouths, and anxious ears they waited for more.

Pauly went on, "We've got this motor home, right? We already have, I guess what we will call prisoners. You remember the truck driver, how much money he had in his wallet, Billy?"

Billy responded, "$400 and some bucks." He wondered what that had to do with the new plan.

"All right, here's my plan. We take off only truck drivers. We get them over to the motor home. I'm sure Charlene will come in handy in getting them over to us. Anyway, we get the truck drivers inside and rob them. No one outside will have the slightest idea what's happening. They become our prisoners too. Truck drivers are usually alone, so we don't have anybody looking for them. Now, we'll have more than half an hour, because we are not dealing with so many people. Everybody with me so far?"

"Boy, am I with you brother, I love it, I could kiss you, and I see what you're thinking. When it is time to go, we take our prisoners with us until we are all safe. Nobody's looking for us because nobody has been missed," excitedly, Bobby said, "Fuck it! I'm kissing you on the cheek."

Pauly pulled back in embarrassment. He had not been sure how Bobby would take his idea.

While Bobby was saying, "I like it, I like it," Jesse joined Bobby in the hug and said, "Now we can all stay together. I was worried about that, being on my own, I mean."

"And don't worry about me being able to get the truck drivers over to us," wisecracked Charlene. "My specialty is getting men to help this poor innocent girl out of a mess. Yeah, it's good Pauly, it's really good," Charlene, commented as she joined in hugging Pauly.

"I guess when some rich dude pulls in with a fancy type car, we can take him off, too," Jesse quipped. This was a surprise coming from Jesse, but it was not a bad idea.

"Yeah, why not?" Pauly answered

Jesse added, "And we can take their fancy jewelry and watches, huh?"

Placing an approving hand on Jesse's head, Bobby said, "We can do anything we want to do Jess, we got the guns, we're the bosses. Pauly, brother, you come through again. I feel real good about your plan."

Perry, Elaine and Kelly had listened to everything that was being said. Perry did not say so but he also thought the plan was good. For the first time, Kelly was thinking clearly. For the first time she could think of the possibility of getting out of this mess alive. She was not so frightened, now that there were other captives. They were not going to kill these two new people or all the truck drivers they were just talking about taking. They had to let them all go, somewhere down the road, Kelly reasoned. Elaine did not understand anything; she just stayed close to Perry, putting her destiny into his hands. She knew that he would see them through the mess. However, she was scared. Just plain scared out of her wits.

"Well, when do we get started?" Billy asked.

"We might still wait till dark, let's just play it by ear for now," Bobby answered.

This was all new to him. He never did believe in his original plan. His plan was to be away from the rest stop before he knew how the old plan would work. He had planned to hang out at the rest stop until someone fitting his description came in. He would take that person along with his car and Charlene and get away from the rest stop before the plan could even get started. He planned for the police to be busy with the rest of the guys while he made his getaway. It was different now that the other guys had the plan, a plan that could work.

PAYBACK

Oh, is not life great when everything is going fine
How easy life is to accept when you are having a good time.
No time to think of bad, I took for granted the way I feel
However, the trip is over and bad times are now real.

I just can't imagine how this could be happening to me
How could I jeopardize all I loved, especially being free?
Now it tears inside of me, I feel so close to hate
I find it hard to believe, that this was my fate.

Oh sure, I've done wrong and sure I should pay
But isn't it enough just for the pain I feel today?
Nope, for what I did one day, I have to pay 2000 more
Humility will be plentiful and sorrows galore.

So eat your heart out sucker, ain't payback a bitch?
I never knew when I was free, that then I was rich.

-Rest Stop- Chapter 12

Monday, 4:02 p.m.
Chief Trevor Haynes, the local Police Chief, met FBI Inspector Mitch Zaga at the small Baker airport. Haynes updated the inspector on all that had transpired

as they drove to the scene of the crime. At 1:35 p.m. today, they received a phone call from a hysterical woman who had discovered the body of the gas station attendant. Two police cars were sent to the gas station and verified the account. In the oil room, they found the body of Arty Thurman. A blunt instrument had crushed his skull. Arty Thurman had managed the gas station for more than 12 years. The cash register was open and all money except some change had been removed. There were no witnesses. The gas pump was still on the ground. A white gas cap was on top of the gas pump. The gas pump was still on, even though no gas was being released.

"What amount did the pump register?" Zaga thought that the answer to this question might give a clue as to the type of vehicle the convicts were driving.

"The amount? What do you mean?"

"The amount, you know, what was the total price of the gas, how many gallons were pumped, the amount."

"Oh yeah, gee I don't know. We are almost there. I'm sure nobody's touched the tank," The Chief answered wondering what difference it would make to know the amount.

"It would be nice to know the answer," Zaga responded. He wondered why it took so long to discover the van. I will not even ask, he thought. He will give me some stupid answer. These small town cops are something else. I am lucky that they discovered it at all.

"I don't know I've been real busy so I haven't been out to the crime scene myself, yet," the chief said, thinking these college trained FBI people think they are so smart.

"Oh yeah, I know how police work can keep a guy real busy," Zaga said. He wondered what could keep a small town police chief busier than the first murder in his city in two years.

They pulled into the gas station. Nothing had been roped off, and spectators were roaming around everywhere. There were three city police cars, two highway patrol cars and a fire engine. The first thing Mitch noticed was that there wasn't a gas pump lying on the ground. He got out of his car. To talk to the chief would be useless, he thought. He did not know anything. He approached one of the police cars and asked the officer, "Which one of these pumps was on the ground?"

The officer looked at Mitch as if to ask, "And who are you?" However, he saw his chief's nod of approval.

"The one on the end," said the officer as he pointed it out. Mitch looked. It was 44.3 gallons. That didn't make sense, but a second look confirmed the amount as 44.3 gallons. Zaga thought, what were they driving, a truck? He looked on top of the pump for a gas cap, but there was none there.

"Wasn't there a gas cap left also?" he asked.

"Sure was, we have it inside so nobody would touch it, we're going to have it dusted, you know, for fingerprints," the officer added as though Mitch might not know the meaning of dusted. Zaga was amused.

"We don't need fingerprints buddy, we know who the murderers are. Where is it?"

"Oh really, they're in there dusting the whole place. It's right inside. Come on in, I'll show you." The officer made his way inside and pointed outthe cap out . As Mitch reached down to pick it up, an obtrusive voice was heard to say, "Hold on there, fellow. What the hell are you doing? That thing has to be checked for fingerprints." Mitch was given a mean look.

The chief blurted out as he walked through the door, "It's all right, George, he's with the FBI. He says you people are wasting your time doing any dusting. They already know who the murderers are."

"No shit. Well fuck it then, close it down, Kurt. Let's get out of here. This FBI guy already knows who did the killing," George answered. George hated this fingerprint shit anyway.

Mitch examined the cap. It sure was not off a truck. Holding it to the chief, Mitch asked, "What do you think this thing came off of, Chief?"

"Can't say, other than it's not off a car. You can tell that for sure. Maybe a van or a pick-up."

"Well whatever it was, it took 44.3 gallons of gas," Mitch added. The Chief realized then the importance of knowing the amount of gas pumped. Mitch said, "I don't think it was a van or a pickup. What would you say to a motor home?" Mitch asked.

"Yeah, in view of the amount of gas pumped, that's exactly what I would say." The observation had given the Chief respect for this college trained FBI kid.

"You say we have no witnesses?" Mitch asked, "You see we are looking for five or six people, maybe more by now, if they have the people who were in the motor home. There are four convicts, and a girl who helped them to escape. I hope they still have a woman who is missing from yesterday's murder scene. That's why I don't think they're in a van or a truck. And, 44 gallons of gas is a lot of gas. Yeah, I feel very strongly they're in a motor home. However, I'd sure like to be able to confirm that. Have your people check around for me, would you, Chief?"

"Sure will. Get on that right away would you, George?" the chief said to one of his officers who had heard the conversation.

"Got ya, Chief. Clean the rest of this up Kurt. I'll get on this right now," George said as he walked out the door.

Mitch went to the oil room. The body was there, lying on the floor. He looked around. Blood was on the floor, on the walls and on some of the cans of oil. He turned to the Chief who had a sick look on his face, "Any sign of a murder weapon yet?" MItch asked.

"Nope, whatever they hit Arty with they took it with them. I sure want to get these people inspector. Arty was a good old boy. Lived around these parts most of his life. A lot of people liked Arty."

"A lot of people want to get these guys, Chief. We have at least four dead bodies so far. I have a feeling that it won't be the last that we're going to have, if we don't get them. Is the van still out back?"

Mitch wondered why he asked as he walked out of the building and around to the back. There it was. A good-looking 1983 two-tone custom van. He went to the side doors and opened it up. He turned to the chief, who had by now become his shadow, "Anyone been through this thing yet?"

"I don't think so. When you called, you said to leave that to you."

"Thanks," Mitch responded as he climbed into the van, "I appreciate it."

It was a nice van. A lot of work went into this thing. The name popped into his head. "Richard Quinton," Mitch exclaimed.

"Huh?" the Chief reacted.

"Richard Quinton, 21 years old. He just got married a day or two before they killed him for this van. And if these guys don't have a 19 year old girl with them, then Richard Quinton's wife is dead somewhere out there, too. Yeah, Chief, a lot of people want these guys," Mitch said as he spotted a pair of panties on the floor. These panties were ripped all to hell. They were damp and had the smell of urine. He never doubted for a moment that if the girl was not killed immediately, that she had been gang raped by these animals. Nor did he doubt that the panties belonged to the girl.

He took out his tape recorder. He did not remember the girl's name and took out a notepad. Kelly Quinton, he remembered before he reached the page containing her name. He looked away. Kelly Quinton, 19, blond hair, wife of Richard? Where is she? His note questioned. He returned the note pad to his pocket and turned on the recorder. He recorded what he had seen. There were no clues except the panties, that Kelly was still alive.

There were paper bags and cups from an Arby's restaurant. He also found an empty casing from a 12-gauge shotgun. The ashtrays were filled with the butts of Camel cigarettes. He did not expect to find anything that would indicate their present whereabouts. He was not sure what he hoped to find. He did know however, that he was not far behind them. There was nothing more that he could do here, so he was anxious to get on the road. He was weary and knew that he should have some sleep first, but he smelled blood and wanted to stay on the trail while it was still warm.

He was sure they had gone north on I-15. He hoped they had been stupid enough to have stopped in Vegas. An earlier vision of them having a ball in Vegas returned.

"Were you able to get me that car, Chief?"

The chief pointed to a white Dodge resembling a police car. Sure did, that's it there. Couldn't get you one with a radio on such short notice. Hope it'll do."

Mitch expressed his gratitude to the Chief, "It would be nice to find out what you learn about the motor home while I'm on the road. My next stop is Vegas. Any information you get, call the Las Vegas Police Department. I'll get the message. Give them and the Nevada State police a call. Inform them of my opinion about the white motor home. The FBI has an office there. I'd appreciate you giving them a call. Could you do that for me?" Mitch asked, uncertain about handling it himself. He had the urge to get on the road immediately.

"Sure, no problem, Inspector. I'll do that for you. The keys should be inside the car. Oh, wait a minute, your bag is in my car, I'll get it." The Chief walked a few feet and instructed one of his officers to bring the bag on the front seat to Mitch. He walked back to the car, which was being checked out by the inspector.

"Wish it had a radio," Mitch said as he looked up at the Chief who was anxious to please.

"Well, let me make a few calls, it won't take long. I'm sure I can get you another car," the Chief said, almost apologetically.

"Na, that's all right, I'll pick up another one in Vegas."

"Thanks for all your help, Chief Haynes, and thank you too, officer," Mitch said as he received his bag from the officer.

The officer just smiled. He, too, would be a G-man some day, he thought. Mitch got in the car and headed north on I-15.

Forty miles ahead of Inspector Zaga was a 1986 Rolls Royce driven by Mike Kudofuzi. Mike was the oldest son of a wealthy oilman from Kuwait. Mike loved being rich, he loved the things that money could buy. Things like the cute young redhead sitting next to him. He was well aware that she was with him only because of his money, but he did not mind. Not 10 minutes ago going down the highway, she had been sucking him. He knew that the $500 he had given her to spend while he played dice had a lot to do with her doing it, but he did not mind. Money had no meaning to him. The forty thousand dollars he had in his money belt was peanuts to him. He had won or lost that much in an hour at the dice table.

Becky Ford, the little redhead seated next to him, had never seen as much money as this guy had. She had just met him the night before at a nightclub in Ontario. He had asked her to dance. She was going to turn him down until she saw his diamond ring. It was like none she had seen before in her life. It probably was not real, but she liked the song that was playing and accepted his offer. After the dance, Mike bought drinks for everyone seated at her table. She was impressed, the next song, a slow one came on, he asked her again to dance. She readily accepted again. What happened next, she thought, happened only in the movies. While dancing he whispered in her ear.

"I would give you a thousand dollars if you would go with me right now and make love to me." She pulled away but kept dancing. She looked into his eyes to see if he was just having fun.

"Are you serious?" she asked.

Without a moment's pause, he said, "Yes, I'm very serious. I will give you the money first if you like." She spent the night making love to him. The sex was terrible, but the $1,000 gave it adequate excitement. The next morning he made her an offer to drive with him to Las Vegas in a Rolls Royce with an additional $500 of spending money. It took her every bit of one second to say yes.

With her cutest smile and most seductive manners, she told him that she had to go to wee wee. He told her to wait a minute. There was a rest area just ahead.

Jim Rushton could swear that was a Rolls Royce up ahead. He was pushing his 1980 Chevy Caprice at 80 miles per hour. He let up off the gas as he got closer he saw it was a Rolls Royce. He wondered if he had a lot of money, like a million bucks, would he own a Rolls Royce. Nah, he thought, maybe a Porsche. But boy, those things are class, he thought, as he got closer. He was catching the Rolls faster than he wanted to. It could not have been doing more than 55. He pulled alongside the Rolls doing about 60. He looked over and found himself doing a double take. At first, he thought the person was alone, but he saw what appeared to be some red hair moving up and down. The driver looked over at him and smiled. Then he saw it again, it was red hair. I'll be a son-of-a-bitch, the guy is getting head. So that's what being rich is all about. Jim stepped on the gas. The lucky bastard, he thought as he went by. He thought about his waitress friend

Debbie. Maybe before the night was over he would be a lucky bastard in a 1980 Caprice. Maybe it will not be as much class, but the results would be the same.

Billy and Charlene were sitting up front in the motor home. Billy had been bugging Charlene to have a talk with him. He was anxious to know why she was giving him the cold shoulder. He had really become attached to her. The thought of losing her had not entered his head until she had pushed him away earlier. He tried to talk softly because he did not want anyone in the back to hear him.

"What's wrong baby? What did I do now?"

Charlene was in no reconciliatory mood. She said, "I'm still pissed at you for what you did to that girl. Damn, Billy, you raped her. That's the same as you cheating on me."

"Geez, I thought you had forgiven me, we made love after that, it was beautiful too, I haven't done it again."

"Billy, that's not it, it's just that you know it has been working on me. It has been bugging me. Just give me a little time. It's just that I can't believe you did that to me. I'm supposed to be your lady."

As this conversation was going on up front, one was going on in the back between Bobby and Pauly. Jesse had fallen asleep in a chair. The three prisoners sat still in the corner. Perry Bartlett tried to listen in so he could hear everything possible.

"What's going on up there?" Bobby asked with a snicker, pointing to the front of the motor home.

"A lover's spat, I imagine," Pauly answered. Continuing, he said, "The way I see it, is after we feel we got enough money, or we run out of room for prisoners it will be time to get out of here. Someone has to drive this thing. We need at least one, and I would feel better with two of us watching the prisoners. That leaves two of us to drive our getaway cars. I don't think Jesse knows how to drive, so he can watch the prisoners." Bobby smiled. "What are you laughing about?"

"Oh, I was just thinking about us driving down the highway with a motor home full of prisoners. It wasn't that long ago that we were the prisoners it's just funny that we turned into cops, huh?" Bobby laughed out aloud. The thought also made Pauly laugh.

"Anyway what are we going to do with the prisoners after we hit the road with them?" Pauly came back saying, "We can't just stop at the Greyhound bus depot and drop them off. Got any ideas? We're going to keep heading north, right? I mean we aren't going back to California, are we?" Pauly asked.

"No, I don't think that would be too smart," said Bobby.

"Then I say we keep going right past Vegas, 20 to 30 miles, there's nothing but desert out there. We find an old road that goes 10 or 20 miles into the desert and drop the motor home and the people off, and we take off in our getaway cars after we fuck up the motor home so they can't drive it out. By the time any of them can get to help, we'll be long gone," Pauly said, impressed with the idea.

"So that means besides the motor home, we got to get two cars; I don't see a problem there," Bobby said without caring. He had his own ideas and they did not include anyone but him and Charlene.

"It's Bobby isn't it, I mean I'm not blind, I seen the way you guys look at each other. I know Bobby wants you and I'm not sure if you want him. Well I tell you, lady, that will never happen," Billy said in a whisper, "Bobby's a brother, and no matter how much he wanted you he wouldn't cross a brother, even if you threw yourself at him."

Charlene thought how naive Billy was. If he had known what had already happened he would not be talking about this brother bullshit.

"It's not that at all, Billy. You just got my head really fucked up. You might have raped Kelly, but it was me who was fucked. Do you know what I'm saying, do you understand?"

"I don't know, I mean, I said I'm sorry. I don't know what else to say. I went crazy. Seven years is a long time to be locked up. I just lost control."

"You always tried to tell me, Billy, that the rape charge that they sent you to prison on was a bum beef, well now I just don't know," Charlene just wanted to end the conversation not start another one.

"Oh, what's that got to do with anything? Fuck it. Do your thinking or whatever you you're going to do, I'm going to the back," Billy said as he turned to leave. Charlene made no effort to stop him. She was glad it was over, at least for now. She laughed to herself again. Bobby would not have her if she threw herself at him. That is funny. She knew Bobby was hers for the taking.

"My wife needs to go to the bathroom," Perry Bartlett said as Pauly, Billy and Bobby, looked over at him. Perry was happy with the plan he had just heard, about what would end up happening to the prisoners. He hoped they would not do any great damage to his motor home.

"No problem, you got to go, you got to go," Pauly said as Perry helped Elaine up. They all looked at Elaine as she made her way to the bathroom.

"Mention my name, you get a good seat," Billy said with a smile as Elaine went through the door. She turned and looked at Billy disgustedly.

Bobby heard a car door slam. He looked out the window and saw an older yellow Chevy, a Caprice. Bobby thought, "This person resembles me." The man got out and headed for the rest room. He was about Bobby's height too. Perfect, just what I need to start my plan.

"All right you guys let's get started," Bobby announced as Charlene joined them in the back.

"Huh, we aren't going to wait till dark?" Pauly asked. Elaine returned from the bathroom and sat down beside Perry.

"No need, besides I just seen a good getaway car pull in. Charlene come here, look at this." Charlene went to the window as Bobby pulled back the curtain. "See that yellow Chevy right there, a blond guy about my height just got out and went into the bathroom. He's alone. I want you to get him inside here, think you can do it?"

"Yeah, no problem. A guy by himself is putty in my hands," Charlene said, looking in the mirror to check her hair.

"Hold it Bobby, don't we want to talk about it more? I'm not sure I want Charlene getting involved," Billy was hoping that Charlene would notice his concern for her.

"Don't want her to get involved, fuck man where you been, she is involved. You were right there when we made our new plans about using the motor home, and Charlene being the decoy," Bobby said with irritation.

"I just don't want her to get hurt," Billy retorted.

"Do you think any of us are going to let her get hurt?" Bobby countered as Charlene interrupted, "Hey, I'm telling you this is my cup of tea, I ain't going to get hurt. I'll have this guy begging me to bring him over here."

"Go get him lady," Bobby said. Charlene took one last look in the mirror and headed out the door.

"She'll pull it off. Wake Jesse up, Billy."

Pauly went to the window wondering what brought the change in Bobby so suddenly. The plan had been to wait until dark. Now he wanted to pull it off right now. Pauly was with Billy as to doing a little more thinking about the plan. It was too late now, it was happening.

Jim Rushton was drying his hand. He crumpled the paper towel into a ball and threw it through the air getting it right in the wastebasket. Two points, he said to himself as his hand instinctively brushed across his pocket to feel the wad of money he had in there. It was fine. Another half hour or so he would be in Vegas. As he walked outside to get into his car, his eyes went wide. The cutest little blonde-haired lady was standing on the path with a troubled look on her face. She looked at him as he walked toward her. Boy, she is a doll, he thought as he came within feet of her. She was the first to speak.

"You wouldn't have change for a dollar, would you?" Charlene asked as she held up a dollar.

"Yeah, I think so, let me see," Jim replied as he reached for his coins.

"I got to call my dad in Las Vegas. I'm bringing his motor home to him, and the emergency brake is stuck. I can't get it to come off," the cute blond said, staring into his eyes with her puppy dog eyes.

"Eighty five cents, but you can have it," Jim said as he handed it to her. He noticed that she was not wearing a wedding band.

"No, take the dollar, I appreciate it," the girl said in her sweetest voice. In addition, she was going to Vegas. Fate, yes, it had to be fate. Debby could not hold a candle to this sweet thing.

"You know what, I've always wanted to be a white knight and help out a lady in distress. Why don't I look at your problem? If we are lucky, we may not have to call your dad. What do you say?" Jim was very cheerful. He was thrilled to see the effect it had on the face of his sweet lady.

"If you don't think it's too much trouble, I sure wouldn't mind. Maybe I am doing something wrong, I don't know. It's that white motor home over there," the blond said as she pointed it out.

She walked ahead of him. Her tight faded jeans seemed to mold around her butt. She was like something out of a magazine. He looked admiringly at the motor home. He was astounded that this little woman could drive it alone. His eyes went back to her butt, it was just the way he liked it, tight and firm. She looked back at him and smiled. She knew what he was looking at and she did not seem to mind at all. He followed her as she walked up into the motor home.

"Go ahead and close the door behind you," she said as she stood at the top of the stairs. "Do you get high?" she asked in her customary sweet voice.

"Weed?" Jim asked. Smiling, she nodded yes. "Yeah, all right, I'd love to." This was incredible, it was like a dream come true. He could not believe his good luck.

"Well, come on back here we'll roll one up," she said as she walked to the back of the motor home with Jim in close pursuit.

The back door opened revealing a person standing there with a sawed off shotgun. Jim's heart skipped a beat. He realized in an instant he was the victim of a set up. He looked behind to see if he could escape from this confrontation before this guy could pull the trigger.

Bobby moved toward Jim with the shotgun pointed at his face, "Don't even think about it, buddy," Bobby said. Three other people backed him up, two of them had guns.

"What the hell's this all about, mister?" Jim asked, knowing he was going to be robbed. He wondered how these people knew he had this wad of money. They couldn't have known. It was just by chance that he stopped to take a piss. Maybe it wasn't robbery.

"Just put your hands in the air, turn around and put them on the wall. Billy, shake him down. Pauly, close that front curtain," Bobby ordered.

"Hey, can't you tell me what this is all about? All I was doing was helping this lady out here," Jim said as he put his hands against the wall.

"You just better shut up for now," Billy said as he spread Jim's legs with his foot. Billy had that part down pat. He had it done to him often enough.

"Did you have any trouble getting him to come in here, Charlene?" Bobby inquired as he kept Jim covered.

"Piece of cake, told him I couldn't get the emergency brake off, and he said something about wanting to help a lady in distress or something, and like I said he almost begged me to come in and help me." Jim looked at her and thought to himself, the fucking cunt.

"What's this?" Billy asked as his hands came to a big bulge in Jim's pocket. It was a stack of bills.

"Holy shit, look at this!" Billy exclaimed in disbelief.

"Let me see," Jesse said as Billy handed him the stack of bills.

"Who would believe that a guy driving an old car like his would be packing that much money? How much you think is there?" Billy's mouth opened wider and wider as Jesse continued to count.

"Four thousand four hundred bucks, every penny I have in the world," Jim said with a broken heart.

While going through Jim's wallet Billy said, "Every penny you had, buddy. It belongs to us now."

Jesse said, "Forty four hundred, he wasn't shittin. I can't fucking believe it. Our first customer and we score forty four hundred bucks." In his enthusiasm, Jesse grabbed his sister and gave her a big hug. The mutual smiles of Bobby and Pauly spoke a thousand words.

"You know The Wizard said you'd run into shit like this. People going to Vegas with enough money to choke a horse, people you would never suspect of having two nickels to rub together," Bobby said with a smug smile, "You were on your way to Vegas, huh, fella?"

"Sure was!" Jim answered still not sure that this was just a bad dream.

"Well, we're going to save you the trip. Chances are you would have lost it anyway. So kind of look at us as the guys who saved you a trip. He clean, Billy?" Bobby asked.

"Yep, nothing in his wallet. Should I give it back?" he asked.

"Let me see it," Bobby said, making plans for this person's ID, "OK, You can put your hands down friend. Get on in the back and meet some other folks that we're saving a trip to Vegas," Bobby said as Jim started towards the rear of the motor home.

Bobby stopped Jim with a hand against his chest and looking menacingly into his eyes, Bobby said, "Now listen, you lost your money, friend, but if your life is important to you don't try to be a hero. You just do as we say, and no harm will come to you. Maybe you heard about us on the radio or something."

"You guys are the escaped convicts from Oregon?" Jim managed to ask.

"Yeah, we are, so you know we're about no games. We got nothing to gain by killing you unless you cause us trouble. We won't think twice about killing you if you do. Do you understand? Bobby asked.

Before he got an answer, Charlene interrupted, "Bobby, check out what just pulled into the rest stop. It's a Rolls Royce--swear to God, a Rolls Royce."

Bobby ordered Pauly to get in the back and keep an eye on everyone back there. "Son-of-a-bitch," said Bobby, "That's a Rolls Royce sure enough. Let's go for number two, what do you say?"

"You ain't thinking about using a Rolls for one of our getaway cars, are you? Cause if you are I want it to be mine," Jesse said, overwhelmed with excitement.

Bobby said, "Don't be stupid, Jess. We want getaway cars that can get lost in a crowd, not something everyone is going to be looking at. No, what I'm thinking is we score 44 hundred off an old Chevy, well shit, Rolls can't do any worse." Bobby saw a cute redhead get out, followed by the driver who looked like an Arab.

"Well, that figures, a sand nigger, they're the only ones who can afford a Rolls anymore."

Charlene asked if Bobby wanted her to do it again. Bobby wanted to know how she would play it this time. He knew that playing a couple had to be different from playing a single guy.

"Yeah, no doubt. But I wasn't sure how I was going to work the guy, either. It is like it just comes to me at the time. I will get them here don't worry. I can do it."

"Oh, I don't doubt you, lady. I'm sure you can," with a short pause, Bobby said, "OK, go get 'em."

Charlene went without a moment's hesitation. Bobby fell in love with her. This woman was one of a kind, he thought. More balls than most of the guys he had ever known. "Where are those sunglasses that were here?" Bobby asked.

"Right here," Billy said, handing them to him. Bobby put on an overcoat, which he had found in the closet.

"What you going to do?" Pauly asked.

"I'm going to back up Charlene. Number one, I don't want anything to happen to her; number two, I don't want this Rolls to get away," Bobby said as he put on the sunglasses and slipped the shotgun under the coat.

"Be cool brother," cautioned Pauly, "your face is a pretty hot item."

"I hear ya," Bobby said as he walked out the door. Pauly looked at the prisoners. The new person sat on the bed besides the rest of the prisoners. Pauly did not figure he needed to be on the floor, so he did not say anything. Billy watched Charlene as she waited on the path for the next victim. He saw Bobby make a wide circle until he got to the lawn. Standing there, he saw Charlene catch sight of Bobby. Billy was deeply disturbed by the smile Charlene threw at Bobby. Bobby just shined it on as though he did not acknowledge it. Billy liked that because it confirmed what he had told Charlene that Bobby would never mess around with a brother's old lady.

"Hey, that redhead chick is coming out," Jesse observed as he peeked out the window.

Charlene was not sure how she was going to play this. She did not have a game plan when she saw the red head walking toward her. She always worked better on impulse. True to her pattern, she got an idea just as the redhead came within a few feet of her.

"Excuse me, can I talk to you a second?" Becky Ford was astounded at first. She assumed the girl was a panhandler. "Sure honey, what can I do for you?" The girl certainly did not look like a panhandler, thought Becky.

"Well I'm in kind of a mess and was hoping we might be able to help each other out," Charlene said with great deliberation. Perhaps, she is a panhandler after all, thought Becky.

"I, well we, my baby and I are heading for Salt Lake in that big motor home over there." Charlene continued as she pointed to the motor home. "Well, we run out of money, but I'm not asking for a hand out or anything. What I would like to know is if I can interest you in a diamond necklace. I'll sell it dirt cheap."

Charlene watched the redhead's reaction. She knew she blew it. A diamond necklace, why did she say diamond necklace, she should have thought of something different.

"No, sorry, really can't afford a diamond necklace," Becky responded.

"A diamond necklace? Who has a diamond necklace?" Mike Kudofuzi asked as he joined the two girls. His eyes roamed up and down the pretty young blonde.

184

"Hi," Charlene said with a big smile. She was at her best with men, "I do. I was telling your wife here about me and my baby being stuck here without enough money to get home on. I don't want a hand out, but I would sell a diamond necklace my ex-husband got me for a very good price. Please say you will at least look at it." Charlene was glad she included the bit about her ex-husband. The guy showed his happiness at that.

"Where is it?" Mike asked.

"Right over here in my motor home," Charlene said, again pointing it out. "You don't know how much it will mean to me, I've been stuck here for hours."

Again, Mike asked, "How much do you want for it?"

"Oh it's worth a $1,000, maybe more, but I just want enough to get home on." Charlene said, using her puppy dog eye approach.

Turning to Becky, "Would you like a diamond necklace?" he asked.

"I'd like to help out this girl and her baby," Becky said, knowing the real interest was in her love for the necklace.

"Well then we shall look at it, please show us," Mike responded, knowing that he would have given the girl $100. However, maybe for the necklace his red haired girl would suck again before they got to Las Vegas. They followed Charlene without noticing the man in the overcoat following them.

"She did it, she's got them coming. We'd better get in the back. Son-of-a-bitch, she did it. My little sis did it," Jesse said on his way to the rear of the motor home. Pauly and Billy followed.

"That's my girl," Billy said as he closed the door. In a whisper Pauly said, "I didn't see Bobby."

With his eye the rest of the prisoners, Billy said, "Yeah, he's right behind them."

Speaking to the prisoners Billy said, "You all keep your mouths shut." This was unnecessary, as they had been quiet since the whole thing started.

"How old is your baby?" Becky asked Charlene as they approached the motor home.

"Baby Billy, oh, he's just a few months old," as Charlene looked back, she noticed that Bobby was just a few steps behind them.

"Wait 'til you see him, he's a doll."

"Are you driving this big thing by yourself?" Mike asked as he gazed at these two fine butts ascending the stairs.

Charlene assured them, "Yeah, it's not as hard as it looks." The two new guests followed her to the middle of the motor home. Becky felt the vibration of someone following them. She observed something out of the corner of her eye.

Mike saw or felt the same thing. They both turned simultaneously. There was some person closing the curtain in the front.

"Welcome to the magic bus, folks," Bobby said.

He removed the shotgun from under his coat and pointed it at Mike's face. Mike reacted instantly by putting his hands in the air saying in a frightened voice, "We don't want any trouble please. We don't want any trouble."

Becky's true character came to light, "What the fuck is this, you assholes."

The back door swung open and three people came out. Two of them had guns. "It's a party, darling. And you people are our guests of honor. You know it's not too nice to call your hosts assholes, now is it?" Billy said.

Speaking to Charlene, he said, "Good job, lady, you're something else."

"This is bullshit," Becky said, "You're never going to get away with it." Mike looked at Becky and gave her a shake of his head to shut up.

"You had better do as your boyfriend tells you, red. This is no game. It would be best if you would just keep your little mouth shut. Not that I don't admire your spunk," Bobby said to Becky.

He looked Mike in the eyes and said, "When you drive a Roll Royce, mister, you must expect shit like this to happen once in a while." Bobby began to frisk Mike. Mike kept his hands raised. He knew the person had felt his money belt. He did not care they could have the money.

"What the fuck you got there, buddy?" asked Bobby as he felt the money belt.

"Look at the size of that fucker's ring. That can't be real, let me see that," Billy said as he reached for Mike's raised hand and removed his ring, "Fuck, look at this thing. Is this thing real, Pauly?"

Everyone was staring at this hunk of jewelry. Billy handed the ring to Pauly. Bobby pulled up Mike's shirt disclosing the money belt, taking attention away from the ring. Bobby, staring in astonishment, asked "I'll be a son-of-a-bitch, how much money you got in that thing buddy?"

"Forty thousand dollars," Mike said as he watched Bobby fall back, leaning against the wall. The entire group, with mouths agape, stood in amazement. Even Becky had no idea Mike had so much money.

"No shit buddy, you got forty thousand dollars in that thing?" Bobby asked, looking at the group while awaiting an answer from Mike.

"Yes, forty thousand dollars--all in one hundred dollar bills."

In the most polite terms, Bobby said, "Take it off for me, would you please," as he observed how the belt was taken off.

Mike reached behind him, unfastened the belt, and handed it to Bobby. Bobby took it and for a second just held it in his hand, moving it up and down.

"If there's forty thousand dollars in that thing, then I'd say this ring is real," Pauly said as he looked at the unbelievable size of the diamonds.

"Yes, it's very real. It's worth as much as the money in my belt," Mike answered as Bobby opened the zipper and looked in the first pocket. There was a wad of hundred dollar bills. Mike said, almost with pride, "There are four pockets each containing 100 one hundred dollar bills, ten thousand in each pocket. Please feel free to take the ring and the money, but please don't hurt us."

"Buddy, I could kiss you, I sure don't plan to hurt you. You and this sweet redhead behave yourselves, and nothing will happen to you. Do you have more money in your car, in your pockets?" Bobby asked with deep respect.

"Nothing more in my car but I have some small bills in my pocket. Can I put my hands down? I will get it for you," Mike said.

"Sure, make yourself right at home. Feast your eyes on this, brother," Bobby said as he threw the money belt at Pauly. Mike took a wad of bills from his pocket and gave it to Billy who was already reaching for it.

"Small bills shit, two hundred, oh here's another hundred, three fifty, three seventy, seventy five, six, seven. Three hundred and seventy seven dollars. Fuck, buddy, what do you do for a living--is it legal?" Billy did not really care. But he and Pauly both had some interest in it. Mike preferred not to disclose the nature of his income. They might hold him for ransom.

"I won the lotto two years ago, $1,000,000," He chose that amount to state.

"No shit, I never met anyone who won one of those things. Well you are a lucky bastard, huh?" Jesse cracked.

"Yes, very lucky" Mike responded, hoping the subject would be dropped there.

"Well friend you made our day, maybe our lives. Now you and your lady friend go on in the back there and join some of our other guests. Just be real quiet and keep still," Bobby pointed the shotgun toward the rear to emphasize his point.

"You will be letting us go then?" Mike asked as he walked toward the back.

"Sure will. We'll be taking real good care of you." He grabbed Becky's arm and looked directly into her eyes, "But remember we're assholes. Don't make us prove it," he said to Becky.

She retorted, "You already have."

Bobby just smiled and let her arm go. As she followed Mike to the back of the motor home, Bobby said, "The broad got spunk, don't she?"

Expressing Billy's thoughts along with his own, Jesse said, "I'd like to give her some of my spunk."

In a more serious tone Bobby said, "Hey, that dude just gave us eighty thousand bucks, counting the ring. We treat him and his lady with respect."

"Yeah, no problem. I was just cracking a joke. Forty thousand dollars, can you believe this shit? It's unreal. I can't fucking believe it," Jesse said in a near scream.

"Hold it down, Jess," Bobby said as he looked out the window. No one was close to them. Bobby gave out a yell as he picked up Charlene and gave her a big squeeze. They all laughed heartily.

Billy and Pauly were busy opening the pockets of the money belt. Just as Mike had said, there were four pockets, each with a stack of hundred dollar bills.

"This is unreal Bobby. I mean it has to be a fluke. I mean we hit two people and we got close to fifty thousand in cash. I wouldn't have figured this reality in my wildest dreams," Pauly said, running his fingers through the bills.

"Let me see it," Jesse said as he and Charlene joined them.

Bobby said, "Let me see that ring. Fuck. I didn't think diamonds came that big." He tried to put it on his finger but it did not fit, "Its unreal to me too, Pauly. I never thought it could be this sweet."

Pauly said to Bobby, "Fifty grand, brother, fifty fucking thousand cash. We could hit the road now. We have enough. There's no heat on us right now; I mean it could not be any slicker than how we've done it. I know we've been lucky. We might have to be here a week to score the next fifty grand. I don't know, I'm just thinking we shouldn't push our luck," Pauly was interrupted.

"Cop, fucking state cop just pulled in," Billy said excitedly. They were all peeking out the window. "What are we going to do? What are we going to do? He's right there by the shitter."

"Just cool it," Bobby said, "Let's see what he is going to do," Bobby said as he popped open the shotgun. Seeing that it had not changed, he closed it. Comfortingly, Bobby said, "He's probably just taking a piss."

That is exactly what the Nevada Highway Patrolman was doing, just stopping to relieve himself. He had heard something on the radio about some escaped convicts from Oregon. However, the radio was constantly blasting out APBs. He simply did not pay attention. His greatest interest for the moment was to get to the can. He did not even register the white motor home parked almost directly across from his patrol car.

"I'm going out. If he gets near his radio I'm going to have to take him. It depends, I guess, I mean they can't know anything about this thing, can they? No one knows we're in a motor home. But just be ready," Bobby said as he put the shotgun under his coat and walked out the door.

188

Pauly asked, "Do you want me to go with you Bobby?" The fifty thousand had given Pauly a completely new attitude.

"No, I can handle one cop all right. Keep an eye on our guests. It would be very bad if one of them would go off now."

"No problem," Pauly said, "we got that covered." Bobby walked slowly toward the rest room. He was anxious to properly time the event. The cop was pulling up his fly as he left the rest room. Bobby thought that this cop had to be the fastest pisser he had ever known.

"The cop's leaving," Jesse said. He went directly to his car without noticing Bobby walking behind him in his overcoat.

Bobby went to the water faucet to take a drink. He watched the cop as he fastened his seat belt. The cop made an entry on a note pad, backed out and drove away without looking around. After watching the cop leave the rest area, Bobby took a sigh of relief and returned to the motor home.

"Fuck. Made me feel like we were back in the joint holding a pound of weed with the man coming down the tier for a shake down," Billy cracked as Bobby returned to the motor home.

"Shit who ever said cops ain't stupid? Hey, we got any weed left. I think I could use one about now," Bobby said as he laid the shotgun on the table.

"Pretty close shave, huh?" Billy said.

"Nah, it was just like I said, the guy just had to piss. I just feel like smoking a bowl," Bobby did not dare to admit he was afraid. This experience did bring back memories of the joint. However, he intended never to go back there. Never.

"I don't think there is any left," Charlene said as the others nodded in agreement.

Perry Bartlett spoke up. "If you look in the bottom of that dresser, in a pair of red socks, you'll find some good home grown there." Elaine gave Perry a disgusted look. She could not believe that Perry had offered his weed to these animals. Perry thought it could not do any harm. Under the circumstances, it might give him an edge later on if the need were to arise.

"I'll be fried, we take your money, your motor home, eat your food, kidnap you folks, and now you offer us your weed. And here I was thinking you were a red neck to boot. Is this guy something else or what, Bobby?" Pauly had difficulty believing that Bartlett held no grudge.

"Well shit, it is hard to believe. The least we can do is to share it with him. As much as I feel like a bowl, I imagine he needs it even worse. What is your name buddy?" Bobby asked.

"My name is Perry Bartlett, this is my wife Elaine. I'm afraid I can't introduce the rest of these people. However, to answer your question, I'd like very much to smoke a bowl."

Perry had picked up the habit of smoking while he was in 'Nam, and had continued to do it for the last twenty years. He didn't smoke as much as he used to, but he always had some around when he had the urge. He used it mostly at night before he went to sleep.

Jim Ruston still could not believe what was happening. His eyes got big when the Rolls Royce people were led to the back. He had heard the convicts say something about a Rolls Royce pulling into the rest area. He wondered if it might have been the one he had passed earlier. When he did see the person, and the redhead with him, he managed an inner smile. The smile did not last long. His mind soon returned to the loss of his money. These fucking convicts had all of his money. He could not believe he hadn't recognized the blonde bitch right off. He'd just seen her photo in the paper at home. He remembered how good looking he thought she was, looked at the photo a few times, then came face to face with her and didn't put her and the photo together until it was too late. He wanted his money back but was not ready to die for it. His thoughts were interrupted when Perry put a pipe in front of him.

"Want some?" Perry asked in a deep voice while holding in the smoke.

"No," Jim answered in disbelief that this guy was getting high with these assholes.

Pauly finished rolling a joint, passed it to Bobby saying, "Well Bobby, what do you think?"

Lighting up the joint Bobby said, "About what, brother? Damn, that's pretty tasty for home grown." Bobby returned the joint to Pauly.

"About us not pushing our luck," Pauly continued, "Take the fifty grand and splitting while everything is still in our favor. Bobby was thinking. Weed always seemed to help him to think. At least he thought so. Pauly was right. The fifty grand they got without any trouble was a fluke. He checked his back pocket and felt the wallet of the guy who resembled himself. He then felt the front pocket where he had put Jim's keys. They were still in place. He looked at the money belt on the table. He took off the overcoat and reached for the money belt. He strapped it behind him under his shirt, carefully tucking his shirt back in.

He was about to ask for the ring when he saw Charlene wearing it and looking at it through the light. Perfect! He saw the $44 hundred dollars they had taken from the first guy. In another pile, there was the money they had taken from the owners of the motor home. He decided to let the guys keep that. He did not want to leave them cold. They were in good shape really. They had their freedom, they had this motor home, and they had close to five grand and a couple of guns.

"Well what do you think, Bobby?" Pauly asked as he observed Bobby engaged in deep thought. He was not sure how he felt about Bobby putting on the money belt, but he thought, well, it had to be somewhere. He took another pull of smoke off the joint and handed it back to Bobby, "Well?"

"I think you're right. I think we scored big and we're lucky. And you are right, no sense pushing it. It's almost dark, so let's get started," Bobby said, as the others gathered around to listen, "Charlene, here's the keys go get that dude's Chevy."

"Got you," Charlene took the keys and left without asking any questions.

"So we're just going to take one car then?" Pauly asked without any real interest in the minor details. One car would be fine. He was just happy that Bobby had accepted his plan that he did not care what Bobby did from here on.

"Yeah, I think for now that's all we need," Bobby responded.

"Who's going to drive the motor home and watch the prisoners?" Pauly asked, thinking about the fifty thousand dollars. Maybe Bobby would let him have $5,000 of it to send to Patty.

Bobby moved up front where he could see Charlene backing the car in by the motor home. He grabbed the keys out of the ignition. No one saw him put the keys in his pockets as he turned around. By the time they could hot-wire the motor home, he would be long gone.

"Oh, I guess it don't matter. Hang on a second, I got to tell Charlene something," Bobby said as he left the motor home. Bobby stopped Charlene as she was entering the motor home.

"Open up the trunk and get back inside the car. I'll be back out in a minute. Don't come inside," Bobby instructed Charlene. The expression on her face revealed how much she wanted to know what was going on but she did not ask. She opened the trunk as Bobby reentered the motor home. Bobby had always been that way. Whenever he got an idea, he wanted to implement it immediately. That was how he intended to do this.

"What's cooking, brother?" Pauly asked.

"Getting ready to move. I'm taking the guy who owns the Chevy and putting him in the trunk," Bobby said as he passed Pauly and Jesse. Billy was in the back keeping an eye on the prisoners. Bobby grabbed the shotgun as he walked by.

"Why you putting him in the trunk?" Pauly asked, not understanding the motive.

Jim Rushton overheard the plan to put him in the trunk. He was interested to know the answer to that question. "Just one less guy to worry about. He won't be staying in there long. Just 'til we find an old road we're going to take where we can stash the motor home and the rest of the people," Bobby said.

One less guy to watch made no sense to Pauly but things were going good and he was not going to argue.

As he pointed the shotgun at Jim Ruston, Bobby said, "Get up buddy, you're going with me."

The thought of leaving under the circumstances gave Jim Ruston no real thrill. He was not excited to be put into the trunk of his own car. However, he got up and proceeded to go outside. Bobby followed close behind him with his shotgun pointed at his back. He had an urge to grab his money lying on the table. He did not pause. He realized that discretion is often the greater part of valor.

"Be back in a second." were the last words Pauly and Jesse would hear Bobby say.

Pauly was still confused about the plans and planned to get some straight answers when Bobby came back inside. Bobby had the shotgun under his coat. There was only one truck in the immediate area. Directing his hostage to the back of the car, he ordered him to get in the trunk.

"Hey, I er, er," was all that Jim could say.

"Get in." The shotgun aimed at Jim provided sufficient persuasion. He climbed into the trunk. Pauly watched Bobby as he closed the trunk and approached the driver's side. The coast was clear.

"Move over," Bobby said. He climbed in, started the car and took off.

"Hey, what are we doing, we leaving right now?" Charlene had no idea what was going on. She had no idea that it would be this fast.

"We sure are, lady. You and me, $40,000 and that diamond ring on your finger."

A light went off in her head. Immediately she understood what Bobby's plan was. It was excellent. She never would have thought of it in a thousand years. She wanted Bobby, she wanted money, and she wanted to be rid of Billy. All the three things happened without any conscious effort on her part.

At the same time, a light bulb went off in Pauly's head. When he saw them drive off, he knew what Bobby's plan was. It was perfect--perfect for Bobby. What Bobby was doing had never entered Pauly's mind. However, as Bobby rolled away, with the money belt with forty grand and Charlene, he could not hold back his laughter. It made perfect sense. What didn't make sense was why he hadn't seen it coming sooner.

"Hey, where they going?" Billy asked without the slightest idea what was going on. Pauly started laughing. He laughed loudly.

"What the fuck you laughing at?" Billy asked. Billy still had no idea what had just happened. This made the whole thing even more laughable.

FOR WHAT? I SAY

Many different people, from many different places,
Many different forms and many different races
All lonely all searching, for their place in life
Many leaving behind children and a wife.

For what. For what I say, what's it all for?
They had all they wanted then wanted more.
Most smart, some dumb, some angry, some fun,
Most hurt, some cry, most live, some die.

For what, for what I say, is it their own will,
Is the money, or the seeking of a thrill
The answer, the reason, the purpose of it all,
I cannot put my finger on it, yet it seems so small.
Then I ask myself, for one of the different people is me
For what, for what I say why couldn't I stay free?

-Rest Stop- Chapter 13

Monday, 5:43 p.m.

FBI Inspector Mitch Zaga had just crossed the Nevada border when he saw what appeared to be a white motor home on the highway about half a mile ahead. He knew the convicts would be beyond Vegas by now, if they had not stopped in Vegas, that is.

Either way, there was no chance that the motor home he saw ahead would be the one he was looking for. He found himself speeding up. He had planned to stop at Whiskey Pete's to have lunch. However, that was forgotten as he drove past the exit. Maybe, the convicts felt so invincible they had stopped at Whiskey Pete's themselves. Maybe they thought they should get off the highway for a while.

Whatever the reason, the Inspector had a strong conviction that the convicts were in a white motor home. When he got closer, his conviction was authenticated. It was a white motor home. He was not certain what action he would take if it were the convicts. He had no radio by which to communicate. He was rapidly gaining on the motor home, and decided to slow down. He looked to see if the motor home had a missing gas cap. The tank was not on the left side, and he could not see the right side.

He drove slowly by the home and observed that the driver was an elderly man. He did not see anyone else, but that was not necessarily meaningful. He knew that probably 90% of motor homes were white. He decided definitely, that he would not leave this motor home before he had determined whether the gas cap was missing. He sped up and passed it. He looked in his rear view mirror for anything suspicious but saw nothing. About a quarter of a mile down the road, he pulled off the highway. The motor home passed and the gas cap was in place.

His stomach growled from hunger, and now he wished he had stopped at Whiskey Pete's. He pulled back on the highway and decided to continue to Vegas for food.

Mitch Zaga tried to think as a convict would think. He wondered if they were all still together or if they'd separated. He figured they were still together. What had happened to the people who were driving the motor home? Were they still alive? He didn't know; he did know they wouldn't remain alive when Smallwood decided it was time to get rid of them. Had the Baker Police Chief, Trevor Haynes, made the call he had promised to make?

Zaga passed the motor home a second time. He took another look at the old driver. It could be someone just like the old man the convicts had kidnapped. He thought about the gas cap, maybe it had been left by someone else. Then he flashed back to the 44 gallons on the gas pump. No. He would not change his strategy; he was looking for a white motor home with a missing gas cap.

He saw the road sign ahead, *REST AREA 2 MILES*. He remembered Smallwood's friend, Ken Rocmel. He would not be surprised if Bobby was at a rest stop now. He needed to go to the bathroom anyway. He might as well check it out.

Billy and Jesse simply could not believe that Bobby had done this to them. Billy would not accept the fact that Charlene and Bobby had planned it. His ego was tearing him apart. Jesse kept insisting that Charlene was not in on the plan. Bobby had kidnapped her. She would never screw her big brother. He had not been convinced that Bobby and Charlene would not pull back in the rest stop any minute now.

Maybe Bobby thought of something that had to be done before they left. They were brothers, and a brother would not do another like Pauly was saying Bobby had done. On the other hand, Pauly knew the truth. He was not shocked because of what Bobby had done because he had accepted it as the truth from the moment it happened. Reality shocked him.

The reality was they were wanted for murder; they were in a stolen motor home with five kidnap victims. He was stuck with Billy and Jesse. He felt that if he were to give each of them half of his brains, they would still be half-wits.

Pauly wouldn't desert them. As crazy as it was, he felt that Billy had saved his life, and he knew that their only chance was with him. He also admired Bobby because he was a survivor. He wondered how long Bobby had been planning this scheme. Perhaps the forty grand had contributed to the decision he had made. Bobby could have taken all the money, but he had been gracious enough to leave them with almost $5,000. He did envy Bobby--he escaped with the money, the diamond ring, the girl and the guy's ID.

Right now, he could kill Bobby. But after all, self preservation is the first law of nature. Bobby had followed a rule that he did not originate. Bobby had the foresight to understand that for all of them to stay together could only provide an insecure future for all. Add this foresight to the means at his disposal, and he had simply done what Pauly himself might have done. Pauly wished he had done the same thing but it had never occurred to him. Before this, they had all been infused with the brotherhood idea. It was that thinking that got Pauly involved in this mess to begin with.

The prisoners in the back were aware of what had happened. They had been mentally tortured by Bobby's unsettled attitude. He had frequently talked about killing someone, anyone. They knew that he had run off with one guy's girlfriend. Perry Bartlett was glad he'd left and taken his sawed off shotgun with him. That shotgun scared him more than him running off his mouth.

One of Perry's friends carried a sawed off shotgun in 'Nam. He knew what a gun like that could do to a man. He saw his buddy use it on a Viet Cong one day. The destruction was devastating. Perry felt that with Bobby gone, the odds were in their favor. There were five hostages and three convicts. He didn't count on any of the others, however. They hadn't found his pistol, and this was his ace in the hole. He didn't consider himself a hero but he was scared for Elaine. Given the opportunity, he'd get his .44 magnum and wouldn't be afraid to use it. He preferred not to use the gun. The abductors' plan to abandon them on some deserted road suited him better. Certainly, it would be better than having to kill one of them. However, he would do what had to be done.

Billy yelled, "I can't fucking believe it. I still cannot fucking believe it. How the fuck could she do that to me. I'm shell shocked, man. I'm just fucking shell shocked."

In defense of his sister, Jesse said, "Maybe it wasn't her doing, you know. Bobby, fucking Bobby, was always talking about the brotherhood, and all that shit. He turns out to be the biggest punk of them all. I bet you Charlene didn't even know it was going to happen." Jesse had come to realize that they were not coming back. He shook his head in disbelief.

Pauly said, "Hey, listen, fuck this shit, it's not doing us any good. The truth of the matter is Bobby's gone. He fucked us and he was looking out for himself. Billy, Charlene is with him. Whether she wanted to go with him or not, she's gone. Now, we need to come back to reality. We got to start thinking what we're going to do."

Seeing he had their attention, Pauly continued, "Bobby did leave us with almost five grand, and that's enough to get us to some place of safety. We're going to need another car, so while we're here we might as well take one along with whatever money we can get from the owner. Then, I think we ought to get away from here, find a safe place to dump the motor home and our prisoners."

"Hey, weren't the keys in the ignition?" Jesse interrupted. Pauly and Billy observed that the keys were no longer in the ignition.

Instinctively, Pauly checked his pockets for the keys, even though he knew he hadn't touched them.

"Fuck you Bobby, you cocksucker," Billy said with all the violent vocal force at his command, "That dirty fucker, why did he do that? Fuck it." Billy stormed out the door.

Pauly, irritated, called, "Billy! Get your ass back here!" It did no good; Billy was walking across the parking lot. He felt hurt and betrayed. He had never felt this type of pain before. Pauly went to the back of the motor home.

"Hey buddy, seems our friend left with the keys, you have another set?" Pauly asked Perry. Perry hesitated to admit that he had another set of keys. Maybe they would just leave them there but that was highly unlikely.

"Hey, do you have an extra set of keys or not? I mean, if you don't, it won't make a difference. But, it's your motor home and if we have to rip it apart to hotwire it, we will," Pauly said.

"Oh no, it's not that, we have an extra set I was just trying to think where they were. Do you know, honey?" Perry asked Elaine. "Oh yeah, I remember, they're in the glove box." Perry decided to tell.

"Great, thanks," Pauly said as he walked to the glove box with Jesse trailing behind him. Pauly opened the glove box and right there were the keys.

"Here take this, keep an eye on the folks. I'm going to get Billy," Pauly said as he handed Jesse the .38 and walked out the door. He saw Billy over by the water fountain.

The first thing Mitch Zaga saw as he pulled in the rest area was a huge white motor home. It couldn't be was his first thought. He kept going past the car entrance to the truck area and slowly pulled in. His heart felt like it would jump out of his chest as he saw a hole where the gas cap should be. A tall man came walking out in front of the motor home and was crossing the parking lot.

Mitch zoomed in on the person as he pulled closer. It was Paul Brown. Another man joined him and began to talk. Mitch then zoomed in on the new person as he pulled to a stop in a stall 20 feet from them--William Atterberry, and the other was Paul Brown. As sure as shit there they were, now what; no radio. They were looking over at him. He looked in the rear view mirror at the motor home.

Where is Smallwood, the shotgun? What should he do, his mind was racing. Pull out; pull out get out of here. They were looking over here. Oh no, Atterberry was coming at him. Atterberry's reaching behind. He's getting a gun. Brown is standing there. Atterberry is still coming. There's no time. I can't get away. It's a show down. Get my gun. Get my gun.

Mitch reached inside his coat for his gun as he kept his eyes on Atterberry. He saw Atterberry pull the gun from behind and point it at him. Mitch hit the door handle and put his weight against the door. He let himself fall to the ground. He heard a shot and the sound of glass breaking. He stayed on the ground and cocked his gun. Atterberry came around the front of the car. Mitch fired his .38 Smith and Wesson.

Billy was not sure what he felt. It was hot--real hot--like someone was burning him with a branding iron. Everything went blank. He forgot what he was going to do. He felt his legs get weak. He had a hard time standing. He had an urge to pull his finger back. So he did. He heard a loud roar next to his ear. He thought he was lying down. He couldn't remember lying down. Hey, I'm not breathing. How could I not be breathing? My brain still works. It's so dark. Oh, there we go. There's Charlene such a pretty lady. There are my brothers. Bobby. Jesse. Pauly. Guys, I'm not breathing. It's a funnel. A spiral funnel. It's going around and around. I'm falling. Falling fast. Mom. Hi mom. Mom.

Mitch knew his shot was perfect, hitting Atterberry in the heart. He saw Atterberry jolt back and, as his hands went up, fire another shot as he fell into a dead heap. Mitch jumped up and saw Brown dashing back to the motor home. Brown turned. Mitch saw something shiny in his hand.

Mitch fired his .38. The shot was not as accurate as he hoped, hitting Brown in the shoulder. There was a shot and the sound like a bee passing his ear. It was not a shotgun. Relieved, he dove under the front of the car. Mitch looked out and saw Brown running towards the desert. Brown went over a barbed wire fence and kept running towards nowhere. Mitch tried to see where the shot had come from. Another shot told him. Someone was under the motor home shooting at him. The gun sounded like a .38. Where was the shotgun? Where was Smallwood?

Perry Bartlett heard the first shot and saw Jesse, who'd been watching them, go running out with his gun in his hand. The rest of the prisoners became scared, not knowing what was happening. Perry got up and looked out the window just as he heard another shot. He almost smiled as he saw Billy fall to the ground. He saw another person he never saw before fire another shot at something he couldn't see. Then another shot sounded like it came from under the motor home. He felt it was time to play his ace. He went to the closet and grabbed his leather case. He got the gun out along with a full clip of bullets and slid the clip in. He wasn't going to be a hero, but he knew no one was getting through the door to threaten him and his wife again. He cocked his .44 magnum and waited.

Jesse was scared shitless. He saw someone shoot Pauly. He saw Billy lying on the ground. Where did this person come from? Who was he? Pauly was running away. He was all alone. Jesse slid under the motor home and fired a shot at the person's head. It missed. He saw Pauly go over a fence and into the desert. Jesse saw the person peek his head out. He fired at him again.

Why was Pauly running out into the desert? What was he going to do? Pauly had the keys. Jesse didn't know what to do. He looked out at Pauly again. He had covered quite a distance. Jesse wondered if he should run out and join him. He got an idea. He would take a hostage. Kelly, yeah. I'll walk her in front of me and take someone's car. The money, yes there was still the money inside. That's all I need to start over. Five thousand was plenty. Maybe he and Kelly could get a thing together. He'd treat her real good.

He crawled out slowly from under the motor home. He had that person scared over there. He was hiding. He went up the stairs keeping his head down. He still didn't see the person. He turned towards the back. He was dead before he saw who shot him. The bullet went into his chest the size of a quarter, and came out his back the size of a baseball.

Pauly was not sure what had transpired in the last five minutes. His urge was just to run and run. He knew he'd been shot but it didn't hurt as much as he thought it would. His shoulder felt numb. He remembered going to get Billy to get him inside. He was showing him the extra set of keys to the motor home. He'd told Billy that Bobby was not as smart as he thought he was. All of a sudden, Billy said, "Cop." Pauly turned and saw someone in a white car. It looked like a cop's car. That did not mean it was one.

Billy went crazy, pulling his pistol out and shooting. Another shot and Billy fell over. It looked like he was dead. Pauly took off running. The next thing he knew he was shot. He didn't know why he was shot. He didn't have a gun, just the keys in his hand. He was running. He still had the keys. He heard more shots and thought the person was trying to kill him. So he ran. He was still running.

He wondered how Jesse was making out. He wondered where he was running. He wondered how it had come to this. How had things changed so fast? He wondered if Patty and Dustin would ever know the truth. He wondered how long he could keep running.

Mitch Zaga heard a shot ring out from within the motor home and dared to poke his head up hoping to see what was going on. The shot did not sound like a .38. More like a magnum. He saw what looked like blood on the inside of the window. He got a cold chill and quickly looked behind him. There was nothing. Some people over on the car side were sticking out from under their car. The chill he felt was not for them, it was for Smallwood. Where was he? He had to be in the motor home. Someone was peeking out a window and he had an urge to shoot. However, his FBI training restrained him. Know what you are shooting at.

He saw someone run to the telephone. Mitch hoped they were dialing 911. He looked around for better cover. He would be just fine where he was for now. What was the shot about from inside the motor home? He hoped Smallwood had not shot a hostage. If only there'd been a radio in his car. He was not going to move until help came.

Willis Clark was asleep in the cab of his truck when he woke up thinking he heard a shot. His first thought was that it was a dream. He closed his eyes again. He heard a second shot which made him jump up and go to the window. At the same time, he heard a third shot and looked outside. He saw a person running. Over by a white car, a man was lying on the ground. Then, he saw a man pop up from behind the white car and shoot the man who was running.

Willis Clark had seen enough. He kept his head down, reached for his CB, and switched to channel 3 for emergencies. He reported what he saw. He was told police were on their way. He kept his head down and made his way back to the rear of the cab. He heard more shots. Some were coming from the white motor home parked beside him.

Mitch watched the state police car pull in and waved them over. He pulled his badge out, held it in the air, and identified himself. The police car pulled up next to him. The officer slowly got out with his gun in hand. He saw a dead body right next to the man showing a badge of some kind.

"FBI," Mitch yelled out, "Stay down, shooters in the motor home." The state police officer bent down and went to the front of his car, pointing his gun toward the motor home.

Perry Bartlett peeked out the window again and saw the state police car pull in. He saw him join forces with the man who shot Billy. At the time, he hoped the person was a police officer, and now seeing him with the state cop, confirmed it. Perry opened the window and screamed out, "There are no convicts left in here. We are all kidnap victims."

"Everyone, come out of there with your hands up, one at a time," Mitch yelled back.

"OK, don't shoot," Perry answered, then looked at the rest of the prisoners and said, "I think it's all over. It looks like we've been rescued."

Elaine stood up, her legs wobbly and threw her arms around Perry. Mike and Becky breathed deeply and smiled at each other. Kelly just sat there, not believing it was over.

"Come on young lady, it's all right. It is all over. The police want us to come outside," Perry said as he reached down to help her up. Kelly looked at him with unbelieving eyes and just sat there.

"Come on, no one's going to hurt you," Perry coaxed. Kelly looked at the gun still in Perry's hand, "Oh yeah, I won't need this." He threw the magnum on the bed and helped Kelly get to her feet. Kelly looked around and everyone was smiling at her. They all made their way to the front of the motor home.

Kelly looked down and saw Jesse. His eyes were still open. He had a shocked look on his face. She looked at the mass amount of blood and stepped over it. Her eyes looked back at Jesse's face. He seemed to be looking at her. Her legs felt weak as she walked down the stairs still staring at Jesse. She seemed to smile back at him.

Pauly had finally fallen to the ground. He looked back and could barely make out the lights of the rest stop. It had gotten dark so fast. He felt wet and thought it was sweat. His shoulder began to hurt. He reached back to feel his wound and came back with a hand full of blood. He looked and saw he was covered with blood. He looked around for a place to hide but he could only see a short distance in the dark. He felt cold and began to shiver. It was the first time the thought of dying had entered his mind. He really didn't care if he did; he felt he had nothing to live for. He would be doing a favor for the people he loved. He began to cry, not for himself but for Dustin. He would grow up without a father. Once he thought about dying, it escalated from a thought to a fact. He was going to die; he was ready to accept it; almost craved it.

The pain grew more intense in his shoulder and seemed to creep down his whole side. He grew colder and the shivering became worse. He looked up and saw the silhouette of a helicopter; its searchlight illuminated the darkness. It was more than a hundred yards away. He decided right then he wanted to live and tried to get up, to show himself, but to no avail. His strength had left him. He was happy that they flew by without seeing him. The only thing he would be living for was the electric chair. He closed his eyes and the cold went away. He thought of Patty and Dustin.

Bobby drove out of the rest stop heading north on I-15, until he came to the first exit, where he pulled off. He got back on the highway going south. He and Charlene both looked over at the rest stop as they passed it.

"You think they'll be all right?" Charlene asked as they went by, barely able to see the motor home.

"Oh yeah, they'll do just fine. Pauly's as smart as I am and he'll take control. Shit, they ain't got anyone chasing them. We left them with five grand, they might even get lucky and pull off another big score like we did with that sand nigger," Bobby answered trying to somehow justify what he did. Not as much for Charlene as for himself.

He knew he had done the guys wrong. On the other hand, he kept telling himself, he did what he had to do. He even admitted to himself that Pauly might hate him for what he did, yet Pauly would understand it.

"It's only Jesse I'm worried about. Will Pauly take care of him, you think?" Charlene asked, wanting Bobby to know that she was not concerned about Billy.

"Sure, Pauly's just that way. Jesse will be all right, they'll all be all right. They are as well off as we are. We're not out of the woods yet. In reality, I'm sure the police want me more than any of them, so maybe I did them a favor," Bobby said as he looked over at Charlene.

The last of the day's light was sinking to the west and seemed to make Charlene's face stand out like a 3D picture of beauty.

"It's you I'm worried about lady. I'm not so sure I did you any favors taking you with me."

"Shit, if you would have left me, I would have hunted you down like a dog and cut your balls off," Charlene answered with a smile.

"Really? You really mean it. I mean, I didn't ask you or anything. I was hoping you would go with me, but I wasn't sure."

"I don't know when or even how, but somewhere along the line I don't know if I should tell you this or not, but I'm going to...Nah, I ain't either, just, I'm real glad you took me with you."

"No, go ahead tell me what you were going to say," Bobby begged, hoping it was what he thought she was about to say.

"No, it is stupid, you'd think it was dumb," Charlene answered, really wanting to tell him. Not that she totally believed it, but just to see his reaction.

"I won't think it's stupid, come on tell me, what you were going to say?"

"If you laugh, I'll be pissed."

"I'm not going to laugh."

"Well, somewhere along the line I fell in love with you. There, I said it, now didn't it sound stupid?" Charlene said watching Bobby's reaction. His eyes lit up, a smile came on his face.

This girl had a way of making Bobby feel like a high school kid. She had done it to him more than once. He felt warmth come over him as he just kept looking at her not realizing he was smiling.

"You just going to sit there with that smile on your face, or are you going to say something? You see, I told you you'd think it was stupid."

"No, lady, it's not that at all. In fact, that's what I was hoping you were going to say, because I'm in the same boat."

"Huh," Charlene said under her breath getting a better reaction than she could imagine.

"It just happened to me a half hour ago. You remember when I told you to go get this car?" Bobby asked, not waiting for an answer, "Well, you didn't ask any questions. You didn't think about it twice and you've been that way since the word go. You're just a one of a kind lady. Anyway, now I feel stupid because I fell in love right then, and I knew I wanted you to go with me. So there, now you can laugh at me."

"This is crazy. The only laughing I want to do is because, oh fuck it, I love you," Charlene said as she moved to Bobby and kissed him on the lips. Her tongue slid inside his mouth and they kissed going down the highway at 65 miles an hour. Her hand went between his legs and she began to rub softly. He had to pull away to see where he was driving. She continued to rub.

"Let's stop and make love right now," Charlene said, having an urge she could not remember ever having before.

"Not yet baby. I'd really love to, but when we do, I don't want it to be like the first. I want it to be beautiful."

Charlene ran her hand up Bobby's belly until she felt the money belt, the fact there was $40,000 under her hand excited her more than any man ever did, but being the diplomat she was, she thought she should make Bobby feel good about something that she just realized had been bothering him.

"The first time, whether you believe it or not, was beautiful. I never had someone crave me like you did. Someone lose all their control over me, as you did when we got together. I remember those few moments with you, yet I don't remember any with Billy. Your desire for me turned me on, and my desire for you has been growing ever since. Whether you know it or not, the way our first time came down was perfect," Charlene said in a soft voice while her hand rubbed all around the money belt.

She did it again, Bobby thought. She made me feel good without even knowing what she was doing. "Thanks, lady. That really makes me feel good. Hey, you ever seen forty thousand bucks? Go ahead, take the belt off, and look. Half of that money is yours."

"No, you're lying. Really twenty thousand is mine. You mean it?" Charlene asked, totally surprised that Bobby would offer her half. She never thought she deserved half.

"Sure I mean it. You and me are partners, ain't we? That's how partners work. Split down the middle. Besides, you're the one that got the people that had the money belt. Sure thing, half of it's yours, I ain't lying," Bobby said as he leaned forward so Charlene could get the belt off.

Bobby watched as Charlene opened up a zipper and pulled a stack of bills out. Her eyes grew big, her mouth came open. She put the bills to her nose and smelled it. "Take ten of those and put 'em in your pocket. Can't have you running around without pocket change."

"Oh Bobby, no one's ever treated me like you do," Charlene said as she counted out ten bills, knowing it was really eleven and put them in her pocket.

"This is just the beginning, babe. Life is going to be sweet from this point on," Bobby spoke out as his hand went to her leg and began to rub. She put her hand on top of his.

"What are we going to do about the guy in the trunk? I've been meaning to ask you. How come we even took him with us?"

"You really haven't figured that out yet, huh?" Bobby answered the questions with a question. Charlene looked at him and shook her head.

"Well, did you notice how much the guy resembles me?" Bobby could see Charlene starting to think. She didn't say anything because she hadn't noticed a resemblance. However, so what, it still did not make any sense why they had to bring the guy along. "Well, I plan to become that guy in the trunk. And, since we didn't leave him and nobody knows he's missing, should we get pulled over or anything—well, I'll have ID, and a car that I own. Which reminds me, check the glove box for a registration or something, would ya," Bobby asked as Charlene snapped up all at once that Bobby was a pretty smart dude. The guy was always thinking. Maybe she really did love him.

"Yeah, here's the registration," Charlene said showing it to Bobby.

"What's the guy's name on it?" Bobby asked as he reached in his back pocket and took out the guy's wallet.

"His name is James Rushton, lives in Barstow," Charlene said as she looked in the glove box for anything of value.

"Look in his wallet, see if it's the same guy," Bobby said as he handed the wallet to Charlene. She reached right in and took out the driver's license.

"Yep, same name. James E. Ruston, 3452 Violet Ave., #12, Barstow, California," Charlene said as she studied the photo on the license. Aside from the glasses, the person did rather resemble Bobby.

"Great. I was hoping the car was in his name. As far as what we're going to do with him," Bobby said, but lowered his voice, in case Jim could hear from the trunk, "We got to get rid of him. We'll wait until we cross the California border, then find some road leading into the desert, and dump him."

"Are we going to kill him?" Charlene asked wanting to impress Bobby, making sure she emphasized we to let him know she was with him, whatever he decided.

"I really don't want to, but I really can't see where I got much choice," Bobby answered, liking the way Charlene said we, "But we can't have the guy running around telling the cops what we're driving, can we?"

"No, don't suppose we can," was all Charlene answered, like the killing of a person was the same as deciding what to order from a menu.

Jim Rushton was trying to make out what the people were saying up front, but there was too much road noise. He was having hard time breathing but was sure it was just his imagination. He wondered how long it would be before they let him out. He wondered what Bobby was going to do with all the people. He felt them pull off the highway right after they left the rest stop, make a left, then another left and back on the freeway. He knew they were now going south on I-15.

The thoughts of these people killing him entered his head. He remembered the article he read about them. They already killed three people, what was one more? He felt safer having the other people in the motor home he thought was following him. Even these people would not kill five people in cold blood.

"If we didn't have the guy in the trunk, we'd stop and do some gambling right over there," Bobby said as they drove past Whiskey Pete's, "Maybe get us a bite to eat, you getting hungry?"

"A little, but I'm fine. I think it would be best if we just kept moving for a while," Charlene answered wisely.

"See that sign, lady? What does it say?"

"California!" Charlene said as she reached over and gave Bobby a kiss on the cheek, then put her arm around him and moved real close, "Where we heading, Bobby?"

"The way I figure, darling, the cops are going to be looking for us every place but where we've been. By now, they found out we were the ones that done in the gas station attendant in Baker. And the cops probably think we kept going south on the freeway. Well, in about an hour we will be driving right by Baker again, going north taking our time. Make sense so far?" He asked.

"I'm following ya," Charlene replied wanting to know the final destination.

"Well, we just keep going exactly the same way back, as we took to get here. All the way to Oregon," Bobby was saying as he saw a shocked look come over Charlene's face.

"Oregon," Charlene answered very surprised, "We can't go to Oregon, can we? I mean talk about going someplace where we have to be hot!"

"That's the whole point, darling. It would be so hot it'll be the last place they look for us. By now, the cops have figured I ain't no fool. So we reverse it on them and do something they would think is foolish. Driving crazy or even going over the speed limit would be stupid, which I don't plan to do. We are just Mr. and Mrs. Joe America going up I-5 through Oregon. You're not hot unless you make yourself hot, and we are in the last place they would think of looking. Make sense?"

"Oh Bobby, you're the smartest man I ever met. Yes, it all makes sense," Charlene answered giving Bobby a kiss on the neck.

Bobby took it all in, believing what Charlene just said. These cops were not going to get a chance to figure out how Bobby Smallwood was thinking. He'd always be a step ahead of them. Charlene was right. He was the smartest man he ever knew.

"What's that up ahead?" Bobby asked, seeing what looked like an old road.

"Looks like an old road going nowhere," Charlene replied.

"That's just what I'm looking for," Bobby said as he looked in the rear view mirror. A car was coming up behind him, so he slowed down to let the car pass. He pulled off the road. There were no street signs. He saw a sign a hundred feet down the road. He drove closer and read: *Private Property. No Trespassing*. He kept going. The road was old and bumpy so they drove slowly. The road seemed to keep going and it was not long before they lost all sight of the freeway. There was nothing to be seen except a dark desert. No signs. No lights. Bobby looked in the mirror. No lights from the freeway.

"This will do just fine."

Charlene was not sure what Bobby meant when he said this would do just fine. Did he mean to make love to her? She hoped so. Or was this the place Bobby planned to get rid of the guy in the trunk. Then she thought why not do both.

Bobby grabbed his shotgun and the habit to pop it open any time he planned to use it happened. The shells were still there. He took the keys from the ignition and handed them to Charlene.

"Here babe, you go open the trunk. Be cool, we don't want another Jack-in-the-box to come out breaking heads, know what I mean," Bobby said as he hit his door and went around to the back of the car. He stood 5 feet from the trunk as Charlene put the key in the lock. She stood back as far as she could and turned the key. The trunk popped open as she jumped back.

"Come on out of there, friend," Bobby said as Jim whose eyes were adjusted to the dark could make out the guy and the girl perfectly. He saw the shotgun pointed at him, plain as day. He did not see the motor home he had hoped would be following them.

"We're not going to hurt you, or you'd already be dead," Bobby said in the kindest voice he could muster up. It gave Jim a sense of relief. It made sense that he would be dead if they wanted him to be. He climbed out of the trunk.

"Now listen, buddy, we're going to be leaving you out here in this desert. We want you to wait an hour before you start walking back to the highway. It's right straight behind us about two or three miles. By the time you get there, we'll be long gone, so feel free to tell the police anything you want. That is the best we can do. We got to take your clothes too, so start peeling them off," Bobby said.

Most of it made good sense to Jim, but taking his clothes, that was another thing. "It's colder than shit out here friend, why you want to take my clothes?" Jim asked.

"Hey, it's not as cold as being dead, so just do it, would ya," Bobby replied, his voice sounding a little meaner.

"Yeah, OK, OK. Just don't see why you have to take my clothes," Jim said as he saw there was no use in arguing with the guy, and leaned back against the car to take his shoes off.

"You're going to let me keep my shoes, right?" Jim asked with all hope.

"Buddy, you better start understanding this ain't no picnic. Yes, we're taking your shoes to slow you down, so the best thing you can say from this point on is nothing. Understand?"

It was right then that Jim really understood this was not a game. They were going to let him live and he just found out this guy might have voted against it. "Yes sir. I understand. I won't say another word."

And, Jim did not. In fact, that was the last thing he said in his life. Jim stripped down to his underwear, and looked at Bobby with hopeful eyes.

"Yeah, you can keep your underwear, buddy. Even I'm not that cold," Bobby, said, looking in all directions. He saw nothing. "OK, start walking out there," Bobby said pointing toward the desert.

"Go out about 50 feet and just sit down and start counting. Wait an hour and make your way to the highway," Bobby finished as Jim reached back, grabbed his glasses and put them on.

"Leave those too, buddy," Bobby said referring to the glasses.

Jim just glared back, finally realizing how much he hated this guy. Why would the guy take his glasses? Was it out of sheer meanness? Jim did not say anything, as much as he wanted to. However, he decided right then, he would do everything in his power to help the police catch these people. He placed the glasses on top of his clothes.

"OK, get going," Bobby said.

Jim started walking. He took one last look back at Charlene. How much he would have liked to punch her in her pretty little face. Jim took about three steps and could have sworn he heard the cock of the shotgun. Oh no, he thought. He turned to look just in time to see the last thing in his life--a bright flash.

The shotgun pellets ripped his face apart. He was thrown three feet back. He was dead while he was in the air. Bobby had pulled both triggers. He had nothing against the guy. He hoped for death to come fast and easy for Jim. Bobby was happy with the results.

Charlene was shaking. She'd never seen anyone die before, and so quickly. The guy didn't say anything. He did not even moan. She thought she was shaking because it was cold.

Bobby walked over to the body. There was no doubt the guy was dead. He just wanted to see what both barrels of a shotgun would do to someone's face. The guy was lying on his stomach. He thought it better to pass on taking a look. He was happy Charlene stayed back. He saw blood coming out of the guy's ear and decided not to turn him over. He really didn't want to see. Bobby saw the guy's watch for the first time, bent down, pulled it off his wrist, and put it on his. He took a quick look at the side of the guy's face. It looked like a face a bloody face, he thought. He turned away and walked over to Charlene.

"You okay, Charlene?" he asked, his eyes looking into hers.

"Is he dead?" she asked, almost as if she did not believe what she just saw.

"Oh yeah, he's gone. You sure you're all right?"

"Yeah, hold me, I'm real cold," she said.

Bobby wrapped his arms around her and felt her shivering. Bobby felt reality creep in. This girl was not much older than a kid. He was mad at himself for killing the guy in front of her. He should have walked the guy out a bit. He held her tight trying to ease the shivering.

"Make love to me, Bobby. Make love to me right now," she said looking him right in the eyes.

"Right here, right now?" he asked, not knowing where her desire came from.

"Right here, right now, in the car. Please?" She asked almost begging.

"Sure babe, whatever you want," he answered as he led her to the car. He opened the door and she climbed in the back. He followed her. Passion took over. It was like two animals tearing at each other. They were both naked in a second. Charlene pulled Bobby on top of her and reached for his manhood, inserting it in her in one thrust.

This time Bobby kept control, and for over an hour they took turns mounting each other. At last, they were making love just a few miles south of the Nevada/California border on an old dirt road, three miles west of I-15.

The end of November, another month, over and gone. Ha, look at me, Ha, who am I in this crazy place? Going crazy right on pace! Shit, I don't care everyday's the same. But, it seems today I feel the strain; ha, I'm crazy, or just getting that way! Because, for years, this place I've got to stay.

Making faces, singing a song, as the seconds tick along.

Ha, look out, of I ever again get free, I won't know what I could turn out to be, for sure not me.

But I don't care. I don't care. I don't care about anything... It's been a ball, but the party's over. Time to clean up. Pass me the broom, never mind I'll put it under the rug.

Thank you.

THEIR BODY, MY MIND

Crazy man, crazy, it's all insane
Crazy is part of this domain.
I make visions that can't be true, appear.
Amusing myself is my new career!
The slightest thought can be a clue,
with my mind, I can see any view.
Women of beauty, so debonair
For my lustful thoughts they prepare.
The brain, strong, and easy to persuade,
My soul to be carried from this stockade.
I move to an island in another hemisphere,
to reality, my mind is a mutineer.
My body is theirs to captivate.
But, my mind, they will never penetrate

-Rest Stop- Chapter 14

Tuesday, 11:00 a.m.

FBI Area Director Peter Brooks was listening to Inspector Mitchell Zaga's report in his Las Vegas office. The director had never met or even heard of Mitchell Zaga before Monday when he received a phone call from the Chief of

Police in Baker, California. At first, Peter Brooks wondered who this FBI agent thought he was. He should have known better than to have an outside agency call him with a report. Chief Trevor Haynes explained that Zaga was in hot pursuit and would arrive in Vegas later that evening. What did Inspector Zaga want the FBI to do? The FBI did not do roadblocks. After receiving the call from Chief Haynes, the director called the Portland office for further information. He was advised that Inspector Mitchell Zaga was in charge of a case involving convicts who had escaped from the Oregon Prison System.

It was now Tuesday, 11 a.m. The young FBI agent sat in front of Director Peter Brooks. Zaga was personally responsible for the capture of three convicts and had freed five hostages. In a way Zaga was a hero. A more accurate statement would be to say Zaga truly was a hero.

Zaga had used his gun in the line of duty more than Director Brooks had during his 23-year tenure with the agency. These captured convicts had been responsible for the deaths of four individuals. The director was filled with admiration for Zaga.

"How you holding up, son?" he asked in the middle of Zaga's report, wondering how he was feeling after such an ordeal.

"I don't think it has really hit me yet, Sir. I'm tired and could use some sleep. We stayed out all night looking for Brown. We didn't find him until 8:30 this morning."

"He was dead when you found him?"

"Yes, sir, not very long I'm told. The coroner said his death was due to loss of blood and exposure. It got cold out there last night. I was really hoping we'd find him alive."

Hoping to ease some of the pain, the director said, "Well don't start feeling guilty about it."

"No," Zaga said, "It's not that at all, sir. Of all the convicts, Brown was the most humane. The young girl whose husband was killed, who was raped by Atteberry and Sweazy, told us that Brown defended her on several occasions during the ordeal. Brown was not there at the time of the rape. Had he been there, I'm sure it wouldn't have happened. A prison guard in Oregon said he would have been killed had it not been for Brown. I think Brown was mixed up in something that he never intended to be a part of. Once a guard had been killed and they escaped from prison, well, it was just too late for him to get out of it. What I'm upset about is that I didn't have to shoot Brown. He wasn't armed. What I saw flashing in his hands was a set of keys."

The director said, "Mitch, don't let that bother you son, you did what you were supposed to do. To come face to face with what you thought were four armed convicts who had killed four people and had shot at you--then someone turns on you with something in his hand, well, under the circumstances--you couldn't stop to think whether he was a nice guy or not. All you think about is staying alive. You did what you had to do. The director in Washington called to congratulate you. He said you did a fine and very brave job. What you did was beyond the call of duty. I'm sure there's a commendation in it for you. This will push you up the ladder, son. The whole agency is talking about you." The director said this, hoping it would lift Mitch out of his despondency.

Mitch felt no guilt for his actions. The real reason he was hoping to find Paul Brown alive was to find out where Smallwood was. He had hoped Brown would cut a deal to help find Smallwood, avoiding the death penalty. He deserved a chance anyway. Then again, he wasn't certain that Brown would have given Smallwood up. Convicts had a code of silence that existed only in their own world. In a sense, Mitch admired their code.

Although he wished he'd found Brown alive, he felt no remorse about killing Atteberry. He had no choice. This convict deserved to be dead. In an effort to appear modest, Mitch said, "It happened so fast, I really didn't have much time to think about it." He never gave a thought to the possibility that his bravery might make a promotion inevitable. Ascending the ladder of success did not interest him at all.

"How did you ever guess that they would be at the rest area?" Peter Brooks asked. He admired Zaga's composure.

"The Oregon State Police had a tap on the phone of one of Smallwood's ex-cellmates. A rest stop came up in his conversation with the cellmate and his brother. That, along with the fact they had used a rest stop to do their first kidnapping. Incidentally, I had to use the bathroom myself. When I pulled in and saw the white motor home with a missing gas cap, like I said, the rest just happened so fast."

"So no one knew where Smallwood was going?" The director quizzed.

"No, not really. Quinton's widow, Kelly, provided the best information. More than all the rest of the hostages, this girl wants these convicts apprehended or killed. I can't blame her. She's been through quite an ordeal. Her husband was killed in cold blood and two of these animals raped her. Information received from her along with the other kidnapped victims was most helpful. This is what I have put together.

"Smallwood has $40,000 dollars in cash which was taken from a, um," opening his note book, "A Mike Kudofuzi. Along with the cash, he took a very expensive diamond ring, valued at about $40,000. With him are Charlene Sweazy and the owner of the car which they are now believed to be driving. Therefore, we still have one kidnapped victim that we're aware of. I'm quite worried about his safety. According to Kelly Quinton, this person bears a striking resemblance to Smallwood. Knowing Smallwood as I do, I can well imagine what's going through his mind now. He's going to become that person. This means we have Smallwood out there with a car, false ID and enough money to choke a horse. We're back to square one trying to figure out who the kidnapped victim is. Smallwood won't keep the guy very long. Even now, I fear he's dead. Smallwood still has a sawed off shotgun and a box of shells."

As Mitch reviewed his notes again, the director asked, "Tell me what you're thinking Mitch, which way you think Smallwood is going?"

"Well, one thing about Smallwood, he's not dumb. He's been a step ahead of me all along. I lost a lot of respect for him."

"What do you mean?" The Director interrupted.

"This may sound crazy, but these convicts live by a code of their own. Well, everything I gathered from the witnesses tells me Smallwood double-crossed his so-called brothers. He took off with the money and just left them hanging out to dry. Smallwood, no doubt, was the brains from the beginning, and when he left them cold, the rest were lost. I thank God Smallwood was not there when the shooting came down with that shotgun of his, because I don't think I'd be here now. So that's what I mean by losing respect for him as far as the code goes. On the other hand, it was the smart thing to do. If they'd all kept running together it would have been a lot easier to close in on him. Besides, forty thousand cash had to have something to do with his double-cross.

"Anyway, to answer your question," Mitch went on as Peter Brooks showed his amazement at how well Mitch had got to know Smallwood, "On which way Smallwood is heading, I'd say Mexico. I've already faxed a bulletin and a photo to all ports of entry. Knowing Smallwood, his thinking is that he was heading north when he was last seen; thus, he's going to change his course the first chance he gets. It would not surprise me if he went to the next exit heading south, going right on past the rest stop." The director was impressed.

"Have you got a description of the car?" The director once again interrupted, agreeing with everything Mitch had to say.

"Yes, and I could kick myself in the butt, because I think I blew it there."

"Now what do you mean?" The director asked.

"Well, before I did much thinking about it, my first thought was that he was heading towards Vegas, which I'm sure is where Smallwood wanted to send us. We blocked the highway and all the off roads we had a cars for--but no older, yellow Chevy. No Bobby Smallwood. After about three hours, I snapped. Smallwood was going south."

"How long was it from the time Smallwood left until the ports of entry received the information you sent?" the director asked.

"Enough time that they could have been in Mexico before they received it. I had all the witnesses to question. We were trying to find Brown. It wasn't until about 2 o'clock this morning that I got word to this office to fax the information to ports of entry."

"What's the closest you can come to the time Smallwood left the rest area?"

"That's the funny part about Smallwood; luck has been in his favor from the beginning. He left within ten minutes of my getting there. So he left right around 6:15-6:30. This gave him seven and a half hours to get to Mexico. I know he won't have his kidnapped victim with him, so that would take some time. My biggest fear is he and Charlene Sweazy are already on the other side of the border."

"A person could make the border in six hours, seven tops, from Vegas," the Director replied in a matter-of-fact voice.

"Yeah, I know. It's just that I got a feeling he's still inside the border. It's like, I feel him, almost like I know I am going to come face-to-face with him. Does that sound weird, sir?" Mitch asked, hoping the director would not think he was weird.

The director thought exactly the opposite. It brought back a memory of a bank robber he once chased. "No, I believe in that kind of thing, Mitch. I was once working a bank robbery, five months I was on this case. He started in California and kept on the move working east. He hit Arizona, Texas three times, but always further east. Worked alone, maybe three weeks tops between jobs. Always worked along Interstate 10. So I knew, after the third job in Texas, he would be heading East on I-10. For no reason, other than a feeling, I stopped at a motel in Louisiana, and there, swimming in the swimming pool, was my man. It was just a feeling. Of course, I was not as brave as you are. When he asked how I knew he was there, I said I received a tip. What I'm saying, son, is if you've got a feeling, you have my approval to go with it," Director Brooks answered, happy to see there were still people that believed in their feelings.

"I appreciate that, sir," Mitch answered, thinking the image he first had of the director was different from what he had now.

"One other point I'd like to make, Mitch. When I saw this person in the swimming pool he was by himself, there was no chance he had a gun. The FBI really does not want heroes. I am far from one. Point is, I called for backup and we took the person without any trouble. Your case, I know, you didn't have much choice. But, I won't endorse you if you can call for back up and don't. You're a hero, Mitch, but you're a lucky hero. We don't want heroes period, we want intelligence. Do you get my point?"

"Yes sir, I do, but believe me, I wasn't looking to be a hero. In addition, as much as these people were animals, I took no pleasure in having to kill anybody. That's the part I think hasn't hit me yet," Mitch answered, in all sincerity.

"It will, Mitch, not that I can say so personally, in 23 years with the Bureau, I've never had to kill anyone. I think you'll be able to deal with it, especially in your case, it was them or you. Also, whether we like them or not, you are a hero and we're all real proud of you," Director Brooks said, meaning every word.

"Who's that guy that shot the convict in the motor home?" The director asked, dropping the subject.

Mitch looked down at his notes, "His name is Bartlett. Perry Bartlett. He's the one who owned the motor home. Ex-Vietnam vet. Put a hole in Jesse Sweazy you could drive a truck through, used a .44 Magnum. The convicts picked the wrong guy to mess around with."

"How's he holding up?" The director asked.

"Fine, felt he had to protect himself and his wife once the shooting started. I put them and the other victims up in the Dunes at our expense. Hope that was alright, thought we might need to talk to them some more."

"No problem with that, in fact, that was good thinking. Who's this guy that carries around $40,000 in cash?" The director asked, wondering how anybody could have that much cash legally.

"We ran a check on him. His folks are big money and oil in the Middle East. The girl with him, ahh," again, Mitch checked out his notes, "A Becky Ford, from Ontario, California, she's just with the guy for the ride. Turned out more than she hoped for, I'm sure. This Kudofuzi person wasn't even bothered about the money. Must be nice to have rich folks."

Before Peter Brooks could answer Mitch about having rich folks, a call came across his intercom.

"A call for you, Mr. Brooks, long distance, California Highway Patrol," a sweet voice said across the intercom.

"Put it through. Thank you, Cari. This might concern you, Mitch," the director said and pushed a button so the call would be on the intercom, "Hello."

"Yes, hello. This is Captain Norm Hunter, California Highway Patrol, who am I speaking to, please?"

"Hello, Captain. This is FBI Director Peter Brooks. How can I be of assistance?"

"We have a memo to contact either you or Inspector Mitchell Zaga regarding either an old yellow Chevrolet or any deaths involving a shotgun."

"Yes, Captain Hunter, Mitchell Zaga is sitting right here. Do you have something for us?"

"We don't have a Yellow Chevrolet, but what we do have is pretty scary. About six miles from the Nevada border on an old dirt road a farmer found the body of a man whose face was almost gone. When I got there, it did not take long to see that only a shotgun could do such a job. That was about an hour ago--took me that long to hear about the memo. Is this the work of our convict friends?" Captain Hunter asked.

The director looked over at Mitch, who was nodding his head with a sad expression on his face. "Yes, I'm afraid so," the director answered back.

"I heard something about you guys nailing the rest of them at a rest stop down by Vegas," the captain replied.

"Well, we got three out of four of them, and you just told me which way the fourth one is going. What's happening down there as far as trying to locate an older Yellow Chevy?" the director asked.

"Oh you better believe we have everyone working on this one. This is the fourth death these assholes are responsible for in California. We'll find him."

"Captain, Mitch Zaga here, any luck on finding any ID on the body?"

"No, the guy was stripped clean. All he had on was his underwear."

Mitch guessed as much. "Get his prints alright?" he asked.

"Yes, sir, already done, got them on the way to Washington, and we're running them in California right now. We should have an answer within minutes, thought I should confer with you while we are doing that."

"Our fault up here, Captain, we had our man running north so we concentrated on that. We should have made sure and put some more information your way. You guys might have bagged him. We just didn't figure him heading south," the director said, taking the blame, which made Mitch admire him more.

"What else do you have that will help us down here?" Captain Hunter asked in a somewhat bitter voice, thinking, these FBI people try to do everyone's thinking.

"Well, he's with a girl, 19 years old, long blonde hair, you already know he packs a sawed off shotgun, and they don't get much more dangerous than what you find in Robert Smallwood. You guys have a description of him, don't you?" The director asked.

Suddenly the director did not like the captain's tone of voice, "Yes, we do. I wish our communications were better. We got the word it ended down here last night and it took us off guard. You guys have a license number on this Chevy he's driving?" Captain Hunter asked, trying to sound professional. He had always disliked the FBI.

"No, sure don't, Captain, older yellow Chevrolet, '75-'80--Impala, Bel Air, we're just not sure--other than we know it's a Chevy, and yellow, and older. I imagine you figured out that Smallwood will be using the dead man's ID," Mitch said from across the desk into the speaker box.

"I think Smallwood picked a guy that resembles him quite a bit. As soon as you find out who the dead man is, you'll know what name he's traveling under. Another thing, Captain, Smallwood is no dummy, and I'm finding he plans ahead. He probably figured on us finding the body. Then, when we see that he is going south, he figures that we figure he is going to Mexico. Chances are he may be. If he was, good chance he could already be there. However, I've been working this person since day one and I have a feeling he may be going north. It's just a feeling, nothing to base it on."

"We're ahead of your feelings. We have the whole state on the lookout. However, even if he was going north, he could be out of the State by now. We figure the guy was killed between six p.m. and eight p.m. last night, which gives Smallwood at least a fifteen-hour jump. He could make the Oregon border in fifteen hours. Hang on a second, we just received the information on the dead man. Yes, we have him. His name is Jim Rushton, he is 180 pounds, blond hair, wears glasses. Lives in Barstow, California. Wait just another second, yes we have his car. 1980 Chevrolet Caprice, license number, 1AYJ782, CA plates. I've got to get this out; I'll keep you up-dated," the captain said in an excited voice. That was the one thing they all had in common, they all wanted Smallwood. Captain Hunter hung up.

"Sir, you said you would let me play my feelings," Mitch said in a wishful way.

"Sure, son, what are you feeling?" the director responded.

"Smallwood is heading to Oregon, I think I even know where," Mitch answered, biting his lip, the feeling was getting stronger.

"Where's that?" the director asked curiously.

"Albany, Oregon. Smallwood has an ex-celly friend I feel he is real close to. The one I told you about who referred to a rest stop on one of his phone calls."

"Yes, so what about it?" The director asked, trying to see how this young person got his feelings.

"I don't know, sir, it's like I said, just a feeling. For some reason, this friend of Smallwood's was in on the plan in some way. Maybe it was something they used to talk about when they were cellmates. I just feel Smallwood is feeling good about himself and feeling safe. Maybe he just wants to brag to his friend. Show the money off, the big diamond ring. Maybe Smallwood doesn't want to travel without a partner of some kind."

"You keep saying that Smallwood isn't a dummy, that wouldn't be too bright of him going back to Oregon where he's hot, would it?" The director said.

"That's why it is bright, sir. It's so dumb he figures it will be the last place we'd be looking for him. Along with the fact that he feels safe, he has what he thinks is a good ID. Like I said, it's just a feeling."

"Go with your feelings then, Mitch. We haven't got much more to go on right now. You'd better get some sleep first, though," the Director said, feeling strongly about Mitch and his feelings, "I'll get you a flight for tonight to Portland. Also, just in case your feelings aren't right, we need to send Idaho, Utah, even Washington, an alert."

"Yes, sir, I learned my lesson last night about risking everything on one endeavor. Ahh, if it's all right with you, could you book me on the next flight to Portland. I'd rather leave right away. I can sleep on the plane. I don't think I'd sleep too well here anyway."

"All right, Mitch, if that is what you want," Director Brooks said, really admiring the young man. He remembered when he had that kind of drive.

Tuesday, 3:14 p.m.

Ken Rocmel's day was going fine. He had already put out one car, and had another deal in the box. He decided to leave as soon as the deal was closed. He would be home by five to watch the news and have dinner with Malarie and Dane.

Ken hated thinking about Bobby. He loved him like a brother, but how could Bobby fuck up so bad? So close to hitting the streets. He planned to get Bobby a job as a mechanic at the dealership. He would have let Bobby stay with him and his family. Ken already knew a sweet girl to fix Bobby up with. He felt he owed Bobby. This would be his way of paying him back.

Bobby had saved Ken from getting a shiv in the back over a gambling debt that was owed to him. The guy who owed Ken couldn't pay his debt. He tried to do Ken in before Ken did it to him. Ken had no idea the guy was creeping up on him--was within inches of sticking six inches of steel into his back--when Bobby stopped the guy with a blow to the head that sent him to the hospital with a concussion. The person went straight from the hospital to protective custody. Point was, Bobby saved Ken's life. Ken would never forget it.

Now Ken would never have the chance to repay his debt. He knew they would get Bobby. It was just a matter of time. The last he heard was that Bobby and crew had been responsible for the death of a gas station attendant. Ken didn't even think about the fact that he had paid Bobby back a hundred times.

Bobby had no one on the street and Ken took care of him. Ken had the gambling concessions locked up in the joint. Even though he was in prison, he was making over $3,000 a month plus all the cigarettes he, Bobby, and everyone in his clique could smoke. Ken furnished all the candy, pastries, stamps--stuff they called zoo-zoos and wam-wams. Drugs that Ken took in trade for debts went to Bobby, except for some of the weed Ken would smoke. Bobby would turn some of the drugs to cash and give that to Ken, but most of it he used himself. Ken did not mind.

Ken and Bobby would play pinochle or dominoes. Two or three hours a day, they'd do push-ups. Ken was in the best shape of his life while he did time. He ate right and did more exercise than he could ever remember. Ken had his own softball team in the joint, with all the best players. His team was number one. He played handball with the best of them. Ken was Activities Director for the convicts and, as all the cons said, had it made. His only job was to clean a closet. Ken had said many times that, if there were women in the joint, he would have stayed. He felt, out of 2000 convicts, not one of them had it as good. Being Activities Director gave him privileges no one else had. He could go play pool or ping-pong anytime he got the urge; pretty much he was allowed to come and go as he liked.

Even the guards liked Ken. They knew he was behind many of the things that went down but they left him alone because he didn't rock the boat. In fact, when there was trouble brewing between the cons, Rocmel was known to patch things up before they got out of hand.

Ken Rocmel went to prison for kidnap and robbery. He and Dee Dee, the girl he was living with, had kidnapped the bank president's wife and held her for ransom. They were both caught within minutes after the delivery of the money. Ken and Dee Dee were in love with each other, more than either really knew at the time. However, one thing prison does is separate people from love. Time had a way of killing their love. One of Ken's biggest regrets in life was ruining Dee Dee's life. Dee Dee had gotten out a year before Ken and they lost track of each other. Ken got out and met Malarie, who brought instant love.

Prison also has a way of teaching if one wants to learn. Moreover, Ken felt it was one of the best things that ever happened to him. One thing prison offers is a lot of time, how you use the time makes all the difference. Ken used it wisely. He went to college, wrote thousands of poems, learned to play the guitar, but the best thing he did was get to know himself. Time gave him that opportunity.

He learned while in prison the true values of life--that the things he missed the most were the things he had always taken for granted--simple things like using the bathroom by himself and taking a shower without a hundred other people, opening up the refrigerator, turning on his own TV.

And Freedom: The importance of freedom, how beautiful a thing freedom is, how he took it for granted, until he no longer had it.

Ken remembered reading stories about Vietnam POWs and the hell they went through. It was a thousand times worse than he had it, yet they had done nothing wrong. They had done what the country asked them to do. To Ken, those were true heroes. They knew the value of freedom.

The one lesson Ken would leave prison with and never forget: he would never gamble with freedom again. He had Malarie and the baby now; they were life's true values. They were what he had been searching for. He had found true peace.

Ken was sad for Bobby. He would never have the chance to find true peace unless it came with death. They were going to kill him or Bobby would kill himself. Ken could see what was going to happen to Bobby. Ken just could not figure out why.

He had tried to get through to Bobby, in every way, to no avail. Ken's last hope was showing Bobby what he could have without needing to rob, steal or cheat--to use his energy doing something legal. It was too late now. Ken's last chance to help Bobby was gone.

"Hi, darling, what'cha doing?" Ken said into the phone.

"Hello, we just got back from shopping. Wait 'til you see the cute little outfit I just got Dane," Malarie answered.

"That's good. Hey, guess what? I just closed my second deal of the day, good commissions too. I'm thinking about coming home early, you have anything for dinner?"

"Sure, told you I just went shopping. I thought you had to work until nine tonight," Malarie answered in her ever pleasant sweet voice.

"When you're top salesman, you get to pick your own hours," Ken answered egotistically. That was one thing that Ken didn't leave in prison, a real strong ego.

"Well good, I'm glad, and what would my top salesman like to eat, chicken fried steak or pork chops?" Malarie said in a way that made Ken laugh. She had a way of letting him see his ego.

"Surprise me, darling. See you in about a half an hour."

"OK, I'll surprise you. Oh, you heard any more about Bobby?" Malarie asked, she knew how much it was bothering Ken.

"No, that's another reason I want to come home, so I can catch the news. See you in a bit Babe, love ya."

"Love you too, bye," Malarie ended throwing a kiss into the phone. She had never thought one way or another about Ken being an ex-con, and never asked any questions about why or how. Ken would speak about it when he felt like it, and she would listen. It was not an ex-con she fell in love with, it was Ken Rocmel.

Ken wanted her to get on Bobby's visiting list so they could all visit Bobby together. She had grown quite fond of Bobby, being the kind of person she was, she never saw an axe-murderer, she just saw Bobby Smallwood. He was polite, always showed her respect and could be quite funny. Bobby had made them all beautiful things in the leather shop. But one piece, a leather picture of two eagles sharing a kill, hung over their fireplace. It was a beautiful work of art. Malarie wondered how anyone who could make something so beautiful could be a murderer.

Malarie went into the kitchen and, deciding on the pork chops, pulled them out of the fridge. They were almost cooked when Ken came through the door. He went right to the TV and turned it on. Walking over to the playpen, he picked Dane up and went into the kitchen. He looked at the clock and saw it was five minutes to five.

"Hi there," Ken said as he went to Malarie and gave her a quick kiss, "Oh, pork chops, what a surprise."

"Rice-A-Roni, and corn too, a regular gourmet meal," Malarie answered, "You see Dane's new outfit? It's on the couch."

"No, come on, buddy, let's go see your new outfit," Ken answered as if he was excited to see it. Malarie was funny about stuff like that. Ken would act excited to please her. He picked it up and saw the price tag--$31.00. Ken remembered buying a suit for him for $50.00.

"Oh yeah, it's real cute," was all that he said. He really didn't mind. He loved nothing more in life than his kid, not even Malarie.

"You want to eat in the living room?" Malarie yelled out.

"Yes, please. The news is about to start."

"Top news tonight, three escaped Oregon convicts killed at a rest area in Nevada, five hostages freed. A fire in Beaverton takes the lives of a mother and two children. These stories and more, tonight on News at Five."

Malarie heard what was said as she was bringing Ken's dinner. She looked at Ken and saw an expression she had never seen on his face before. She herself, was in shock, and almost dropped the plate from her hand.

"No, fuck, no!" Ken yelled as he slammed down his fist on the couch. Ken never swore in front of Malarie. The TV was introducing the weather and sports broadcasters, then went to a commercial. Ken stood up and handed Dane to Malarie as she laid the plate down. Ken had just lost his appetite.

"Honey, calm down, there's nothing you can do," Malarie said.

"I can't believe he did it. That rest stop thing, that was my idea," Ken said in an irate voice, almost under his breath.

"What was, what are you talking about, Ken?"

"Nothing, tell you later," Ken said, as he stood right in front of the TV.

"The manhunt for four convicts who escaped from an Oregon State Prison facility on Saturday--killing a prison guard in their escape and also responsible for the deaths of at least three other people in California--ended in the death of three of the convicts last evening. The event occurred at a rest stop on I-15 just south of Las Vegas.

Five hostages were freed unharmed. One of the hostages, a Perry Bartlett from Billings, Montana was responsible for the killing of one of the convicts. A single FBI agent killed the other two convicts. A fourth convict, the known leader of the pack, was not present at the time of the shooting. There is a nationwide manhunt on to find Robert Smallwood, convicted of an axe-murder in Eugene eight years ago.

The dead convicts were listed as Jesse Sweazy, William Atteberry and Paul Brown. The convicts are tied to the murder of a newlywed man from Seattle, Washington; a truck driver father of three children from Fife, Washington; a prison guard from Salem, Oregon, father of a newly born baby; and a gas station attendant from Baker, California. All of these victims were apparently killed in cold blood.

There are unconfirmed reports that one of the kidnap victims had a large sum of money with which Robert Smallwood absconded.

It has been confirmed that Smallwood is traveling with Charlene Sweazy, a 19-year old woman who aided in the prison escape.

Smallwood is described as 37 years old, blond hair, muscular build, with tattoos covering most of his body. Sweazy is 19 years old, 5 ft. 5 in. tall with long blond hair. They are both heavily armed and considered extremely dangerous. It is believed that Smallwood is responsible for the death of all the innocent victims. An all points bulletin has been issued in six western states. Police authorities believe that the pair is likely to head for the Mexican border. They fear that Smallwood might have made it to the border before the alert went out.

The trucking company for whom the dead truck driver worked has agreed to pay a $10,000 reward to Perry Bartlett for his heroism. The company offered an additional $10,000 reward for information leading to the capture of Robert Smallwood. The FBI at this point declines to disclose the identity of the agent who killed the two convicts. Little information has been made available about the five hostages who were held inside a motor home, other than that they are safe.

Unconfirmed reports say that the wife of the newly married man is safe but that she had been brutally raped.

Anyone who sees or knows the whereabouts of Smallwood and Sweazy is asked to call their local police authority immediately.

A fatal fire broke out in Beaverton, today..." Click. Ken turned off the TV walked to the couch and sat down.

"Oh Bobby, Bobby, Bobby," Ken spoke into his hands as he rubbed his face.

"Honey, you all right," Malarie said as she walked over and put her arms around him.

"Oh, it's sad, babe, just real sad. Jesse, Pauly, and Billy are dead. It's only a matter of time before they get Bobby. It's just sad that it had to end this way. Yet, when I hear of four people being killed, a couple of them with kids, the rape of that poor girl whose husband had been killed, it was what they deserved. It's sad that any of this had to happen. It just doesn't make sense. All of them would have been released within months. Why did this have to happen? Why?"

Malarie had never seen Ken so heartbroken before. She squeezed him as she gazed at a beautiful art piece that seemed to bring some relief from the pain.

Seventy miles to the south, Bobby and Charlene were driving north on I-5 in the 1980 yellow Caprice. Having heard the news, Bobby turned off the radio. Charlene was crying.

"Oh Bobby, Jesse is dead, they killed my brother, the motherfuckers killed my brother!"

"Easy, lady, easy. Fuck, I can't believe it. What could have gone wrong? How did the Feds find them? I knew that asshole who owned the motor home was the hero type. Damn it. Fucking damn it. Oh lady, I never figured this would happen," Bobby said most sympathetically. It came from the heart.

"Bobby, I got to call my mom. She'll be going crazy by now," Charlene said with tears streaming down her cheeks.

"Okay, but not just yet," Bobby said with deep understanding of her sadness. He couldn't have her make that call now. He needed time to think.

They'd driven continuously, stopping only for food and gas. They'd made love for over an hour, while the body of Jim Rushton lay about twenty feet away.

Luck still seemed to be with Bobby. He'd left the rest stop minutes before Mitch Zaga arrived. He'd encountered no roadblocks or Highway Patrol cars. The state of California was on alert for them. The authorities had given a vivid description of the couple.

Bobby thought how successful he had been. He was regretful that the guys had been killed. He reasoned that, had he remained with them, he too would have been killed. This rationalization gave him some comfort. He had done what he had to do for his own survival. He loved Pauly as much as a man could love another man. The Wizard was the only other man to whom he had been closer. By traveling north instead of going south he felt he had outsmarted the police again.

Charlene was still crying. Bobby wanted to ease her pain, but how could he? According to the news, a single FBI agent had killed two of the convicts. He wondered which two. The news report had said nothing about a body being found or about the vehicle they were driving. He felt safe driving the Caprice with his fake ID. They had been careful not to exceed the speed limit.

Bobby's goal was to get to Canada, but he had to make one important stop first. He had to stop to see The Wizard. Kenny Rocmel would be very happy when he showed up with the $40,000 and a diamond ring big enough to choke a horse. Maybe he would give the Wizard a couple grand. After all, the rest stop idea was all his. He might stay with Ken and Malarie a few days while things cooled down. He knew Kenny would do anything for him. He had saved his life.

Bobby decided it might be best to allow Charlene to cry away her pain. He wished that he could weep for the boys, but he couldn't. She'll be all right, he thought, when we get to The Wizard's place.

Time is not all it seems, for tomorrow comes in the form of yesterday. Time slowly turning years into long lasting days. Reminiscing seems to be a big past time lately.

RESCUE ME

Wind of night, through long day flight
And secrets you never tell
Come forth and say, you'll blow me away
From this piece of hell
Remove the chain, of yesterday's strain
Pain I can't ignore
Pains time inflict, as bars restrict
Feelings I can't restore
A living tomb of endless doom
And me with no excuse
To gamble free, on a little spree
Now, memories seduce
I played the game, no one to blame
For a crazy plight
But, mighty wind, once my friend
Rescue me, White Knight.

-Rest Stop- Chapter 15

Tuesday, 4:15 p.m.

FBI Inspector Mitchell Zaga arrived at the Portland airport at 4:15 p.m. He'd slept so soundly on the plane the flight attendant had to wake him up. He'd slept little more than an hour of the last forty-eight. He thanked the flight attendant and retrieved his overnight bag from the storage area.

Lt. Camode had been waiting twenty minutes for the flight to arrive. When Zaga first interviewed him he felt it was a waste of time. He was also envious. Ten years earlier he'd been rejected when he tried to join the Feds. What could this young person do that he couldn't do?

Now the lieutenant was awaiting the arrival of a hero. In his view, Zaga was responsible for the deaths of three convicts and the release of five hostages. He never would have guessed that the guy who had interviewed him could possibly have such esteemed ability.

"Inspector Zaga," said the lieutenant as he reached out his hand to Zaga. Mitch knew that he would be met at the airport by someone from the Oregon State Police but had no idea that it would be someone that he knew.

"Lt. Camode, remember?" Mitch remembered immediately. It was a difficult name to forget.

"Hello Lieutenant, how are you? I knew someone from your department would be picking me up but I didn't know it would be you," Mitch was happy it was someone he had met before. He remembered that the lieutenant was gung-ho about catching the convicts.

"Just fine Inspector, thanks. Hey, we all heard what you did down in Nevada. That was really something, Inspector."

"Mitch, call me Mitch," he said, surprised that the news had spread so fast.

"OK, you got a deal if you call me Harold," the lieutenant replied.

"The reason I'm here to pick you up is that I was asked to do so. I feel the only reason that you should be here is because you must think Smallwood is coming this way, is that right, Mitch?"

"Think, is right, Harold. That's the only reason I'm here. Has he been seen or do you have any other information about him?" Mitch asked.

"I haven't checked in during the last hour but there was nothing before that. It's as if Smallwood and the old yellow Chevy have disappeared. I'd say that he's headed north, and that he's switched cars by now," Harold said as they left the airport, "Do you have any bags Mitch?"

"Only what I'm carrying."

"Good, I'm parked right out front. It pays sometimes to have a state license plate on your car. What do you want to do first?" Harold asked as he unlocked the door on the passenger side for Mitch.

"Well, I'd say first, get on your radio and see if anything has happened during the last half hour. For some reason, I believe Smallwood's still driving the old yellow Chevy. I made sure this time that the news media didn't know what car they were driving. I made that mistake in California, and all I did was make them get another car. It might have cost the life of a gas station attendant to boot. They could be held up somewhere because the car hasn't been seen. An old yellow Chevy shouldn't be hard to spot," Mitch said as Harold got on the radio to check in.

"This is Lt. Camode checking in from Portland airport. Time 16:34."

"Lt., do you have a report?" a voice asked over the radio.

"FBI Inspector Mitchell Zaga was picked up and is with me. Any information on escaped convict Smallwood?"

"Negative. Your destination, Lt. Camode?" the voice said as the lieutenant looked at Mitch.

"Albany," Mitch responded and Harold smiled. He knew what the connection was. He too, had been suspicious of the ex-con Rocmel.

"Albany," Harold said as he looked at his watch and thought about the rush hour. ETA about 6:30, over."

"Ten four, Lieutenant, over and out."

The radio went silent.

Malarie walked into the bedroom where Ken was lying on the bed looking at a photo album.

"What ya got there, babe?" she asked as she lay down beside him.

"Pictures from the joint," Ken's voice showed that he was depressed.

"That's Jesse, huh, you told me about his different color eyes."

"Yep, that's Jesse," Ken said, "He had one blue eye and one brown eye. He was a good kid, really. He just allowed others to do his thinking for him. Once on my birthday, Billy thought he'd do me a favor. He sent Jesse to my cell to give me some head while Billy kept point. That's one thing prison takes away, the touch of another human being. It's just an empty feeling I can't find words to express it."

"I think I understand what you're saying, Ken," Malarie said. She was always interested whenever Ken chose to talk about his past. This was the first time he had shared his photo album with her. She was dying to ask if he had let Jesse do anything to him, but thought it better if he were allowed to tell only what he wanted to tell.

"No," he said, "I really don't think anyone can understand it unless they've been there. I don't mean just sexual feelings or touching. I mean like when your mom gives you a kiss or a hug, or even a close friend you haven't seen in a while. I remember my dad used to run his hand across my face, real soft and just smile into my eyes. I used to love that feeling. It was so real and meaningful. I'm glad I didn't know you before I went into the joint. That would have made time so much harder."

Malarie disliked interrupting Ken when he was in a talking mood. However, she wanted to cheer him up. "If you had known me before," she said, "You never would have robbed a bank in the first place." Ken was speaking from his inner soul. It wasn't often that he talked so candidly. Malarie's well chosen words did cheer him up. He expressed his solace with a kind laugh.

"You're probably right," he said, "My life hasn't been the same since I met you. I'm not complaining babe. I've never been happier," He spoke softly, turned and kissed Malarie.

"See? That's what I mean. You don't have that in the joint a person needs it. It contributes to one's contentment."

Ken's eyes went back to the photo album. Malarie did not plan to say anything more about Jesse but the words just came out of her mouth.

"So what happened with Jesse?" she asked. Immediately she regretted having asked. Ken laughed at her. Well at least she was cheering him up.

"I knew you were going to ask. Women try to be so cool but they are unable to control their curiosity," Ken jested.

"No, I don't care. You don't have to tell me if you don't want to," she was dying to know.

"Well did you?" she asked.

"Ha, ha, ha," Ken laughed and finally got serious.

"Well, it had been four years that kind of thing works on you. When Jesse walked into my cell and said, 'Happy birthday from me and Billy, I'm here to please you.' Well, I knew what he meant. Jesse told me it was cool, Billy was keeping point. I was lying on the bed and Jesse came and sat down beside me. Four years I had heard stories about these things. People had told me that some kids were better than girls were. How this kid gave better head than girls you may know. They said, you just close your eyes and think of some girl and let it happen. Well, that is what I did; when Jesse sat down by me, I just closed my eyes and thought about Dee Dee. Then he touched me and my eyes popped open. I was looking at Jesse. I jumped up and grabbed Jesse by the neck before I knew what I was doing. Jesse just looked at me wondering what he'd done wrong. I let him go and said, 'Nothing Jesse, it's just not me, thanks for the offer anyway. I accept the thought as your birthday present, Jesse. It's just not me, guess I got to wait till I can get some pussy.'"

"You were just afraid your voice would get higher," Malarie said, trying to be funny. "Who's that?" she asked pointing to a photo.

"That's Pauly. Big old teddy bear Pauly. One of the best cookers in Oregon," Ken told her. He knew firsthand how good his stuff was. Patty had smuggled in some of Pauly's stash a few times.

"Cooker, what do you mean, cooker?" Malarie innocently asked. This was one of the things that endeared her to Ken. That he had information about things she had no clue about.

"Crank. He made crank. But he made it right. Pauly was a true artist when it came to cooking."

"Oh," Malarie pretended to understand. She knew it was some kind of drug.

"That's you. You look good in a beard. Is that you there with all those muscles? No, it can't be. Your belly, it's too flat." She knew it was him. She had met Ken just a month after he was released from prison. He had a great build for a guy only 5 ft. 6 in. Ken reached over and lovingly tickled Malarie under the chin. They both laughed. She was so happy.

"Being witty again, huh? It's your fault, you're such a good cook," he said as he rubbed his stomach. He had gained ten pounds during the two years since his release. He continued to turn the pages of the album.

"There's you, Bobby, Jesse and Pauly. Who are those two guys?" Malarie asked. She was looking at a group of scary looking people with their shirts off. They all had tattoos except Ken.

"That's Billy and the fat ugly dude is none other than the notorious Maggot. He had a bugger patch on his wall. He was so proud of it that he used to bring people to his cell to show it off. I never met anyone that a nickname suited so well as Maggot."

"Oh, icky, that's gross, Malarie said as she felt her stomach turn over. She was looking at Maggot. Ken watched with amusement. He said to Malarie, "That's the grossest individual you could ever meet. He used to think it was funny to fart in his hand and throw it at you."

"No, stop it! You're making me sick," Malarie said.

"If you don't believe me I can invite him to dinner," Ken said. Malarie's expression amused him.

"No way, he's a pig. How come everyone has a tattoo except you?" Malarie asked, hoping to drop the subject about Maggot.

"Never believed in them. I thought they were stupid. I used to think it was funny that many of the convicts were anxious to get out of prison so they could go back to a life of crime. The tattoos on their bodies were like road maps. I must have known twenty people while I was in prisons that were identified by their tattoos. It is strange that robbery victims usually don't remember the faces of their assailants but they remember their tattoos. It is even stranger that these same convicts will wear a mask and a short sleeve shirt and expose their tattoos. The cops record tattoos like they do fingerprints."

"Is this your softball team?" Malarie asked pointing to a photo.

"Yep, that's the mean machine. Everyone on the team was in for murder except Billy and me." Malarie asked why Ken wanted all murderers.

"They were the best players and had the most pride. They didn't have much to live for, so the team was important to them," Ken responded.

"What was Billy in for?" Malarie found the subject fascinating. She also hoped that talking about it would help to relieve some of Ken's tensions.

"Billy was probably more dangerous than any of the murders that I knew. He didn't care about anyone but himself; he had no regard for anyone's feelings. I never liked Billy. He was a back stabber. He stabbed a couple of people while he

233

was in the joint with me. He had no fear and he was crazy to boot, and this was probably the greatest cause of his downfall.

"Bobby let him join the clique for that reason. There were times when it was necessary to frighten or even do bodily harm to someone. In such cases, Billy came in handy. Anyway, he's gone now and I guess I shouldn't be talking bad about him," Ken said not wanting to talk about some of Billy's acts that were more notorious, "He raped a young kid in his cell. The kid was so distraught that he committed suicide by hanging himself. When he heard about it Billy said, 'What a weak punk, he's better off dead, for everyone.'"

The baby crying interrupted Ken's reflections.

"That's your son," Malarie said, "I guess he's hungry. He didn't eat before he went to sleep." She went to the bedroom to take care of the baby.

Ken's thoughts went back to the album. He just flipped through the pages not taking any particular interest in any of them. His thoughts were mostly on Bobby. He thought about the news he'd heard, about the $40,000 that Bobby reportedly got away with. He thought, maybe the plan for getting the money was easy, getting away with it was the problem. He wondered why Bobby was the only one to get away. That thought plagued Ken. Did he leave the rest of the guys out to dry?

Malarie returned with the baby and sat down on the bed. She was undoing her blouse to breast feed Dane.

"You see your daddy? Yes, that's your daddy," Malarie said to Dane. Dane looked as though he did not care one way or another.

"Who's the older guy in the suit?" Malarie inquired.

"That's Warden Glass, our fearless leader. I don't know why I got his picture. Did I ever tell you about the time I got a write-up, and had to go to a kangaroo court they have inside the joint to hear write-up complaints?"

"What's a write-up?" Malarie asked.

"When you break one of their funky rules, they write you up."

"Oh," Malarie said, and thought about not asking any more questions. But, another question just slipped out. She inquired about the nature of Ken's violation.

"Well, if you will hold your horses I'll tell you," Ken replied.

"OK, I'm sorry!" She swore she would keep her mouth shut.

"Anyway, everything in the joint is bells--bells for dinner, bells for lunch, for towel out, yard, school classes--bells for everything. I used to hear bells in my sleep. Anyway, I was playing dominoes with this guy when the bells went off for lunch. You have three minutes to get to the chow hall. We finished our hand of dominoes and I had to take them back to my cell. I was a couple of minutes late when I went to go eat.

"So I'm going across the control room floor on my way to the chow hall when one of the guards stopped me and asked where I was going. Shit, why is the guard hassling me, I wondered. He did, so I told him I was passing out towels. That was one of the duties of an orderly. They were usually a few minutes late, and the guards didn't bother them. This guard said all right and told me to get to chow. Well he either knew me or found out that I was not an orderly.

"When I got back from chow, there was a write-up on my bed. It was for disobedience to an order and lying to staff. It seemed ironic that there were murderers, rapists, armed robbers, and child molesters, and I got a write-up for lying. However, it wasn't funny at the time. I was in "A" block at the time, which was the honor block. For any kind of write-up, you are sent back to the main population. Therefore, it's going to be a drag for me to move and have to wait for 30 days to come back to "A." There was nothing I could do. A few days later, I was ready to go to court on the write-up charge. My belongings were packed, I was ready to move. When I got to court there's like five guys ahead of me when Bobby comes over and says..."

"Somebody mention my name?" stopping Ken in mid-sentence. Ken and Malarie turned to see who it was. They both were frightened. It was Bobby Smallwood.

"Bobby, what the fuck," Ken managed to say, in shock.

"Hi, Bobby," Malarie greeted Bobby as though she had just seen him the day before.

"The door was open so we just came on in, didn't think you'd mind," Bobby said in jest. Charlene came in from around the corner wearing a big smile.

"Bobby, Bobby, what the, where...Jesus, how did you know where I lived?" Ken was still in shock. He hardly knew how to act or what to say.

"I've been writing to you for two years at this address, just asked one person if he knew where Lawnridge was, and here we are. Hey, what is this? You turned cop on me or something? Forget the questions and give me a hug and a hello fit for brothers. Bobby's here, you mother fucker."

Bobby let out a small yell and Dane began to cry. Ken jumped off the bed and gave Bobby a giant hug and kiss on the cheek.

"What, damn, talk about surprise, you got to be out of your minds. You can't turn on the TV or pick up a newspaper without seeing your guys' pictures all over them," Ken said, "Oh hi, you must be Charlene. I'm Ken, this is my wife, Malarie, and our baby, Dane."

Ken reached out to shake hands with Charlene but she pulled him into a hug and then kissed him right on the mouth, "Shit, Bobby has told me so much about you, Wizard, that I feel like I've known you all my life."

Charlene went to Malarie and gave her a big hug. To reciprocate, Malarie gave Bobby a hug. It was like a family gathering at Christmas.

"Hey, Dane, how you doing, buddy? It's your uncle Bob," Bobby took Dane from Malarie and held him above his head. For the first time, Malarie became nervous. Bobby sensed it, lowered Dane and gave him a kiss.

"Boy, he's really growing huh?" Bobby returned Dane to his mother. She didn't respond to Bobby's statement. She was glad to have Dane back in her arms.

"So you been following the newspapers and TV, huh?" Bobby asked, with his eyes fixed on Ken.

"Can't watch TV these last few days without you being a on the news," Ken responded, wondering just how happy he should be that they were in his house.

"Well, it's all bullshit, brother. Remember when we had the riot, how the cops rushed in shooting anything that moved? The news people came to interview us and promised to print our side of the story, too. When the article came out, it told everything but the truth. It praised the cops as heroes and shit. Well this is the same bullshit. They ain't telling it as it is."

Bobby showed how pissed off he was.

"Pauly, Jesse and Billy, did they really get them? Are they dead?" Ken hoped that at least part of this story was a lie, but he could not imagine how the press could tell everything but the truth.

"I don't know that for sure but probably," Bobby said, "Me and Charlene went to get some food and when we returned, we saw the place was full of cops. We turned around and headed here, and we've been driving until now." Bobby knew that Ken wouldn't like that he had taken off on the guys. "But it worked, brother, it worked," Bobby announced as he opened his shirt and removed his money belt.

"It was just like you said it would be," Bobby continued, "except you're not going to believe this, we got over $50,000 and we only took off two guys. One of the people, a sand nigger, had $40,000 alone and this diamond ring. Show Kenny the ring, babe," Bobby proudly said as he displayed the ring to Ken,"Is that some kind of a diamond or what?"

"Damn, fuck, is that thing real?" Ken by now had found it easy to swear in front of Malarie.

"Fucking "A", it's real. A guy packing 40 grand don't wear no phony diamond," Bobby said.

"Here, feast your eyes on this," Bobby said as he handed the money belt to Ken.

"This is 40,000 bucks?" Ken asked moving the belt up and down in disbelief.

"Open it up and take a look. You never saw anything so pretty, four hundred one hundred dollar bills. It will give you a hard on," Bobby said as Ken looked at Malarie. She was not used to this kind of talk. However, the money belt drew her attention.

"Let me hold the baby," Charlene said to Malarie, "Money can be real pretty." Malarie handed Dane to Charlene. It did sound strange, this girl calling Ken The Wizard. Ken opened the money belt.

"Go ahead and pull a stack out. Two thousand of it's yours--rest stop was your idea, so you earned that much, at least. Bobby watched Ken's expression when the figure two thousand was mentioned. It amazed him that Ken showed no excitement.

"Nah," Ken said, "I don't want none of it." He thought of it as blood money. Seven people were dead over this money. He felt it but didn't want to say it.

"Bullshit! you earned it. We never would have had it if it wasn't for your idea," Bobby said with the pretence that he was hurt by Ken's refusal to take the money.

"Hey brother, don't say that," Ken responded, "If that's true then it was my idea that killed our brothers. Maybe it was because we sat on our bunks one night and discussed stupid scams that might have led to your escape. Tell me, Bobby," Ken went on, "This part I can't understand for the life of me. With three or four months to go, why the fuck did this even happen? Every one of you guys was ready to hit the street," Ken looked Bobby in the eye and asked softly, "What happened?"

"You remember Gary Duggan?"

"Yeah, the black guy. It was on the news that you stuck him, but why? What could he have done to make you blow your life? Pauly, Jesse and Billy...I can't think of anything he could have done to cause all this shit to happen," Ken was not sure that this came out the way he intended. Bobby was offended and became angry.

"Oh bullshit!" Bobby said almost yelling, "Now it's my fault, you laying the guilt on me. You saying I killed the brothers. Come on, Kenny, I don't need this shit from you," Bobby said looking right into Ken's face. His eyes were filled with rage.

Ken didn't like it. He was uncomfortable in his own house. Bobby was different. He saw that Bobby was not the same Bobby he had known. Ken's thoughts turned to the safety of his family. He knew and understood the potential danger of the situation. Bobby and this bitch with him weren't his concern. His family was. He needed to take control while he had the opportunity. Ken was one of the few people who could control Bobby.

"Oh Bobby, you dumb fuck," Ken said in a more mellow tone, "That ain't what I'm saying. I love you. Fuck, brother, you saved my life. You can't do no wrong by me. I'm just hurting for you, Bobby, not for me. I know all this shit that happened wasn't planned. I know that if you had it all to do again it would be different. Do you know how excited I was to know you were getting out and coming to live with us? I already had a job for you. Man, I don't know what I'm trying to say. I'm just hurting with you bro," Ken was saying exactly what Bobby wanted to hear. His eyes lit up as Ken spoke.

"You asshole, I love you too," Bobby said, just what Ken wanted him to say also. Bobby pulled Ken to him and hugged him. Ken did not remember Bobby's strength; those arms were stronger than Ken remembered.

"Hey, you got any smoke?"

"Stupid question," Ken said, "would I be The Wizard if I didn't have weed. Even when we were in the joint it wasn't often that I didn't have the bag, right? Well, it wouldn't make sense not to have it now," Ken was happy for the way Bobby's attitude had changed.

"Right, right, Wizard, sorry I asked," Bobby said. He smiled as his hand went softly across Ken's face. It was the way his father used to do. This reminded Ken that he did love Bobby. Nevertheless, as big and tough as Bobby was, he would lose it if Bobboy came between him and his family.

"Hey, you guys were talking about me when we first came in. What were you talking about?" Bobby asked as Ken went to the dresser and pulled out a bag of weed and a pipe.

"Oh yeah," Ken said, "I was telling Malarie about the time I got a write-up for lying. Remember we were in "A" block together?"

"That's one of the funniest stories, finish it, I want Charlene to hear it."

Ken loaded the pipe and gave it to Bobby, repeated the story, as he had told it to Malarie, and continued, "So I'm waiting to go to court on this write-up, there were like five people ahead of me. Bobby came over to tell me he had just copped some Hawaiian bud he had been telling me he was going to get. 'Let's go smoke some,' he said. I told him I had to go to court and asked him to hang on to it until I'm done. 'Let's do it now,' Bobby said, 'it's going to take a half hour before you get in, let's do it now.'

"I said, 'I don't want to be stoned when I go to the Kangaroo court.' Bobby said I was going to plead guilty and I could do that stoned. I looked down the line and it wasn't moving, so I say, 'Let's go.'

"So we get to the cell and smoke a doobie, and shit, it was knockout stuff, I mean I'm really stoned. So I go back to the court and sit down. I'm not there ten seconds before my name is called. So I go in, and sitting on the panel of three judges is Warden Glass, Assistant Warden Lockney and some other dude. I don't know whether it was because I was stoned but suddenly I do not want to plead guilty.

"They asked me how I wanted to plead, and I say that the whole thing is a misunderstanding. 'Just tell us how you plead,' the warden cracked. I say, 'I guess I'm pleading not guilty.' The warden told me to go ahead and tell my story.

"'I was sitting on the pot when the chow bell rang. I try to hurry but sometimes you can't rush nature. So I'm a few minutes late going across the control room floor. The guard asked me why I was late getting to chow. Well, I try to be as etiquette as possible, not wanting to say I was taking a shit. So I say I was passing my bowels. The next thing I know I get a write-up for lying about passing out towels. I don't pass out towels. I'm not an orderly. And that's why I say it was just a misunderstanding. I could have straightened it out but the guard gave me a write-up without even talking to me.'"

Bobby, Charlene and Malarie got a hearty laugh.

"The judges, I'm looking at them and I can tell they want to crack up but, they hold it in. Anyway, they send to me to this little room to wait while they reach their verdict. So I got my ear to the wall, and I hear them something like, the little fucker is lying through his teeth, but what a story. They found me not guilty. Thanks to Bobby getting me high, because I do not know where that story came from, it just popped in my head."

Bobby was still laughing when he handed the pipe to Malarie.

"No, thanks," she said. Malarie did not do drugs. Bobby passed it to Ken.

"You were always that way, rhyming shit, bowels, towels, that's why you're The Wizard. You still writing poetry. Boy, you ought to hear some of Ken's poems babe, he can write some first class stuff."

"I'd like to hear some," Charlene said, as she filled the pipe again.

"You still got that poem, about the seventies, about John Wayne and Janis Joplin? I can't remember, something about Elvis, you know. Read that one to Charlene, would ya?" Bobby pleaded.

"Are you serious? You want to hear a poem when the whole world is looking for you?" Ken answered, not believing that Bobby was in the situation he was in and wanted to talk about poetry. He took the pipe from Charlene and took a toke.

"Yeah, I do, come on, Wizard, just one poem," Charlene was pleading now.

"Besides, you said it. They're looking for me, and have no idea where I am. I have a strong feeling the cops think I'm in Mexico by now. The last place they would look for me is right here," Bobby said.

"You know the cops came to see me the day you escaped, and asked me a lot of questions," Ken said. He did not want Bobby to feel too comfortable or safe here.

"That makes sense, figured they did, and it wouldn't surprise me if your phone was tapped. That's why I ain't called you. You people are on my visiting list, we are ex-cellies, sure they're gonna come to see you. So read us that poem, I miss your poems," Bobby said.

Malarie could not believe that she was sitting in her bedroom with people who were wanted for murder. She had just seen them on TV. That girl whose picture she had just seen on TV was holding her baby. A nationwide manhunt was being conducted for the very people sitting on her bed, and all they wanted was to hear one of Ken's poems.

Ken went to the box on the bed and took out a thick black book, "This is crazy, but here's the poem," He began to read it.

"DECADE

As timeless as waves, comes a new age
I wonder if I am ready.
Is it conception or instinct rejection
That no answers come steady
And through inquiry of a decade diary
I live it one last time.
****

I was just twenty one, when the last begun
I remember the lost cause soldier.
Hippies at their peak, yet marijuana reeked
The war that was not was over.
Long hair took a dive, disco came alive
Acid was an intellectual high.
The Beatles split, Dick went and quit
Kent State still asked why.
The laborer soiled, to see prices of oil
Man walked on the moon.
Duke and the king did their final scenes
Janis and Jimmy died too soon.
And coming to close, our president chose

The Shah over fifty yanks
But most of all, the seventies were a ball, So to whoever, I say thanks"

"There. You happy?" Ken asked, remembering that this was one of his favorite poems, too.

"That was really good," Charlene said, "You have any more like that?" She was very impressed.

"Shit, he's got thousands of them," Bobby said, "We would be talking or something and all of a sudden, he would say, 'I got to write a poem.' He'd hop on his bunk and start writing. A half hour later, he'd be reading me a poem. They were always good." Malarie also knew Ken wrote good poems.

"He still does that," Malarie said.

"Read another one Kenny," Charlene asked.

"This is too much, here we are telling old war stories, smoking weed, reading poems like there's not a care in the world. It's just too much. Maybe I'm paranoid," Ken said, and he was. He wanted to ask Bobby what his plans were but he thought maybe it was better not to know.

"You're more paranoid than I am, that's for sure," Bobby said, "Listen brother, I feel really comfortable here. The cops don't have the slightest idea that I'm even close to Oregon. We were within a couple of hours of the Mexican border, and that's where they're looking for us, I just know it.

"This is what I'd like to do, if it's cool with you. Charlene and me would like to kick back a few days, just in case there is heat. Give it a couple of days to cool down, and then we'll head for Canada. Besides, I'd like to spend a few days visiting my closest people. I don't know if we'll ever be able to make it back this way."

Malarie gave a look at Ken that said no, in no uncertain terms. Ken didn't like the idea either.

"I don't know Bobby. You think that's smart? You got them looking for you in Mexico now. Maybe it's a good time to keep moving. Maybe they'll figure you went north when there's no trace of you in Mexico. And, as you said, they might even have my phone tapped," Ken said, hoping Bobby would think the smart thing to do was to keep moving, "If that's true, maybe they'll be watching the house. How did you guys get here anyway?"

"Car. Got it parked down the street about two blocks away, on a side street. We drove past here about four times, took our time walking, no sign of your house being watched. Now that you said so, you could be right. Maybe we should keep moving. Besides, I couldn't live with myself if I ever brought shit down on you guys," Bobby said. He thought it might be best for them to move on. He sensed they weren't welcome guests. Ken was relieved by this new attitude.

"Hey, there's no rush. You guys hungry?" Ken asked, thinking Bobby would be leaving in an hour or so with no hard feelings, "We still have some cold fried chicken. You guys want some?"

"Yeah, that sounds good. It'll go with these munchies I'm having," Bobby said.

"I'll go get it. You want some corn bread with that?" Malarie asked.

"Whatever you put together is fine with me," Bobby replied.

"I'll give you a hand," Charlene said, following Malarie out of the room.

"Oh, take this," Ken said to Bobby, "I can always get more." He handed Bobby a bag of weed.

"Thanks, brother," Bobby said.

He picked up the photo album and started flipping through it. Suddenly, he exclaimed, "Son-of-a-bitch, there's Donny Ray. Did you hear that he got blown away during a robbery in Utah?"

"No shit? No, I didn't hear about it. Donny was always a good ol' boy."

"Yep," Bobby said, "No shit. It wasn't too long ago either, just a couple of months." Bobby continued to skim through the album. Chills ran up and down his spine, he was trying to forget the joint.

"It's hard to believe that I was walking that yard just a few days ago. It seems like a hundred years since I was there. That bums me out about Donny Ray."

"I remember him telling me how this was his last time he would go down. He said he'd go straight when he got out."

"Come on brother, how many times you heard that, and then see the guy coming back a few months later."

"I know, but for some reason I believed Donny meant it."

"He probably did, but they let him go, gave him a hundred bucks and told him to go and sin no more. Shit, man if a guy ain't got someone out there, what is he going to do with a hundred bucks? In three days, he's hungry and he's busted. He ain't going to starve; he's going to do what he has to do to survive. And, like Donny Ray, what did he know except robbing people? There's too much money in the prison system. They don't want people to make good, they want them back. Well as you know, most of the time they get them back," Bobby answered, true to life.

THE CHANGE

The eagle was free to roam,
Make the sky his home.
Over valleys, over trees
He was completely free
Then like a flash of light,
He was trapped one night,
In a cage he was left to stay,
They took his freedom of play.
Move when he was told, Give up his bold.
Eat from an unwanted hand,
Never make his stand.
For he was an eagle no more,
Just a bird without form.
When they took away his free
He now can never be
His purpose in life,
Making the wind his wife,
So the eagle's life is now a lie,
Time for the eagle to die...

-Rest Stop- Chapter 16

Tuesday, 6:08 p.m.

FBI Inspector Mitchell Zaga and the Oregon State Police Lt. Harold Camode had just finished their dinner at the lieutenant's favorite little restaurant. The food was good and, besides, he could eat there for free. The owner would comp the police when they came in. He felt safe with the police around. Of course, the lieutenant always offered to pay but he knew the owner would always say, "On the house, lieutenant." Still, he felt obligated to make the offer. He didn't want it to get around that he took graft.

They'd both decided to eat. The lieutenant offered to buy dinner for Mitch at this restaurant in Salem, 20 miles from Albany. He'd used his radio to change his arrival time in Albany from 6:30 to 7:30.

As they got back on I-5, Mitch thought about Ken Rocmel again. "What do you know about this Ken Rocmel?" he asked Harold.

"He did four years for a bank robbery in Eugene about six years ago. For two of the four years, he was Bobby Smallwood's cellmate."

Mitch interrupted, "That's the part I don't understand. Bank robbery is a federal crime. How did he end up doing state time?"

"I'm not sure myself," the lieutenant confessed, "But I think they dropped the bank robbery and just hit him with kidnapping and robbery. I don't think he ever entered the bank. He and a girlfriend kidnapped the wife of the bank president and had the bank president deliver the ransom money."

Again Mitch interrupted, "And he ended up doing only four years. Boy, you state guys are easy on your criminals."

The lieutenant said, "I checked on that myself. Oregon has the matrix which determines how much time a person can do for a crime. Another person doing the same crime could get ten years. The system is based on the past record of the offender. Rocmel was clean, that was his first felony conviction."

244

Mitch asked, "Why does he have a rap sheet?"

"Yep, a pretty good one, but no convictions."

"Is he hard core, is he still into things?" Mitch asked.

"I checked with his parole officer," said the lieutenant, "his employer and the local cops. They all spoke well of him."

"Is he still on parole?"

"No, he's been out two years now. He only had a one year parole," said Harold.

"Geez, you guys are easy here. One year of parole for robbery and kidnapping."

"He kept his nose clean," the lieutenant said, "He worked the whole time, married a local girl and paid his taxes. What can I say? I don't make the laws."

Mitch thought the report was too good to be true. "What does he do?"

"Car salesman, the best one on the lot. He makes four to five grand a month. After I saw that I knew I was in the wrong business," the lieutenant said. He knew he did not have a salesman's qualifications.

"What's your feeling about him?" Mitch knew the lieutenant had interviewed Rocmel.

"I felt he knew more than he was telling. He was just too smooth. You know we found the prison van in Sweet Home, a small town not far from Albany. My first thoughts about Rocmel were that he was helping the convicts to hide. I was the one who got the wiretap on his phone. We also had him under surveillance 24 hours a day until we heard about the killings in California. We kept the phone tap active but stopped the surveillance."

"I just don't know what I'm basing my suspicions on. And I know this could lead to a dead-end. I have no evidence Smallwood is on his way to Oregon or that he would try to contact Rocmel. Harold, I could be wasting your time," Mitch admitted.

"Weren't you inclined first to think he went to Mexico? After all he was only a couple of hundred miles away."

"Yeah, that would seem to be the logical answer. We still think it's still a possibility he might be there or at least en route. There isn't much I can do there that isn't being done. Smallwood is no dummy. We've tried to be logical but he's been illogical and has kept a step ahead of us. My feelings are based on his track record. The most illogical thing he could do would be to return to Oregon," Mitch said. This made good sense to Harold. He would sure like to be in on the bust of Smallwood.

Looking out the window, Mitch saw some gigantic smoke stacks. The most ungodly odor penetrated his nostrils.

"Wow, you shit in your pants or what?" Mitch managed to say.

"No, that's the pulp mill, smells like shit. Thanks for asking, I thought the same about you at first." They both had a good laugh. Harold had come to like this young agent. Turning on the blinker Harold said, "Here's Albany."

"You got any dominoes?" Bobby asked Ken right out of the blue.

"Dominoes?" Ken answered in surprise.

"Yeah, dominoes. I ain't leaving until I whip your ass in a game of dominoes and make you do 50 push-ups," Bobby replied.

"Shit, you'd be here till Christmas. Why do you think your arms are bigger than mine? Because you had to do a million push-ups trying to beat me in dominoes," Ken responded, knowing this was one game he wanted to lose. He would gladly do the fifty push-ups. His heart began to pound and he began to become paranoid.

"Honey, where are the dominoes?" Ken asked Malarie who gave him a strange look.

"I'm going to teach this home boy a few tricks."

"The only trick you're going to show is how a fat boy like you can do fifty push-ups. Get the dominoes!"

Harold and Mitch were arriving IN Albany.

"This is Lawnridge," Harold said as his turn signal went on.

"What's the set up here? House, apartment, or what?" Mitch asked.

"I've never been to his place before. I interviewed him at his work. His address should be on the clipboard right there."

"You have about twenty sheets of paper and notes here," Mitch noticed as he thumbed through the clipboard.

"Right there on the page, about half way down, it should say Ken Rocmel. His address is under his name."

"Yeah, here it is. Ken Rocmel, 2917 Lawnridge." It was dark and Mitch had difficulty seeing the house number.

"You see an address on any of those houses?" Harold asked. He could not see the numbers either.

"No, not yet. Wait a second, stop, back there is an address on the box!" Mitch thought he saw 31 on the mailbox. Harold backed up to the box. Mitch was right. The number was 3116. Should we go on or turn back the other direction?" Mitch asked.

"I don't know." said Harold.

"Slow down, here is another mail box," Mitch said, "We're going up. This is 3124, we've passed the number."

"Shit," Harold said as he went down to the end of the street, turned in and stopped. He turned off his dome light and backed up to find the address. He backed around the corner and Mitch caught a glimpse of a yellow car. He tried to get a better look, but Harold had turned the corner too fast. He dismissed the thought that this might be the Chevy he'd been searching for. Maybe I'm too jumpy, Mitch thought. They drove by again but he still didn't get a good look at the car. He dint say anything about the car to Harold. He thought it might turn out to be embarrassing.

Bobby and Ken were engrossed in their game of dominoes. Bobby slammed the dominoes on the table and said to Ken, "I'll take 15 points. You know I don't think you could do fifty push-ups, old man."

"Shit you ain't won this game yet, asshole. I'll take twenty. You forgot about the ace, six, huh," Ken said and laughed loudly.

Ken loved dominoes. He hadn't found one person on the street who knew how to play. He decided to play his best. What the hell, nobody knew Bobby was there. The time it took to play a couple of games couldn't hurt. Ken could play dominoes all night.

"Lucky shit, you've always been lucky, fuck," Bobby said reaching into the bone pile for a domino. He didn't have a five or six. The first bone was double five. "Yes indeed, give the master twenty-five. I'm the lucky one today, feeling good and alive," Bobby said in an effort to rhyme like The Wizard.

"One pull, you talk about me being lucky, you pull one bone and it's the perfect one, shit," Ken said, really pissed.

"Twenty more points and the only look there's going to be is you trying to do fifty push-ups," Bobby laughed. He loved beating The Wizard. He remembered that Ken would beat him two times to his one but he did not care. Ken took it more seriously than he did. Bobby would like to see him get pissed off.

Bobby picked up a chicken leg and stripped off the last morsel of flesh. He was really enjoying the game. He had played a lot after Ken got out, but he never enjoyed the game as much as when he played with Ken.

There was a knock at the door. Bobby and Ken looked at each other, and lost interest in the game.

"You expecting anybody?" Bobby asked. His countenance expressed anxiety.

"No, it could be Steve," Ken said, "He just drops by whenever."

Bobby knew Steve had been a one-of-a-kind brother while Ken was in prison. Many times when Bobby and Ken were smoking a bowl they would say, "Here's to little brother Steve," toasting the one who smuggled the weed in to Ken.

Steve was responsible for getting Ken an eight-month reduction in his sentence. He showed the parole board that Ken would have good family support when he was released. Steve stuck with his brother all the way, even went to see the Governor once to plead his case.

"Better check it out. I'll go back with the girls in the bedroom. Bobby said in a soft tone. He got on his hands and knees in order not to make a shadow as he went to the bedroom. The girls had also heard the knock at the door and were looking out the window. Bobby pushed them back and closed the door.

As was his habit, Bobby popped open the shotgun to be certain it was loaded. This made Malarie extremely tense. She impulsively took Dane from Charlene.

There was a knock at the door again. Ken wondered who it could be. He knew it was not Steve's knock. He became apprehensive when he saw the bedroom door closed. He knew Malarie and Dane were in there with Bobby and his sawed of shotgun. Ken opened the door and saw two men standing there dressed in suits.

"Ken Rocmel, remember me? I'm Lt. Camode. We met a few days ago at the car lot where you work." The lieutenant looked over Ken's head to see as much of the inside of the house as he could.

"Sure lieutenant, how you doing? Any luck in finding Bobby?" Ken thought he came across quite well but his legs felt weak.

"We'd like to talk to you about that, Ken. This is FBI Mitchell Zaga. May we come in?"

"Sure!" Ken opened the door wide enough for them to come in. He did not know what else he could have said or done. His heart pounded heavily when he thought of the possibility of Bobby flying out of the bedroom and blowing off the heads of these cops. He closed the door. A quick look outside showed only one car parked in the driveway besides his own. He didn't see any police cars.

"FBI in on this now, huh?" He spoke loudly enough to be heard in the bedroom by Bobby. He made a great effort to keep cool and not show anxiety.

"We've been on this case since the escape was discovered," Mitch replied as his eyes scanned around the room.

"Hey, I'm not trying to be disrespectful or anything, it's just that I've never seen an FBI badge before. May I see yours?" Ken was trying to buy time to think this thing through. He also wanted to give this FBI agent an image of being a nerd.

"No problem with that, Mr. Rocmel. This is my badge and ID."

"Wow, that's quite a badge. How long you been with the FBI?" Ken was still trying to stall. The lieutenant interrupted.

"Ken, we need to ask the questions. First, have you heard from your friend, Bobby?" Harold asked. Mitch wondered where the State Police got their training.

"Haven't heard anything from him, personally. I've been following the news reports. He hasn't called me, if that's what you mean, and you guys know he's not in Oregon," Ken was trying to ascertain whether they had any idea that Bobby was in Oregon.

"That's just it Ken, we think your buddy Robert Smallwood is on his way back to Oregon," Harold Camode said as he watched Ken's reaction, "He could be here right now." Ken's heart skipped a beat. Ken knew Harold meant in the state of Oregon, right now. However, when he thought of Bobby being only twenty feet away with his shotgun, he laughed nervously.

"Something funny, Rocmel?" Harold asked. Mitch just took it all in.

"Well, not funny, but in a way, it is funny. I mean, I know Bobby pretty good and one thing I know about him is that he's not dumb. Coming back to Oregon would be one of the stupidest things he could do. I just think you guys called it wrong."

Bobby had heard the people when they first came in the house. When he heard Ken say something about the FBI, he cocked both barrels of the shotgun.

"No, Bobby please don't," Malarie said in a frightened whisper.

Bobby said, "No, don't worry, just in case is all." He hoped this would put Malarie at ease. It did not have that effect.

Just in case of what, she thought.

Bobby put his ear back to the door to listen. Malarie watched the back door and wondered how she could get out that door with Dane.

"Mr. Rocmel, what can you tell us about Robert Smallwood and the plan for the rest area?" Mitch raised this question, primarily to watch his reaction. Ken was cool. He showed absolutely no reaction.

"Plans? I don't know anything about plans. I heard it was a rest stop, where Billy, Pauly and Jesse were killed. If that's what you mean."

"Rest stop. Yeah, that's how you said it, not rest area," Harold thought he had stumbled on to something.

"Excuse me," Ken pretended he didn't understand the point. He knew that somehow, he had fucked up.

"When you and Smallwood were cellies you guys would talk about a score at a rest stop. Tell us about that," Harold expected to catch Ken off guard.

Oh shit, the motherfuckers tapped my phone, is what ran through Ken's mind. There was no way these cops could know such a thing. Ken and Bobby were in a cell alone. He knew that Bobby hadn't told them. They had to pick it up on the phone.

"It wouldn't surprise me if Bobby was at a rest stop right now."

"I'll be a son-of-a-bitch," Ken said aloud and gave the officers a dirty look. "You guys tapped my phone, huh?" Ken just looked at them. The expressions on their faces confirmed his suspicion.

"We didn't say that."

To Ken, this was as good as an admission. He thought to himself that convicts were much better liars than cops were. Regaining his composure, Ken thought, "So what? They tapped your phone. The damage is done. I didn't really say anything to cause any damage. Bobby's in the bedroom with my wife and kid. I have to get them out of here. I have to get the cops out of here now. Even if I have to go with them."

"Hey you guys got a warrant?"

"What are you talking about, Rocmel? This is a murder investigation. We don't need a warrant. We can take you downtown to talk to you if we want to. So don't start any shit you can't handle," The lieutenant said in an effort to frighten Ken.

"Hey, save that kind of talk for the suckers. That downtown shit don't scare me. I'm not on parole any more. I have all the rights you do, my friend. You know, what scares me is people like you can wiretap someone's phone whenever you get the notion. Well, I take that personally. You want to take me downtown, well, you go ahead and do it. But, if you're not, and you don't have a warrant, then I want you out of my house right now. I'm getting on the phone with my lawyer about that wiretap as soon as you leave. Boy, I pray you people didn't do it legally," Ken's voice demanded attention. Both men just looked at each other. They acted as if they didn't know what to do.

Mitch looked into the kitchen and a cold chill ran over him. He wasn't sure what it meant. When he saw the dominoes on the kitchen table, he immediately felt the presence of Robert Smallwood. He decided to take over.

"Mr. Rocmel," he said, "the FBI is completely unaware of any wire tap on your phone. We are obligated to honor the rights of fellow citizens. If you would like for us to leave your house we'll do so." Mitch stopped there but thought it might have appeared that he was asking permission to leave. He wanted Rocmel to demand that they leave.

"We'd like to ask a few more questions but we don't have a warrant."

Ken had not expected this turn of events. His first thought was to have them take him downtown. He wanted to get the cops out long enough for Bobby and the girl to get away. By the time he returned home, all would be well again. Bobby had brought him a nightmare. Now, the cops were saying they would leave if he requested them to go.

Yeah, I would feel safer being here with Malarie and the baby. I can control Bobby. I can't control him if I'm downtown.

"I'd like for you guys to leave right now. Please just go, you had no right to tap my phone, and I'm going to call my lawyer as soon as you leave," Ken demanded as he watched the reaction of the two officers. Camode seemed to tense up.

Harold could not understand why Mitch would give in to this ex-con. He would have taken this guy downtown in a second. But he knew that the FBI was responsible for his being there, so he would play it down, at least until he got outside.

"Thank you for your time, Mr. Rocmel, if we need to talk to you again, we'll be sure to have a warrant," Mitch said as he pushed Harold toward the door.

"You do that. One more question, Lieutenant Camode, if the Feds didn't tap my phone, that means you guys did it."

Harold turned to Ken and responded, "If you want to talk to me, asshole, you get a warrant." Maybe it was improper but it made Harold feel better, no matter what that FBI kid had in mind. Mitch gave Harold an unkind look as they walked to the car. Ken closed the door.

Harold got in and unlocked the door on Mitch's side. He was anxious to express his discontent with Mitch's handling of the affair.

"What was all that shit about rights and warrants? We should have taken the asshole downtown. He knows more that he's telling us. I know he does."

Mitch looked at him and marveled. Harold had no idea as to the reason for Mitch's action. "You know, you might think I'm crazy, Harold, but do you want to know what I think?"

"What?" Harold snapped as if to say go ahead and tell me.

"I think Smallwood is in that house right now. He's probably looking out the window with that shotgun in his hands. As Mitch spoke, Harold took another look at the house.

"What? You're crazy," Harold said but kept his eyes on the house. His voice sounded like he had a lump in his throat. "What makes you say that?"

"When I first started with the Bureau my job was transporting federal prisoners. I must have been to fifty different prisons. They all had one thing in common. Did you see the dominoes on the kitchen table?" Mitch asked to see if Harold was putting it together. Mitch knew from his response he had not.

"No. Dominoes? What are you talking about Mitch?"

"There were dominoes on the kitchen table."

"So what do dominoes got to do with Smallwood being there?" Harold asked.

"I'll tell you while we back out. We're being watched. Someone's peeking out the window. Wait! Don't look," Mitch was beginning to think that the Governor must have been Harold's uncle for him to have made the rank of lieutenant. Harold backed out of the driveway.

"Go to the spot where you backed around the corner. You know, when you passed the house." Mitch suggested.

"We can't get out that way," Harold said.

"I think I saw a yellow car back there. I should have checked it out then. When I saw the dominoes, it all seemed to come together."

"There you go with the dominoes again. What about the dominoes?" Harold was confused.

"There wasn't one prison that I ever went to where there weren't dominoes," Mitch remembered.

"So, are you saying that you saw dominoes and that means Smallwood's there in the house? Other people play dominoes besides convicts," Harold wondered what methods these Feds used to reach such conclusions.

Mitch made no response. He remembered how one side of Jim Rushton's face had been blown away. He knew what a sawed of shotgun could do. This made him extremely cautious. Mitch was anxious to call for back up. But first, he wanted to turn the next corner to ascertain whether the yellow Chevy was there.

"This is where we turned around, isn't it?" Harold asked as he turned into the street. Sure enough, they saw a yellow car. It was a 1980 or 81 Chevy.

"California plates," Mitch said with both fright and surprise. Reviewing his notes, he found that Chevy bore Jim Rushton's license plate number.

Bobby had heard the conversation between Ken and the cops. When the cops left, he went to another bedroom and peeked out the window. The cop who was driving looked toward him. Bobby quickly closed the curtains, dropped to his knees and peeked through the bottom of the window. He heard the cops talking but he knew they were not on the radio. They backed out of the driveway and Ken saw them going in the direction of Bobby's car. Ken saw Bobby come into the living room. Charlene was standing near Malarie who was holding the baby. Ken feared for the safety of wife and baby.

"You did real good getting rid of the cops, Kenny. One of them was from the FBI, huh?" Bobby wanted to know what Kenny had said on the phone that brought the cops to the house in the first place.

"Sure was," Ken said as he wondered why the cops had gone toward the end of the street. He knew this was a dead-end street. Was it because they believed that Bobby was in the house?

"Do you think they have your phone tapped?" asked Bobby. Ken knew that Bobby had heard his conversation with the cops. He believed that Bobby must have known that he had screwed up on the phone.

"Yeah, I think I fucked up, brother." he said.

"How did you fuck up?" Bobby asked.

"Well, on the day of your escape, my brother Steve called to see whether I had heard the news about you guys. I told him I'd heard the news and that I thought you guys were long gone by now. Steve asked where I thought you'd be going. I said, 'It wouldn't surprise me if you guys were at a rest stop right now.' That's all I said. It didn't occur to me that my phone was tapped. I still wouldn't have known if the cop hadn't said that I was quoted as using the term rest stop rather than rest area. But I still don't know how that has anything to do with the cops thinking you were here."

"Well, it don't matter, we better get the hell out of here," Bobby said, "Sorry brother that I brought this shit down on you."

Bobby knew he was disappointed in Ken. He wasn't as smart as Bobby thought he was. They'd better get the hell out of his house, as Bobby had just put it.

Those were the most welcome words Bobby could have spoken Ken thought. However, the cops had not left the area yet. "Where did you guys stash the car?" Ken asked Bobby.

"Same way the cops went," Bobby said, "but we pulled it down a dead-end street. I'm sure they didn't see it. Even if they did see it, they won't know what the hell we were driving. We'll give it a few minutes and then split."

Bobby embraced Ken and Malarie and said, "Listen, I just want to say, out of all the people in the world, you two are my favorites. You guys hung by me while I did my time. You know, brother, what it's like to have people on the outside while you are doing time. You guys were the only ones I had. I guess what I'm saying is, I just had to stop and say good-bye before we split. I don't think we're coming back this way for a long time. Oh shit, I don't know what I'm trying to say. Just give me a hug, would ya's?"

Ken and Malarie gave him an affectionate hug. Malarie was so glad they were leaving. Ken watched the window as he joined in the hug. He hoped the cops didn't know the area. He hoped when they discovered they were on a dead-end street they'd turn around and pass his house a second time. He had to hold Bobby there long enough for the cops to pass by.

"Well buddy, it's too bad, because I think you might have won the domino game," Ken said with an eye still on the window.

"That's all right. You can owe me fifty push-ups, on demand, whenever I see you again," Bobby managed to give a phony laugh. He was anxious to get out of this house, get on the road, the hell with Oregon. Now he knew it was a mistake to come here. Why did Kenny continue looking out the window?

"You worried about something, Kenny?"

Ken couldn't mask his anxiety. He was caught off guard by Bobby's question. He knew Bobby was conscious of him looking out the window, and decided to reveal his worst fears to Bobby.

"I got a feeling that the cops are still out there because of the direction they went," Ken said as he pointed the direction the cops had gone.

"Yeah, what about it?" Bobby asked.

"Well, that's a dead-end street. At first, I just thought they didn't know the area—they'd come to the dead-end, turn around and come back this way. They haven't come back this way yet. You say you parked your car down there?" Ken felt better now that he had revealed his thoughts to Bobby. Before Bobby could answer, a car slowly drove past the house. Bobby turned off the lights in the living room. The car kept moving.

"Whew, you had me worried Kenny. I knew they couldn't know what car I was driving," Bobby said as the car's taillight disappeared into the darkness. "I'm getting suspicious and I think we better hit the road." As Bobby finished his statement, a police car with lights on the top drove by slowly.

"What the fuck is this?"

"You got me Bobby?" Maybe it's just a fluke, cops drive down this street all the time," Ken responded. He was also getting fearful. Had he done something that tipped off the police?

"You sure they don't know what car you're driving?"

"Fuck yeah, I'm sure. Are you sure you didn't fuck up somehow when they were here?"

This put Ken on the defensive. "Bobby, what kind of question is that? I certainly didn't do anything that would put the cops on you."

"Talking too much shit on the phone might have done it," Bobby said. He did not think that anything Ken might have said on the phone could have anything to do with what was happening then. However, Bobby had a natural tendency to impute his own wrongs to others.

"Oh bullshit, Bobby. Don't start that shit. I didn't know you guys were coming here. I didn't say that much on the phone anyway. Besides, we're all probably apprehensive for no reason. That cop car is most likely just on patrol. It could also be the neighbor down the street who often calls the cops on some kids," Ken said in a way he knew Bobby could understand. He just wanted Malarie and Dane out of the house as soon as Bobby and Charlene left.

"Well, I got bad vibes. We're splitting. We'll go out the back way. Let's go lady." Charlene walked out behind Bobby. She smiled at Malarie and gave Dane a pat on the head as she walked past them.

"Nice meeting you both," Charlene managed to say as Bobby opened the sliding glass door in the kitchen. She thought they were all too wary.

Bobby looked outside and thought he saw a shadow moving around the side of the house. Someone jumped over the wall. He cocked both barrels of his shotgun. The person who jumped over the wall was holding a rifle. He was surprised when he saw Bobby standing by the door.

"Hold it right there," he ordered. He was too late. He heard the explosion of the shotgun as his legs gave way and he fell to the ground. He was in great pain. As he fell, he returned fire from his rifle. He wasn't sure what he was firing at. He heard the sound of shattering glass. He looked but saw no one.

"There are cops all around this fucking place," Bobby said as he crawled across the floor. His face was bleeding profusely. Ken was lying on Malarie and the baby in a corner away from the windows. Charlene stood in another corner. She was uncertain what role she was to play. The phone rang. Bobby knew it was the cops. He thought about answering the phone but allowed it to continue to ring.

"You want me to get it, Bobby?" Ken asked. He knew it was probably the cops, too. His wife and baby were in the house, and he wanted to get them out before they were hurt.

"No, let it ring. It's the cops wanting me to give myself up. They are dreaming. Motherfucker, how could they figure I was here? Fuck!" Bobby screamed as he wiped blood from his face.

Charlene came to his side. Bobby pulled her to the floor. "Get down, lady, there's guys out there who are trying to kill us," he told her.

Bobby couldn't think straight. His mind was going a hundred miles an hour. He asked Kenny to look out the window and tell him what he could see. He asked Malarie if they had any guns in the house.

She could only say "No," between nervous spasms.

Ken heard her voice and was enraged. Fucking Bobby! The phone kept ringing. Bobby reloaded his shotgun. He thought about shooting the phone but crawled over and answered it, "Yeah, what do you want, cop?"

"Smallwood?" Mitch asked.

"Yeah, this is Bobby Smallwood. What do you want?"

"I am Mitch Zaga, Bobby. I'm with the FBI."

"Yeah, you're the fucker that was just in the house. I should come out shooting and blow you and your cop friend away."

"Maybe you should have, Bobby. However, it's over now. You are through. There are forty cops out here with shotguns just waiting for you. You shot one of their boys. You know how cops are."

Bobby cut Mitch off, "Listen, asshole, by now you know I don't play games. I got women in here and I have a little baby."

It was Mitch's turn to interrupt, "Now you listen, Smallwood, there aren't any games being played on this side either. Rocmel isn't going to let you hurt his kid or his wife. Even you wouldn't use a kid as a shield."

"Hey, you asshole, you don't know me. I'm staying alive. If you kill me, I ain't going alone. You better believe that." Smallwood's senses returned to him.

"What do you think we're going to do, let you go? Rocmel was in this thing with you from the beginning. You can't use a brother as a shield."

"You know what cop? Fuck you," Bobby hung up the phone. Ken heard the phone conversation. Malarie began to cry when Bobby told Mitch that he had a baby in there. Ken tried to comfort her.

"Bobby would never hurt us. He was just saying that to the cops," he told her. However, Ken was no longer sure what Bobby might do. He was sure however, that his family was in danger. When Bobby hung up the phone, Ken crept over to him.

"Bobby, I want Dane and Malarie out of here right now. They're going to gas us," Ken said as he looked into Bobby's blank eyes, "You know that, brother. Don't put my family between you and me, brother."

"Can't do it, Kenny, not right now. I need time to think. You know they won't come storming in while there's a baby in here," Bobby was cut off by Ken this time.

"Bobby, will you listen to yourself. This place is surrounded by cops. They got you. It's over, brother. It's up to you if you want to die. But don't put my family in the middle of this mess."

"They won't storm us while there's a baby in the house," Bobby argued.

"Bobby, that's my baby you're talking about. You want to second guess what the cops will do with my baby's life? Well, then you don't know me at all, because you should know, I won't let you do that," Ken looked at Bobby to determine whether he was getting through to him.

"I'm sending Mal and the baby out. Malarie take Dane and go."

"No, stay where you're at. Kenny, don't make me turn on you. You're the last person in the world I want to hurt. But I will. Don't fuck with me now. I ain't going back to prison. Do you understand what I'm saying? They can kill me, but they can't get me back to prison. Just let me think a minute. They won't do nothing right away. They got to think about it too," Bobby spoke with the look of the devil in his eyes.

Subconsciously, he turned the shotgun toward Ken with both hammers cocked. Malarie remained where she was. She was too afraid to move. The phone rang again.

Luck, percentages, odds, the balance, the bottom line? You toss a coin in the air and twenty successive times it could come up heads every time. There is a fifty-fifty chance that the next toss will be heads. However, in the end it has to average out. Bobby had a run of luck. He tossed the coin and got heads twenty times in a row. Luck was on Bobby's side since the escape. He had continued doubling up, but eventually had to repay all his winnings. The coin came up tails.

It was simple luck that Mitch Zaga stumbled upon Bobby. If he had kept going without stopping in Albany, Bobby might have made it to Canada. Had there been no dominoes on the table, Mitch would have left without any suspicion that Bobby was there. Had Lt. Camode not driven past Ken's house. Had the street not come to a dead-end. If he hadn't turned at the very spot where Bobby had parked his car.

Bobby might have taken an hour longer to come to Albany. Mitch Zaga might have taken the advice of the FBI Director and waited until morning to fly from Las Vegas to Portland. Were these events pure luck? Whatever view one takes it adds up to the fact that the time had come. It was time for Bobby to pay his dues.

Ken found it difficult to believe that this was the same Bobby that he knew in the joint. This guy was pointing his loaded shotgun at him. He had put his family's life in danger. He was a wild animal, wounded, and trapped in a corner. His survival was the only thing that mattered to him.

Ken looked at Malarie. She'd covered the baby with her body. She looked at Ken with a countenance of horror. Her eyes had filled with tears.

Bobby grew tired of hearing the phone ring. He answered it with all the arrogance he could muster. "Now what do you want, pig?" he snarled into the phone.

"Bobby, this is Mitch Zaga. Let me talk to Ken Rocmel."

"I'm the one you have to talk to. He ain't got no say. This is my game, no one else's."

"What game are you talking about Bobby? I don't see this as a game," Mitch had finally realized he was talking to a lunatic.

"It's my game. You people think you can get to me without innocent people being killed. It could be the last game I'll ever play. Sure, I might be dead, but I'll win the game 'cause I ain't going out alone. Understand what I'm saying, Fed?"

Mitch understood precisely what he was saying. Ken also understood only too well. Bobby knew it was over for him. He knew he was going to die. He knew he did not plan to die alone.

Now Ken knew what he had to do. The only question was how he would do it. Bobby no longer had the gun aimed at Ken. He went to Malarie and Dane.

"Bobby, why don't you let the women and the baby go. I understand what you're saying. You don't want to go back to prison. You're willing to die first. In a way, I understand your reasoning. You want to take a few people with you. Well, why not try for a few cops? You have the opportunity. You know they'll be coming to get you. In fact, I'll give you a shot at me. I'll be one coming in after you. Go out in a blaze of glory not like a scumbag using a baby as a shield," Mitch stated, hoping he had taken the proper approach. He hoped he'd spoken a language Smallwood understood.

Bobby did understand. It even made sense to him. Go out in glory, he mused. Bobby liked the sound of the proposal. The people in the joint would be talking about him for years to come. In his meditation, he didn't notice Ken going to the kitchen. The Fed had given him a personal challenge. He thought of the shootout at the OK Corral. It would be like Ike Clanton and the Fed Wyatt Earp. It had been more than a hundred years ago and they still talk about it. Ike Clanton went out in glory.

Suddenly he returned from fantasyland. Wasn't it just a few minutes ago that he'd told Ken and Malarie they were the only friends he had, that he would never forget them. He looked around and saw Malarie embracing Dane fearing for their lives. Over the mantel, he saw the leather picture he'd made that they had so proudly displayed. That was a good piece of work. He had worked on this picture in the leather shop for two years. He did it with love, knowing it was to go to Ken and Malarie. His reasoning had returned.

How did it come to this? Pauly, Billy and Jesse are dead. Now it was his turn. So be it. He decided to let them all go, including Charlene. He looked at her. She was such a beauty and just a kid. Poor girl. They'd come down on her hard. He decided to tell the Fed she'd been forced to do the things she'd done. He stood up and pulled Charlene close to him. His hand went softly to her face and he smiled at her. He looked at Malarie with soft and gentle eyes and smiled.

Malarie saw the softness in his eyes, but was confused. Was this the look of death? She saw Ken creep up behind Bobby with a knife in his hand. Bobby heard the Fed say something. He turned to look behind him. He felt an intense pain in his back. Both his hands went up. He dropped the phone and gun simultaneously. He couldn't get a grip on the knife. The pain was causing him extreme mental agony. He felt the knife stuck between his shoulder and neck. He turned. He saw Ken with his mouth open like he wanted to speak. Bobby forgot all his most recent thoughts.

"You son-of-a-bitch...in the back...you," Bobby grabbed Ken by the neck and lifted him off the floor. He pushed him against the wall. Ken had forgotten how strong Bobby was. He threw a punch that struck Bobby's forehead. It was ineffective.

Ken tried in vain to loosen Bobby's hand from his throat. His breath was cut off and he grew weak. Ken was able to reach the knife sticking out of Bobby and miraculously pulled it out. Bobby was now feeling pain he'd never known before. His grip on Ken's neck relaxed enough for Ken to get a deep breath.

"Fuck, Kenny, let's die together," Bobby said as he used his waning strength to squeeze Kenny's neck. Ken was about to black out. Ken looked into Bobby's eyes as he raised the knife into the air.

He wanted to say "Sorry, Bobby," but nothing came out. His windpipe closed. He brought the knife down with all his strength. It went through Bobby's shirt, into his chest and through his heart. Bobby let go of Ken and fell to the floor. He stared at Ken. He wanted to speak, but was unable. He knew Ken had just killed him. In a way, he was glad.

Charlene wasn't sure what was happening. It all happened so fast. She was terrified from the moment of the first shots outside. Seeing Bobby's bleeding face had left her in shock. The window near where she was standing was shattered before her. Everything went blank. She didn't see Ken come up behind Bobby.

When she saw the knife sticking in his back, she realized that Ken had done it. She was startled. She knew it was over.

Ken sat on the floor. He lifted Bobby's head into his lap. He was in agony. "I had to do it Bobby. You made me choose between you and my family. You lost it. You didn't know what you were doing. You went off. I was left with no choice. Oh God, Bobby, I'm sorry. I loved you like a brother, I really loved you," tears ran down Ken's face as he spoke. Bobby raised his hand and softly ran it along Ken's face. He smiled. His hand fell. Bobby was dead....7:11 p.m

-THE END-

ONE MORE DOWN

The bell rang, is it sheet out today?

No, that just happened yesterday
It must be breakfast, do I want to go?
I didn't sleep too good, no, I don't think so.

Ten fifteen, ah shit, I'm late again
What happened to my wake up friend?
Pencil and paper, a book or two
Thirty years old and off to school.

Macaroni and cheese, a slice of bread
Now play some dominoes or go back to bed
Maybe write a letter, I'm two behind
Seems the one thing I have is plenty of time.

The bell rings, it's time to be counted
Good little cattle in bars surrounded
Led by a ring attached to the brain
I'm not in agony, just in pain.
Just another day.

EPILOGUE

Mrs. Cox looked at the photo of her husband and pointed it out to her two-year-old son. "This is your daddy's picture," she said to him. It was a picture of John in his prison guard uniform. She had used his life insurance money to purchase the house of their dreams. Two years after John's death she still cried herself to sleep at night. She thought she would never fall in love again.

Prison Guard Turnbell had returned to work after a six-month leave of absence. He was the godfather of John Cox's little boy. He never went to work inside the prison again. He worked in the tower instead. When he had his rifle, he often wished that Smallwood had been caught alive and returned to prison. Many times, he envisioned watching Smallwood walking the yard, sighting his rifle and pulling the trigger.

Warden Glass had been fired for a cover-up in a missing supplies scandal. The escape two years before had not worked in Glass' favor as he had thought it would. He pointed the finger at the wrong people when he tried to show how resourceful he was. The people he accused were powerful, and successfully brought about an investigation of his administration. Although Glass was not a party to the theft of supplies, a cover up was discovered with the help of Assistant Warden Lockney. The new governor fired Glass and appointed Lockney as the new warden. Lockney ran a tight prison during the past two years.

Dick Ellis, aka Maggot, was back in prison. The FBI had traced the weapons supplied to the escaped convicts to him. He became a kind of hero inside the walls, having contributed to the most notorious escape ever known in the Oregon system. He had been interviewed on TV, and his picture was in the newspapers. He spoke well of all the convicts who were killed. He let his fellow inmates think that it was he who gave Smallwood the idea to rob a rest stop. He didn't argue that he had masterminded the escape. What stories he would tell were about how Bobby went out in glory. He never got his GTO back.

Patty Brown married her paramour, Danny, a year and a day after Paul had been killed in Nevada. They had a good marriage, and Danny adopted Dustin. Pauly had it right about Patty and Dustin never knowing the truth. Patty did not really care. The love she thought she had for Paul was lost when she heard what transpired during the escape. She was shocked because she always wanted to think that deep inside Paul had a good heart. She guessed that she had never really known him. She never knew where the $2,000 came from that she received in the mail, a week after Paul died.

Mike Kudofuzi got $37,786 of his $40,000 back. He went back to the Middle East. He thought it was less violent than it was America.

Becky Ford still bragged to her friends in Ontario, California, about the adventure she had two years ago. She loved to show off the diamond necklace Mike had bought for her in Las Vegas. She often wonders what happened to him.

Sid Clifton was working in his garden. His wife Mary Clifton sat under a shade tree knitting. Mary knew Sid was itching to get back on the road in their motor home, do some fishing, and see the kids along the way. She thought about the people they had met at the camp and wondered what ever happened to them. She always thought they were in some kind of trouble. "Oh darn," she said to herself. She hated it when she missed a stitch.

Perry and Elaine Bartlett were enjoying the hot tub with a few of their friends from Billings. They had used the $10,000 reward money given to them by the trucking company to build the hot tub and the patio. All their friends knew that Perry never liked to talk about their hostage experience. He wanted to forget the event. The State of Nevada invited him to come back all expenses paid for the citizen of the year award, he declined. He was never proud of shooting the convict in cold blood, but he knew he did what had to be done. That was the end of it as far as he was concerned. Of course, he did enjoy the hot tub.

Captain Harold Camode was one of the people who were happy that there had been a Robert Smallwood. He had received most of the credit for the capture of Smallwood. He was a hero in the state of Oregon. He was certain that his promotion to Captain was due to the Smallwood matter. He would always be grateful to the FBI kid who allowed him to take most of the credit.

Kelly Quinton lived with her father and mother in Seattle, Washington. Her parents kept a watchful eye on her. She had attempted suicide a little more than a year ago. She seldom left home. She had an opportunity to meet Rich's dad, Joe Quinton, at the funeral. They had supported each other when both broke down and cried. Joe gave Kelly some fishing pictures of himself and Rich. She hung the pictures above her bed. Kelly never felt clean even though she took daily showers. She had no desire ever to be with a man again. More than anything else, she disliked going to sleep at night. She wished that just once, she could see the face of Rich in her dreams, but it was always Billy and Jesse's faces that haunted her.

Malarie Rocmel was breast-feeding her new baby. She looked at the clock. It was a quarter to twelve. Ken would be home for lunch in fifteen minutes. She was happy that Ken was now sales manager. Besides getting the additional salary, he was able to spend more time at home with the kids. The leather picture still hung over the fireplace. Malarie remembered that a guy offered them $2,500 for it. He had heard about the picture during a newscast two years ago. Malarie could not forget the nightmare they had experienced in their home. Ken was arrested for aiding and abetting an escaped felon. She was very grateful for the efforts of the nice FBI person who was instrumental in getting the charges dropped. She learned to love Ken even more after that last night with Bobby. Many times Ken would wake up in a cold sweat calling Bobby's name. However, she knew that Ken did what had to be done to save the life of his family. The $2,000 that Bobby gave to Ken was never found by the police. Ken sent it to Paul Brown's wife without any indication of its source.

The Allied Trucking Company notified Ken that he was eligible to claim the $10,000 reward money it had offered. Ken suggested that it be given to the wife and kids of the truck driver who had been killed. When it was reported in the news, Ken became a hero in his own right.

Ken received a letter from Charlene Sweazy about a month ago. She said in the letter that some day he would have to pay for stabbing Bobby in the back. Ken just shook his head and threw the letter in the garbage. He felt that he had been paying for stabbing Bobby from day one in his own conscience. Hardly a day passed that he didn't think of Bobby. The Wizard died with Bobby.

Gary Duggan was at Prigg Cottage with only two weeks left to parole. He had developed a different attitude than the one he had before he was stabbed. He'd spent 73 days in the hospital and undergone three operations. His life had been saved. When Gary first entered the hospital, he wasn't expected to recover. The prison did not provide adequate facilities to give proper attention to such cases. Dr. Swartz, took a personal interest in Gary's case. His professional services contributed immensely to Gary's recovery. Gary had come close to death. While hospitalized, he had time to think. He thought about his past and his future. He became a new man. His thoughts were on what he would do when he was released. His bitterness had left him. What he wanted most was to start his life over. He wanted to become a useful and productive citizen. He no longer thought of law-abiding citizens as suckers. He wanted to marry, have children and work to support his family. Gary rejoiced when he first heard about the death of Bobby Smallwood and his friends. Now, two years later, he felt sadness and a trace of guilt. It was ironic that, two years before, a carton of cigarettes had caused the tragic deaths of nine people. He'd almost lost his own life. Now, he saw values in people. Whereas before he had never noticed. He promised never to return to his old ways that had sent him to prison.

FBI Inspector Mitchell Zaga was working another escape case, his fifth in two years. All the escapees had been caught. The last guy, a federal prisoner from Atlanta, reminded him of the Smallwood case. The convict had killed a guard with his bare hands on a trip to the doctor's office and escaped with the second guard as his hostage. Mitch was not as lucky as he was in the Smallwood case. The second guard had been found dead, also.

Mitch had a special attitude toward escaped convicts. He was able to understand things about them that other agents could not. That was perhaps the reason why the FBI made escaped convict cases his specialty. Mitch knew that an escaped convict was the nearest thing to an animal. Escape required intelligence combined with desperation. This made an escapee all the more dangerous to society. All escaped convicts had one thing in common; they all swore that they would never be brought back to prison alive. Mitch had better luck than he did with the Oregon case. In that case, four convicts escaped, and four of them died. Only one of the four he had caught during the past two years had been killed.

He was worried about the convict he was chasing at the present--another die hard, the Smallwood syndrome. He was as calculating as Smallwood. Mitch was closing in because he knew how the escapee was thinking. Mitch loved his work and he loved the FBI.

The God damn bells. Two years of God damn bells. That was Charlene Sweazy's thought for the day. Every day. An electric shock running through her every time the bells went off. The wake-up bells were always the worst. They started ringing at 4:30 a.m. to wake up the cooks. Then at 5:45, they rang to wake up everybody for breakfast. Most of the time, Charlene could not go back to sleep after the 4:30 bell. The bells would continue throughout the day: work bell, school bell, lunch bell, put your towel out bell, count bell, supper bell three different times, movie bells, night yard bell and lights out bell.

What bothered Charlene most was that she was going to hear the bells another six years before she would be eligible for parole. Bullshit, that's what you people think. A few more months and the plan would be ready. I'll be out of here. After the bells, these were Charlene's first thoughts. Repeatedly, Charlene thought about Bobby's rest stop idea on lonely nights. She came out with a better plan. She called it *Bus Stop*.

"You going to breakfast, honey?" Story asked as she stuck her head down from the top bunk.

"What are they having, you know?" Charlene asked with a smile. She loved Story. Had it not been for her she would have gone crazy. They had been cellmates for the past year. As strange as it might seem, she used to be friends with Pauly Brown's old lady. Charlene also loved the way Story made love to her. No man had ever made her climax as much as Story.

Grits and bacon!" Story answered.

YOURS TO CHOOSE

Be timid, don't fight
Take shit not right
For the lamb sheds its wool to clothe
Kiss ass, buy time
Look ahead, not behind
For what tomorrow brings, you mold

The lion can't survive inside a cage
For trapped, he is no longer king
But never learning to give up his rage
Will mean never hearing freedom sing

The man plays with cards stacked
If you gamble, you have to lose
You are alone, and his game is backed
The lion or the lamb, it is yours to choose

Be wise, not quick
Be smart, not slick
For the lamb,
Will again
Have his wool.